SUN-BEARER

by Anita Berk

ISBN 978-0-620-96279-7

CONTENTS

Chapter 1   **7**
The Choosing   7
The Drawing   12

Chapter 2   **15**
Lesson for the Day   15
Arrival   18
Hope and a Shaded Window   23

Chapter 3   **27**
A Walk and a Secret   27
Departure   31
The Naming   34

Chapter 4   **36**
Shrouded   36
Wires and Screens   39

Chapter 5   **43**
Homecoming   43
Herding and Batting   45
Jewel   51

Chapter 6   **54**
The Assembly   54

Chapter 7   **61**
Harbouring a Grain   61
Closing Words   65

Chapter 8   **68**
Victory   68
The Opening   71

Chapter 9   **74**
Hidden Sky   74
Findings and Conclusion   76

Chapter 10 — 85
The Visit — 85
Burst Container — 89
Unguarded — 91

Chapter 11 — 98
Hands Dipped — 98
Berth — 104

Chapter 12 — 108
Evening Birds — 108
Prying Time — 112

Chapter 13 — 114
Bestowal — 114

Chapter 14 — 123
Unveiling — 123
Nativity — 126

Chapter 15 — 128
A Song — 128
Revival — 130

Chapter 16 — 133
Gengun — 133

Chapter 17 — 143
Chamber Day — 143
Unoccupied Chair — 149

Chapter 18 — 154
Return — 154
The Spectator — 158
Sleeping Dogs Wake — 161

Chapter 19 — 174
Friable Reunion — 174
The Thorn — 176

Chapter 20 — 180
Awakening — 180
A Girl's Room — 187
Stopover — 188

Chapter 21 — 191
A Bed Made — 191
Bats — 196

Chapter 22   202
A Princess's Birthday   202
Inheritance   208

Chapter 23   210
Breakout   210
Tea and an Answer   219
Spotting from Above   223
Beginning Snuffed   224

Chapter 24   231
Girl Held   231
Righting   234
Inching Shadows   235
Trouble   239
Empty Tank   240
Unexpected Caller   242
The Island Awaits   245

Chapter 25   252
Return of the Messenger   252
Distance Crossed   254
Prelude   259
Ingress   260
Cars in the Library   263
An Afternoon Snack   265
Crewless Kitchen   267
Approach   268
Encroaching Storm   269
Talkie Whispers   271
A Meeting of Old Enemies   272
Preparing for a Truth   274
Scent   275
Unlocking   277

Chapter 26   280
The Battle Within, the Battle Without   280
Stray Guard   301
Exit Strategy   302
Game Up   304
Passage   305

Chapter 27   313
A New Order   313
Uneasy Peace   314

Chapter 28   **318**

Procession   318

Deliverance   322

Lessons by the Sea   324

Glossary   **330**

Translations   **331**

About the Author   **332**

CHAPTER 1

The Choosing

30/10/2050

As they leave, dawn is no more than a suggestion of light, drawing the unyielding Karoo-scape out of the darkness like a holy land. Keesa glances through the rear window. All she can make of her father is a lone waving hand and nervous face as they pull off. Their annual girls'-only road trips are the one thing that her mother insists on, regardless of Kaleb's objections. Aedan's way of holding onto a small piece of independence from his over-protectiveness. She knows his misgivings aren't unreasonable. He's been steadily collecting fuel from various Genguns in the vicinity over the past four months to ensure they won't have to stop to refuel en route. Invariably, electrical maintenance is required at the stations and Kaleb's expertise has always proved a fruitful exchange. The 20-litre barrels are secured at the rear of the four-wheel drive. Kaleb has rigged the Jeep to resemble an army tank more than a car. It won't be seen as an ideal target. Nevertheless, Aedan always has her shotgun at the ready, lodged between her seat and the driver's door.

Their village, Hale, gradually recedes out of sight and the trip down to the coast unfurls. The seared, semi-desert plains eventually give way to the lusher regions near the land's fringes of sand. The air is infused with moisture; the light seems more skittish. As much as Keesa is fond of her life in Hale, she is glad of the respite from chores in her mother's dairy, schoolwork, and the rainless veldt. Evergreen trees and bush flurry past the car; Keesa drinks in the hues of leaves. Flashes of colour in the Karoo are a rarity, shocking though their shades may be. Although her mother has a rule that all the windows of the car must stay closed for the sake of safety, she occasionally allows Keesa to open hers a little. The girl lifts her nostrils to the gap and takes deep draws of the coastal fynbos scent; it settles her stomach of any motion-queasiness.

She notices that her mother becomes jittery as they travel through empty towns but this cannot be avoided; travelling on any back road would slow the car down too much. Only a handful of towns remained populated here after the rapid and uncanny global spread of a vicious new mutation of meningitis, for which there was no cure at the time, in 2041. The Karoo was one of the few areas to escape being infected.

Roads are not maintained as they used to be; journey times are always at least an hour or two longer than they had been before. Although the drive to her sister's place on the coast only takes about three hours, Aedan drives fast wherever she can. Slowness and hesitation only increase the risk of being ambushed by Baboon Gangs.

Rusted signs forlornly welcome Keesa and her mother to the quiet. Names of towns no longer carry meaning. This one is George. Keesa pictures people in the last village they passed through and the word George is present.

We're going to George on Friday to do some shopping, one friend says to another.

A time when the word was formed in the air and bounced between people. Now the name floats above the ground on a board of eroded metal. Half-scavenged cell phone towers decay and telephone lines slouch, unused for a decade.

Keesa catches sight of a mother kudu with her baby. They have made their home in an enclosed front lawn, now full of overgrown bushes. The doe freezes as the car passes, her face riveting in its beauty and fear. Their speeding car feels hurried and odd to Keesa in the eerie stillness of the forsaken towns, streaking past her like powdery, resumed Gardens of Eden.

An hour or so later they arrive in the town where her aunt lives. The new town name, Beginning, has been pasted over the old one on the welcome sign.

'What did this town used to be called again, Mom?'

'Plettenberg Bay but, we just used to call it Plett.'

'That's right. Plett. I like that better than Beginning.'

'Maybe don't mention that while we're visiting, okay? People here are trying to make a fresh start.'

'Okay.'

8

They approach the security checkpoint. A man and teenage boy stand outside a shack next to a roughly put together boom that blocks the road into Beginning. The man bowls a faded red ball to the boy, who hits it with an old cricket bat. Keesa recognises the actions. Her and her friend from Hale, Elijah, have been taught how to play it by his grandfather, Brick. The man and boy are laughing. As they sense a car moving towards the checkpoint, they toss their cricket gear into the shack and pick up their rifles that are leaning up against the metal sheet. Their faces harden to an unwelcoming resolve.

The interaction is brief. The man quickly recognises the two of them; they have been visiting the town once a year ever since Keesa can remember. He signals the boy to open the boom, wishing the two of them a good vacation. As they drive on, she turns to watch them through the back window resume their cricket practise, their bodies humorous once more.

She can see candles and some lights in the windows of houses, mothers talking, children jousting, a young girl and boy walking holding hands, nervous smiles on their lips. Then the magnificent ocean as they come over the hill. They pull in to her aunt's driveway; her mother hoots briefly twice. They are welcomed with strong hugs by Aedan's sister, Ruth.

'Oh my word, just look at you, Keesa. Ten years old already. Such a pretty thing,' her aunt remarks, cupping the girl's chin. The sisters go into the house, continuing a stream of chatter.

Keesa savours the time on holiday with her mother. She is able to do more exploring out of the reaches of her father's heedful eyes. Lagging behind in the driveway for a moment, she drinks in the quickly falling night air. The salty smell rolls in, then recedes again, as though the ocean is tugging at her hair, her clothes. Her mother calls from inside; the girl goes in reluctantly, stirred that the water is merely metres away.

The three of them spend a perfect day at the sea; the relief of skin comforted by sun and held by ocean. In the balmy late afternoon Keesa is playing at the edge of the water. Aedan and Ruth are beneath a beach umbrella a short distance away up the incline of sand, laughter bursting from their direction every so often.

A sudden gust of wind takes the air around the beach, upsetting picnic baskets, spiralling newspapers up to the sky, and abruptly shutting Ruth's umbrella. Keesa turns back to look and sees her mother and aunt being swallowed up by the navy and white striped pin-wheel. That is when she hears the sound lifting from the ocean. She turns back to look at the water, drawn in. A solitary note that plunges and whips up again. She looks back to her mother once more, takes in the sight of the umbrella attempting to digest the two adults scrambling to see if Keesa is alright, and returns her eyes to the ocean.

The hullabaloo around her begins to fade away, until all she can hear is the song. The notes floating out of the water begin to suck her in. Her legs jerk out of the wet, sinking sand where they are planted and advance into the surging eddy, as though they know what they are doing, even if she does not. Before she has time to think, she is wading through the warm liquid up to her waist. The wind that had seemed to be centred on the beach billows out onto the ocean now, snatching areas of it up into waves that heave and break in pounds on the shoreline. A wave draws up and hangs suspended before Keesa and, for a moment, it occurs to her that she might die in it. Then it is crashing down on her and sucking her down into the depths.

After what feels like a long time being pulled and pushed by the mad sea, hurtling along the inside of a giant tube of water, she comes to a slow stop, gently touching down on the ocean bed. In front of her is some kind of reef, which blocks out her view, as though she is facing a wall. Even though the light down here is murky, her sight is clear. It strikes her that she should be having trouble breathing. She lifts her hand to her mouth, unaware of how she has been managing till now. Tentatively, she takes in what feels like a breath. The sensation is warm and a bit salty but it seems to work. She blows out onto her fingers and sees she is exhaling seawater with bubbles in.

The sound she heard on the shore rings out again, this time so loud and close it feels her bones are reverberating with it. This is when she realises: the wall in front of her is not a reef; it is the dark hide of a whale. Keesa looks up as the whale edges slowly backward, until she is craning her neck back and looking into its eyes. A speck before a gargantuan beast.

She considers that this is the second time today she could be about to lose her life. An odd feeling comes over her. She is afraid of the whale—it could inhale her, let alone eat her but, at the same time, she feels calm. The whale lets out more notes and, at the end of each phrase, Keesa has the sense that it looks at her. As it sings, it is as though her bones are pulsing bigger and smaller inside her. The whale finishes, looks at her a last time. Keesa detects a hint of a smile in the dark pools gazing down at her. Then the whale turns and begins swimming away, causing such a ripple that Keesa is flung back into another tunnel of water, back and thrashing and up this time to the shoreline, onto which she is eventually spat out.

Her first concern is that her mother is going to be exasperated that she went so deep into the water alone. She becomes aware of the windstorm still enduring. She turns to look at her mother and aunt, expecting to see them running towards her. But instead, she sees them struggling beneath the umbrella, exactly as they had been before she went into the water. The same man is chasing his newspaper and the same dog is scurrying after its wind-dancing toy. It dawns on her: all is as it was before, because it is before. It is still the moment she heard the singing. Except now all she hears are surprised shouts and barking dogs.

Just as quickly as it whirled in, the wind drops, and within seconds is no more than the breeze it had been before. The people on the beach appear ragged now. Aedan and Ruth have finally managed to extricate themselves from the umbrella's jaws; they scramble up and run towards the shoreline shouting, 'Keesa! KEESA!' Aedan is stumped as they stop and realise that there is no more wind. 'That must have been the shortest storm ever.'

She is relieved that Keesa has not come to any harm. As they make their way off the beach with the mangled umbrella and what could be salvaged from the picnic basket, Keesa decides to keep what happened to herself. She wonders whether anything happened at all. Whether it had been an unusually clear daydream. She recalls the deafening notes engulfing her. The towel wrapped around her hides that she is still trembling. Her mother will think she's merely cold from her swim. Her feet tread tired, taking comfort in the dry sand still warm like charcoals from the afternoon sun.

The Drawing

31/10/2050

Her cloak of deep mulberry trails through the semi-desert sand, a bleeding bruise against the golden grains. A grey and burgundy robe twines her body; black jewellery frames her features, her alarming beauty. Her stride is purposive, her pace swift. The moon rises heavy and yellow over the hills in the east, barely visible now but for their blackness against an ink-blue sky. Queen Regan of Night walks towards a simple structure that rises out of the sand. Made of clay, it consists of a square slab as its base with four pillars protruding vertically, one from each corner of the foundation, each of these joined by a beam. She steps onto the pedestal, glances down, kneels and touches the faded floor. She had discovered it abandoned to erosion when she was five years old.

Regan stands up, steps out of the structure, removes her cloak, and casts it over the skeletal clay cube. Fixing all her attention on the space at the centre of the frame, she faces her palms towards it, and begins drawing on the void in herself with the magnetism that her grandmother taught her as a young girl. Their Nox Dark family has held the throne for centuries. Slowly, pieces of time and space begin to assemble underneath her cloak, all wanting to make up the same scene. Her focus is sharp; the particles cohere steadily. One of them begins pulsing out sound intermittently. Regan becomes aware of her mother's spirit close now; it momentarily derails her concentration. This lapse causes a break in her magnetism and the swarming pieces of the semblance to be played begin drifting back into the veldt night. Clenching her fists, she clears her inner vision and forces the uncomfortable emotions to the periphery, to lodge once more in her muscles and dreams. More determined now, she hums up her magnetic draw and beckons the living image to amass once more.

The vision begins converging in on itself again, this time with more speed. Sounds escape from the pieces with more frequency—the cry of a man, the sound of her cloak flapping, gunshots, horse hooves drumming the ground. Although she feels her mother's presence once more, she manages to push her out to hover on the perimeter of the magnetic sphere that is now almost electric in energy. At last, the mirage cements before the Queen. It hangs in the air for a few seconds, and she gets the same feeling she always does at this point; that she is peering into a moment that is somehow always about to happen.

Suspended before her is the frozen image of a man, a soldier, twisting his face away, his body contorting to avoid something. He wears a uniform of red and blue. There is an arm and hand seizing at his shirt. It looks like that of a woman, a sleeve of white with a black cuff. From the single ring on the forefinger, Regan realises the woman is herself. She has called up many visions in her life; all of them featured only other people. She is aware of the dangers involved if the vision features her own destiny; her mother had banned her from looking into these. She considers dissipating the vision, knowing that to be the safest course of action. Her desire to know is too strong; she allows the vision to breathe.

As soon as it starts rolling, the still night air is invaded with the grisly sounds that frequent a battlefield. The thud of metal on skulls, horses snorting in panicked tones, rattles of gunfire, hurried orders being belted out in the hope that some will hear. The soldier is on his knees, tipped back and stretching for his weapon that must have been knocked away when he was struck. Her hand yanks the soldier up from the ground by his shirt, his arm still flailing for his dagger. Her other hand delivers her concise, bloodied sword just under his rib-cage with the precision of a dance move. He breathes in sharply, looking into her eyes. She retracts her sword and, as she tosses him limp to the ground, her ears are taken by a woman summoning her to fight. The voice is laden with a thirst for vengeance and calls her by her first name—a rare occurrence. The impropriety of it bristles the Queen, even as she watches the flickering light before her.

'Regan!'

Her view swings sharply in the direction of the voice, taking in a messy battle vista. Although it is happening at night, massive fires illuminate this war in the semi-desert. Once the view comes to rest again, all she can make out is a lone figure with a lava-red cloak riding away from her on a battle horse.

The spike in her emotional state has broken the continuity of the vision. When it resumes, she is higher off the ground with the rider still in her sight, mere feet away. For some seconds the cloaked woman on horseback judders up and down with the movements of the Queen's own horse as she pursues her. They have ridden up an embankment of sand and Regan flings a look back at the battle now; she has been led away from its main stage. The rider stops a few feet from the Queen, and nimbly disembarks her horse. Regan follows suit in the vision; outside the cube looking in, she is impatient to know the identity of the shrouded figure. The woman spins around, loosens her cloak to the ground, and draws a golden sword, holding it aloft in threat to the Queen. She is younger than Regan had anticipated and, judging from her battle attire, has royal status.

There is something familiar about her features, but Regan cannot place it. The vision freezes on her striking warrior figure and, after a few moments, dissipates into its many bits, which shoot off back into the motiveless night sky.

The Queen is left with the same feeling of emptiness that always comes over her when her visions end. If only she had caught this imperial's name. Her anomalous garb of red and blue confounds Regan. The gold weapon indicates a Light representative. She is not aware of any daughter born of royal blood in the Chamber of Light. Perhaps the unidentified royal signal that began transmitting hours earlier? Could add up, but the heraldry still doesn't make sense. As the temptation to try force another vision rises up like an uncontrollable itch in her, a voice from behind startles her.

'You are lucky your emotions merely dissipated the vision this time, Your Majesty, and you were not—'

'Yes Valtere, that will be quite enough, thank-you.' She removes her cloak with a swoosh from the cube and turns rearward.

'Your Majesty does not appear to gauge the severe dangers involved, given that you have crossed the threshold that your mother warned you of.'

'Unless you wish to lose your position in the court as my helper, I suggest you refrain from raising this subject with me now or at any point in the future.'

The eagle flaps his wings deliberately once, a slow shrug of defiance. Nonetheless, the Queen knows she has put him in his place.

'Come now, perch on my shoulder while I walk back to the Chamber. I want to hear details of the scouting mission for the new water source. We will need to send a team out to secure it soon. Also, a new royal frequency signal began transmitting earlier. An unknown female youngling. I'll need you to investigate this for me.'

With that, Regan throws one last look towards the clay cube, so empty now, pricks of starlight blossoming into the horizon behind it. Fear pulls at the sides of her mouth; it sits awkwardly on a face that seldom shows it. She turns towards the west and begins walking, the comfort of Valtere's talons brooching her shoulder as she does. Although she is reluctant to admit it to herself, he is the only friend she has in the world.

CHAPTER 2

Lesson for the Day

02/12/2031

Regan looks out the window. Knotted branches of creeping vines with an occasional fleck of sunlight stealing through the brush. Her leg is jittering under the desk. She silently plans where she will explore today, if she can manage to sneak out. She tires of all this hiding. Not that she has ever known any different. Concealment of her royal identity renders a normal childhood impossible. She is only permitted to play with children of members of the Dark royal court, or those attendant on it. Her ladies-in-waiting watch her constantly but she is a calculating girl and prides herself on outwitting them frequently. They are never keen for her little escapes to be revealed to the King and Queen of Dark and thus her bits of freedom stay as firmly under wraps as the rest of her existence. She takes pleasure in the power she has over the ladies; it passes the time.

It has been centuries, some say millennia, since the royal Forces could operate openly amongst humans on earth. Regan is exposed only in very small doses to what life on the planet is like; she is barred from access to television and communication networks, or any contact with outsiders. On the other hand, she has entry to her mother's main medical quarters almost whenever she pleases, and observes the Queen working there as often as possible. The medical quarters are located a short distance from the main homestead. The main laboratory was converted from a sheep-shearing shed, and her mother's smaller, but considerable private laboratory was originally a large barn. No one, not even Regan, has access to this private laboratory, nicknamed the *Initium* by the Queen, whose father had a fondness for Latin. Queen Signa is in sole possession of the keys to it. She has been working on a series of experiments that she claims will enable the Dark Force to preside over the planet, ever since Regan can remember. She has asked her mother to reveal some of its particulars but Signa is as unyielding to anyone on this subject as a dog's jaws clamped around a bone.

The Queen hopes that her daughter will someday follow in her footsteps and become a pioneering surgeon. It is too early to apply pressure; the girl is only ten, but she is nonetheless in the habit of heavy hinting. Regan watches her mother working on bodies when she is allowed. They are always those of old people or sometimes animals. Her mother delegated one of her workers to take employment at the morgue in the closest city and he ensures a steady supply of unclaimed corpses. A body that has aged is interesting to Regan; it is rare to see elderly people in the royal court.

Regan has always preferred the assortment of glass vials and tubes in the laboratory to the corpses. She is intrigued by the tinctures and concoctions they contain and what effect each one will have. Her mother plans to commence her lessons in medicine in five year's time. Regan found an old copy of *Alice's Adventures in Wonderland* at the back of one of the cupboards soon after her parents moved into the run-down, sprawling homestead five years ago. She fancies herself drinking the contents of one of the tubes, shrinking into tininess and going on adventures in the cities nearby, without anyone knowing.

'Princess Regan! Your lessons in philosophy are no less important than grammar or mathematics. I shall be setting you a test for tomorrow, so I suggest you pay attention or suffer the consequences of your mother inspecting your poor results.' Her tutor, Mister Alton, has been in her mother's service for 10 years and is one of the Dark Queen's most avid admirers. As much as she finds this tack annoying, it works. Mister Alton continues.

'One of the keys to being a Dark royal is detachment. To feel or show love for another being places one in direct violation of the Dark creed. Members of the family are in no uncertain terms forbidden to do so. In the event of a momentary lapse of compliance with this law one must immediately disengage from the target of that love and cease all contact forthwith. Of course, parents will experience a sense of obligation with regard to their offspring, as might occur between siblings as well.

Love is the primary source of disappointment, pain and betrayal on the planet. The only way to enduring peace within is for each person to be an island, completely self-sufficient as regards emotional fulfilment. An intricate and powerful web of lies has been fed to the human race by the followers of Light

Bearers for millennia, one which begins with the notion that we all need to love and to be loved in return, in order to actualise as human beings.'

Regan's ears take these words in, some familiar, some not. They swim around her head, planting themselves into her spongy brain, forming into groups: what to do, what not to do. A row of shiny bottles with labels on. 'Drink me', 'Do not open' and 'Smell, but do not consume'. Her official person. Her mind returns to her scheme for the afternoon. Will it be the edge of the city today? Or the fields bordering on the veldt? She wants the quietness today. Sometimes she tires of the city childrens' questions. The familiarity and fascination of what the veldt holds for her is far more alluring.

Arrival

07/11/2050

A week has passed since the day at the beach. Aedan and Keesa made the return drive the day before. The girl is up at dawn, as usual, and pulls on a tunic. She takes a moment to line her miniature animals up on top of her chest of drawers, their order having been disturbed by the packing and unpacking process. These are artefacts her father has collected for her from deserted houses and shops over the years, to service her delight in little things. Then there are skeletons of tiny creatures—birds, mice, a baby snake. The inside of bodies and what holds them together is a source of fascination for Keesa. Her mother abhors this morbid lot, and used to go on episodic confiscation missions. These upset Keesa, and she has settled for soaking them in water steeped in bicarbonate of soda or a bleaching agent.

Her first daily chore is to drive with her mother to help load fresh milk from the farm next door, some of which Aedan will use for making cheese. It has taken her mother 10 years to learn the craft and refine her range of cheeses, which are in demand by the local villagers and farmers. They bring the milk back to their farmstead in four big pails, two of which are taken straight to the dairy shed, and the others to the kitchen. The homestead is an old one, which has been for the most part well maintained. Hale was established close to a town that used to go by the name Steytlerville.

Next Keesa tips those in the farmhouse into a steel double-boiler pot that stands on the kitchen stove and turns the heat on low. There is a wide stool that she stands on to do this. Then she washes her face in an enamel bowl placed in the bathroom sink, so as to use as little water as possible. She dresses for school, ties her cocoa-brown hair into a ponytail, and sits down to breakfast with her parents around the Formica table in the kitchen.

Once Keesa has finished helping with cleaning the breakfast dishes, she collects her school-bag. Most mornings she walks to the village school with her friend, Elijah, a twelve-year-old boy who lives on the next-door farm with his grandfather, Brick. They keep goats, and Aedan and Brick have a trading relationship. Brick provides her with a number of pails of milk each day, and she provides him with cheese, and sometimes yoghurt, if she has made extra. Today Keesa is walking to school on her own, as Elijah had to go searching unexpectedly for a goat that has gone missing.

Keesa waves goodbye to her father as he sets off for work in the Jeep. Kaleb is an electrician, highly reputed in the region. He has rigged their farmstead and the village with power from generators. It is a commodity used sparingly. Aedan sees Keesa off from the front door. The girl unhinges and opens the wire mesh and steel gate that edges the front garden. It squeaks its two notes, as always, as she shuts it behind her. She starts off on her walk. She is at ease in the quiet of the veldt. The only sounds that pierce it are the crush of building heat on her ears, and her feet crunching sand and rocks. Her dark-green eyes scour the ground for any dead creature.

Despite the consternation following the outbreak, and the threat of gangs, the people of Hale have managed to create a degree of peace in their village. It is one of the few that has warded off being attacked. Keesa likes to believe it is safe to explore her vicinity.

As she walks, she registers something different about her walk this morning. A sense that something is moving under the ground. A thing that courses and ripples. Like a huge snake, or an undercurrent. One that her body perceives, rather than her mind. Just at the point it seems to be tipping over into something she can hear and see, it vanishes, leaving the veldt around her looking absurdly normal. She passes the ring of aloes; 10 minutes from the village school now.

She notices something on the side of the road, sitting next to a lone tree. A small kitten with fur the colour of amber and honey, each hair ticked on the end with a fleck of black. Ears that have tufts of fur sprouting off them. A locket is suspended around its neck, surface winking each time the sun hits it. Keesa looks around for an owner. Only the hardy vegetation with the well-worn path through it. Normally she might have tried to pat it, walked on. Keesa takes a step forward, then stops herself. The kitten's sharp eyes hold hers.

Abruptly, approaching it feels like a bad idea. Her legs feel constricted, and are turning now, carrying on walking to school. She makes it to the school-house in a short amount of time, not turning to see whether the kitten is still looking at her, or perhaps following her. The sense of unsettledness grows as the day wears on. Elijah comments that she is not looking herself.

It takes an interminable amount of time for the final bell to be rung, letting the children out of school. Keesa pretends to dawdle for a few minutes (a frequent occurrence anyway) so that Elijah will walk ahead of her home. Once she has made sure that all the other children are well beyond her on the road, she starts back towards the farmstead. As she turns the corner about halfway there, she sights the solitary tree, the kitten next to it like a statue. It swings its head in Keesa's direction, and keeps its eyes on her until she is within a few yards of it. Her feet turn her away from the kitten again, heading quickly on to home. A voice that sounds like purr and boy at the same time sounds behind her.

'Would I be correct addressing you as Keesa?'

Keesa halts. She turns to see where the voice has come from. There is no person in sight. That is not possible, thinks Keesa. Being trawled through waves to a benthic encounter flashes across her mind. She feels gauche and dream-like, but curiosity pushes words from her mouth.

'Did you just speak?' she asks the kitten.

The kitten blinks. 'Yes.' That same voice coated in purr.

'How did you know my name?'

'I am your helper, if you name me such.'

As sphinxian as its words are, Keesa is struck by how smoothly they glide through the air and canals of her ears.

'How did you get here? Does this have to do with the whale?'

'It is the whale that sent me, yes, but only you can accept.'

Keesa pauses. The notes the whale sang to her rebound in her head. She looks around again, half-expecting its lumbering mass to be beached on the caked ground. Just the dry breeze, and dip in birds' tweeting from nearby bushes. Then an echo in Keesa's ears of what she is about to say before she forms it.

'I accept.'

Her voice has a surety to it. She notes the disquiet inside her has evaporated. Keesa turns to go.

'Shall we?' she asks, looking back to the kitten, a new tone in her voice, one of kindness and command. The kitten breaks its marble cast, and walks alongside Keesa on the path.

Keesa and the kitten sit across from Aedan in the lounge.

'But what about that very expensive-looking collar? Surely there is an owner?' Aedan asks.

'That's my bracelet,' Keesa improvises.

'Yours? I've never seen it before.'

'I found it on the beach on our holiday. I forgot to tell you.' Close enough to the truth, Keesa thinks. Aedan hesitates. She has always felt there are things Keesa declines to tell her.

'Please Mom, if you let me keep the kitten, I'll lay the cloths on the cheese every afternoon when I come home, and go sell at the market every Saturday, and then maybe you can make more, like you said you want to,' Keesa urges.

'Well...' Aedan feels her resolve wavering.

'And I promise the kitten won't make messes or anything,' Keesa adds for good measure.

'That's debatable,' Aedan points out, but finds herself almost believing Keesa, given the intent look the kitten is giving her.

'Please, Mom?' Aedan can see how much Keesa wants the animal. It is not often that she asks for anything.

'All right,' she surrenders.

'Thanks, Mom,' Keesa beams, gets up, and starts making her way out the lounge, looking back towards the kitten every few steps with her hand out. The kitten follows, taking pauses to sniff out its new dwelling.

Keesa's father arrives home shortly after the fortunate decision and, as he kisses Aedan hello, asks after the kitten being coaxed through the hallway by the girl.

'That's the newest addition to our household, my darling,' explains Aedan, in a voice that declares the matter closed, yet with a look that appeals for approval on the matter.

He smiles. 'If it makes her this happy, then it's good with me.'

He follows his wife in and, as he turns to shut the front door, a feeling of unease comes over him, a sense that he is being watched. Kaleb looks up into the baobab tree in the garden. Settled on its uppermost branch is a large eagle. His eyes meet those of the bird. The eagle gives him a look that is now threatening, now sad. It flaps its wings and lifts off into the darkening sky. It has been many years since Kaleb felt panic rising in him as he does this evening. He makes sure not to show this to his family as he enters the cheerful space, locking the door behind him.

Hope and a Shaded Window

01/03/2036

Valtere looks at Regan as he preens his wing feathers with his beak. She is beginning to look like a young lady now. The eagle was assigned as her helper when she was four years old. He has noticed that the Princess has taken to wearing her hair loose more often now, and he can tell by the way she speaks to the court girls that they are discussing boys. As neutral as he is required to be about the Princess, he cannot help feeling a degree of pity for her. The other girls will have their chance at dancing with a boy, stealing a kiss in some furtive locale, perhaps get asked to be his girlfriend. Regan is aware that her talk, plans and giggles of such activities are futile. She will only be permitted certain formal activities with boys of Dark royalty. The pool of such candidates on the planet is not extensive and they all live on different continents. This has long been a safety strategy of Dark royalty—splitting the wider bloodline up physically in order to confine any harmful incidents to satellite families, and so ensure continuation of the pedigree.

Meeting dates and times between the Princess and the candidates were scheduled years in advance. It is incumbent on Regan to choose the one she feels is fit to become the future King of Dark. For anyone to be welcomed into the Nox Dark family is a feat of note. Before any candidate is allowed time in the Princess's company, her mother will already have gruelled them through a screening process. One of the reasons Regan still manages to slip out on regular expeditions away from the Chamber is the firm trust that her parents place in Valtere as her helper and protector. They know that wherever Regan might wander, he will not be far behind.

Her tutor is not in a tolerant mood today. 'I will not have this constant tittering while I am teaching. If you do not focus on the lesson, I shall set you extra homework tasks for the weekend.' The girls settle immediately. They don't direct attitude to Mister Alton; Regan is the only one who does this; she likes to push edges. The court girls know how quickly they can lose their place and shatter their parents' prospects as courtiers through one short-sighted incident.

Mister Alton points to a phrase written in capitals on the chalkboard:

EMBRACE THE VOID.

He reads it out. 'A maxim you have heard before. You will have to learn to practice this in thought and action in your lives. It entails first embracing the void of emptiness inside yourself, and then, the meaninglessness of life around you. There are a million human sayings that all pose 'love' and 'light' as the catchall answer to anything negative. The reason this argument receives so much support, is that humans refuse to accept the fact that fate is an impartial force, and that the only certainty one can count on is that life is born out of and ruled by nothingness, an empty void.'

Regan raises her hand. 'Yes, Your Highness?'

'Surely adherence to the Dark creed displays an equal degree of refusal to believe that we might be born out of Light, out of everything?'

Valtere stops his cleaning and observes Regan. She should practice more caution. Mister Alton studies her face.

'Dark breeds choose not to latch onto salvation through Light as a result of superior faculties of logic, not out of fear. We are not suggesting that living by Light is 'bad'. The labels of 'good' and 'bad' are considered discriminatory and archaic. We simply regard Light customs to be ineffective with regard to economy of energy expenditure. A society that lives in accordance with the Dark code functions more smoothly. There are not countless people wandering around in a perpetual state of loneliness, depression, pain, and disappointment, expending unreasonable amounts of energy on processing those emotions in order to find a way out of the tunnel of such self-created turbulence. Dark devotees do not set up expectations of actualising as a being of Light and love or, of 'finding love' in some other counterpart. Such conjecture is bound to lead to a misfit between idyllic fantasy in the mind and empty reality on the ground. Instead of a human race withering on a spectre of belief, you could have a people flourishing by nurturing their own inner power, not in the name of love but in the name of acceptance of reality.'

The court girls sit neatly, taking in these words with blank, alert faces. Regan's eyes are racing with thought; she struggles against the notions and what seem like their dead ends.

'But, what if—' Valtere lets out a squawk, flapping his wings and fixing his eyes on Regan. She casts a blistering look his way and turns back to her tutor with doggedness in her eyes. 'As I was saying, what if you—' A bell is clanged with verve outside the classroom door, a duty assigned to the youngest courtier children.

'Your question will have to wait until our next lesson, Your Highness, or perhaps by then you would have answered it for yourself?' Mister Alton is reluctant to enter into murky philosophical territory with the Princess. He has strict orders as to the limits of his lectures. Questioning of the Dark creed is not encouraged in the Chambers. Almost any answer he might give now could be interpreted as such.

The court girls file out of the classroom in a suitably deflated state. Regan exits last, with Valtere taking wing after her. He settles on her right shoulder; she attempts to shrug him off. He holds tight with his claws. 'I will dismount soon enough but first you must heed these words, Your Highness. You need to decide how important these questions are to you. You know the risks involved. Your natural ability as a Dark Princess is notable; why risk your future Queendom for the sake of arguing?'

'Surely as Queen one should agree completely with the laws? I am just trying to understand them more deeply.'

'Concurrence with the rules is a luxury. Obedience must be unquestionable. I fear that your contact with the outside is proving hazardous.'

They talk in hushed tones, making subtle checks of the passage for any courtiers or servants. 'I do not care for your opinion, Valtere. I have sworn you to secrecy about my movements. You still have to accompany me wherever I go; you cannot refuse my command.'

'You know I am at your service as long as you live, Your Highness. Your secret is safe with me. But that does not mean that I do not have strong reservations about—'

'My outings are simply entertainment for me. You concerns are unfounded, I have no interest in hearing them.'

'Do not forget that I am your helper, Princess Regan. Your curiosity and stubborn posture are proving risky traits.'

Regan purposefully walks close by a low-hanging chandelier, forcing the eagle off her shoulder. He settles on top of a cabinet in the passage. She turns to face him; her green eyes burning. 'You should not forget that as a Dark helper you are enslaved to me forever. I am ordering you to desist from this line of conversation, Valtere, or I will have your wings clipped and your voice removed. Then I will choose a new helper who understands the desirability of silence, who you can observe from the confines of a cage for the rest of your existence. Do I make myself clear?'

'Quite, Your Highness.' They both know that the selection of a helper is out of either of their hands. Regan has threatened the eagle, no more. Nonetheless, a threat from a Dark royal, no matter how young, is never a thing to be taken lightly. She strides down the passage, her carmine and black skirt swishing pertly after her. Valtere admires her coolness; it is one of the qualities that will take her to Queendom. But her rebellious demeanour hangs like a thorny snag in the air. It is only a matter of time before it hooks into her glowing prospects.

CHAPTER 3

A Walk and a Secret

08/11/2050

Once Keesa's mother has packed all the cheeses into her steel carry-box with ice scattered in it, it is loaded onto a hand-cart for Keesa to tow behind her as she walks to the market. Keesa and the kitten set off to call Elijah from his grandfather's farm. She places the cart under the shade of a tree while they make the detour. As soon as they are out of Keesa's parents' earshot, the kitten starts speaking.

'Keesa, you must name me. You have one day in which to do this. If the name fits, I will stay with you. However, if it takes you longer than one day, or if the name doesn't fit, I will return to where I came from.'

'But...' Keesa is thrown. 'How can I know what to name you? And where did you come from anyway? And why are you wearing that locket? And—'

Before any more questions can topple out her mouth, the kitten interjects.

'I was wondering when you might start asking questions. The truth is, I don't know all the answers. I either would like to know the answers myself, or I am not permitted to tell you them—not yet, anyway.'

'But, why not?'

'You're going to have to be patient, Keesa. I too wanted to know everything before I came here. But we will hopefully find out more as we go along, and I'll tell you what I can, when I can,' the kitten replies.

More and more questions teem around Keesa's head. They spot Elijah approaching them halfway between the two farms. Striding alongside him is a dog with a sleek, black coat, who is almost as tall as Elijah.

'I'm not sure I like the look of this...' says the kitten.

'Oh, that's just Nefer, Elijah's dog,' reassures Keesa.

'That's a dog?' the kitten's fur is standing on end now.

'Yes, it's a cross between a Doberman and a Great Dane, I think,' Keesa offers. It doesn't seem to alleviate the kitten's fears.

'This is my new kitten,' Keesa explains, once up close. 'I haven't decided his name yet.'

Nefer's short tail begins wagging slowly. His movements are generally quite deliberate, as are Elijah's. He has been given responsibility from a young age. His family live in a town a fair distance from Hale. He is a tall boy, with a lean, strong frame, spry energy, and dark blonde hair that reaches to below his earlobes. He was sent at age six to assist his grandfather with the management of the family farm, and it is Elijah's wish to take over from him one day. His school attendance sometimes becomes patchy because of his chores but, during those times, he tends to get help from Keesa with catching up on schoolwork. On occasion, Elijah has brought his herd of goats to school so he can keep an eye on them from the classroom window. The dog and cat size each other up for a few more moments.

'I think the reason he's not chasing your kitten is that he's happy for animal company that isn't a goat,' says Elijah.

As the kitten doesn't look quite as convinced that Nefer could be a potential playmate, Keesa tells Elijah to keep a bit of distance between the two animals for now. They collect the cheese cart from its shady resting place and make their way to the village.

'Did you hear about the attack?' Elijah asks.

'Baboon Gang?' Keesa's mind veers from the guesswork ticking in her head.

'Jah, two villages away, night before last. A whole family was mauled.'

The Baboon Gangs are bands of survivors who turned down opportunities to join any of the village communities and, instead, rove from village to village, raiding homes for supplies.

'Miss Stein says that Hale is like a fortress compared to other villages.' A quiet girl, Keesa often listens in unnoticed on adult conversation.

As a method of insurgence, the leaders of the gangs hold packs of baboons in captivity, and use them to create a distraction by releasing them at weak points of guard around villages. Given that baboons have been an unrelenting pest for years, they are a logical decoy. The baboons are starved for the few days before a raid.

'Maybe.'

Keesa had hoped for something more reassuring from Elijah. She tries to stop the images in their tracks; applies her mind to naming her kitten.

They load the cheese off at the woman who trades it for Aedan in the bustling market-place. Money no longer has currency; the planet has reverted to a barter system. Keesa keeps one block, as usual, to use for her own purposes and this serves as her pocket-money for the week. They while away part of the day hunting the stalls for relics brought in from the scorched cities. Keesa finds an old medical text and snaps it up.

'What? I like the pictures,' she says, addressing Elijah's questioning look.

Later, they join a soccer game thrown together by some of the village school pupils. The play is an approximation of the sport, but encourages frivolity amongst a generation born into an all-too serious world. The kitten and towering dog watch the antics from the sidelines, slowly growing accustomed to each other's presence. The four of them make a happy band wending their way home at the end of the day, Keesa carrying the kitten for his tiny legs. Elijah notices that the circle engraved into the kitten's pendant is glowing green, brighter and dimmer in turns.

'Why is that thing around the kitten's neck shining like that?' he asks.

Keesa looks down. Nefer, also focused on the locket now, begins a high-pitched whining.

'Put it down,' the boy says. Keesa does so with care, disturbed by the kitten's eyes, which look to be in a state between waking and sleep. He remains so for a few more moments, then abruptly opens his eyes fully as the locket's illumination fades.

'What the hell was that?' Elijah asks. He gathers from Keesa's expression she is not as surprised as him.

29

'I'm not sure,' she says.

'I know when you're lying. What's with this kitten and its freaky locket thing?'

The kitten looks warily from Elijah to Keesa.

'Do you promise to keep it secret?' she asks.

'All right,' Elijah assents.

'The kitten can talk.'

Elijah throws the girl a concerned look.

'Go on, show him,' she instructs the kitten.

'This is not a good idea,' the feline says, in a concerned tone.

Nefer cocks his head to one side. Elijah's face goes white. He opens his mouth in disbelief and tries to get some words out.

'Don't worry, I'll explain later. I mean, we must be patient...it will all be explained to us at the right time...he means us no harm...just don't worry right now!' Keesa says.

Elijah swallows, now confused as well as in shock.

'If I'm any later than this getting home, my dad will probably ground me next weekend. I swear you don't need to be scared. Trust me.'

They walk the short remaining distance to Keesa's home in uncharacteristic silence. As they get to the gate, they see Kaleb's car in the distance. Keesa turns to Elijah and lifts her hand to his shoulder reassuringly.

'You'll be okay?' she ventures.

'Sure,' he returns, at a loss as to what else he could say.

Better if I don't make a big deal of it, she thinks, *it only makes the madness of it seem worse*. She picks the kitten up and swiftly opens the gate, slipping into the front garden as inconspicuously as possible. She gives Elijah a quick wave as she heads for the front door. The actions of normality are imperative now.

30

Departure

21/09/2039

The mood in the late morning classroom is jubilant. School will break for an early vacation of 10 days today, after which it will resume with shorter hours for the remainder of the year. The bell was rung by a 10-year old aspiring court girl 15 minutes before, excited for her moment. Her fervour was dampened when she realised that the Princess was not even around to notice. Her Highness has been known to give tokens of encouragement to the bell-ringers, if she feels they are showing notable promise as future court girls. A piece of ribbon for their wrists, a spray of her perfume. The court girls in the classroom are keyed up, whispering about how they will spend their holidays. Mister Alton is doing some paperwork, keeping his eye on the door for the Princess. He assumes the Dark Queen is having a talk with her, given the significance of the day.

'Princess Regan approaches!' The court child relishes watching the girls in the classroom taking order upon her words. They all assume their usual places and turn in their seats towards the door, smiles touching their lips. Regan enters the room, followed shortly by Valtere. The girls break out into applause and the word 'congratulations' peppers from their mouths. Mister Alton stands, beaming at his most exalted pupil. Their vim tails off as they take in Regan's appearance. Her countenance is chalky, apart from her eyes, which are hot and blotchy with tears recently shed. Her usual air of confidence has disappeared, her hair is untidy; she attempts a smile for her subjects. The brittleness it exposes is unmistakable and unnerving for those witnessing it.

'My apologies for being late; thank you for your wishes. Please continue with the lesson, Mister Alton.' A few of the girls sitting closest to her rise unsurely to help Regan in some way, uncertain how.

Mister Alton's tone is careful, an unfamiliar sound in the classroom. 'Your Highness, are you unwell, should I call your Mother?'

Regan strains to harden her demeanour, stop the fuss in its tracks. 'Please! Sit, ladies. Mister Alton, I am perfectly well; kindly resume the lesson.' She seats herself slowly at her desk, moving like bits of shattered glass held together with skin. Valtere is on edge; he perches himself on the seatback of her school-desk.

Mister Alton pauses, considering whether or not to mark the day, as is expected of him. He wonders what could have transpired to cast this pall over her. 'Your Highness, six weeks have passed since your 18th birthday, and later today you will leave the royal Chamber for your year of solitude. There, you will develop the ability of your choice. You must harness your strength now and apply all that you have been taught.'

The Princess is looking down at her desk. Control is everything, her mother has said so many times. Containment is paramount. She smoothes her hair down, smoothes her dress down.

'Even though your helper is permitted to escort you, your tolerance for isolation, an essential Dark skill, will be tested to the utmost. Channel any struggle you may have with this into perfecting your special capacity. We all wish you well in your coming year; your presence in the classroom will be missed.' Regan looks briefly at the girls, their faces of concern, and drops her eyes again. This is not what she can look at now. It draws the emotion out of her like a distasteful osmosis. 'Now, there are a few more issues of administration to deal with—'

'May I be excused, Mister Alton?' Regan is on her feet again, still casting her eyes down. The tutor senses that the Princess's state is not a good example for the court girls.

'Of course, Princess Regan...we shall all be there later to see you off from the Chamber.'

She makes it to her room, still forcing the tears back. Once at her door, she turns to Valtere.

'I wish to be alone now.'

'But does Your Highness not require some refreshment? Perhaps, I could—'

'No, just to be alone.'

Regan turns, feeling the eagle's anxiety hanging in the dim passage. She turns back towards him and looks into his eyes with rare gentleness.

'Thank you Valtere, your services shall not go unrewarded. It pleases me that you will accompany me during my year of solo training.' Despite his awareness of the illegality of her state and what led to it, he is touched by her words, which are seldom offered with such naked respect.

'I am forever at your command, Princess.'

Once in her room, she attempts to quell the brokenness that jags in her chest. She is a Dark royal; this must be the last time she ever comes so close to that kind of display. Her heart is screaming that intolerable sound again. She swallows it down again and again until it spews out of her mouth onto the floor. This grants some relief and helps her place herself again. She cleans the vomit off the floor with her bath towel and soap, repeating the process three times so as to leave no trace of mess or smell. The court girls saw enough. Their tongues are no doubt already wagging. She will have to come up with yet another lie for her mother. This will not be difficult; she is getting better at it all the time. Soon she will be far away from all of this. The timing couldn't be better. She will keep telling herself that. Just the farewell speech from her mother that afternoon, a car journey, and then away on the ship. Away from this house hidden by ligaments of thicket, away from the ever-watching eyes of her parents and the court, away from him. He must be wiped from her being like an amputation. There is no other sane route to take.

The Naming

Early the next morning, the sun has not yet touched the tree in front of Keesa's house. She walks across a sand-blown expanse towards a slate-grey, square tower, which has the face of a clock at the top of each of its four sides. As she peers up, light strikes the highest point of it. *Dawn*, she thinks. She detects faint sounds in the distance, coming from the east—people cheering, drums being beaten, and a low bagpipe hum. Curious as to the source, she begins climbing the inner stairs of the clock-tower to view the surroundings. As she makes her way up, the sounds take on a tinny quality, bouncing off black varnished iron. Looking up, she sees that the clock facing east is warming yellow now and the sounds are growing clearer. Feeling that she'll miss out, Keesa speeds up, her calf muscles struggling to keep up with her haste. Finally she reaches the belfry, edged by the reverse sides of the four clock faces. She pauses for a moment, her legs biting for a break, taking in time the wrong way round. At last, she spots the uppermost trapdoor leading onto the roof. Scaling the last short ascent, with great effort, she pushes open the heavy wooden lid, which falls down with a dusty thud above. The sound of excited voices and instruments being played swells through the hatch. Keesa heaves herself up.

The top landing of the clock-tower has wrought iron benches lining each side of its quadrant, only a railing behind each bench. They look weather-beaten, unused. She quickly moves to the east-facing lookout and takes in a view of the parade, still from a fair distance, yet close enough to make out its principal constituents. The moving mass is anchored by a central procession, made up of a number of dignitaries who surround a female figure elevated on a golden chariot, drawn by four horses. *Some kind of queen, perhaps*, Keesa thinks. Walking on all four sides are what seem to be formal musicians, all dressed in attire matching the colours of the cortège—red, blue, gold and white, with grey and black trims. It is the first time Keesa has seen the balloon-like bags with protruding pipes they carry that give a full bass note. This focal retinue wends its way in slow time, with gravity.

Surrounding and exhilarating off it is a drove of people abandoning themselves to what seems to be a celebration. They flurry and skip around the procession like moths around a flame. Their musical instruments are rudimentary—pots and spoons, fiddles and drums. Dust swirls up, stirred by their treading and dancing feet, caught in the clean dawn's rays. Despite all the flinging, Keesa's eyes are drawn back over and over to the central imperial figure. She struggles to make out her features, yet even from such a distance, she has an uneasy sense that she looks familiar. Just as Keesa determines to stay on the tower as long as it may take to get a good look, she wakes up in her bed.

Still dark out. She looks down towards the kitten curled up on a cushion next to it.

'Toekoums,' she says.

These words draw the feline from his drowsiness. He gets up, faces Keesa.

'You have succeeded. I am your helper for as long as I live.'

With that, he bends one hind leg, and makes a low bow to her. She lifts her hand and places it on his inclined head. They remain so for a few moments, after which she drops her hand to her side. Toekoums looks up; the two stare at each other, not quite understanding what has just taken place, or how they knew what to do. They break the woodenness with an outburst of laughter. It trails off. They look at each other with wide eyes.

'So, what happened earlier? When your locket lit up?' Keesa asks.

'That's when my name came through.'

'Of course.'

Keesa does not get back to sleep before day breaks. As pleased as she is that it somehow brought her helper's name with it, the dream has left her feeling dislodged.

CHAPTER 4

Shrouded

09/11/2050

Regan's guards await in cars. Such trips are not frequent. Today's was an unexpected emergency call-out. They arrive at the patient's house. The woman is almost fully dilated. It would have taken days to call the closest midwife, four villages away, let alone the time it would have taken her to travel here. The woman is clearly in pain; shrieks escape her mouth every now and then but, she is inhibited by this doctor who wears something that amounts to a burka. The patient's sister is a courtier in the Dark Chamber and made the appeal personally. It is common knowledge amongst insiders that if you are in need of urgent medical assistance, an appeal to the Dark Chamber may be your only chance, with their fuelled vehicles and skilled doctor.

Over the last 10 years Regan has gradually become a doctor, not in the conventional sense, but those rules no longer apply. Her mother had provided a thorough base. Regan treats mostly in the Chamber but is occasionally required outside. Reversion to antiquated or natural methods, equipment and medicines has been necessary, given the lack of medical supplies. The Genguns are an intermittent source of the latter, but unreliable. A year after the scourge, some of the few surviving doctors tried to form Samaritan-type medical centres but, they were taken out in hits ordered by the Gengun heads so as to maintain their stranglehold on rare supplies of any description.

The umbilical cord is coiled around the neck of the foetus like a cosy adder, reluctant to emerge into the uninviting world. Regan performs a caesarean. The mother loses consciousness immediately after the incision. Anaesthetics are hardly ever available now and, if accessed, are generally too risky to use, given the rudimentary nature of their synthesis. The mother eventually wakes, and welcomes the neonate onto her chest.

After scrubbing her hands, Regan, guarded heavily, leaves wordlessly and waits in the assigned car for her attendants. It is not an operation she is comfortable with. She would rather deal with any trauma, any disease, than be confronted with the groping vulnerability of a newborn. On the way back, the smell coming through the air-vents alters as they pass what used to be Port Elizabeth. Here it is laced with the acrid scent of burnt earth, faded now, but still winding the road like a ghost. The bigger cities had undergone mass burnings, once the disease had taken its toll on their inhabitants, to deal with decomposing corpses and prevent the reinfection of survivors.

Back at the Chamber, Regan averts her eyes from the disapproving looks of courtiers, staff and Mister Alton. Many in the Dark Chamber still believe it is not fitting for a Dark Queen to perform work, let alone of an altruistic nature, and outside Chamber walls on top of it. As much as they take security in having access to a doctor, their Queen's consistent departure from tradition unsettles them. Regan goes to her bedroom now, shuts the door behind her and leans against it, lifting the black muslin off her face. She remains still until the disturbance inside her has abated to its hiding-place.

Regan's bedroom forms part of the rear portion of the homestead. When her family first moved in, the closest town had been Graaff-Reinet, now barely existent. French windows open up to her private garden area of trees, bushes, a light covering of tough grass, and a few flowering plants. There is a pecking on one of the panes. It is Valtere. Regan lets him in.

'Did you locate the youngling?' she asks him.

'I did, Your Majesty. Her name is Keesa. She is living in a village named Hale, about three or four hours' drive from here. She lives with her parents—both commonplace human. No other siblings. She recently acquired a kitten.'

'That's not a good sign. Could be a helper. I don't want to attract too much attention. It is essential that the girl not be harmed. She will be of no use to me dead. She has quite the shield around her—I still haven't been able to pinpoint her origins. Certainly high-born, though, with the signal she is giving out. If there is to be an heiress to the Dark Throne, steps must be taken soon. Her potential to be moulded into the role is plain.'

'I know there would be risk involved, but we could search out a Dark suitor for you in lands across the seas.'

'The process would take too long. And, judging by the poor array of candidates that cloyed my youth, I can only imagine the wearisome lot they've grown up to be. I have no desire to rear any of their spawn, let alone go chasing across the globe in search of them. The Chamber of Light will no doubt be eyeing the foreign royal for their own purposes as we speak. Nonetheless, she is extremely young, by both Chamber's standards. I could risk ruining any chance of winning her over by moving in on her too soon. Let us bide our time for now but, keep an eye on her.'

Valtere nods. 'Your Highness wishes to retire for the evening?'

'Stay a bit. Eat here with me. I want to hear details of your observation of the girl.'

Wires and Screens

It is a tranquil Saturday morning, and, although the sun has barely risen, Keesa is up and dressed, and about to begin her chores in the dairy for the day. The sooner she is done with them, the sooner she and Toekoums can go play. Keesa begins skimming the top, thick layer off the buckets of cream. Her father enters the dairy in his work clothes and makes his way over to a corner where he stores some of his trade tools.

'Morning Kees,' he says, kissing the top of her head.

'Hi Dad,' she replies, without taking her eyes off the task.

Her father pulls a roll of thick electrical cabling out from a shelf above his head. 'I'm pleased to see you helping your mother more often lately, Keesa,' he comments, 'and I know that she is impressed with how quickly you seem to be learning the skills.'

'Thanks Dad.' Keesa looks at her father. It is rare to receive a compliment from him.

'Your mother tells me that you take your kitten playing with you in the veldt and village,' he comments, wrapping the heavy bundle of cables with thin rope. Toekoum's ears prick up; his tongue halts its cleaning.

'Yes,' replies Keesa. She feels her cheeks becoming flushed.

'Isn't it a bit odd for a cat to go out walking like a dog?'

Toekoum's shoots her father one of his purposeful looks and jerks back into cleaning as Kaleb's eyes meet his.

'I didn't know that cats couldn't go on outings.'

Her father pauses, resists the urge to scold Keesa for her disrespectful tone. 'No, I don't suppose you've had much experience of cats," he says. A shadow crosses his face momentarily. It is not the first time that Keesa has sensed a part of her father that she cannot fathom.

'Did you have a cat when you were little?' Keesa is keen to steer the conversation away from herself.

'In a manner of speaking, yes, for a time.'

'What do you mean?'

'Never mind, just the usual childhood friendship with an animal. Where exactly did you go on your excursion?'

Toekoum's skin on his back twitches as he regards Kaleb. 'We went to the market with Mom's cheeses and then played in the field near the village for the afternoon.'

'You only got home at 6 o'clock.'

'Yes, I lost track of time—Daddy! Look out!' Keesa exclaims, pointing towards the high shelf of cabling above Kaleb's head. He ducks, spinning around to look at it. Everything appears normal. He turns back and raises an eyebrow at Keesa, who still has her eyes fixed on it.

'That's an odd way of getting out of telling me where exactly you... Keesa! Look at me when I'm talking to you!'

A forceful gust of wind picks up outside and blasts through the cracked plank situated directly behind where the stacks of wires are. A moment later, a roll of wire precariously balancing at the top of the pile rolls off the shelf, hits a hook on the wall, twists vertically, and goes hurtling down towards the floor, exactly where the top of Kaleb's head would have been. The wire-stack slams into the floor and thuds to a rest, leaving gouge marks on the wooden boards. Kaleb stands looking at it, shaken. Toekoums' tail stands upright and bushy. Keesa resumes her chores; she is stirring the milk now.

'Keesa...how did you know that was going to happen?'

'I don't know.' She keeps her eyes on the milk.

'Has that happened before—that you've known something before it takes place?'

'Not really...'

Her father steps closer to her now, 'What do you mean by that? Keesa, how many times must I tell you; look at me when I'm talking to you!'

Toekoums pads to Keesa's side.

'Why should I tell you anyway? You never tell me anything except what I shouldn't do and where I shouldn't go!'

'You don't understand yet how important it is for me to tell you those things, especially after what I just saw you do!'

'But isn't what I just did a good thing? Those cables could have landed on your head!'

Kaleb kneels down before Keesa, and places his big hands around her shoulders. 'Of course it was a good thing, Keesa, you just need to be aware of the dangers... of how and when it is appropriate to use that skill.'

'So teach me what to do, Dad. I'm scared of it. I don't understand why it's happening.'

'My girl, I wish I could do that but, believe me when I say that the best and safest course of action for you now is to ignore those feelings, keep them to yourself. Do not tell even your mother, or else you could be inviting great danger into your life.'

'But if I'd ignored it, you could have died!'

'That's not what I meant now,' Kaleb returns.

Keesa wriggles out of his arms. 'What have I done that is so bad?'
She starts to run out of the dairy; Toekoums follows her.

'Keesa, come back here! I'm saying these things because I love you! Where are you going! Come back here!'

She is already out of his sight around the corner of the dairy, making her way to the front gate of the garden. Toekoums pauses for a moment to look back at Kaleb, who has spun back to the cabling lying on the floor.

'Damn it!' He kicks the cabling in frustration. Small sparks skip across the bundle of wires, making the sharp buzzing sounds of live electricity. He senses that he is being watched, swivels his head and sees the kitten observing him.

'What?' Kaleb blurts out. Toekoums takes in this strange scene for a moment more, then patters off quickly to find Keesa. He catches up with her as she is footing across the garden carrying her knapsack. Her mother is busy watering her desert flowers that dot all of the beds around the front area of the house. Keesa pauses briefly at her mother's side.

'I'm so sorry I haven't finished my chores this morning, Mom, I promise I will as soon as I am back. Please can I go to Elijah now?'

The tone in her voice and heated tears in her eyes unnerve her mother.

'All right Keesa, you can finish later. What's—'

'Thanks, Mom. Come, Toekoums.'

She walks hastily out the front gate; Toekoums struggles to keep up with her. Aedan knows there is only one person who can work Keesa up in that way. She will have to have a word with her husband. She turns to find him, only to see him at the side of the house, watching as Keesa leaves. He starts towards the front gate.

'Kaleb, let her go. We both know you're not going to make anything better if you try talk to her now. What happened this time?'

'I'm just trying to protect her.'

'From what? There is no-one for miles around this village. You cannot expect her to spend every weekend sitting in the house. What are you so afraid of happening?'

'I don't want to talk about this now, Aedan. I have to go work.'

Aedan watches her husband pull off in his truck with the same sense of too many questions unanswered that she has carried for years. She accepted his enigma a long time ago, because, in return, he brought security to her child's life. Yet now the mystery is less the thrill of mist and more the feeling of being blindfolded. Her freshly watered flowers are opening to the morning sun now, their bright oranges and pinks a welcome otherness to the swathe of beige that surrounds them.

CHAPTER 5

Homecoming

21/09/2040

A small welcoming party of the Princess's ladies-in-waiting stands in the entrance hall of the Dark Chamber, headed by the Dark Queen. The door opens and Regan enters, escorted by a cluster of guards. It has been a year since she has had any human contact. Even the Dark guards stationed around the abandoned temple that she lived in for the duration had strict orders to refrain from laying eyes on her, unless absolutely necessary for security reasons. No such incidents had occurred.

The Queen immediately notices a change in her daughter. Something in her has broken. Her eyes look different. It is not so much that they have lost some of their mettle, but that they have altered in quality, deepened. As determined as Regan is to control her emotions, the simple yearning for her mother's arms overwhelms her. Tears begin to sting her eyes. She walks forward disjointedly, feeling small and foreign on the ground that once felt so much like her home. She feels the eyes of the court ladies following her.

She is wearing the slate grey and black dress that she wore for her embarkation. She is unused to it now, as her training year was spent mainly in short, functional wear. The thick skirt catches under her foot, and she lurches forward, falling into the Queen, grabbing at her waist. The Queen looks down at this mess of a daughter, her mouth grimacing, and steps back woodenly. An inconvenient wave that pulses with the year of deprivation and a life of withheld affection from her mother takes Regan by surprise. She hangs onto her mother's waist. The Queen hastily motions the guards to take her away. They do so with difficulty. Her ladies-in-waiting look on in silence. As Regan is carried to her bedroom by the five guards, she looks back to her mother.

The Queen is dusting off her skirt whilst giving quiet orders to the ladies. They all curtsey and make their way from the hall except one, Charlotte, who stays behind and walks with the Queen into the reception room. Regan balks at the fact that she has done precisely what she had promised herself never to do again. This unutterable show of emotion was far worse than a year ago. She will have to work hard to find her way back from it. She must cease this childish hankering for once and for all. There is no space left for any more mistakes. Walls of the coldest order are called for.

Herding and Batting

20/11/2050

Toekoums struggles to keep up with Keesa's quick feet as they make their way to Elijah's farm. Keesa is silent at first, but Toekoums can feel words blistering her tongue.

'Are you all right, Keesa?'

Keesa halts her stomping.

'Can you give me answers yet? Can you tell me what's happening to me and why? Or why my father thinks it's dangerous and wrong? And why I should trust your word over my father's?'

The kitten's frame deflates visibly. 'It pains me to tell you that I cannot give you those answers. You must find them for yourself.'

Keesa throws her hands and head up to the sky and begins pounding towards the farm once more. Toekoums darts behind.

Elijah is herding his goats when they arrive and has to stay on the farm for the day as his grandfather had to go into town to get supplies. He notices Keesa's bad mood and suggests a game of cricket, something she never refuses. She assents, but even the prospect of cricket doesn't pull her out. He knows that if he asks her what it's about, she will only get worse. He sets up the wickets close to where the goats are milling around so that he can keep watch over them during the game. Nefer knows the drill as soon as he sees the wickets and cricket bat come out, and positions himself in the fielding area.

Elijah picks Toekoums up and takes him to stand next to Nefer as a second fieldsman. He considers asking Toekoums what it is that is bothering Keesa but, the notion of asking a kitten a serious question causes him to close his mouth. He just hasn't got there yet. He goes to the pitch—really an area that has a thin layer of grass cover where they can get the most bounce on the ball. He is aware that Keesa's mood is probably the result of a fight with her father. He has been noticing an increase in these lately. The Great Dane can see the kitten is in low spirits and nuzzles his snout softly on the top of the kitten's head; he is growing fond of his little friend.

'Hey, Nefer,' Toekoums says. A growl of indignation escapes Nefer's throat; he is having trouble adjusting to the voice that keeps popping out of the kitten's mouth. Toekoums starts a little, then meows. The dog lets out a single, approving bark.

They begin the game. Toekoums notices that what cricket generally consists of is that Elijah throws the ball towards Keesa in a funny, Ferris wheel kind of way, she hits it with the bat and Nefer goes running madly after it. Once he has his huge jaws around it, he uses his neck and head to whip it back to Elijah. The children keep yelling things like 'four' and 'six', usually accompanied by Keesa doing a little dance, or 'wide', said in a low, accusatory tone. Keesa's mood is lifting as they play. Toekoums does a great deal of running around, becoming frustrated with being too small to catch the ball. Whenever he does make an attempt, mimicking Nefer's technique, he ends up jumping out of the path of the whizzing orb, so as not to be wrecked by it. On these occasions, Keesa yells words of encouragement from across the field. She feels bad for her conduct with him earlier. It isn't Toekoum's fault that he doesn't have the answers to her questions.

At the end of the fifth over, they pause for drinks, which entails Keesa taking the cooldrink bottle of water out of her knapsack and pouring some for Toekoums and Nefer into a steel bowl that she carries for this purpose. She and Elijah and each take a sip from the bottle. He notices that she is slightly pale as she sits at the base of a tree and goes to sit next to her. She holds her hands out to Toekoums, who regards her open palms, licks his fur a few times, then gingerly makes his way to her hands and finally, to the seat of her lap. She strokes his fur, sad that her manner has made him wary of her.

Once they begin playing again, Elijah is batting and Keesa is practising putting spin on the ball, so as to get him out. She has been trying for months; once she has a particular goal in mind, she becomes determined. Elijah hits a soaring six now, which heads in the direction of the goats.

'My spin-bowling is pathetic!' Keesa exclaims; she has never seen such a big hit from Elijah. They all squint into the sun to see where it will land.

'LION!' bellows Elijah, spotting something that the others haven't and begins tearing towards the herd.

The others look at each other quizzically for a moment, then make a dash after him in unison. As they near the herd, they spot the ears of a lion in the midst of the goats, who are all hysterical now and scattering outwards in all directions.

Nefer keeps getting caught between his function of controlling the herd and his duty to protect Elijah from the big cat.

'Oh, no!' the others hear Elijah crying out as they are nearly upon him. They find him kneeling next to a limp goat on its side on the ground. The last of the startled goats bolt from the area now, exposing the lion disconcertingly close to where Keesa's little group is gathered. However, the lion is not a lion, they all quickly realise. He is a sturdy, handsome man who has certain features of a lion, such as his ears, a tail, and hair that resembles a short, tawny mane. His clothing is spruce, but nothing out of the ordinary. Nefer threatens the stranger with growls. Elijah looks from the motionless goat to him and blurts out, 'You killed it!'

The stranger is unfazed by this accusation. 'Actually, I'm afraid you knocked it out with your six. Hit the left side of its head. I'm sure it will come around soon,' he says, in a voice like dark honey, produces the red cricket ball and holds it out towards Elijah. Nefer lurches forward towards the lion-man, snarling. Elijah can see now that the goat is still breathing, and orders Nefer to stay.

'We had better get the goat to the town vet. Keesa, can you go fetch the wheelbarrow from the shed?' Elijah hastens.

'If you'll allow me, I can try a technique that I've had good results with in bringing creatures back from an unconscious state,' the man proposes gently.

'Seriously...?!' Elijah scoffs. Keesa, who has been regarding the man all this time says, 'Let him do it.'

Elijah stares at her. 'This is not a joke. If my grandfather loses one goat, he loses trade. All this wacky stuff that's been happening lately...it's all becoming a bit much, Keesa. I need to be responsible here.'

'We don't have time, Elijah, just trust me; let him do it.'

Elijah lifts his hands up in disbelief, 'Fine! Go ahead, let a complete stranger who looks weird kill my grandfather's goat. No problem!'

The lion-man goes to the goat's side tentatively, given that Nefer is still showing his teeth. He stabilises his hands around its jaw, places his thumbs on the space between the goat's mouth and nose, and applies a great deal of pressure. At the same time, a barely audible roar sounds in his throat.

'See! As good as dead! Ridiculous!' Elijah is pacing around now in disbelief. Nefer starts barking again and looks set to attack the stranger's rear-end with a vengeance. The stranger then gives the goat a hard thump on the base of its spine. It comes abruptly awake, startles at the creature kneeling over it, leaps up, and bolts off unsteadily to rejoin the herd.

The lion-man stands up and dusts himself off. 'It should be all right now; just keep an eye on it for a day or so.'

Elijah shifts his weight and, looking at the ground, mumbles, 'Well, thank-you.'

'Pleased to be of assistance, young man.' Nefer whines. The lion-man looks from Elijah's glower across to Keesa. She is scrutinising him, considering everything her father has told her of the perils of trusting strangers. Yet, against her better judgement, when this striking man looks at her, a smile escapes the sides of her mouth. Toekoums, in her arms, lets out an unassuming meow.

'That's a sweet kitten you have.'

Elijah is at the end of his rope. 'Sorry to intrude on your cosy moment but, who or what are you, and what are you doing on my grandfather's property?'

'Forgive me, in the hubbub my manners seem to have lapsed. You can call me Lion, at your service. I am on a prospecting visit to your area; I want to farm olives. Apologies for my trespassing; there were no fences or signs. I got carried away while exploring.' The stranger's manner is marked by an intrinsic sense of decorum.

Keesa enquires, 'Not meaning to be rude but why do you look like that?'

'Oh, that's a long story and it seems I have offended your friend here through my intrusion, so I had best be on my way. Farewell...I'm afraid I didn't get your names?'

'Elijah' the young goat-herd says, followed by a single belligerent bark from the dog. 'And this is Nefer.'

The lion-man nods in Elijah's direction and smiles towards Nefer. The dog's ears turn up and his tail gives a confused wag. Lion turns to the girl again. He finds her features mesmeric.

'I am Keesa and this is Toekoums.'

'It has been a pleasure to meet you.'

'Why don't you stay and play some cricket with us? It's not often that we have more than two players. Do you know cricket?'

'I do indeed, and would be honoured to join the play. Elijah, are you in agreement?'

Elijah is still distrustful of the situation but, this man certainly seems to lift Keesa's mood and he does not seem to have untoward intentions. Most of all, Elijah doesn't want to be the grump in the group. 'All right, who's batting?'

Play lasts another hour. With the extra time, Lion has a chance to study Keesa more closely for affirmation of royal frequency. He is a little rusty; it's a technique he learnt early on in his training. A window can be opened in a moment of exhilaration, he remembers. He sets his mind upon coaxing the girl into achieving something she didn't expect. As they play, he gathers that Keesa is working on her spin, and offers to help her with it. They have a practise session while Elijah and Nefer have to herd a small group of straying goats closer to home. Once play resumes, within three balls, Keesa integrates the coaching perfectly into her bowling, puts just the right amount of spin on the ball and gets Elijah out by cracking the wicket wide open. She turns and shrieks 'OUT!!!' With that, Lion picks up the signal he is hoping for. A light that resembles a miniature sun opens out in the centre of her forehead. It appears to his eyes that is, but he is aware that the others are unlikely to pick it up. Elijah is dumfounded; he's never seen such a quick improvement. Just before she turns around to get the ball, Lion notices something different about this sun, something he has never seen before. By the time she turns back, the image has faded; that is its nature. Nonetheless, he coached her, she got it; the reward of this displaces any unease for now.

They play on for a while and, when Lion smells a female human making her way towards them on the other side of the hill, he says his goodbyes to the group and begins walking away. Keesa runs to him, a distance from the group.

'You never told us why you have lion in you. There have been strange things happening around me lately; are you a part of that?'

'You already know the answer to that.'

'But—'

'It will all be revealed in time, Keesa. For now, it would be best if you did not mention our meeting to your parents. Can we keep this a secret, just between us cricketers?'

Keesa hesitates. 'Okay, but only if you promise to come back soon.'

'I cannot promise that but I will do my best to make sure of it.' With that, he raises her hand and kisses it. Keesa is flooded with the sense again, as when she met Toekoums, one of dueness and amity. He begins his quick descent down the northern side of the hill.

Although not easily, Keesa gets Elijah to agree to keep the interaction with the lion-man confidential. 'We seem to be keeping more and more secrets. I'll do it but I'm not happy to.'

'Oh, come on, Elijah, lighten up! You have to admit that it's all quite exciting?' Keesa is in no mood to consider consequences now. They spot her mother coming through the gate. Lion has hidden behind the thickest bush in the vicinity and now attempts to scan Keesa's mother. It is not easy because of the distance, but the signal he instantly receives is pure human. *Perhaps when I return to this area,* he thinks, *the father will be in the vicinity too.*

He makes his way to his car, a 2040 overhauled Land Rover, a lucky find a few years ago. Most were destroyed in the fires and the car he'd had since he was 16 had given in. He had found this one protected from flames in a closed garage in an affluent Cape Town suburb and nursed it back to life. His gallons of petrol line the back seat in an assortment of jerry-cans and drums for his journey home. As he drives, the air is broken by a sound that has become foreign to him. He realises he is singing. He turns the music up and allows his fallow voice to climb over the sound of tyres on sand.

Jewel

22/09/2040

There is feasting and toasting in the Dark Court tonight. The ballroom, adapted by smashing out the walls of four intersecting rooms when the Family took occupation of the homestead years ago, is transformed with lit candle chandeliers, sumptuous platters of food, and the wafting scent of neroli. A coming of age celebration is traditionally thrown upon the return of a young Dark royal from their training. Applause dapples the room; Regan has just finished an expected, short demonstration of the technique she honed on the island. Given the convivial context of this night, she did not draw on any sensitive material, sticking to past Dark Chamber activities. The vision shared was of Queen Signa's coronation. It's veracity was remarkable and went some of the way to restoring Regan's stature for those who had witnessed her fragility the previous morning. The ladies-in-waiting and guards had been sworn to secrecy regarding the incident. The music starts, much to Regan's relief. She is still drained from the journey home and starts making her way to a quiet corner. Her mother intercepts, gently pressuring her to engage in courtly conversation.

'My daughter, the visionary.' The Dark Queen curls her arm around Regan and smiles like a snake at the circle of courtiers. 'Not quite what I had expected but, impressive nonetheless.' She touches her daughter's cheek as though it were that of a porcelain doll. 'You shall help make possible the downfall of the Light family for once and for all. They cannot hide from us now. Well done, darling.' The words should please Regan; she has hungered after her mother's praise ever since she can remember. The Queen's words ring hollow now. She brushes Regan coolly off her arm and returns to her mingling, her eyes and jewellery glittering with her creation.

Regan can see that her mother is surprised by how strong her daughter's ability to manifest visions has become. Nonetheless, she knows that she is a great disappointment to the Queen. The power of seeing is a talent that Regan inherited from her grandmother on the Queen's side, who became one of the most skilful at it of all the Dark Queens in her time. Regan's abilities have fast matched hers. Queen Signa, on the other hand, had always taken more to her father's powers of extracting and manipulating sera from all manner of creatures, with the aim of wiping out the Light Force on the planet. His vision had been to create a second *tabula rasa* on the globe, to simplify the palette for the Dark order to take root. It was cut short when he was assassinated by Light royals. Queen Signa stepped up as heir, set on bringing his research to fruition.

Regan's keen interest in chemistry and pharmacology is one of her only redeeming features, in her mother's eyes. She had expected a daughter who would share her passion for experimental surgery. Signa reserved respect solely for science. She had scorned her own mother for this reason, bonding more with her father. She was viewed by her father and the court as a brilliant candidate for Queen of Dark; the hardness of detachment had never been embodied as perfectly in anyone before her.

Regan glances at her father now, King Dallon of Dark, who is, as usual, surrounded by men who talk to him in a way that allows him to feel he has a say in courtly proceedings. Everyone, however, including the King himself, is aware that he is nothing but a puppet in the Court. Queen Signa will tug his strings when necessary, but her word wields unilateral power in all respects in the Chamber. She chose him for his uncalculating character, making it easier for her to bend him to her will. Other than his superior physique, he is notably unheroic. Soon after Regan's birth, the Queen made it clear that any parenting was to be left to her. She wished to raise a daughter who would emulate her side of the family. To Signa, King Dallon is an adherence to tolerate, nothing more than a source of Dark sperm, and a token, male figurehead for the Chamber. Her radical lack of interest in her husband makes her an exemplary leader for the Dark Force.

Leadenness seeps through Regan's body now; one of her ladies-in-waiting notices and offers to bring her some food and drink. Valtere settles next to the Princess in the tenebrous corner she has chosen. She smiles at him and strokes his head. The Queen detects this affection instantly; her indignation pierces Regan from across the room. She senses the crack in her daughter again. Signa has glimpsed the intactness of a hard outer shell around Regan throughout the day, which is encouraging but, there is something swampy about her daughter's interior that concerns her. The Princess shoves the bird away; composes herself to receive attention. The court musicians have assembled an odd combination of instruments—they have to make do with what they can get their hands on. Haunting electronic melody is punctuated with rhythm from fiddles and clappers and occasionally one of them sings, or delivers a solo on trombone.

When her mother is not looking, Regan casts a warm look in Valtere's direction. She had expected to feel relief at being back but the court feels vacuous, and the court girls distant, even smug. He flaps his wings and returns her comforting look. Their bond has strengthened and softened through her time away. It has grown beyond trust and loyalty into something highly illegal in the Chamber: a friendship. Neither of them is particularly comfortable with this; unaccustomed to such things as they are. Regan attempted to stem the change that was occurring in her before she left but did not succeed completely. It is not uncommon that a helper is influenced by their master. They are both aware that containment of any good humour between them is essential in order to avoid thin ice in the Chamber. If a helper is killed as a punitive measure against their master, replacement is forbidden. Slitting the eagle's throat would be a perfunctory action to the Dark Queen.

CHAPTER 6

The Assembly

27/11/2050

The dignitaries are filing steadily into the venue. The lion-man who Keesa met a week earlier is assigning a few last duties to his attendants. He is King Maen of Day. He looks the part today for this assembly in his formal attire. The Light officials are to be given a drink for refreshment and he has chosen a berry and lime juice blend. Fairly rare now, the fruits are grown in royal orchards in a fertile area about two hours from here.

He enters the conference hall of the royal Chamber of Light. Even though they have been holding the annual meeting of Light in this location for 10 years now, the splendour of the setting still astounds him. The seats are set out in a horse-shoe shape, the cream-coloured velvet freshly brushed. A vaulted ceiling lends the room grandeur and a sense that one's thoughts can expand. Small, simple bouquets of flowers common to the area are scattered throughout the hall. The King of Day enjoys the spacious aspect of affluence but has little interest in waste for the sake of ostentation.

The Light Chamber is situated along the west coast close to where a settlement known as Eland's Bay used to be. With a mountain as backdrop, the Chamber leads down to a glittering white-sand beach. The conference hall is on the first floor and the circular windows on its north-west-facing wall look directly out onto the ocean. Each one has a steel shutter attached to it—security in the Chamber has always been of utmost importance. The Aduro Light family, which Maen was born into, has presided over the Light throne for centuries. Their powers have remained unmatched in that time.

The chairs all face a giant transparent vessel that is filled with sea-water a few days prior to the annual conference. The tank has an extended spout reaching out through the wall; the external section of the spout, also steel, is fitted with an airtight door with a circumference of 20 metres at its sea end. Slowly circling the massive pool are two huge sperm whales and four dolphins. A special device lifts each of them out of the ocean nearby and places them into the cradle of the spout. From there, they slip down the chute into the great bath.

Once everyone is seated, a large celluloid screen to the right of the water bubble illuminates. The sound of static accompanies an image struggling to come through. It flashes on and off a few times; then settles. It is of Elke, former Queen of Light. Applause breaks out in the auditorium and there are smiles in her direction. The dolphins lift their heads out of the water and kreech out their greetings, as the whales blow gentle jets of air from their spiracles. Her look is one of modesty, yet great authority. She is seated on a simple wooden chair in what looks like an old stone farmhouse. There is a yellow bird perched on her shoulder, flexing its tail feathers. Her exact location is never revealed. The frame features only her head now. She looks towards someone off-camera.

'Thank you, Danie, I think it's transmitting clearly now.'

Maen looks at his mother's enlarged, floating face. Even at the age of 70, it has an unaccountable glow of youth to it. He does not applaud but holds a respectful stance. He sees her eyes flicking quickly through the gathering, looking for the member that he knows is not there. She hides her disappointment ably. When she catches the King's eye, a moment of awkward warmth passes between them. He swiftly lowers his eyes, sensing the attention of many. The Queen maintains the requisite neutrality of a royal in public and quietens the group down by raising her hand.

'My dear fellow Light beings, it is as always a great joy to see all of you here, particularly at this critical time. As you all know, we are approaching the juncture at which a handover of royal guardianship of Light is nigh. My years in flesh form are coming to an end and, soon I shall take on the supreme mandate of becoming the planet's next Sun-bearer. Unfortunately, the process of producing a female capable of becoming the Sun-bearer to follow my reign is not something that can be forced or engineered. The ingredient of authentic love between the prospective high-borns is essential. That Earth's population was all but wiped out by the contagion has not helped. While it distresses me that I may not live to see my son find that, one must at some point be practical with regard to these matters.'

Maen's expression turns stony. Discomfort pricks the air in the auditorium and eyes dart towards him.

'It appears as though we may have found a solution. Albeit an unorthodox alternative, the predicament we find ourselves in is dire. Light Royalty have now officially been an endangered species for 30 years. Once my time has come, if we have not established a female successor to begin her training as the next Sun-bearer we risk the psyche of the planet regressing once again to a radical form of separation. Whatever happens now will determine the new order of life on the globe. I leave it to the sea-borns to let you in on the details of the situation. I give you over now to our trusted interpreter, Erin.'

A small wave of applause patters the room as Erin lifts herself out of her chair. She has the look of an absent-minded professor. Although she clearly attempted to neaten her shock of white hair for the day, it is not complying with the arrangement she had in mind. She looks uncomfortable in her chalk-blue, full pencil skirt and matching jacket. Her usual attire consists of something that resembles a private girls' school uniform, circa 1950. She has a deep respect for uniforms as a practical alternative to wasting valuable time fussing over what to wear every day. Erin gives the crowd an unassuming nod, then adjusts her bearing in order to best listen to the sea mammals. She elongates her spine and tilts her head to the right.

The sea-borns have been focused on Erin through this, and now all turn to face the gathering. The largest whale dips its head down and up again, throwing out a pattern of heraldic sounds that fill the hall and ears. Erin interprets:

'We greet you, humanoids, and bring tidings of hope in a form new to our kind. At the end of September, we detected a high-born of unknown origin on the planet. Although her physical appearance is human, she has a highly charged identity shield around her that could only have been cast by another high-born. It was thus only through the royal readiness signal she began to emit two months ago that we were alerted to her potential. Her powers as a royal and capacity as Sun-bearer were confirmed upon contact. Her sound frequency is one of the most potent we have ever heard.'

The dolphins add their voices now, bursting their fricative clicks against the glides and whoops of the whale. The two smaller sea-mammals start and end sentences for each other, their thoughts seem shared.

'We subsequently sent her a kitten-helper, son of a trusted cat-helper who has worked for high-borns of the highest order. She has passed the first two helper tests and the King has met her. We are proposing that the girl be moved to the royal Chamber of Light as soon as possible, where she will undergo her schooling as a Light royal of Planet Earth.'

Erin comes out of her listening posture, turns and smiles at the sizeable creatures, then sits down in her seat in the front row. A flutter of response travels through those gathered, ranging from excitement to indignation.

'Are there any questions?' The Queen looks out with her child-like eyes. Maen notes that her mere presence invariably seems to comfort those near her. He is feeling hot and orders one of the attendants to open more windows. An aged man wearing a suit and tie, who has an air of authority about him stemming from a life as a powerful businessman, raises his hand.

'With all due respect, Your Highness, who is this girl? Where is she from? Why should we trust her?'

Surprise, agreement, and disregard show in gasps and the shaking of heads. It is not often that royalty are questioned on anything by their subjects, apart from by the sea-borns.

The Queen measures her words carefully. 'In all honesty, there is an element of risk in this course of action. Her sonic frequency contains definite elements of Light royalty, and I would even venture to say these seem to resemble the earth-affiliated family that I am part of. However, there are other elements to it that, at this point, I am unable to ascertain the origin of.'

The whale who has been silent until now intones a short series of pitches. Erin stands immediately but looks hesitant to relay its content to the Queen. The Queen looks at her expectantly. Erin smoothes down one of her wayward strands of white.

'We notice that the Prince of Rising Star is yet again absent from our meeting. Have you had any word from him?'

The room goes quiet. The buoyant look on the face of the Queen drops, and for a moment, a black hole of untended sadness renders her eyes hollow. She recomposes herself like brittle steel.

'No, I have not had word from him. As much as I try, I cannot pick up his signal at all.'

Erin reports the same whale's response. 'Is there not a possibility that this girl child could be his? It seems quite a coincidence that he has been missing for the same period of time that she has been alive—10 years.'

'There is that chance, yes. However, my son, the King, has observed her mother from a distance and picked up immediately that she is pure human, no royal frequency whatsoever.'

A young woman from the audience raises her hand. 'Surely, given that the child's form is human, she might be the result of a union between the Prince and a human woman?'

Maen observes his mother's reaction closely. The Queen flinches at this suggestion.

'It is highly unlikely that my son would have taken such a path.'

The King feels queasy with the taste of anger. The young woman persists, 'But, it is possible. If this were the case, would you accept her as the new trainee? We all know that this has never been allowed in the past, for good reason.'

'Her signal appears to us to be of pure royal frequency.'

'Yet, you yourself said that there are certain elements to her signal that you cannot identify—could these not be as a result of her being a human-royal mix?'

'I cannot say for sure. However, she is our choice. The decision has been made.'

The man in the suit comments, 'This is preposterous and puts us all in danger.'

The Queen seems to be tiring now. 'I'm afraid that all I can do is ask for you to have faith in me. My intuition tells me that this girl has the capacity to be Sun-bearer. Unfortunately, more than ever in these times, all we have to go on is our intuition. If we delay taking action now, you will all be in far greater danger from Dark royalty.'

'You yourself saw to it that the Dark royalty is in tatters now. There is only the Queen of Night left; one person hardly constitutes a threat,' the man retorts.

The veneer of Elke's evenness shatters. 'It is never a wise move to underestimate the power of a Dark royal,' she says.

A young mother holding a baby stands. 'Indeed, especially one set on avenging the murder of both her parents.'

A woman sitting close to her responds. 'What was she supposed to do? The former Queen of Dark carried out the brutal murder of her husband! It was after the loss of the Lion of Light that everything started to go wrong.'

The largest whale stops this escalating rally of blame with a jet of spuming water and Erin speaks for him. 'You all know that Queen Elke came under severe criticism for her decision to exterminate the Queen and King of Dark. Revisiting the topic now is not going to solve the task ahead of us. Suffice it to say, retaliatory killings are no longer an option for Light royalty on the planet. The Queen of Light has paid for her actions. Over 10 years in virtual seclusion away from one's children is hardly an idyllic life.'

The words of the whale have had the intended effect. The mood in the hall has begun to cool now, taut faces have loosened into something more pensive. A man with the weathered look of a farmer stands now, 'I, for one, stand by your decision, Your Highness. Your protection has served us all for a great deal of time.'

There are displays of support for this sentiment from around the room. Sceptical glances are still exchanged but these are in the minority. The Queen, slightly punctured now, closes that part of the discussion and moves onto the other items on the agenda of a more logistical nature.

Once the proceedings are wrapped up, the guests are served a late lunch, consisting mainly of vegetables, salad, rice and bread. With cheese and meat both being scarce commodities, there are only small amounts of these included on each plate. The whales and dolphins are fed a selection of their favourite fish, brought fresh off the boats' fishing trip before sunrise that morning. They are heaped onto wheelbarrows and trundled in by the ground workers, who then mount the two tall, steel ladders on either side of the lucent pool. Passed up in bucket-loads from there, the fish are tipped into the water. Most of them are already dead but some of them begin to splutter back to life once they hit the water, twitching into a directionless, sinking swim, only to sense the colossus ahead, feebly attempt to change direction and become part of a swift current being sucked into parted jaws. Maen is always taken watching the few younger members of the gathering who have not witnessed the sea-creatures being fed before. They become transfixed by the image and seem to lose self-awareness for a few moments. Afterwards, they eat their food slowly, referring back every now and then to the satiated sea-mammals.

CHAPTER 7

Harbouring a Grain

30/09/2041

A year has passed since Princess Regan returned from the island. Her beauty is sharper; she carries an air of acceptance. She has tamed her adolescent cheek; her performance of courtly etiquette now seamless. She does not indulge in idle chatter with the ladies of the court but keeps to herself, practising her powers as seer, or working on the laboratory project that her mother has placed her in charge of. She no longer observes Queen Signa in the main laboratory. For at least a year now, her mother has worked only in the Initium lab, access to which is still restricted solely to the Queen herself.

For six months, Queen Signa has had Regan working on a compound to be used in a new batch of experiments. She is to focus on an offshoot strain of the meningitis bacterium that will temporarily interrupt a victim's ability to receive or comprehend light. Queen Signa has told Regan that she will use the substance in dart bullets to overcome humans and Light workers. 'They will quite literally forget what light is,' she had said, 'a state perfectly conducive to recruitment to the Dark Force.' The spine, brain, and retinal nerve endings are the targets of the concoction.

Regan stands in the empty ballroom. She likes the largeness of it for practising her vision gathering. She has closed the doors and has lit 10 of the huge candles lining the room. She is focusing on calling up a vision of potential recruits for her mother in the Eastern Cape region. Queen Signa has received a tip-off about a string of households where firearms and explosives are being manufactured illegally, positioned on the outskirts of a port city. The leader of this backstreet company would be a useful connection for her, particularly since it would give her an ammunition source reasonably close to the Chamber.

Regan raises her hands and angles them towards the area in front of her. She concentrates on the section of land outside the coastal city. The ocean there has a harsh edge, bordering a throng of industrial plants. Regan can feel the molecules of the vision coming towards her now, like a speeding up of atoms in the space that her hands face. She steers the particles towards the ammunitions house by expanding the sense that she is there already. The vision materialises; it opens above a street, the sign visible: 'Tait St'. The eye of the vision pulls closer and hangs over one of the houses, ordinary and aging, that might have been built in the 1970's, with a peeling number '20' affixed to the fence. Regan immediately senses that the vision has settled on an area close to the one she was aiming for but has not hit her target. This district is not affluent but is still safer, more suburban than the savage neighbourhood she had been trying to draw. Regan is irritated; it has been a long time since she miscalculated like this. *Perhaps I am distracted*, she thinks, and is about to dissipate the vision, when she senses something in the house, a force of kinds. The eye of the vision descends now, through the roof and into a sitting-room. All the furniture has been pushed to the sides, clearing the way for what appears to be a lesson of kinds in progress. A small group of people is standing in a semi-circle, listening attentively to a teacher figure. The vision rotates to take in the person addressing them. Regan catches her breath. It is a lion, larger than any she has seen in the wild or in books, his fur shades of gold and caramel-brown. Sheer power emanates from his being. She knows that this must be the Lion of Light. He speaks:

'I conclude the teaching for today. Tomorrow we will go over how you can transfer these skills to your children. We'll also cover how to set up your home stations to pick up the whale's signals. This will help you detect alerts quickly. Communication via email has proven too risky lately. It will now only be used for the most urgent of messages. Thank-you.' The women and men in the gathering before him all bow and curtsey briefly. He tips his head, looks back up with inquisitive, yellow-green eyes. The vision freezes.

Regan's heart is thumping against her ribs; her knees trembling. She suddenly becomes aware of a presence in the room, and the faint scent of formaldehyde. She turns and looks behind her. It is Queen Signa; she has a way of creeping up behind people without a sound. Regan had not even heard the door open. The Dark Queen's eyes are fixed on the motionless image of the Lion of Light, about to dissipate.

'A felicitous vision, indeed, my daughter.' She shifts her gaze to Regan, her lips curling back to reveal her teeth. 'I hope you don't mind, I took the liberty of an impromptu observation of your practise session—and a fortunate visit it has proven to be. Is this the first time you have seen him?'

'Who?' Regan's mind is racing now; she strains to focus it, find some words to turn the moment.

'Oh, no need for modesty, my girl, the Lion of Light, of course.' Regan looks back towards the vision, which disperses outwards now. She turns to the Queen.

'We can't be sure it is him.'

'Of course we can. I thought your powers of intuition were stronger than that. I saw the location; I will leave with my guards immediately.' She turns and starts towards the door, zeal in her step.

'Mother,' the word jumps out of Regan's mouth, aimless and panicked. The Queen pauses, swivels back, impatient. What Regan wants to say is stuck in her throat like a barb.

'Good luck.'

Signa's eyes narrow; she picks up something off-centre in Regan. She discards it as her daughter's tendency to attach rearing its head again. 'Yes, yes,' the Queen raps out. Then, as an afterthought, 'oh, and thank-you; your hard work is paying off.' She must ensure the continuation of Regan's productivity.

The Princess watches her mother leave the room, reeling at how her night has taken an unexpected, ghastly turn. She reverts back to the space where the vision had appeared, empty and innocent now. Even if she wanted to contact the Lion of Light to send him a warning, she has no computer access for that purpose. One of the few elderly courtiers had told Regan that Queen Signa had banned any technological equipment that could be traced back to the Chamber site soon after Regan had been born. Not that she would have known where to send a message.

Regan goes to her room and begins her toilette. It is as though she is lagging somewhere outside of her body, trying to grab back at a moment. Why did she choose to practise in the ballroom instead of her room tonight? It is unlikely her mother would have entered the Princess's bedroom uninvited. Regan can tolerate collecting intelligence on nameless dark recruits for the court—after all, she is bound to perform her duties as Princess. However, had she viewed tonight's vision in solitude, she would never have given Queen Signa information on the Lion of Light. She is aware this makes her a problematic member of the Chamber. She hears the helicopter whirring upwards and away. An off-hand decision to use the ballroom tonight, and the Lion of Light will be murdered within a matter of hours.

DON'T KILL HIM. The words she had wanted to say to her mother. Like the final coating around a grain of sand in an oyster that renders it a pearl. The culmination of all her doubts, her suspicions of the Dark order that her mother is choreographing, like a perfect waltz performed by disfigured dancers. This dormant, opalescent orb is a bomb. It will change everything; it will be the end of Regan's Princesshood, of having any place of belonging.

She lies in bed, her eyes open and adjusting to the dark. She tends her thoughts, sees herself plainly. Regan is an oyster working backwards now, unpeeling the ivory sphere to expose the tiny pith that everything formed around. Her attempt to smother her passion two years ago has failed, and worse, has backfired on her. She can no longer deny her lack of commitment to her mother's strategy for the Dark Force. She questions the reason she stays in this Chamber in a family of no love, in a place of no friendship, with a father collapsed into himself and under the Queen and a mother who appears to feel nothing for her daughter. Signa seems to sustain relations with her only to use her for her own aims—visions to track potential recruits to the Dark and chemistry to wipe out the light.

That's it. The speck comes clear. *I don't belong here.* It is impossible to belong in a place where any tendril of warmth between creatures is forbidden. *I don't belong anywhere. Bombs must be handled carefully,* she thinks. If she wants to stay alive, she will choose her moment of when and how to detonate it. *My life belongs to me. My royal blood, my Princesshood, belongs to me. It is time to craft it as my own.*

Closing Words

27/11/2050

All the guests have left and the sea-borns have been hoisted up and slipped back into the ocean. The last attendants are leaving the hall now, having cleared the tables. They will return for a final clean but know to leave the King alone to spend some time with his mother's projection before the signal is cut. The rigging of that cell tower signal annually requires a huge amount of generator power and, with scarcity of resources, it is cut immediately on the closing of the assembly. Maen stands close to the screen; he turns to watch the hefty hall doors being closed. Bryce, the King's most trusted confidant in the Chamber, is the last to leave. He casts a reassuring look in Maen's direction; he has observed the unsteady relationship between the King and Queen Elke for many years. Maen takes momentary comfort in this look, his ears lifting upright. They fold back as he turns to face his mother's emanation. Although she is weary now, the relief of getting a few private moments with her son is apparent in the smile breaking out on her countenance.

'You have so much of your father in you. It's still strange to me how you were the only son to manifest his physicality.'

The warmth of her comment falls into blank air. 'Mother, is there anything you want to tell me about the youngling that you could not say in public? Do you still want me to bring her to the Chamber?'

Elke modulates. 'There is something about her that concerns me, yes, but I can't seem to put my finger on it.'

'We could wait a while, try and find a more suitable candidate.'

'There is no other alternative. We must go ahead with her training.'

'But, what if something goes wrong and—'

'Maen, we can no longer afford this conversation! If it weren't for your steady evasion of your royal duty to marry and produce heirs to the throne, we would not be in this predicament.'

'I have told you repeatedly that I have simply not been able to find a candidate who I love.'

'Between your weak excuses and the rumours that your brother might be the father of the Sun-bearer candidate through union with a human, I'm not sure how much more embarrassment I can be expected to field.'

'Yes, it is terribly inconvenient for you that Colter has abdicated his royal responsibilities. For all we know, he might have been slaughtered by the Queen of Night years ago...why you keep hanging onto hope is beyond me.'

'Maen!'

'It is time you took responsibility for pushing him away. Not only have I had to run the Chamber all the time you have been in hiding due to your thirst for revenge but, I have also lost my brother.'

'If you had simply made more effort to find an appropriate female partner, we would not be in this precarious situation of having to rely on an outsider, possibly from another Light realm altogether, to solve our succession quandary.'

'Have you considered the possibility that your sons do not share the royal values of old with you, that perhaps there are different, more forward-thinking responses to the state of royalty on the planet?'

The bird starts to twitter at a rapid pace, flitting nervously around the Queen's shoulders. The old woman's complexion has drained to a shade of grey. Her feathered helper is programmed to warn when her system is close to decline. The King slumps into the chair behind him, head in hands. When he looks up at his mother again, the vitriol has evaporated, uncovering his affection for her. The Queen chuckles softly.

'Saved by my canary in the mine-shaft.'

Maen's tone is gentle now, 'I did not want to fight with you again, Mother. You must go and rest. We will resume communication through our letters as usual.'

The Queen's eyes soften. 'I want you to know that your devotion to the Light Chamber and its work never goes unnoticed, my boy. I may not always show it but, I am proud of you for it.'

'Thank-you Mother.'

'Fetch the girl and begin her training. I shall make contact with her through the kitten at the appropriate time to arrange for her to visit me. Go in light, Maen.'

'I shall carry out your bidding, Mother. Look to your health. Go in light.'

The bird trills a farewell and, with that, the screen fades. The King goes to look out one of the portholes. Taking in the ocean always calms him. He tells himself that all is as it should be. His task is clear.

CHAPTER 8

Victory

01/10/2041

The passages buzz with excitement as Regan strides towards the Dark Queen's quarters. The corridor is dim, as usual, even though it is afternoon. As courtiers catch sight of her, their faces register respect and they congratulate her in low tones as she passes. Regan acknowledges them with quick glances and expressionless nods. As Charlotte goes by, she simply fixes the Princess's eyes and tips her head almost imperceptibly, unable to hide the displeasure. Regan enters the Dark Queen's study. Signa is at her desk, making notes in her laboratory manuals.

'You wished to see me, Mother?'

The Queen looks up. Her mind is clearly far away, her eyes intoxicated with victory and momentum. She draws in a breath, closes the book in front of her, rises and comes to stand before Regan.

'I wanted to congratulate you personally, my daughter. It was thanks to your last vision that I pinpointed the exact location of the Lion of Light and ended his days. You have proven yourself worthy of the mantle of Dark.'

Regan inclines her head, unspeaking.

'I am pleased to see that your shaky patch after the training period has passed; you have consolidated your Dark capacity. I was concerned for a while that you might be too soft.' Tiny flecks of red indignation begin to rise in Regan's countenance. She holds her mother's slicing gaze.

'With this crucial link in the royal Light chain broken, I am poised to complete the work that my father began. I am promoting you to become my right hand.

You will work with me in the Initium laboratory on the next stage of my strategy.' The Queen folds her hands into one another, pleased with herself; everything is in its place.

'Are you referring to your father's plan for a 'Second *Tabula Rasa*'? The courtiers laugh about it; they all think your father had become a senile, old man with a crazy scheme that would amount to nothing.'

The Queen's lips tighten and her eyes flash. 'I would ask you to take a tone of more respect when addressing your Queen, my girl.'

'I thought you'd want to know what they think, Mother, given how out of touch you've become with your court.'

'My father was a great man, one who had more mettle than any Dark king before him. The Dark Force had been slipping down a feeble slope for centuries. He showed the resolve and genius that was required to haul us back onto the playing field. I will complete his cherished dream for the future. That is my destiny.'

'How are you going to do it? No disrespect, but to wipe out the Light Force on the planet is an impossible feat.'

'You'll find out what my plan is in due course. You underestimate your mother, Regan but you and all the courtiers will see. It would be far more fitting for you to have simply thanked me for the honour I've awarded you. If you're not careful, I may decide to rescind it.'

'And rather give it to Charlotte?'

The Queen's head jerks back slightly. 'What do you mean?'

'I know that you were priming her to be your right hand while I was away. I got it out of one of my ladies. You still appear close. You could have had more faith in me; after all, I am your blood.' The Queen is taken aback by Regan's assurance. It's been years since she heard this tone in her daughter's voice.

'As Queen, one must take precautions, Regan. One day when you reign, you will understand.'

'I am replaceable in your scheme?'

'I'm obliged as your mother to provide what is necessary to keep you alive, no more. Replacing you wouldn't have been the ideal choice for me but, I would have done it for the greater benefit of the planet. You know this to be Dark law. What, exactly, are you getting at?'

'I was merely a pawn in your hands all this time. There is not one fraction of love for me in you.'

The Queen breathes in sharply, as though she has swallowed poison. Her razor voice scratches the air, quiet and cutting.

'My dear daughter, may I remind you that you are not supposed to love your mother. You are a Princess of the Dark Chamber. You know as well as I do that love was never supposed to be one of your capacities, nor mine. Indeed, by all measures, I should have you chastised for saying that.'

The words fall from her lips like small deaths. Regan's eyes dull and something in her flickers.

'However, given your latest achievement for our family, I will overlook your confusion this last time. Report for duty at the laboratory tomorrow morning.'

'Yes, Mother.'

Regan moves to the door, hesitates, turns back to the Queen.

'Did he say anything?'

The Queen is annoyed with all this talk, sighs impatiently. 'Who?'

'The Lion of Light, before you killed him, did he have any words?'

'He did. He said, 'Open your heart and the Light will enter'. Why?'

'Just curious.'

Regan moves through the Chamber passages like a shell of thoughts that close in on themselves. She shuts them off, one by one, rendering her mind vacant.

The Opening

01/12/2050

Keesa is on a wander. She has left Toekoums sleeping in a restful nook in the backyard. As she walks, she tries to quieten her thoughts by counting the bushes and trees that she can see. Twenty bushes so far. Keesa is thankful for the solitude of the veldt right now. She passes a tree. Number six.

A baby bird lies gasping for breath on the sand next to the tree. It lies half on its side, its body featherless and raw, a translucent grey-pink. Its beak is soft and defenceless, gawping in a strange slow rhythm at the world. The mother bird does not seem anywhere in sight. *She must not want it anymore*, Keesa surmises. The first time her mother caught her cutting open a mole she had spotted in the veldt, she banned her from these activities. She claims it is an unhygienic pastime that will lead to Keesa never finding a man to settle down with.

Keesa gives a token look around; she knows her mother doesn't frequent this part of the veldt. An image rises of herself as crone struggling with her last breath in the farmhouse alone. Her curiosity is too strong. She takes out the Swiss army knife that her father gave her for her ninth birthday. Kneeling down, she carefully lifts the beak upward while softly pressing against the chest, so exposing the throat. She cuts a perfect line across the thin flesh; dark-brown blood oozes from the opening. Its legs begin paddling the air and its beak opens and closes with more urgency now. Keesa makes a second, swift incision down the front of the body, gently squeezes out the excess blood, then pins the body open with two long thorns. There in the chest, just slightly off centre, is the tiny beating heart, jerking in slow, uneven time now. Keesa carefully severs the veins and arteries running from the organ, removes the heart by balancing it skilfully on the blade and cups the heart in her soft fist. The bird's beak and twig legs cease moving. Keesa's actions have taken on an involuntary quality. Her eyes close. A surge of energy travels from her hand into her body. Her skin grows hot and the top of her head feels tingly. As the flow circulates inside her, nausea rises sourly into her stomach. After a short time, the rush seems to settle and a cool relief opens in her throat. She extends her arm forward, uncurls her fingers, and opens her eyes.

A few metres away, on the sand in front of her, a tall woman leans over a steel table. She holds medical instruments in her hands and is engrossed in an investigation. Her subject is a human being, lying face down. She has opened the body with a vertical incision, exposing the spinal cord and all its tributaries.

71

Her hands move deftly, cutting here, lifting there. Her eyes seem to burrow into the faded pink, purple and yellow mass before her and see things that a naked eye could not. She pauses now and looks up from her work. Her icy grey eyes settle on Keesa. An expression of intense interest comes over her countenance and a smile breaks out that sits strangely on her mouth. A wave of admiration and yearning for her approval swells up in Keesa.

'Would you like a closer look, my little one?'

Keesa's legs jerk forward. Her walk is stiff, like a child that cannot keep pace with its own inquisitiveness. In this haste, her hand opens and drops the bird-heart. She looks down to see it land on the ground. A feeling of deflation comes over her and a dull sense that she has done wrong begins throbbing in her head. She looks back up to the woman at the table, who instantly seems to recognise the change in Keesa. Her expression contracts to one of disdain. A voice that sounds unimaginably loud to Keesa speaks behind her.

'Gee whiskers, Keesa, it took me ages to find you; what have you been—'

Keesa spins round to see Toekoums stop dead in his tracks as he spots the pinned bird and the hapless, miniature organ lying in front of her. The fur on his spine and tail rise. He looks up to her eyes, starts pawing backwards. Keesa turns back to the woman. All trace of the vision is gone. Nothing but sand and empty space, as it was before. She suddenly feels very alone. She turns back, an irritable tiredness seeping over her now. Throwing a guilty, yet defiant, look in Toekoums' direction, she kneels down and starts digging a hole in the sand to bury the remains of the bird in. She takes care to cover the sections of sand soaked in blood.

'What were you doing here, Keesa?' Toekoums asks with a heavy voice.

'Oh for God's sake, I don't see what the big deal is. You're a cat. Aren't you supposed to want to eat the bird anyway?' Her harsh tone thinly covers the panicked culpability that lies beneath. She finishes patting the sand down on the buried parts, then rubs some sand between her hands in an attempt to clean them of the brown-red stain. Getting up, she sees the kitten's distress. Her heart tightens and self-reproach inks in.

'I'm sorry, Toekoums.' Keesa goes down on her haunches and holds out her hand to the feline. Even though the smell of blood sets his hackles rising again, he brushes his cheek gently against her hand.

'Let's go home,' Keesa says, straightens up slowly and begins the walk home at a pace slow enough that Toekoums can keep up. Once she is there, she manages to slip behind her mother busy in the kitchen, giving her usual greeting, and making her way straight to the bathroom. After some washing, the blood stains are gone.

Keesa's sleep is disturbed that night. She dreams of long passages lined by many doors. There is a clean smell of surgical disinfectant, which agrees with her. At the end of the passage stands the ice woman from her vision, looking expectant. Keesa becomes aware of a clawing on her shoulder. She twists her head to see what it is and, there is the little bird that she killed, still wobbly with newness but its eyes are blinking at her. It opens it beak and tries to sing; she can hear the tiny outbreath escape its lungs. Keesa tries to flick it off; it feels like raw, moist meat under her staccato hand. No matter how many times she tries to rid herself of it, it just digs its claws deeper into her flesh. Keesa wakes. She touches her shoulder. Toekoums stirs, sensing her fear. He meows to her. For a moment, she is simply a young girl with her kitten meowing at her. She reaches out and strokes his fur. She sees he still smells something on her skin but covers it up with his scent by rubbing the side of his face against it.

'Everything will be all right.' Keesa sounds the words in the most comforting tone she can manage for both of them. She doesn't believe it but has heard adults use the expression and hopes that saying it might quell the incertitude swelling the ranks of her being.

CHAPTER 9

Hidden Sky

03/12/2050

Kaleb is working a distance from their village today. He'd camped in the area the previous night; he wasn't able to finish the job he is busy with by sunset, as planned. The work he is doing on the pylons is his pet project. The other tasks he carries out are generally for the people of the village, from fixing faults in home generators, to restringing used light bulbs. The trips he takes to search for electrical hardware often take him a week or more at a time. Cabling is one of the things that has tended to fare quite well in the face of the burnings. The ruins of buildings in the scorched cities have proved quite fruitful for him.

He was lucky to receive his truck some years ago. An old woman who lived on one of the farms near the village had died, shortly after her long-standing husband had. An occurrence taken for granted before but now, death as a result of old age is viewed as a relic. At the next town meeting, the villagers had taken a unanimous decision to furnish their local electrician with a vehicle. They knew that access to better cabling could enhance the makeshift electrical wiring of their town. The truck enables Kaleb to transport his long ladder with him on his trips. He is working his way toward rigging wind turbines, which would lead to many of the domestic generators in the village being done away with. It is a long-term scheme of his, one that he chips away at when things in Hale get quiet .

He enjoys working on his own out in the openness. Not being much of a social creature, he prefers working without the constant stream of conversation from the villagers he is working for. Their overcompensation for living in pastoral isolation with the memory of previous bustle and quick words in the city. He is on the uppermost rung of his ladder now, securing the final wiring connection to complete a segment of closed circuit running between around 50 poles. As he finishes, he considers the normal process entailed in checking whether the circuit conducts current evenly. Given the present state of disarray of so many power grids, it would involve the rigging of a generator in order to fire the circuit, after which he could test its strength.

Kaleb takes an habitual look around, despite the obvious absence of people for miles. Nothing but veldt, slanting light, and the sound of a breeze lifting and dropping like breath. He turns back to the intertwine of wires, places his right hand over it, lowers his head slightly, and closes his eyes. The breeze around him picks up and the air takes on the clarity it has just before a storm is about to break. His hair starts to rise with static. A faint, high-pitched humming sound laces the air, building quickly in volume until it snaps. At the same time, sparks of blue light begin escaping the sides of his down-turned palm. The electric charge skitters quickly along the cables between the poles; it seems joyous for its release. Small streaks of dry lightning fork overhead, from a sky of no clouds. Kaleb opens his eyes and looks to the left. The entire circuit of poles is humming with current, small stray sparks flitting off into the air like little skips. He is satisfied that once he has set up the turbines and rigged a central distribution board, the circuit will function and can be slowly linked to the village power system.

He notices the lightning becoming more frequent, closes his eyes and yanks his hand back from the wires. The pulse dies down quickly; sparks stuttering every now and then, a few snips of lightning, then silence. He lifts his eyelids and checks to see that all is as it was before. Sand, hush. He disembarks the ladder, pleased with his day's work. He thinks of how Keesa would enjoy watching him do that. She must never know. Too many questions would follow. Aedan would never trust him again. He opens and closes the fingers of both hands; they are always a bit stiff afterwards. The sun is low now; time to pack up and head home.

A heavy residue lingers from his fight with Keesa. Despite this, as he drives through the glorious sunset, the prospect of sitting down to eat with his family is warming. Sometimes, just for that comfort, he feels he must be the luckiest man in the world.

Findings and Conclusion

02/10/2041

Regan stands in front of the door to Queen Signa's Initium laboratory. It's the small hours of the morning; the Chamber sleeps. She has instructed Valtere to guard the door while she is inside and to ensure he stays out of view. He has flown up onto the roof and is nervously ogling the strip of veldt that lies between the main medical quarters and the Initium lab. The eagle thought the Princess had tamed her disobedient streak since returning from the island but her endeavour tonight has come seemingly out of nowhere, her riskiest yet. She enlisted the help of two of the Dark guards to pick the five locks on the door. Even though many of the guards chosen by her mother come from dubious backgrounds, Regan made sure to choose two who had done time in prison. Even so, it took them 20 excruciating minutes to do the job. As hardened as they are, their terror of the Dark Queen was patent as they struggled with the locks, throwing out repeated, furtive looks in the direction of the passage. As soon as they got it done, Regan ordered them back to their quarters, forcing them to swear not to tell anyone about her request, else she tell her mother that she saw them breaking into the Initium lab and demand their execution.

Regan gives Valtere one last look, turns the worn, brass door handle, and opens the door. It is pitch-dark inside. The scent of disinfectant, formaldehyde and something heavier beneath that she can't identify hang inside. She pauses. Crossing this verge is irreversible, not only for what she may find but more as a drastic act of insubordination against her mother. The Lion of Light's eyes flash across her mind. Regan removes the box of matches from her pocket, and steps inside. The air is cold as a fridge; her mother has air conditioning running inside all day long—Regan has seen the outlet vents near the roof on its exterior. As nights in this area are generally chilly, what with little cloud cover to trap the day's heat, the laboratory likely stays cool from evening on, even with the air con turned off. The windows have all been blacked out with paint; as a girl, she would try peer through them. The sun's rays could not have touched this space in at least two decades.

She lights a match, and looks around the entrance for candles. The medical quarters are the one part of the Dark Chamber powered by solar panels as well as generators, but the latter are switched off when no one is working inside. The noise of them would have woken everyone up tonight. Her mother had

76

wanted to keep the homestead off the electricity grid, and had thus stuck to using generators, solar power, gas and fire for most of the running of it. A good supply of candles is planted in almost every room for this reason, and the Initium lab is no exception. There is a collection right by the door where the lab desk begins that trails around almost all four walls of the space, as well as a few torches. Regan lights one of the candles, closes the door behind her, grabs the biggest torch, and switches it on.

It is a vast room, almost as large as the main laboratory. She begins making her way along the right wall, shooting the torch beam into the dark as she does. She quickly comes across a surgical table to her left, the soles of two bloodless feet hanging off the edge of it. She turns in, treads slowly along the side of the table. The narrow shaft of light reveals a corpse lying prostrate, its head swivelled to the side. The skin has been neatly peeled back to divulge the spine. Some of the vertebrae towards the centre of the back have been sawn in half to allow examination of the spinal cord. It looks like a thin horse's tail in grey. Regan flashes the torch on the face of the cadaver. It appears to be male, the head has been shaved of hair. He could not have been more than 30 when he died. Regan has never seen a corpse this young in the main laboratory. She lifts the torch and casts the beam into the rest of the room. Her stomach sinks. Row upon row of bodies filleted in the same manner fill all the available space.

Regan begins moving through what are narrow aisles between the steel tables, the bobbing torch beam alighting again and again on these nameless, youthful, undone bodies. They have all been basted with some kind of ointment that preserves them. Although it must be potent, given that there is no visible decay occurring in any of the corpses, as she gets further into the room, an insistent smell of exposed innards latches the air. The left hand wall of the room is lined with shelves showing glinting vials and flasks with glass stoppers that contain what looks like different specimens of body fluids and sera. Regan feels the blood draining from her head, and a giddiness coming over her. She bites her teeth together, presses her nose into her sleeve at the bend of the elbow, and draws a filtered breath. She is close to the other end of the room now, and the scouting beam hits the back wall, flashing over hundreds of laboratory manuals stacked tightly into the shelves that cover its entirety. Regan would like nothing more than to leave this room of glistening gristle and never return, but she knows these bound pages are sure to contain the details of her mother's plan. She approaches the library with swift pace. Everything has been filed meticulously using a system of tags, which she begins hurriedly searching through. The longer she stays in here, the greater the risk of being caught.

After some minutes she finds two tags, one named 'Main Findings' and the other, 'Central Theses'. She takes the most recent manuals from these sections, sets them down on the long, rectangular block of laboratory desk that forms the only separation between the library area and the bodies. She finds more candles in one of the drawers, lights them, sits down on a high stool, and begins poring over the documentation. An hour goes by. Regan becomes increasingly appalled at what she reads. She battles to control an irrational fear that one of the bodies will rise to life, walk over, and begin to strangle her with unsightly, oozing eyes. Her imagination as a child was always keen. She plastered it over with logic and sense, but it still finds an outlet in her vision gathering. Tonight, though, it feels as it did when she was little, as though if she holds the image long enough, it will happen. She shuts these thoughts out, takes a squashed breath filtered by her clothing, and finishes her reading. I know enough, she thinks. I know too much. Too much for a daughter to know of the woman whose body she incubated in.

She slides the manuals back into the shelves, making sure they are lined up exactly as she had found them. She blows out the candles, waits some minutes for the wax to harden, returns them to their drawer. Her mouth is dry, and her head has begun to ache from the pungent odour. As she is placing the stool where she found it, she hears Valtere give out a call, using the avian version of his voice. Regan freezes. Someone must be approaching, probably a guard. She snatches up the torch and starts towards the door, making her way along the right hand wall of the laboratory. If she can just manage to get out before whoever is approaching reaches the door. She breaks out into a run, her hand clutching the torch, its frenetic light snatching at unsealed bodies, faces that droop towards their beds of cold steel, and innocent, accusing feet. She is at the door now. A quick outbreath and the candle is out. Torch off, placed next to candles. Another squawk from Valtere. Her hand is on the door handle, when she hears a key being thrust into one of the locks. She jerks her hand away, as though burnt. She takes a few steps back, terror seizing at her gut. I do not belong anywhere, she reminds herself. I am not hers. She can hear confusion in the scratching key as the lock is tried. A pause, silence. Another brief attempt. A realisation that the door has already been unlocked. Another pause. The door is opened.

Regan is the one scrutinised by torchlight now. She puts her hand in front of her eyes. Queen Signa lowers her torch. Her caustic voice barely contains the rage beneath.

'Why don't you light a few candles? I presume you know where they are? I think we need to have a little talk.'

Regan stands motionless for a moment, then moves to the candles, lights them, as Signa closes the door behind her. She turns and faces the Queen, holding her fear at bay like a wriggling cat, her eyes defiant.

'What are doing in my laboratory in the middle of the night, and without my permission?'

Regan is wordless.

'How did you get through the locks?'

'That is irrelevant.'

The Queen balks. 'What has gotten into you?' Her voice is laden with disappointment, but for the first time, Regan detects a trace of hurt in it too.

'How could you?' The words leave Regan's mouth like rotten food that can no longer stay down.

'How could I what?'

'How could you consider this course of action? I read enough to gather what it is you are plotting.'

'I am doing what a Dark Queen is supposed to do—lead her people to a new world.'

Regan's voice is rising. 'A new world? You mean a dead world. Mother, there is no other way to put this: what you aim to do is wrong.'

Signa whips the Princess's cheek with her bony hand. 'How dare you?' Her voice is livid now. 'I am carrying out the orders of my father, a Dark King who would be shocked to see how his grand-daughter has turned out.'

Regan reins her voice in. 'Mother, I am appealing to you as your daughter: Do not release the bacterium. What power, what satisfaction can you possibly gain from killing off human life on the planet?'

'It is not your place to question my methods. You will be told information as and when is appropriate, not before.'

'Did you not think it 'appropriate' to tell me that you would alter the compound you have me working on so that it will not merely cause a temporary episode, but will permanently disable the victim's ability to perceive light? And how did you come by all these youthful bodies?'

'That is none of your concern, and, furthermore, should not matter to you, my girl.'

'Mother, we both know that Dark and Light royalty have co-existed on the globe for centuries. What kind of a crippled world are you trying to create?'

'Am I to understand that you see a world without Light as crippled?'

Regan takes in a breath and releases it slowly, clenching her hands, letting them open. 'Dark royalty is supposed to encompass a form of Darkness above a common criminal. Lower order Dark beings are hardly likely to appreciate the Dark royal code. If they escape the pandemic, they are likely to turn to lower Dark methods to survive. You honestly want a planet of rapists, murderers and thieves?'

'Your valour is admirable, Regan, despite being thoroughly misplaced. As for your whimsical sentiments, you remind me more and more of my mother the older you get. Weak. Soft. Even your powers are bloodless, like hers were. The two of you and your visions. If only you had exhibited more of my father's genes. I had such hopes for you. But, I digress.'

Again, an expression that Regan has not seen in her mother before, this time it is one of loneliness in her quest. The partner in crime is not complying. For a moment, she looks like nothing more than an old woman, alone and sad.

'Even though I would never consider your appeal; it is too late anyway. The meningitis eximius bacterium is being released as we speak. I have dark workers in every major city on the planet dispersing it right now on suicide missions. They are real Dark workers, workers my father would have respected, who understand the meaning and beauty of sacrifice for the greater cause.'

The room swims around Regan's head. She takes a few unsteady steps backwards, leans against the laboratory block, and brings her hand up to her mouth. She shuts her eyes, opens them slowly, lets her hand down.

'I used to look up to you. My mother, the great surgeon. The Dark leader of our times. You are not a surgeon. You are a vivisector, a monster. You are not a leader. This strategy and the methods you are using make you no better than a common thug.'

For a split second, Regan sees that her words have wounded her mother, something about the way her body has stiffened. But the moment passes quickly, and the Queen lifts her chin, her eyes flashing like knives.

'For the sake of saving myself yet another conversation with you, let's get to the point: are you or are you not going to take your place as my right hand in my plan or not?'

Regan is unforthcoming.

'Well, for once, my argumentative daughter has nothing to say. Then let this be my final word on the subject. By all measures, I should have you killed at daybreak. Only because you are my daughter, and because I believe that it would benefit the Dark Chamber more to have royal blood on the throne than not, I am going to give you one week in which to make a decision on the matter. If you decide to join me, you will be rewarded. You shall succeed my reign and rule as the next Queen of Dark. If you choose not to join me, you will be executed. I would urge you to consider this matter seriously. I am hoping that you will come to your senses.'

Regan can tell that her lies do not see the murder. They have grown so thick and murky, that she can no longer see out of them. Signa opens the door, turns towards her daughter. 'Now, I would appreciate if you would leave me to the work I came here to do.'

Regan exits the laboratory. As she passes her mother, she senses chasms of distance between them. The veldt night air has never smelt so sweet. Her feet move back towards the homestead in strange, uneven paces, like an animal stunned after being hit by a car. Her eagle wings alongside her. He asks her no questions.

'She is not my mother, Valtere. I am not her girl.'

She knows they are only words, but they give her something to hold onto. And if you sound words over enough times with your lips, they can come to hold a truth of their own. Regan lies in bed that night imagining the disease spreading. Her mother has always prided herself in being part of a long line of Dark royals who have channelled their powers into pursuits of intellect, of science. This is her opus.

81

She has altered the fundamental workings of and invigorated an organism with power that it should not ordinarily have. Regan knows from the manuals that the meningitis eximius bacterium, as Signa has coined it, grows exceptionally quickly. It begins its effect as Influenza A, quickly escalates to pneumonia, and finally develops into meningitis. The speed of the process has been designed to be so swift, however, that most people will experience it as an almost instant process of deterioration. The bacterial cells divide every five to ten minutes. She has made use of recombinant plasmids as vectors to amplify the ability of the pathogen to be virulently infectious, to spread rapidly through airborne droplets, and to evade an array of human immune responses. It will produce an unheard of amount of pili, guaranteeing resistance to destruction through phagocytosis by a host cell.

It redefines the term professional invader—bacteria that successfully invade the upper respiratory tract as opposed to a secondary invader, which only causes disease when the host is already impaired. She has combined the most effective attributes of Streptococcus pneumoniae and Neisseria meningitis into one microbe. This preternaturally robust mutation of Pneumococcal meningitis is no longer restricted to effecting mainly children and the elderly; any age group is vulnerable. Its incubation has been shortened to 30 minutes, and the symptoms develop over the next hour, rather than between two to fourteen days, as in the case of the original strain. As a final touch, it now has a microbial shedding period at the end of its cycle—where there was none before—so as to ensure further infection in other hosts.

Too late. Again, too late. The scourge breaks the next morning with venomous force. Messengers to the court begin arriving with reports of states of emergency being declared in every country. Within a few days, the smell of burning starts seeping in from the cities. Chemical fumes of melting synthetics, woodsmoke, the deplorable stench of burning flesh. The sky becomes shrouded in a pall of black smoke.

Regan makes herself scarce, holing herself up in her room. She turns the matter over and over. If she defies her mother, and is executed, what hope for the Dark family then? What prospect for the planet? At least if she is alive, she can attempt to contain the damage her mother is inflicting. She wants nothing more to do with the Dark Queen's experimentation, and cuts her hours in the laboratory completely. The Chamber is under lockdown; all members are given immunisation injections, thinly disguised as 'boosters' for a flu that is circulating. Signa administers them personally. That is the last and only time Regan will see her mother after their altercation in the Initium lab. Signa is more distant than ever, unable to read. She injects her daughter as an impersonal doctor would in a hospital. She finishes up, gives Regan a look of expectation, devoid of any sentiment, anger, or even contempt. A look of certainty. Then she motions her daughter away, and turns her attention to the next in line. Perhaps she surmises that a firm presumption of Regan's obeisance is the most reliable approach.

Just before the week is up, with Regan's decision imminent, Queen Signa and King Dallon are found murdered. Their bodies are severely burnt, almost beyond recognition. They had been taking a rare walk not far from the Chamber. Fifteen Dark guards were taken out getting to them. Neither of them had kept up their martial skills sufficiently; they had become complacent given their faith in their security contingent. The burial ceremony takes place the following day, officiated by Mister Alton. There are no religious overtones.

No one but Valtere knows of the words that passed between her and Signa that grim night, or of the awful understandings that Regan now possesses of her mother's scheme. There are rumours. But then, there are always rumours of one kind or another in the Dark Court. Regan keeps it that way. She has the house guards board up her parent's room. A few days later, she orders the two lock-picking guards and two others to carry all the unsealed bodies out of the Initium lab, shrouded in the darkness of night. They all wear protective suits that Regan finds in the laboratory cupboard, herself included. She and her four henchmen carefully wrap the bodies in sheets from the Chamber, and transport them to the incinerator a distance from the laboratories to the west of the homestead. The noxious procession feels to last a lifetime.

After this, Regan transfers all reserves of the original bacterium, the eximius mutation of it, and immunisation sera to the freezer facility of the main lab. She leaves the stocks of the offshoot strain that she had worked on in there too. She needs to preserve all the bacterial material in order to evolve and keep stocks of antidotes. She then locks the Initium lab and takes the keys. She would like nothing more than to raze it to the ground, but refrains. She cannot afford to appear to be disrespecting her mother's memory at a time like this. Now is the time she must work to gain the respect of her court. She will have to be fastidious in concealing work on antidotes. It will become necessary to make contact with humans who can assist her with administration of immunisations and treatment. She resolves to create a new order, one that returns to the original, more mystical Dark Force, rather than the unutterable empire of the dead that her mother has wreaked.

The following day, Regan undergoes her coronation as Queen of Night. The ceremony is subdued. All of her time in the weeks and months to follow are spent creating an eximius antidote. That her mother and father are dead feels odd, like a familiar presence now hollow, the husk of it still lingering. Regan looks forward to the time when it is safe enough to venture into the open veldt again. To run into the nothingness. To sleep in the shade of a tree with her eagle nearby. She wonders if the Dark order she is creating anew is yet another falsehood, a gentler one, but a deceit nonetheless. The lie doesn't see properly. It can't move quickly. It gets stuck and then can't find the answers to get out of the mud again. She shoves these thoughts down into a place that she boards up as she did her parent's room. Remaining still is out of the question, she tells herself. I will lead as best I can. I am Princess of Dark, become Queen of Night.

CHAPTER 10

The Visit

10/12/2050

It is too hot to play outside today. Aedan has opened every window in the house, and is in the kitchen making something sweet for the children. This is how her mother would soothe her if she was hurt. After the last fight between Keesa and her father, the girl has been edging away from them both, spending more time on her own. She seems jumpy, and when Aedan checks on her sleeping at night, she finds her moving in fits and starts.

Since it is so stifling out today, Aedan has given the children permission to play in the dairy, the coolest part of the homestead. Their history lesson by Miss Stein at school today had touched on the practice of marriage through the 19th century. A group of adults rotate at being teacher at the village school. None of them are qualified, but their former work consisted of a position of enough authority that they have been deemed fit to teach.

Elijah and Toekoums have managed to distract Keesa from her troubled mood. They have coaxed her into a game of wedding-wedding. Keesa is the bride, Elijah the groom, Toekoums the organ player, and Nefer is the non-denominational priest (Miss Stein is adamant the children get a rounded perspective). Toekoums is practising his organ-playing—the sound of which is pitched somewhere between his meow and talking voice, not the most lilting of accompaniments. Keesa finds relief in immersing herself into another character. She pretends to prime herself at a mirror, prodding her hair, and swivelling her body while keeping her head fixed on the reflection.

'Oh my God, I look terrible.'

Toekoums starts to giggle. Keesa is a keen observer and is quite taken with the teenage girls at school. Elijah stands stiffly at the altar—a large wooden box full of dairy equipment. 'I'm waiting, my bride,' he says in a cheerless tone. This sets Toekoums laughing, which interferes with his organ tune.

'But I'm not ready yet...' Keesa hurriedly finishes her styling, and sashays with exaggerated happiness to the altar. Toekoums' bizarre bridal march rises. Keesa faces Elijah and they take hands.

'I think you look very pretty,' Elijah says in his earnest way.

'I hope I'm still pretty when we get divorced; Katy said that actually divorce was bigger than marriage by the end, they just didn't want us to know,' Keesa responds. Toekoums collapses with laughter now. Elijah blushes. Nefer barks, trying to bring Toekoums to order. He has taken on the humourless nature of his master.

'We're supposed to be having a wedding here!' Elijah pulls his hands away, throws them up in the air.

Keesa starts giggling now, 'You always take things so seriously, Eli, we're just playing!' The more Keesa and Toekoums laugh, the louder Nefer barks. Elijah stands to one side, shaking his head at the marital deterioration before him. He notices Toekoums' locket beginning to glow green.

'Keesa! Nefer, keep it down! KEESA!' he insists, pointing to Toekoums. Keesa sits up in stages from rolling on the ground with her kitten, wiping the hysterical tears from her eyes. As she sees the shining, her face sobers. Toekoums realises something is up, senses the pulsation on his chest, and sits upright, a little nervous now. Nefer starts whining and backs off. Toekoums closes his eyes. Elke's face emerges in the pendant circle. She looks around the room, spots Keesa, and addresses her.

'Are you the youngling by the name of Keesa?'

'I am.'

'And can your present company be trusted?'

Keesa looks at Elijah and Nefer; the boy's eyes do not leave the spectral countenance.

'They can.'

'I am Queen Elke of Light. I greet you in peace, and deliver a royal request for your presence, within the next week. I will explain the reason for this once you are here. As soon as you assent, I will inform you as to my whereabouts. I must stress that this is a matter of the highest urgency. There is something valuable I need to give you. Do you accept?'

The joviality of minutes before has drained from Keesa now; a clammy unease pales her cheeks. Her body looks stuck, like prey paralysed.

'No. I mean, no, thank-you, Queen.'

Queen Elke's face clouds over. 'You realise you have been chosen for this...that the change in you will affect the path that earth is on?'

Keesa is hurtling back into herself now, thoughts shouting in her head. 'I don't know who you are. Things are happening to me that I don't understand. What if I don't like the change? What will my parents say? They would never let me go, anyway.'

'It would be best to keep this between us, Keesa. I can assure your safety.'

'I can't do it. I'm sorry. I hope that everything works out.'

Queen Elke's brow wrinkles. 'I see. This is disappointing. If you should change your mind, you can contact me through this pendant. Your helper will know how. Go in light, young Keesa.'

With that, the Queen's image fades, and the pendant returns to its original hue. Toekoums opens his eyes. The three friends regard Keesa.

'I'm going to go help my mother in the kitchen,' she says, heading for the dairy door.

Elijah catches her hand, 'You know that we would all come with you if you wanted to go, don't you?'

'Thanks Eli.' She pauses, still facing the doorway. 'You know, you made a handsome groom.' Out into the bright heat.

She enters the kitchen, offers to help her mother, hugs her firmly, and starts mixing the batter in the bowl. Aedan is surprised, but doesn't ask questions. She simply takes pleasure watching her daughter's small hands finding their way around the spoon. Keesa does not think of choices, of men who look like lions, or of shining pendants that bring messages of change. She stirs the mixture, her eyes moving from it to the flour strewn over the baby-blue kitchen table, and back. She tells herself that this is her place, this is her family, she is this little girl.

Burst Container

11/12/2050

The King of Day stands outside in the strip between the Chamber and the ocean. Lined up 10 metres away from him is a row of objects; a glass jar, a desk drawer, a couple of old door locks, and a rusted car engine. It is late afternoon of a warm day. He loves the beginnings and ends of days. He focuses on one of the glass jars, and lets out a small growl. The glass shakes briefly, then shatters into tiny shards on the ground. He takes in a breath, focuses on the desk drawer, and lets out a slightly longer growl. The wood of the drawer warps, curling like a piece of paper being burnt. He raises the volume towards the end of the sound, and the drawer bursts into chips of wood. The door locks pop quickly with two short low grunts from deep in his throat. He gives his attention to the car engine now, and draws in a deep breath.

Quick footsteps on the gravel behind him disrupt his flow. He exhales and turns to see Bryce approaching swiftly. Once close, Bryce observes the split objects, addresses the King.

'Forgive the interruption, Your Majesty, but I have an urgent message to deliver.'

Queen Elke's face flashes in Maen's head. *Accept each moment in peace. This is the light way*, she would tell him as a boy. 'Go on.'

'It is an invitation for you to meet with Queen Regan of Night, Your Highness, at a location of her preference. She stated that the white flag code of conduct would prevail for its duration, and that guards from either side would not be allowed to attend.' The King's stomach jolts. He stands unmoving, looking at Bryce's face.

'Your Highness, I said that a message—'

'I heard what you said, Bryce. Have Shep and his men ready the cars.' Bryce is astonished. Maen turns back to his objects. Bryce hesitates a moment before interrupting the King's practise session once more. His role as advisor to the King has always been in an informal capacity, as his valet. Light helpers, who are expected to advise their royal charge to a degree, are only assigned to potential Sun-bearers.

'Sire, if I may, it would be highly advisable for you to refuse her invitation. The Queen of Night's word on white flag protocol can hardly be trusted.'

'I have given you my answer, Bryce.' He keeps his back to his attendant.

'Surely Your Majesty is aware of the kind of risk implied in this situation.'

'I am aware of the dangers, Bryce. Ready the cars. I leave at first light.' Maen speaks this to Bryce's face, in a voice that bears a hint of the lion in him. The valet can feel the tremor of it in his stomach and under his feet.

'Certainly, Your Highness, I will make the necessary arrangements.' He makes his way back to the Chamber, his hand lifting to his brow every few moments.

Maen's thoughts are racing; it feels as though his blood is moving too quickly for his heart. He stares at the sea for a few moments. He turns again to the car engine, pulls a well of breath into his lungs, and lets out a deep roar, so intense it causes Bryce to jump, and the birds around to go quiet. The engine explodes instantly; a small shower of metal rain follows. His body is shaking. A neutral meeting. He will have to work hard to keep it that way.

Unguarded

The location given is simply a set of co-ordinates: 33.29 ° S; 23.54 ° E. His guards work out where to go using an old compass; they accompany him until about half an hour away from the destination, as they did when he went to meet Keesa. This displeases those in the Chamber who know of his trip. The King has ordered that it be kept secret and that, above all, his mother should not be informed. The last thing he wants is for her to worry; not with her health at present. He is relieved to drop the guards off; they have everything necessary with them to keep themselves comfortable until his return. Driving on his own is a rare pleasure.

The sun is setting; it is as though a gigantic thumb has smudged the sky orange near the blazing half-disc. He is close now. This route is still familiar to him, after all this time. He drives, trying to still his thoughts, quell his nerves. They are like opposing currents, restless, pulling him this way and that. He breathes in the dusk, bush air. There is nothing like it, he misses the simplicity of this place.

And suddenly there it is. Its structure is silhouetted; the familiar black lines criss-crossing. Her outlined figure inside cuts the red sky behind it with grace. He hadn't needed the guards to work out the location but the less they know the better. He parks his car, walks slowly towards the lattice. As he gets closer, the dwindling light catches more of the Queen. Taking in her womanhood with his eyes is torture; he steels himself. He reaches the edge of the structure and bows to her from his sternum.

'Queen Regan.'

She takes a low curtsey and returns to standing in one elegant sweep. 'King Maen.'

Regan drinks in the King's features. His furry ears, russet hair, comely face, his mesmerising yellow-green eyes. The relief of being in his presence floods her; it is as if she has been drowning, and now comes up for air.

'Ten years since we met here that last time. It's good to see you.'

He strains to remain impermeable. 'What have you summoned me for, Regan?'

'Please enter.'

Maen surveys the empty space; the clay pillars rise bare to the sky. His tail swishes, ears fold back. He steps onto the clay base.

'Anyone would say I was insane to come here today.'

'You can trust me. You know that.' She is achingly beautiful up close.

'And why should I trust the daughter of the Queen who murdered my father? I'm not sure I want to know how much you had to do with it.'

'Your mother assassinated both my parents; my mistrust of you should be double-fold.'

'And the meningitis outbreak? Your mother engineered the mutation, did she not?'

'You knew even then that she didn't let me in on her medical experimentation. I didn't know what she was planning until it was too late. We are not our parents. I am not my mother. We were always different from them.'

'We were young and reckless. I have come to understand my responsibilities far more clearly since then. Tell me why you called upon me.'

Regan takes his hand in hers. The current between them flares. He should pull away, but has thought so many times about this moment, of touching her again, he is unable to. Regan pauses. This was easier when she was a teenager. She has grown accustomed to the comfort of convention since then. *You do not know what will fill the space next*, she tells herself. *Embrace the void.* She fixes his eyes, takes a breath, hurtles herself forward.

'I love you, Maen.'

The sound of her velvet voice uttering those words cleaves his heart in two. She sees the crack in his eyes. When she speaks again, her tone has sureness, where there was apprehension before. The admission has opened her throat, she is intoxicated with telling a truth that should not be uttered, one that has been screaming to be heard from its burial place for what feels like an eternity.

92

'You know I could be killed for saying that; that should show you its strength. I have asked you this once before and now, I offer it again. Marry me. Together, we could put an end to the senseless carnage of the past. A union of the Chambers of Dark and Light could deliver them both from the brink of extinction.'

Maen lets go her hand, turns away, lifts his exasperated hands to his head, drops them, turns back to her. Her lips, her crimson lips. His voice is like a tightly twisted rope about to snap. 'We went over this 10 years ago. What I said then still stands. We both know that what you are proposing is unprecedented, treasonous, and fraught with peril. We cannot fathom how it may affect life on the planet; the risks are indescribable.'

'And the alternative? If the Chambers continue on the path of opposition and vengeance, either the planet will be imbalanced by one side being wiped out, or we will eventually annihilate one another, leaving anarchy in our wake. It is time to move forward.'

'Why must you always question rules? Can you not see that they provide the structure necessary to maintain balance?'

'There was a time when you questioned them too. You just didn't have spine enough to go through with it.'

'You don't know how far I took our proposal, the consequences of which almost lost me my kingship.'

'What do our reigns mean if we cannot even produce heirs to our thrones? The royal Light code is already being corrupted. I have knowledge of your foreign incomer. I know that you too have not chosen a marriage candidate. Why is that?'

'I simply have not found a candidate who I...' He swallows a word; his tail flicks.

'Who you what?'

'A candidate who I love.'

'Do you not love me?'

'But you are not a candidate!'

Maen lets out a growl of frustration, a small bush nearby explodes. He paces now, struggling to contain his desire.

'Who says? Your mother? We both know she is coming to her time. My parents no longer have a say. You were so concerned a decade ago about what our union would do to our parents but what did it help to stop ourselves? Look at the state of things now. Our generation has to make our own choices, according to what we believe fitting for the times.'

'What you are proposing is an impossibility!'

'You still have not answered me, Maen. Do you love me?'

He turns to her, his eyes firing. 'I have always loved you, Regan. It may be high treason and I have tried with all my strength to stop, but it is as undeniable now as it ever was.'

An expression breaks onto Regan's face that has always been his favourite. It is tenderness that does not know itself, that she is so unused to that its depth seems to surprise her. He steps forward, places his hands around her waist, pulls her into his body and kisses her fiercely. The moment is theirs, they have opened possibility. Their bodies find each other again, the sweet relief racing their blood. She yields to his searching lips, which brush over her collarbones, the creamy skin of her chest. He kneels, pressing his mouth against the silk covering her stomach. She watches him, transfixed. She touches the point where his hairline meets his brow, stoops down and kisses it, the mind beneath it. He looks up into her eyes. Their meeting gaze respires the bond between them, a feeling that the air around them is somehow clearer given their entwinement. Maen drops his eyes.

'Regan,' he whispers, placing his hands in a slowing gesture on her belly. 'We have to talk.'

Regan strokes his ear. 'I know.' He stands again and enfolds her in his arms. A minute passes. The pleasure of hearing his heart beating beneath his skin is indescribable. *I am your Queen.* The words pulse through her like a knowing that does not require formulation. Maen gently pulls away.

'There is something I have to know.' His hand briefly touches her shoulder, drops again. 'Did you play a part in my father's death?'

Regan looks to the darkening sky, back to the clay underframe beneath her feet. 'My vision the day before. It pinpointed his location.'

Maen is silent, unmoving. She reaches her hand towards him delicately. 'Maen, I—'

'NO! This is why I should not trust you!'

'You could never know how sorry I am that it happened that way. I thought I was alone in the room but my mother had come in unnoticed. I would never have given her that information willingly. But, don't you see? I did it precisely because I was following the rules you speak of so fondly! I was a ghost of myself at the time, moulding myself to my mother. Anything to shut out the mess inside. I am asking you now to forgive me. I want to begin fresh, to show you how I have grown past what I was then.'

'NO MORE!' He lets out an agonising roar now. The earth beneath them shakes violently then slowly subsides. He hauls himself back to a teetering semblance of calm. Regan stands with her head lowered, her heart sinking.

'This is madness. We have to lay this to rest once and for all, Regan.'

'How can you do this? When you know how much there is between us?'

'We both knew that what we shared could never last. We agreed!'

'Things change, Maen. Don't you see? You changed me! You made me question my Dark heritage, the code that used to give me purpose, made me feel like I had a place in the world. What place do I have now? Sitting between two Forces, never feeling like my life has begun. Hungering after you every day. Pulling the mask tighter over my face so that no one will sniff out the stench of emotion.'

'You chose to play it out that way, Regan.'

'Are you telling me that you don't feel anything like this yourself? That you never wish for me?'

His voice is cold now. 'It does not serve the Light for me to answer that question.'

'Why close your heart now? I am offering you the opportunity to create a royal family once more. I give you my word to halt the Dark plan for destruction, to forge a path that includes the best of what each side has to offer. I am giving you a window, one that is unlikely to come around again in your lifetime. All you have to do is say yes.'

'I already have a family. You embody the greatest threat to their well-being.'

'What family? From what my sources tell me, your mother has been in hiding for a decade, who knows where your brother is, and you run the Chamber without a wife or children. If distance and detachment are two cornerstones of the Dark code, your family looks like a textbook exemplar of it.'

'You know that is not true.'

'Is it far from it, though? My mother told me your father's last words. He said, open your heart and the light shall enter. I am ready to do that. Are you?'

The King is quiet a few moments. A breeze has come up. The serenity of the night veldt seems ludicrous to him now, given the madness that shouts its way around his head, and the plummeting of his heart. He watches Regan sweep a lock of her ebony hair away from her face and place it behind her ear, an involuntary gesture, her fingers move with innocence. What other actions do those hands perform? What concoctions, what incisions? Her eyes wait for his answer like beacons now, like shining chance. The words he must say feel like bile rising in his throat.

'My decision is made. It would be thoroughly irresponsible to place my trust in you. A union between us is out of the question.'

The words hit Regan like mute bullets. Once they are in, they separate out from skin to bone to organ. She can't seem to put the phrases back in a row again. She closes her eyes, lowers her head, waits for sense to come back. She can almost hear her mother's caustic laughter. *This will not happen again*, she thinks. *Not like last time.* She opens her eyes, lifts her head. His answer has drained the verve from her eyes, the colour from her lips. The familiar process of shutting cranks back into gear.

'As you wish, Maen. The white flag code ceases at daybreak. I bid you farewell.'

As much as he knew his decision would have an effect, he feels an appalling sense of loss as the practised coolness in her voice slices through him now. 'I admire what you did this evening, Regan. I wish that there were some way that

I could—'

'Please leave, King Maen.'

'Of course. Farewell, Queen Regan.'

He steps off the structure, walks back to his car. Every second he wants to turn back, change his mind. *That will lessen*, he thinks. *Remember who you are; you stand for the Light*. Light? His life feels more like a prison of closing now than something that opens enough to let light in. He gets into his car. It is almost night now but his lion eyes see well in the dark. She has her back to him, her face turned towards the rising moon in the east. He drives, concussed with what he has done. Everything outside of that square space, those exhilarating moments, feels unreal now.

After some minutes he passes a low tree that glints a pair of eyes. Valtere. The King nods as he goes by and the eagle flaps his wings in return. Maen is glad to know that she is watched, guarded. After the countless secret meetings he kept safe for them, Valtere feels more like an old friend to the King than a Dark helper. He watches in the rear view mirror as Valtere's head jerks towards his disappearing car, jerks in the direction of the clay structure, then settles forward again. Something in his energy puzzles the King; he almost looked disappointed with the paucity of their contact in that passing moment.

He drives on, nearing his men now. He lets the sound of tyres on gravel fill his head, as though he is a spectre that things can pass through. All other thoughts are too risky to have in this confined space with it sitting like an armed grenade in his throat. Things are likely to move quickly now; there is much to do. The youngling must be brought to the Chamber; she must come under their protection and begin her training. She must be taken to his mother before it is too late. But for now, rubber rolling over small stones and the smell of dark veldt air.

CHAPTER 11

Hands Dipped

14/12/2050

Keesa is out collecting rocks. She is turning over a new leaf. This week's teacher taught them that expression and she likes it. It sounds so final and open at the same time. She is going to be a good girl now. Help her mother more with chores. Do her homework on time. And no more skeletons. She has soaked them all in water doused with bleach from her mother's dairy, placed them in an assortment of boxes, and pushed them under her bed. Now she picks up rocks. She chooses those with the brightest colours on them; phosphorescent green, far-fetched orange. Keesa wonders how these colours come to adorn matter whose source is a place as dark as the ground. The plants and flowers of the veldt sometimes appear more like a seascape than a landscape to her.

She comes across a lone flower bursting with pinkness and thinks of her mother's flower-beds. She takes out her Swiss army knife and carefully acquires a cutting of the flower, the way Aedan has taught her. She positions it among the accumulated rocks in her school satchel, which is her carry-all today. She reaches the western fence of Elijah's farm, a short way down from the front gate. Climbing over it is easy; the wire is weathered and pliable. She has spotted a mass of colourful rocks on the other side. As she picks her way through them, the sound of panicked bleating draws her attention. It is coming from over the ridge that opens out on one side to a small patch of level ground, and dips away to the lower part of the farm on the other..

She scales the ridge and spots the herd grazing in the grassland enclosure of the lower pasture. The bleating, which had gone quiet for a few moments, starts up again, more fretful now. It is a young goat kid directly beneath her, struggling intermittently to pry its front right hoof from where it is trapped between a boulder and the side of a craggy rock outcrop. It must have wedged its foot while hurrying to keep up with the herd as they made their way downhill.

The farm is empty today. Elijah and Nefer have gone into the village with Brick to organise an expedition to fetch grain-feed from a village west of Hale. Elijah told Keesa his grandfather wanted to visit friends after, so he would drop by her house late afternoon.

Keesa climbs down the ridge and approaches the calf. She wants to help it, free it. Something else wants to be done, though. Her hands must carry out what is expected of them. The kid is frantic now, there is blood around the hoof that it is tugging, over and over. Keesa has a sense that it is trying to get away from her. She reaches into her pocket for her knife. She knows her orders. They fill the air around her, as though she is inside a tunnel of unseen liquid that moves her hands, her thoughts, to enact its oozing desire. She can hear the message faintly already, beating in the kid heart.

Toekoums hears Keesa calling to him from behind, her voice urgent. He turns to look for her but she is not there. Instead there stands an aged woman who must have been alluring as a youth but whose skin is now grey as a fish. Her eyes are remote and merciless. Her lips hardly move as she speaks.

'Here, kitty.'

Her voice hangs with unspeakable secrets. It sits out of place in the air, dredged from a malign past, refusing to budge. Toekoums notices a tapping, clicking sound that repeats in uneven time. There is something moving behind her long skirt that sputters its confused way out from behind the folds now, flapping like a fish out of water. It is a live spine that must once have belonged in a body. The vertebrae are dry and old. The sets of muscles clinging to them have lost any radiance they may have had and now resemble small, sapless clusters of hair.

Toekoums wakes up from an afternoon slumber so deep he feels drunk with it. The dream is still with him; he sits up. He licks the fur on his stomach, extends his right leg on the floor, cleans the length of it, the hind paw. He looks around for Keesa. Perhaps she is in the garden. He pads outside; no sign of her. He stands in the dairy doorway, giving his eyes a moment to adjust to the dim light. Only Aedan, finishing wrapping 20 blocks of cheese in mutton cloth to barter with at the next market. She notices the kitten; it doesn't often come to her on its own. It follows her into the house. She calls out to Keesa; the house is quiet. Her daughter's room is even neater than normal. The kitten is still following her.

'You looking for Keesa, Toekoums?' She talks to a feline as most humans do—with no expectation of a response, yet with an irrational belief that something of what she says is understood. 'I thought she had taken you with her.' A cloud of concern passes across her face. Toekoums meows. They hear the front garden gate closing. Elijah is stopping in on his way home. He asks after Keesa.

'She went out collecting rocks a while ago. I need to pick up some eggs from your place; how about we go over together? I'm sure we'll see her along the way,' Aedan suggests. She's determined to stay calm. It's not the first time that Keesa has been out longer than expected. Kaleb is away for two days this time. Keesa has bent the rules in his absence before. She knows the leash is longer with her mother. Aedan drives over to the neighbouring farm in her car now, Nefer and Toekoums on the backseat. The kitten is so insistent with his meows that Aedan brings him along.

<hr />

The goat kid put up quite a struggle. The noise it made sounded different to Keesa than before. Once she is carrying out her orders, everything around her becomes more distant, as though a space opens up between her and her surroundings. Sounds are novel again, as when she was baby, yet she is detached from the meaning of them. She had to use two hands to make the incision this time and there was more cutting involved in getting to the heart. She cradles the glistening organ in both hands, gets up off her haunches and moves to stand next to the goat, the section of even ground before her. Holding the heart out, she waits. The image in front of her is altering. Molecule of one view is exchanged for molecule of another, as though one portion of reality is swapped for a different one.

The Dark Queen stands on a small patch of operating theatre floor, shining out in contrast to the ochre sand and dry grass surrounding it. Keesa recognises her from the day of the little bird. Again the woman has a subject lying face down on the theatre table in front of her. This time it is an animal, a large lion. Judging from its size, it must once have been a powerful creature. Now it is fastened down to steel rails lining the table, its front and hind legs splayed to the sides, and its face protruding through an opening in the centre. Its mane is knotted with dried clumps of sweat and its tail hangs limp off the end of the slat. Signa is shaving the large cat's fur along the spine with a razor. Her hands work scrupulously and with a fondness for the action that seems to soothe her. Keesa notices that the skin covering the area where the base of the skull meets the spinal column has been circled with what looks to be charcoal.

Signa senses her presence, her eyes lift and meet Keesa's, observe the heart in the girl's small hands, and trail to the kid, mute and leaking on the ground. Her lips curl up and affection pulls at the unwilling muscles in her face.

'Ah, you again.' There is victory in her tone. She lets her arms rest on the lion's back. 'I accept your offering, little one. Your skills are progressing rapidly. I see promise. A natural talent with the knife, what's more. You have earned the chance to prove yourself, to become a part of the one family that will survive. It is time for you to come to your new home. I have much to teach you. Beware the attachments that prevent your rise to power.'

Suddenly, the lion jolts back to life again. He jerks his head up out of the opening, twists it with difficulty to the side and drops it back down onto the steel, looking Keesa full in the face now. The Queen regards the creature derisively and, unhurried, exchanges the razor for a blinking surgical knife from the small table next to her. The lion's eyes scream with wanting to tell Keesa something. He attempts to roar now, craning his neck with the effort. No sound comes out as he releases, just a whistling as the air wheezes from his lungs. He tries again and again, his eyes growing ever more disbelieving at the lack of sound, his limbs struggling with increasing frenzy against the leather restraints. The Queen lifts the knife with both hands now and plunges it deep into the centre of the charcoal circle at the base of his skull. The lion's eyes widen in surprise, then go dull, still staring into Keesa's. His body is, once more, inert. Keesa becomes aware of a faint, repetitive, sound coming from behind her. The Queen removes the knife, looks at Keesa with eyes that challenge. Then her face whips up to the space above the ridge. The unremitting sound comes clear. A dog's bark. Nefer.

'KEESA! What are you doing?' Aedan's shriek shatters her immersion. Keesa flinches and drops the heart with a moist thud. Looking at the spent organ on the sand, the blood dripping off her hands, she grasps what she has done. The vision before her disappears. She half-turns slowly to see her mother, Elijah and Toekoums standing on the ridge, watching her in astonishment. Toekoum's fur is raised; Nefer is growling. Her mother's face is flushed with anger. Elijah has paled with shock; Keesa can hardly look into his eyes.

'I'm so sorry, Elijah.' Keesa's voice feels small and the words insufficient. She unplants her feet from the sand and starts to run down the hill. Toekoums patters down the ridge and follows her as quickly as he can. Nefer starts sprinting towards her, baring his teeth. Elijah yells for him to come back, to stay. The dog strains against these actions but obeys his master. He whines, confused.

Elijah speaks quietly to Aedan, who is still as a statue. 'I can go after her if you would like me to.'

'Let her go. I'll deal with her when she gets home tonight; she hardly has anywhere else to go.'

Elijah's anger is clouding any caring feelings in this moment. They watch Keesa run in a stop-start panic around the bend at the bottom of the hill, out of their view, the kitten a little way behind. Her satchel lies discarded in the blotched sand, carefully chosen rocks spilling out, the lone flower out of place now with its cheery pinkness.

———◆•◆———

As soon as Keesa is out of the other's sight, she pauses a moment, kneels down, and tries to wipe away some of the blood on her hands by rubbing sand on them. It takes away the excess liquid, but the stain remains. The bitter stench of hands that have dipped into innards is overwhelming.

'Keesa!' Toekoums is not far behind. She starts at his voice, looks around swiftly to see him approaching, hastens up and starts running again. He shouts to her again. Keesa's legs are already growing tired and, it occurs to her that she has no idea where she will run. She scrambles over the farm fence and heads in a direction that will take her north of the village. At that moment, two cars moving at high speed tear out from around one of the low koppies close by. Keesa freezes, and the stories she has heard of baboon gangs rear in her head. Toekoums catches up to her. Keesa can't face looking into his eyes. She thinks about running back, but paralysis and confusion have got the better of her. She waits, thinking perhaps she deserves the fate of the vicious baboons.

The leading vehicle is a Land Rover, which pulls up next to her, sending a cloud of dust over the two of them. The other vehicle comes to a halt a short distance away. The driver stays in the front seat and opens the passenger door from the inside. The dust clears slightly. Keesa recognises the driver. It is Lion.

'You shouldn't be out on your own, youngling, it is no longer secure. Allow me to take you to a place of shelter.'

Keesa suddenly feels fatigue sweeping over her, yet still she hesitates, reluctant to break more of her mother's rules by getting into a car with a man she knows little about. She turns her head to Toekoums; he looks up, nods surely. Keesa points to the other car, another four-by-four that looks like it's been restored. 'Who's in that car?'

'Those are my guards; they will help make sure no harm comes to you.' Keesa keeps her eye on the second vehicle, trying to make out the figures inside.

'I promise to bring you back,' Maen adds.

The thought of going back and facing the incensed onlookers at the top of the hill turns her stomach. Keesa walks forward and climbs onto the passenger seat. Toekoums pauses next to the passenger door.

'Can my kitten come too?'

'Of course.'

Keesa holds out her hand to the kitten, registers the ruddy colour sunken into its skin and retracts it quickly, folding it into her other hand.

'My hands are dirty.' She fixes her eyes on the dashboard. The little feline hops up onto the side bumper, into Keesa's lap. He begins licking one of her hands clean with his tongue. Silent tears roll from the girl's eyes.

'We'll have you in a bath in no time, Keesa. Never mind.'

There will be plenty of time to talk later, Maen thinks. He doesn't want to ponder what Regan might have conspired to cause the blood on the girl's hands. He can never allow the youngling to come to harm. Her life depends on him now. The responsibility gives him an odd, off-balance feeling of lightness when he would have expected it to weigh him down. She has a difficult road ahead of her; she has much to learn. Her nascent powers need to be shaped, directed. Training a Sun-bearer this young, and of unknown origin, will make for thoroughly uncharted territory. Yet beyond this assignment, he finds himself hoping to someday watch her practise spin-bowling again as a girl simply playing at life.

Berth

14/12/2050

Maen notices a little head appearing in the rear view mirror. Keesa has surfaced from slumber. He had stopped the car a few hours ago to move her to the back seat, where she could lie down on a blanket he took from the boot. She sits up slowly, displacing Toekoums from his ball of sleep at her belly. Dark is fast approaching outside now; Keesa notices the vegetation here is sparser than in her area.

'Did you rest well?'

'Kind of, thank you.'

Her dreams have left her tired. She can't remember them but can feel that they were constricting and seemed to go round in circles. She watches the scenery. They are on a seldom-used dirt road, judging by the roughness of its condition. She would never have imagined she'd be riding in the back of the lion-man's car today. She knows that her parents will be worried. She feels disjointed in the situation, yet not overly anxious. Inexplicably, there is something about lion-man that puts her at ease. Within minutes, Maen pulls the car onto the side of the road and stops.

'We have to walk a little way from here.' He goes to the open the back door for Keesa and helps her out. The other vehicle parks close behind theirs. Five guards step out. They all wear practical clothing in the tones of the veldt, with the odd item visible that would at one time have been standard army issue. Although the men are all hefty and carry intimidating artillery, Keesa can tell they have honest faces. Maen goes to instruct them to stay with the cars for the night and guard the outer entrance.

Keesa carries Toekoums in her arms as Maen leads her through an area of thick, dry brush, stooping where it has grown too low. The path is on a slight gradient and, after a few minutes, they come out to a small clearing where they are met by six armed guards. The clearing is surrounded by more brush and further out, a number of koppies. As soon as the guards see Maen, they bow and step aside. Keesa sets Toekoums down on the ground. In front of them is an old stone cottage, so overgrown with sunned foliage that all that is clearly visible is the front door. It is opened by an old woman. Keesa recognises her.

'Queen Elke,' she says and makes a low curtsey.

'Hello, little Keesa.' Despite her age, she exudes the stature of a monarch. She wears an unembellished gown that hangs off a yoke in ivory cotton with white silk detail. Her healthy silver hair is swept up in a loose bun. Her eyes are the colour of a fawn's coat. Maen goes to embrace his mother.

'Good to see you, my boy.'

'And you, Mother.'

'Please come in, all of you. This must be your helper.'

'Yes, Your Majesty, Toekoums is my name.' He bows gracefully.

'Charmed to meet you.'

Inside, the house is simple and neat. A single wrought iron bed with a light-blue silk throw on it, a wooden table and two chairs, a few kitchen utensils, an old coal stove. A free-standing bath and different sized white enamel buckets and jugs stand in the corner. A low door leads off the rear of the main room to a smaller, second room with just enough space in it for another single bed. On nights when a scouting guard has detected human presence in the vicinity, one of the guards will sleep in the small room as a precautionary measure. A small bokmakierie is perched on one of the wooden chairs, the same bird that had appeared on the screen in the assembly, it lets out a few notes. Although its movements are brisk, its eyes have an aged look to them.

'This is Ninev, everyone.'

Toekoums had noticed Ninev straight away; his jaw is chattering now. Ninev flits up onto one of the kitchen shelves. The Queen's sharp eyes quickly register the kitten's hankering.

'You will have to rise above your carnal desires, little cat. Ninev is not food, she is my helper.' Toekoums controls his jaw with difficulty, sits back on his haunches and licks his lips with an expression of disenchantment. Keesa looks from Toekoums to Ninev to the Queen with a puzzled look.

'How old are you, Ninev?' The bird tilts her head sharply to one side, back up, and chirps.

The Queen smiles, 'Ninev is the same age as I am—seventy years old. Helpers live for about 100 years. Not all of them can talk. Ninev and I communicate in other ways.'

'How?'

'We grew up together; I have learnt to read her notes. There will be time for questions in the morning, little one. First things first: wash, eat, and bed. We will begin before daybreak, so that you and Maen don't drive too long into the night.'

'Begin what?' Keesa has never been good at containing questions. Queen Elke catches her son's eyes. Maen goes to Keesa, lowers himself onto his haunches.

'My mother is going to hand something over to you, Keesa, something that has been in my family for years. But you must be refreshed for the process.'

Keesa's eyes widen in fear, dart towards the Queen, then back to lion-man.

'I think I want to go home now.'

Maen places both hands on her arms. 'How about you rest here tonight and after we've explained everything to you in the morning, you decide whether or not you want to go through the process?'

Keesa looks gingerly at the Queen, who assures her gently, 'You have nothing to fear from us, Keesa.'

'Okay, I'll say in the morning.' The events of the day are catching up with her; her jittery state is plummeting toward exhaustion now. Queen Elke heats the water for Keesa's bath on the stove and fills the tub.

'Would you like me to help you?' she asks the girl.

'No, thank you, I bath myself.'

The Queen and Maen leave her to it; Ninev darts out the door after them. Toekoums sits next to the tub cleaning his fur. It feels odd to Keesa to be bathing in someone else's home other than her aunt's by the sea. The soap is translucent green and has a funny, rough shape; Keesa sniffs its foam each time she lathers it. It smells of lemons and roses; the scent is soothing on a day that seemed to shout at her. She wonders if Elijah will ever speak to her again. She remembers the pink flower she wanted to give to her mother. She thinks of the opened animal lying next to it; wishes she could put it back together and make it alive again.

'Am I bad, Toekoums?'

Toekoums pauses the cleaning of his belly, straightens up, blinks at Keesa.

'I don't know. But I know that there is good in you.'

'Do you think Queen Elke is good?'

'Sometimes your head gets so filled with questions, you can't hear the answer that's in you.'

'I think she's good.' Keesa watches Toekoums resume licking his amber fur. 'Thanks for coming after me today.'

'I am forever at your service.' Toekoums bows his head; Keesa nods hers in return. The two of them revert to their toilettes.

CHAPTER 12

Evening Birds

14/12/2050

The Queen and her son sit in the front courtyard on a bench of wood and rocks that her guards assembled for her years ago. Her parents had loved their sleek furniture, their jewels, their splendid Chamber. Even though she occasionally misses the home she grew up in, her little stone cottage in the Karoo suits Queen Elke better. When she first came here, the closest town was Die Hel. *Apt*, she had thought. There is nothing left of it now. She casts a sideways glance at her son. It is never easy seeing him. His features are a flagrant reminder to her of his father. That she misses her husband has become as much a part of her being as her Queenhood is, or her love of royal etiquette. The loss of him and, soon after, the disappearance of her younger son, Colter, has taken the wind out of her sails. Her bones have begun to feel brittle with carrying the vacuums left.

The Lion of Light used to joke that Maen got the lion's share of his genes. Colter, on the other hand, is the spitting image of Queen Elke's late father— dark hair, eyes the colour of the ocean on a cloudy day and a tendency to brood. Queen Elke likes to think of her younger son as alive, despite the prevailing opinion that he is long dead. She touches the wood of the bench. She knows that superstitious behaviour is ludicrous given her station but, when it comes to Colter, she struggles to curb an array of it that she learnt as a princess from her ladies-in-waiting. A lifetime ago now.

'Did you tell the girl to curtsey to me?' she asks Maen.

'No.'

'The genes are strong in her. Or perhaps she is just a good con artist.'

108

'You can't fake a royal frequency signal.'

'No, but hers is still not undeniably of the Light. The identity shield around her is impenetrable. I'm not happy with that.'

'Happiness is a luxury, I'm afraid. We are out of time.'

'I know. But, if you had simply taken the time to look harder for a suitable wife...'

'Or if you had been receptive, all those years ago, when I put forward what could still be the most practical solution to the royal crisis, the situation might be very different. Instead, you turned it down on the grounds of etiquette.'

'It is a matter of genetics, not etiquette.'

'Mother, I did not come here to discuss your disapproval of me and the choices I have made. Need I remind you that the last decade has in large part been taken up with re-establishing links with our network of human representatives in court and with assuring a means of survival after the plague. That didn't leave me with much extra time on my hands to sail to other continents in search of marriage candidates.'

'No, but I could have gone as your ambassador.'

'Mother! You know as well as I that your security is paramount. You would be a sitting target on a ship. Were anything to threaten your safety, I need to know I can travel to you in a matter of hours.'

'The whole point of splitting the family up is to thwart the risk of all of us being taken out at once, of total extinction. You must never try to save me. And anyway, I can defend myself with my powers of fire.'

'You are the one who constantly told Colter and I to beware of underestimating the powers of the Dark!'

Ninev, perched in a nearby tree, pipes out a few sharp chirrups, prodding the royals to engage in more constructive talk. The Queen averts her eyes from Maen's intense stare; she looks at the dusty ground, her lips pressed together like clamps. Maen drops his head into his hands; lifts it again and sighs resignedly. 'We are not getting anywhere with this. My instincts tell me we can trust the girl, that she is genuine Light royalty. Where she has come from I don't know but, she is all we have. Hopefully she will assent to the transmission in the morning, and then we'll be on our way. You won't be reminded of what could have been.' He gets up to go back into the cottage. The Queen grabs his hand. He pauses, turns to her; her eyes ask him to sit again. He complies. This may well be the last time he sees her.

'As important as it is to me to help generate the next Sun-bearer, I miss being a mother to my sons, a wife to my husband. I'm so angry with myself for making choices that led to me ending up as the old Queen dying out her life in the Karoo.'

'Mother, you know that that anger will not serve you as Sun-bearer.'

'Of course I do. I work with it every day. We may be high-borns but we still have human physicality, human emotions. We will always be flawed. I think all this missing has made me into a moody old woman.'

'You were always a bit moody. And you never were the greatest mother—not like the ones in the movies you and Dad use to show us. You were always working on your powers, or out establishing networks. But I always knew you loved us. I always knew you had our backs. And that was enough for me.'

She takes his hand in hers. Maen embraces his mother. He can feel the bones protruding from her skin through the fabric of her dress. That she still takes the trouble to dress elegantly all the way out here in the desert saddens him. She draws back, her expression urgent.

'Maen, there is something I need to ask of you before I...before you leave. When you came to me and your father asking for permission to marry Princess Regan...I have come to see since then that we all make mistakes, we all stray from time to time away from the Light. Despite the fact that the relationship amounted to high treason, I should have recognised that you loved her. I am not saying that I would ever have given you permission, perhaps my sense of royal custom is simply too stringent for that, but I had no right to treat you like an immature boy. I should have shown you more respect. I know that it caused you great hurt. Can you forgive me for that?'

Maen is looking at his mother with an expression of disbelief. The mention of the screaming match between him and his parents that night so long ago turns his stomach to stone. He pushes this down, smiles at his old mother.

110

'I work on it every day, Mom.'

The Queen smiles back, a few tears escaping her eyes.

'Anyway, I always thought it was a pretty conservative argument coming from a woman who married an animal.'

The Queen lets out a wry laugh. 'Yes, I can't say my parents would have been captivated by that idea.'

Their laughter trails off to a comfortable quiet. The Queen adds softly, 'I suppose they could have been convinced by his animal god status, though. He had 10 times the Light and heart of any of the human candidates at the time.'

The birds are calling to their mates for the evening, settling into their nests, warming their young. Maen stands, holding out his hand to the Queen. 'Shall we see if Keesa is ready for bed?'

The two of them make their way inside to light candles and prepare supper and beds. Queen Elke and Maen walk with a calmness tonight. They have found a bit of peace in the harshness of a merciless decade. And for this they are grateful.

Prying Time

15/12/2050

Regan stands in the enclosed garden, her back to her room, scanning the fresh vision before her. Her brain aches. She has been gathering these refractions all through the night, slipping into sleep as if into a coma between times. She has always been more of a nocturnal creature, resting in bouts during the day but she has never pushed the visions with this frequency. She knows it is time to stop, perhaps try to eat something. The thought of food makes her stomach twitch. Peace always feels just around the corner, if she could only find the right vision, the one she knows she's been searching for a decade now, even though she's refrained from admitting that to herself. If she draws a vision that features herself and focuses enough emotional energy in that moment, she can be sucked into the time and space of it. Her visions are to further the new Dark code, she has told herself.

The semblance before her now is almost black with night. There is something familiar about the room it opens onto; the glint of glass and steel and slabs of dark wood. Regan hears a door opening in the vision and the soft glow of candlelight illuminates the blinking medical equipment. Even though she has only entered it a few times, she recognises now that it is the Initium laboratory. Animal sounds start at the turn of the door-handle; the chatter of simians. A person carrying a lit candle enters and locks the door. It appears to be female but wears a hooded cloak, obscuring the face. The figure opens the manuscript lying on the central wooden unit at a page marked with a pen, and briefly glances at it. The person removes four corked vials from the cabinet and lines them up on the laboratory desk. Then opens a drawer, takes out a syringe and lays it next to the vials. A clicking sound starts now—perhaps the door being opened again? The shrouded figure checks in the direction of the entrance, looks towards the animal sounds, removes cloak, and starts rolling up sleeves. Regan's skin goes cold; the woman in her vision is herself. She looks the same age she is now. The vision freezes; this means it will dissipate soon.

Regan tries to work out what she might be about to inject, and why, and none of the answers are comforting. She had never returned to the Initium laboratory once she locked it up after her parent's death. She only has a weekly routine of checks in the main laboratory to make sure the stocks of all the variants of the meningitis bacterium are intact, or goes there when necessary to synthesise remedies. She alone keeps the keys to both laboratories.

Regan watches her static self crackle apart now and a piece of time and space scatter up, outwards, and away. The first hint of dawn is touching the sky, reinforcing the queasy sense that she has pushed herself too far. She goes to the kitchen and makes herself some breakfast. The staff are asleep but the kitchen coals are still warm enough to stoke up the fire again. She takes comfort in the act of preparing food for herself. After two eggs, a hunk of bread smeared with butter, and a strong cup of tea, she feels as if she might sleep. She holds the questions arising out of her vision at bay, returns to her unmade bed.

As she begins to drift into slumber, the vision that she has been seeking all night swims to her. It is of herself and Maen together. They are by the sea; there is fresh morning light all around. She is laughing about something and he smiles at her, takes her head in his hands and kisses her brow. She feels a delicate arm at her hip, someone smaller than her. As she turns to see who it is, she comes awake. Being yanked from this snippet of easefulness into a room filled with greying dawn is an intolerable reality. Regan closes her eyes and sleeps like the dead.

CHAPTER 13

Bestowal

15/12/2050

Keesa wakens to the sound of match striking flint. Queen Elke is lighting some candles. The stove fire has been stoked up, the dancing light moves skittishly on the floor. Keesa slept like a log. She notices that the makeshift bed of blankets on the floor next to her that the lion-man had slept in, has already been cleared away. The front door opens and Maen comes in from checking in with his guards. This rouses Toekoums from his warm spot on the bed behind Keesa's bent knees. He begins his series of morning stretches and yawns. It is still dark out and Keesa can feel the morning here is colder than at her home. Maen notices Keesa's eyes blinking at him.

'Morning Keesa, I was about to wake you. Are you feeling more rested?'

'Yes, thank-you, Lion.'

This pleases Queen Elke. Despite her misgivings about Keesa, her cottage feels happier for the presence of a young girl in it. 'Good,' she says, 'I have made some porridge and tea. No good starting today on an empty stomach.'

Once they have finished, it is still before five in the morning. Queen Elke and Keesa sit facing each other now by the kitchen table. Elke has been explaining the royal family's structure.

'My son, who you know as Lion, is King Maen of Day, King of the Family of Light.'

Keesa, taken aback, turns to Maen, 'You're the King?'

'Yes, Keesa.'

She turns back to the Queen. 'So, is Lion...I mean, King Maen your husband... and your son?'

The Queen smiles. 'No, my husband was killed by the Queen of Dark when you must have been a tiny baby. I instated Maen as King then, even though that would normally only have taken place after my death.'

'How come he looks like a lion?'

'Well, this may be difficult for you to understand, but his father was the Lion of Light, an animal-god. He was an animal that had special powers and could talk like a human.'

Keesa swivels on her chair towards Maen, 'Do you have a queen? Did you make children like that with her?'

There is something about being asked this question by a child that makes Maen's solitary life feel even more desolate. 'I don't have a queen or children.'

'I think you're a nice man. Don't worry, there's lots of fish in the sea. That's what the mature girls at my school say.'

Maen and Elke respectfully contain their laughter. Elke continues answering Keesa's questions, eventually reaching the subject of the scourge.

'We suspect that the meningitis epidemic was orchestrated by the former Dark leader, Queen Signa.'

Keesa has a puzzled expression. 'How did she do it?'

'That I do not know. But I know that she, like her father before her, was a brilliant scientist and surgeon.'

An image is swimming up into Keesa's mind now, one that causes her to feel at once unseemly and intrigued. 'What did she look like?'

Elke hesitates. 'In the later part of her life, she had dark grey hair, which she wore very short. Her eyes were blue, cold as frost.'

The hair on the back of Keesa's neck prickles up and Maen notices the fur along Toekoum's spine rising. 'Why do you ask? Do you think you may have seen her?'

Keesa goes quiet, holding words in her mouth. Her eyes dart to Maen, down to the floor, she shifts her weight in the chair. 'I couldn't have seen her. She's dead.'

Maen moves to Keesa's side, brings himself down to her level. 'The Dark family is capable of many things, Keesa. They operate in ways we do not fully understand. It's important that you let us know if you have seen her.'

Elke and Maen's inquiring eyes are on her. 'Maybe once, in a dream.'

'Can you tell us about it?' Maen probes again.

Keesa repositions her feet on the wooden rung of the chair. 'Can I hear the rest of the story first?'

Elke and Maen exchange a discreet look of concern but they know that to push the girl to talk now may cause her to bolt. It is critical that they keep her soothed, to maximise the chances of her assenting to the transmission.

'Of course, Keesa,' Maen pats her shoulder gently, stands again, 'Mother, please continue.'

Maen turns his eyes away from his mother, towards the courtyard. Day is creeping in; muted light touches the trees. He notices that there are clouds in the sky; they will not give rain, they rarely do in this area but they will provide a degree of coolness.

'Who killed Queen Signa and her King?'

At Keesa's question, Maen's head swings towards his mother. In a knee-jerk, protective reflex, he goes to quash a question that he knows will cause her anguish. The Queen sees this and lifts her hand to still her son's tongue.

'I'm afraid to say it was I who killed them both, Keesa.'

'But, I thought you said that Light people aren't supposed to kill other people.'

116

'It's not something that I am proud of.'

'So...does that make you bad?'

'I'm afraid that what makes one good or bad is not as clear-cut as I once thought it to be. I am still a royal. I still strive to uphold and protect the Light Force on this planet.'

Keesa looks intently at the Queen, her brow furrowed. Elke senses fear in the girl now, as she did when she first visited her through the locket.

'I promise that I will never harm you, Keesa.' This does not appear to put Keesa at ease. Maen notices the increasing light outside.

'Mother, I don't mean to interrupt but time is short.'

'Yes,' Elke resumes, 'the most important function of Light royalty on the planet is to maintain the balance between Light and Dark. Our time here is seen as a preparation for what comes after. Once we become spirit at the end of our lives our critical role commences. As the reigning Queen of Light dies, she will become the next Sun-bearer. That is, if she has undergone the necessary training during her life.'

'What's a Sun-bearer?' Keesa asks.

'We act as representatives of planet earth on the sun. The new Sun-bearer will position herself as mediator between the earth and sun and will act as a filter of all the choices that humans are making on the planet. Choices like to help someone, or to hurt someone, to be truthful, or to be deceptive. Whichever it is, the queen will capture the energy of that moment and transmute it back into pure Light, so that it has the potential to be used to spread more Light onto the planet. This serves to keep the energies on the globe aligned in the direction of Light, rather than Dark. It does not mean that the person concerned will definitely make a choice in the direction of Light in the future but, it does gently nudge them in that direction. Each Sun-bearer presides for 100 years.'

'You said it's queens who become Sun-bearers. Wouldn't I have to be a princess to become a queen?'

'Given the signal you are giving off, it appears that you are a princess, wherever you've come from. Are either of your parents are royals?' Elke asks.

117

'They're just normal parents.'

'I can clearly see that your mother is pure human but I don't get a discernible picture of your father. What are their names, my girl?' Elke throws the question out with feigned nonchalance. Maen knows what his mother is attempting to confirm. If one wanted to believe so, the girl could have a resemblance to Colter.

'Kaleb and Aedan Cross.'

Elke's chest sinks in slightly but the hope that her son is still alive is not erased. If he is hiding out somewhere, he would not be using his real name. Maen brings himself close to Keesa. She can smell the animal part of him, the scent of clean fur, a bit like the veldt. 'It is time to make your decision, Keesa. Will you give permission for my mother to transmit the seedling powers into you?'

Keesa's eyes are wide open.

'What will happen to me afterwards?'

'The unique powers that are growing in you already will be magnified and I will also grant you special ones to enable you to become the next Sun-bearer.'

'I want to speak to Toekoums.' Keesa says, reads the urgency in Maen's eyes and adds, 'Quickly.'

'Of course,' Maen says.

Keesa gets off her chair and goes to stand a little way outside the front door. The clouds overhead are thickening fast, uncharacteristic for the region. Keesa has seldom witnessed this weather in her lifetime. Toekoums patters to her; she kneels beside him and speaks in a low tone, 'I am going to say yes to the Queen. I'm scared of it but I want it. I need to know if you have any bad feelings about it, though.'

The kitten looks at her with certainty, 'This is your destiny, Keesa.'

'Good.' As she starts to get up, Toekoums speaks again.

'There is one spirit who doesn't want you to go ahead with this. She came to me in a dream yesterday, before we found you.'

118

Keesa avoids Toekoum's eyes and an uncomfortable heat prickles under her skin. 'Yes, I feel her too.'

'She sees your Light and wants you for the Dark Force. The only chance you have of not being taken by her, is to go through with the transmission.'

Keesa looks at the kitten and nods. She gets up and makes her way in. Something is trying to stop her legs from moving forward, as though she is wading against a tide. She forces herself inside the cottage, the heat under her skin beginning to burn now. Maen and Elke look towards her expectantly. Keesa takes in a breath to speak; it has the same sensation as those she took in the ocean with the whale hanging suspended before her—as though it shouldn't be possible, yet it is.

'I am at your service, my Queen. That which you bequeath shall be my honour.'

The sound of her voice delivering the words seems to allay the heat under Keesa's skin and a flutter of relief opens in her throat. It also generates a sharp wave of nausea from her stomach. A wide smile breaks out on Queen Elke's face.

'Good girl, Keesa. I was hoping you would say that. Let us begin.'

Maen places his hand on Keesa's back for a few moments and says, 'I'll be in the room, Keesa. Don't worry, you're going to be fine.' He clears the kitchen table and chairs out of the way and goes to close the front door. He stands by it, indicating to Toekoums to join him there. Ninev alights on the floor next to Toekoums. The kitten's head whips around to the dainty, yellow-green bird, prompting a defensive chirp from it.

'I won't eat you, Ninev.' Toekoums offers. The bokmakierie gives out another cheep, punctuated by her tail feathers lifting up in a self-righteous manner. The kitten's tail involuntarily mimics the flick.

'You two, settle down now,' Maen whispers in their direction.

Queen Elke takes the blue throw from the bed and lays it on the floor. It feels as if an icy, sour hand is gripping Keesa's stomach, the nausea is becoming unbearable.

Queen Elke steps onto the cloth and indicates the area before her. 'Stand before me, Keesa.'

Keesa sets foot on the blue silk. Queen Elke appears to be going into a trance of sorts. Keesa can sense that the Queen's energy is being wound up into a ball at the very centre of her being. She extends her arms in front of her, angled forward and slightly downward. Keesa does the same, hers angled slightly upward so that her fingertips touch those of the Queen. With this contact, the nausea lifts and she begins to harness her energy in a way that mirrors Elke's. The Queen begins to radiate light. It races outwards, upwards and downwards, flowing like an electric current into Keesa's arms, up into her feet and zooming into the top of her head.

Three circles of light begin glowing like neon, one that flows along their arms, one along their spines, and a third one along the interface between the Queen and the girl. Keesa can feel that the substance being poured into her from Elke is thick with knowledge of performances, each performance a complex sequence of thoughts, intentions, actions. The pressure is steadily building at the crown of her head, the tips of her fingers. At the same time, it feels as though certain areas of her body are heating up, whirring into life.

Maen, Ninev and Toekoums are all riveted to the decantation taking place. The room is as warm as an oven now. Maen hears a crack of thunder sounding outside, above the loud humming emanating from the whirling circles that fills the room. At one point it seems to culminate, when the circles spin so fast, they appear on the verge of bursting into flame. Ninev begins chirping agitatedly; she can feel that this is pushing Elke too far and her heart is on the verge of faltering. The circles begin to slow down at that point and the light from them starts to cool and soften. It is difficult for the three observers to judge how long it has been going for; a pocket of time feels to have yawned open in the room to accommodate the transmittal.

Eventually, the circles stop spinning, until only faint traces of their paths glow dimly. Keesa and Elke are holding their positions, still as figurines. Then, both of them gasp a breath into their lungs, as though they had been underwater all this time. The remnants of the circles vanish in that moment and the two open their eyes. They look exhausted but, their faces are flushed with colour and their eyes are clear.

'The bestowal is complete.'

'Thank you, my Queen.' Keesa makes a low curtsey. Elke moves forward and touches the top of the girl's head.

120

'You did well, Keesa,' she says. Ninev stirs into flight now, up to the kitchen table, letting out pinched notes in the direction of the Queen and Keesa.

'Yes, Ninev, you are quite right,' Elke says, 'We must replenish our structures before you leave. Just one more thing.' Elke moves to Keesa's side, places one hand on her chest and gives the girl's coccyx three firm thumps. Keesa startles. Elke reassures her, 'It helps with pushing the new information through.' She starts towards the stove but Maen quickly orders his mother and the girl to sit; he will prepare something simple for them to eat. He opens the front door, letting in gentle gusts of cool wind. The storm seems to have passed; it did not last long. Keesa is glad of the cold. Her body is still warm as an ember.

Queen Elke and Keesa rouse within half an hour of slipping into sleep after eating, each feeling somewhat recharged. The group stands in the courtyard. Keesa turns to the Queen, 'Thank you for having me and Toekoums to stay, Queen Elke.' Despite the persistent reservations that she has concerning Keesa, Elke has warmed to the girl and bends down to hug her. Then she pulls back and places her hands around Keesa's shoulders.

'It is my pleasure, youngling. Now, keep in mind that this is not the way it was supposed to go. I was supposed to train you for the next 10 years but so many things have not gone according to plan. We may not be the perfect royal Light family, we have our flaws, but we do the best we can and our hearts are in the right place. You hold our future in your hands. You have yet to prove yourself worthy of the title of Sun-bearer. Listen to what Maen tells you and apply yourself to your training. I wish you well.'

She turns to her son. Maen can sense that her body is strained from the transmittal but that she would not like to be asked about it. He pats her back, prompting a courageous smile from her that masks an insistent fear.

'Mother, thank you for everything. Please be careful, and listen to what the guards tell you to do. I will come visit again as soon as possible.'

'Of course you will, my boy. It has been so wonderful to see you and to meet the newcomers. Travel safe, now.'

Their words are comforting, despite a lack of truth in part. They embrace, both aware that this is likely the last time they will see each other in the flesh. The Queen bids farewell to Toekoums with a stroke of his fur; he bows to her. Ninev lets out a sweet string of goodbye notes to the three travellers. Toekoums meows to Ninev, rubbing against her feathers with a purr. The bird allows this. For all their bickering, the cat and bird have grown used to each other. The King, the youngling and the kitten set off down the path towards their car. Maen turns to look at his mother. She looks smaller than when they arrived the evening before. Her eyes betray the pain of watching her son leave. She jerks her hand up and waves, evading the moment, trying to look like the happy mother. Maen waves back, turns, and leaves, making a fist so tight, his nails almost penetrate the skin of his palms. Keesa must not see his despair now. It will not do. Today, he must be her King. It is alarming to him that in instants such as these, it is Regan he misses. He is relieved for the journey ahead; for him the road is still the best salve to stay his thoughts.

CHAPTER 14

Unveiling

15/12/2050

Her bedroom is the largest one in the Dark Chamber, barring her parent's old bedroom, which is still sealed up. Tonight Regan's room feels tiny to her. She circles around it like a panther in a zoo. Since the meeting with Maen, Valtere has insisted that security be tightened and that she be confined to the Dark Chamber. Her skin is prickling. The mix of hurt and sadness after her rejection two days before was easier than what it has given way to now. Her inherited instinct to detach helps; she observes: the spine that refuses to arch as a queen's should, the trickling eyes and the strange shaking that sometimes accompanies this. Rather than moving through her unabated, the emotion chokes out of her, she mechanically restrains it, it erupts forward in splutters.

She has mostly remained in her room since the meeting, terrified of the courtier's or servant's stares should she mistakenly let on the untidiness simmering beneath her surface. Tonight she paces so as not to feel. Embarrassment and anger burrow their way through her now. Once you uncork feelings, they become more difficult to shut down, she is realising. Ever since she met Maen, she has glorified the freeing of emotion. Another adolescent fantasy. She admits now: Mother was right all along. *What had I been thinking? That I thought it might be different in my case is laughable.* Each time she replays the scene in her head, she looks more and more like a dumb dog seeking out love regardless of flagrant logic and law. Sickening need, as her mother might have put it, unfortunate liability.

Valtere wings in through the French windows and settles on his perch in her room. Regan takes the glass of water she is drinking from and sets it down on the perch. The eagle takes a few needed gulps.

'Have you any news?' Regan is relieved to be in company she can talk to; her confinement to the Chamber is reminding her too much of her period of isolation on the island.

'I'm afraid you will not be pleased by it. I spotted the youngling heading west in a car with King Maen. His guards are following behind.'

'DAMN IT!' She lifts her hand to her forehead and smooths her fingers along her eyebrows. Her anger is getting in the way of clear thinking.

'The girl will bring power to the Light Force, they are a far greater threat now. I can't believe I delayed moving on this for some dream. It is critical that you fetch the girl and bring her to me. Rest tonight but you should leave at first light. Time is short.'

Regan begins readying herself for bed. She takes her nightgown out of her cupboard, lays it on the bed. The eagle half extends his wings, folds them in again.

'What is it, Valtere?'

'There is something I have to tell you, Your Majesty, something, I'm afraid to say, I have kept from you for many years.'

'Go on.'

'The girl...the youngling...she...'

'Come now, Valtere, it is late, I'm tired and you need a decent sleep before your journey tomorrow.' She folds the blanket to the end of the bed.

'Yes, Your Highness. Well, there is no easy way to put this...she is your child.'

Regan's eyes snap to the eagle. She freezes midway turning the sheet back.

'But that's impossible. You took her away and had her...dealt with. She is dead.'

It is the first time since that direful day that she has spoken of it. The words hang like pieces of bloody meat in her boudoir.

'I did take her away, yes, but instead of killing her, I left her on the doorstep of a childless woman.'

124

'You disobeyed my orders?' The colour is seeping from Regan's face.

'I did, yes, but only because I thought there may come a time when you might regret your decision.'

'But why have I not detected her presence? Where was she?'

'In a rural village. The identity shield you cast around her—'

'Of course, I didn't lift it...at the time there was no reason to.' Regan feels faintness about to envelop her. Her knees submit, she takes a few unstable steps backward, and sits on her bedside chair with a bump. 'Our baby is alive.' She covers her face with her hands, attempting to stifle the sounds that escape her mouth. Valtere is always disturbed seeing her like this; it has been a decade since the last time. The memory of the day she implemented her decision floods back to Regan now.

Nativity

Regan sits on a reed mat in the abandoned temple on the island, her quarters for the last nine months. She holds her newborn daughter in her arms, unable to take her eyes off her baby. No matter how many times she tried to think of a safe way to allow the child to live, she would hit a brick wall. Producing a child from a union between Dark and Light royalty is deemed unconscionable. The punishment for the mother would be life imprisonment and the forced utilisation of her powers to advance the reach of the Dark Force. The child would be slain instantly, to ensure zero pollution of the Dark bloodline by Light genes.

Even if she chose to give the child away, she knew there would come a time when the girl would begin enacting orders of the Dark Force without her conscious awareness, usually around the age of 16. It would not be long before she would be detected, and either killed or imprisoned along with her birth mother, for the purposes of siphoning her powers. She had considered abortion, but knew she couldn't carry it out herself.

Regan placed an identity shield around the foetus the minute she felt its presence inside her. What with her powers of seeing, she knew within hours, just before making her way to Queen Signa's study for her farewell address before departure to the island. She reinforced the shield daily, right up until this morning. The bond between her and her unborn is unmistakable. She swings between resisting it, as she knows she should, and giving in to it. The labour lasted only three hours and she took herself through the birthing process. As a precautionary measure, Valtere kept watch at the door to the temple.

Regan managed to control any vocalisations of pain as the baby made its way down the birth canal. To her, physical pain pales in comparison with the pain she carries in her heart. After the birth, she carefully cleaned her daughter, wrapped her in an inconspicuous blanket. She sits cross-legged on a mat in the area that must previously have been the altar, rocking her baby in her arms. She has already given Valtere his orders. Regan knows that she cannot kill this child herself. The eagle is dreading the task. Until now, he has not been required to carry out exterminations—the Dark guards generally see to those. To end the life of a Dark royal, albeit a halfling, feels instinctively wrong to him. He waits now as Regan feeds the baby from her breast, patting the child's back, tears streaming down her face. Once the girl has drunk her fill and begins drifting in and out of sleep, Regan looks up to Valtere. He gently flaps over to her. Regan's voice is strangled as she conveys the final instructions.

'Wherever you take her, make sure she is comfortable when you give her the capsule. And be certain to administer it quickly, the way I showed you. I don't want her to experience pain.'

Regan had the potent fusion of arsenic and sedative ready-mixed before leaving the Dark Chamber, knowing it might come to this. She specially synthesised the outer covering of it to be harder than normal, so that it would not puncture in Valtere's beak as he fed it down the baby's throat, the same way he would feed his own young if he had any. She removes the pouch containing the capsule now, slung around her wrist on a string. The eagle bows his head and she slips it around his neck. She gives the girl one last kiss on the forehead, folds her up in the blanket so that she is no longer visible and holds her out to Valtere. He places his talons gently around the bundle, and lifts off. Regan gets onto her feet, still dizzy from giving birth and staggers towards the door to open it. She grips the long steel door handle with both hands, as a way of stopping them from flinging out to grab her baby back. Back from a decision she already hates herself for.

Valtere thrusts himself out of the door and up into the bright afternoon. It is as though her very life is being sucked from Regan by an impartial tempest that knows not of its destruction. It does what it is meant to do; it destroys. It strikes her that everything in that moment feels poisonous to her: the blinding sunlight beyond the door as she closes it, the damp darkness of the temple that she will call home for another three months, the thought of consuming food so as to stay alive to someday become queen, the sound of her tortured voice as it heaves with regret, over and over, until she wants to cut out her own heart so that she will not feel, rip out her own vocal cords so that she will not hear the mutterings attendant on her deed.

By the time Valtere returns, squeezing his way through a small, high window in the temple wall, he finds Regan in a heap on the ground, next to the temple door. For weeks he feeds her food and water from his beak, between her long bouts of sleeping, sometimes restless with terrible dreams, sometimes so deep he suspects she may have stopped breathing. Once her strength is regained, she slowly begins practising her vision-gathering again. Now her approach to it is robotic; her former enthusiasm has wilted. Nonetheless, she continues improving her skill level. When she was younger, she remembers anticipating the years following solitude as the time when she would begin blooming into the queen she was born to be. Now she sees it as doing what is expected of her.

CHAPTER 15

A Song

15/12/2050

Keesa catches a glimpse of half a sign reading 'Huguenot Toll'. She has been awake half an hour now, after a heavy, dreamless sleep on the backseat. She knows the singed smell of cities from family road trips. It is night outside; she must have slept for the better part of the afternoon. She feels bolt awake, her body alive with impetus she has never felt before. Keesa glances at Toekoums stretching and sniffing at the incoming air.

'How much longer till we get there?' Keesa asks, peering into the veldt flying past the car. She can make out bushes and rocks distinctly, even the occasional dassie or veldt shrew scampering away from the streaking vehicle. She doesn't remember being able to see this clearly at night before.

'One stop soon and then another two or three hours, more or less. Do you like music?' Maen slows the car and reaches over to the cubbyhole.

'I love music.' Keesa leans forward and watches Maen rifling through some CD's. 'When we go on trips, my Dad sometimes lets me look in burnt city shops and houses for CD's. If it's safe. He says it's only okay to do that if the people in the house or shop are gone. Dead and gone. If the body's still there, you must leave.'

Maen chooses a disk and slides it into the front-loading player on the dashboard. 'So you collect music?'

Her face lightens. 'Yes. When I can. When I grow up and can drive, I'm going to go on trips just to look for CD's.'

128

'I collect music too. I have much more at my home; I could lend you some, if you like.'

'That would be great, thanks.' Maen hears excitement in the girl's voice. It's been so long since he shared his music with someone, shared in joy. Keesa sees the words *Mandolin Orange: From Now On* come up on the digital display.

The song begins. Guitar and mandolin, then a woman sings. Keesa keeps rhythm on the car seat with her hand. Toekoums leans against her side. The music loops up into the night sky.

Revival

Regan stands by her French doors, looking out at her night garden. Valtere is on his perch in her room.

'Your Majesty, as much as what I did might seem like disobedience, I had your interests in mind.'

Regan looks to Valtere, registers his words, turns to the foliage again, breathes in its familiar scent.

'I should have you executed. My mother had her helper killed for far less.'

'I do not mean to be insubordinate but might I remind you that I have kept your secrets unquestioningly ever since I was assigned as your helper. I could choose at any moment to bring the Dark Court up to date on your covert life.'

'Helpers are incapable of betrayal. They are slave to their servitude. The Dark ancestors see to that. You will be struck dumb before you open your beak.'

'And Dark queens do not break cardinal rules. You seem to have managed undetected, nonetheless. I suspect that your acts have already changed the playing field, whether you intended it or not.'

Regan takes a long look at the big bird's black eyes. 'I believe you may be right. I am aware of the leverage you hold against me. Perhaps foolishly, I considered our bond to go further than simply Queen and helper. The truth is that what you told me is the best news I have heard in years. You may have disobeyed my command but you did the right thing.'

'It pleases me to hear that, Your Highness. And you are not wrong about our bond.'

'However, by keeping my daughter's existence from me all these years, you betrayed my trust. How do I know you will not take matters into your own hands again behind my back? How can I trust you?'

'I'm afraid that all I can give you is my word, my Queen. I swear to you, that is the only time I have ever gone against your orders. Since you never brought the subject up again, I assumed you wished to move on. The more time elapsed, the more inappropriate it seemed to dig up the past. It was only when I could see that your plan for the Dark family was deviating from your mother's approach, that I felt my news might serve your vision.'

'Do you believe in my mother's vision?'

'I believe in you, Queen Regan. As your helper, I am, and always will be, at your service. I may have reservations about your strategy but I will stand by you, no matter what.'

'For now, I am going to place my trust in you again, Valtere. I am grateful for your service all these years...and for your friendship.'

The plain-spoken acknowledgement of their friendship takes the eagle by surprise. Regan notices his head cock back and smiles softly. He will need to get used to her using words in a manner that contravenes the Dark code.

'You must sleep soon. There is, however, something else I need to ask you. Have you seen me visiting the Initium laboratory recently?'

'Yes, Your Majesty.'

'How often have I been there?'

Valtere pauses. 'Perhaps three nights a week.'

'When did it begin?'

'Forgive me, but I don't understand why you—'

'Answer my question, Valtere.'

'I would say it started around the end of September.'

'About the same time as a royal frequency was detected emanating from the youngling.'

The eagle thinks back. 'Yes, about that time. Do you not remember visiting the Initium lab?'

'I'm afraid not. I suspect I have been acting under my mother's orders without realising it.'

'I didn't think to say anything. Any mention of the medical wing by Chamber members has always been forbidden.'

'From now on, if you ever see me making my way there, I want you to stop me.'

'How do you want me to do that?'

'Let me figure that out. The resistance of Dark orders has never been recorded. I may be the first to attempt it. One of my biggest concerns now is the kind of influence my mother may already be exerting on my daughter. She must be brought to me at the soonest possible moment. She has a part to play in the destiny of the Dark family.'

'I shall leave at daybreak, Your Majesty.' He spreads his wings to fly into the garden.

'Sleep in my room tonight. We cannot afford to take chances. I cannot send Dark guards to get the girl. You are the only one I trust with the task, as well as the most inconspicuous. Our safety is paramount now.'

Valtere can see that the Queen's will to live has returned, after a period during which it had seemed to lag. Regan gets into bed, tries to imagine what her girl may look like now, how she positions herself for sleep at night. It strikes Regan that she may be more afraid of coming face to face with her own daughter than she ever was of her mother. For a moment, Regan catches herself missing her own shadowy mother, wanting to ask her for guidance. She knows, though, that her appeal would have been quickly evaded. She tries to relax her muscles. Her daughter has a laugh that sounds, teeth that sink into bread, hair that is lifted by the wind. *I must become her mother*, Regan thinks. *I am her mother.*

CHAPTER 16

Gengun

15/12/2050

Half an hour passes. The smell of stale cinders gets stronger. A solitary clump of lights blinks into view ahead. Maen pulls to the side of the road, turns the music off, fetches two coats with a large hoods from the boot. He pulls his on and hands Keesa the smaller one, before resuming the wheel.

'That may be a bit big for you, it was lent by one of the Chamber worker's children. Put it on, hood up. We're going to be stopping to refuel at a Gengun now. Whatever happens, I want you two to stay in the car with me. Keep your windows rolled up and the doors locked. My guards will take care of filling the cars with petrol.'

'Do you always hide like this?' Keesa enquires.

'From people who have no connection to the Light family, yes. I'm afraid you're going to have to be cautious from now on too.'

Keesa puts the coat on; it is a dark-brown colour and is made of thick canvas. She pulls Toekoums closer to her as their car rolls into the station. As he always does on trips, Maen parks close to the pump—there is always only one that works—and the second vehicle parks close behind. The five guards disembark and take various positions in the station. One of them stands by the pump, ready to refuel Maen's vehicle; two of them stand close to the cars, keeping a lookout and the other pair remove a few generators from their boot and make their way inside the makeshift shop. They will need to negotiate the transaction before any fuel can be taken. Only once the Gengun owner has approved their offer as fair exchange, can the cars be filled.

Keesa doesn't recognise this Gengun. There are a few that her parents always pass through on their trips to the ocean, which can also be eerie, but this one feels somehow more coarse than those. Everything in it is weather-beaten and precarious. The disused pumps are rusted; the station building is in a slow process of crumbling, pieces of wooden plank or corrugated iron nailed to parts of it, like Band-Aid strips holding it together and fending off the elements. A layer of grime pervades the establishment, and Keesa notices bullet holes in the pumps and scattered on the walls. The only clean thing is the window to the area that used to be a shop but is now more of an office. Presumably it's important for the owner to be able to see what's going on in the station when he's inside. The faint sound of a generator sputters somewhere at the back of the establishment and diesel fumes eke their way in through the car's air vents. There is a skewness about the place that Keesa cannot put her finger on.

Maen is keeping a sharp lookout onto the road to his right, focusing on the bushes across from the Gengun, which are relatively thick. His concern is for an attack by Dark guards. There could well be a search out for them by now. Keesa looks out the window to her left, watches the guards talking to the owner inside the office, lit by fluorescent lights. The owner has grey hair, skin leathery and red from the sun and holds his head slightly rearward above his shoulders in a bearing of arrogance. He looks nervy with the guards. An old, plastic Coke bottle sits in front of him on the counter. The liquid in it is a nameless shade of brown. There are two children playing with a soccer ball on the floor of the office, a girl and boy. The boy is older and is outmanoeuvring the girl at every turn, as she tries to get the ball from him with her feet, her hands. Keesa can hear muted tones through the shut car window as the owner yells something to the back of the shop. As he inspects the generators the guards have presented, a woman who Keesa presumes must be his wife comes out of a door at the back of the office and goes around the counter to collect the children and shunt them with her out of the room. Her face is the colour of coffee and her eyes are like coals. She must have been beautiful once and this echoes in her daughter but her clothes and skin hang off her thin body now in haggard inattention. The girl resists being taken out the room, pointing to something outside the front door. Her pleas are ignored; she looks back anxiously as she is herded out. Keesa notices an old Barbie doll lying on the station floor, a little way away from the front door. Its colour is faded and cracks criss-cross its body. The hair is dry and old but neatly brushed back into a ponytail.

The owner has made his decision. He nods wordlessly towards the guards, one of whom comes out and gives the green light to begin filling the cars. Keesa senses a bitterness in the owner; she cannot imagine a smile turning the hard edges of his mouth. He catches her gaze for a moment, seems to get irritated with it. It is as though he picks up that she is seeing into him. His rankled eyes dart around from their car, to guard filling car, back to Keesa's gaze, to second guard leaving the office, to the bushes that border the left hand side of the station building. The bushes. Keesa trails her gaze to that hedge, blocks the fluorescent lights from her view with her hand and peers into the darkness among the shrubbery. The car shakes a few times as the petrol cap is re-fastened; Keesa's peripheral vision takes in the guard switching to the second vehicle, starting to fill its tank. Her eyes adjust to the black in between the leaves and buckled branches now. She picks up movement close to where the hedge meets the building, races her eyes to the spot, blackness. Whatever it was is out of sight. Toekoums lets out a low growl; Keesa feels his little tail whipping against her thigh.

That's when she sees it. In a small opening near the middle of bushes. A baboon with a rag wrapped around its mouth to silence it. She notices that there is a wet patch forming where the opening of the mouth must be. Its bulbous eyes are locked on Keesa. It tips its head upwards in three quick jerks, sniffing at the air. Keesa recalls what she overheard her father saying to her mother; that the baboons are starved before attacks. She thinks of how Nefer starts drooling as Elijah prepares his food. The baboon looking at her now has hunger like a madness in its eyes and the wet patch in the gag is growing. An arm interjects from behind the brush and yanks the baboon out of sight by its neck.

'King Maen, there is something in the bushes,' Keesa says in a low voice, her eyes darting to the office, where the owner has moved around the counter and is closing and locking the front door.

'I don't see anything.'

'Not those ones, the bushes by the office. I saw a baboon and someone with it.'

Maen swings his gaze, slowly takes up his rifle from where it is lying on the floor by the front seat. The guard has finished filling both cars now. Maen pulls his hood down low over his face, opens his door and gets out of the car. He clicks it shut, tapping the window for Keesa to lock it. He is joined by one of his men, they exchange whispered words. That guard removes his weapon from his jacket, starts making his way to the bushes by the office, indicating to the other guards to make haste, they must all leave immediately. The owner is slowly backing out of his shop. He opens the back door, edges into the back room, still watching the station area, and starts shutting the door in front of him. Toekoums is standing on the back seat, every strand of fur on his body

135

raised. His locket is humming green but there is no face in its centre. His eyes are staring ahead. Even though he is too small to see out of the car properly, he looks as though he is seeing something.

'A message is coming through for you, Keesa. You must find the place of stillness now. Connect to all that you were given.' The kitten's voice sounds strange, like an extension of his growling before. Even under the heavy coat, goose-flesh ripples over Keesa's arms, legs, skull. She feels panic welling up in her like a scream, breathes into her stomach, and closes her eyes.

At first nothing seems to happen. However, within less than a minute, the sounds of the Gengun around her begin to fade away. The space inside her quietens. Then a sensation comes over her, as though she is held by water. She opens her eyes. She is under the ocean again, just as she had been months ago on holiday at the seaside. This time she floats in front of the whale, her arms and legs lifting outwards, buoyed by the salt-water, like a human star. She senses that time has suspended. Hanging before the mammoth is terrifying, all the more without the soaked sand beneath her feet. Yet, it also feels to be the safest place she knows.

He greets her with a single note that slants up at its end; Keesa's snip of a frame reverberates as though struck by a gong. Then he begins parting his jaws. Watching is like witnessing the birth of an abyss. A school of fish swimming by gets sucked in as water spirals towards the back of his throat. A brilliant light begins to shine inside the chasm. Gradually it comes clear. It is the Lion of Light, vigorous and free, standing on all fours on the hulk of whale tongue. He draws in a deep breath, in turn opens his jaws, and lets out a roar so thunderous it pushes a wave that sends Keesa hurtling backwards in the water out of the whale's mouth. As she twirls through the surge, she catches glimpses of the Lion, who has become so bright she can no longer make out his features. Sunlight emanates from him now, dancing in the water, touching Keesa's skin and warming her bones. She closes her eyes. The pulse of another sound is beginning outside of her, one that she knows she must be present to. It is a man's voice, full of fear and untoward intent. Keesa lifts her eyelids back into the sealed car. As she swings her head to take in the owner clicking the back room door shut, a fraught man's voice screams from the bushes opposite the station.

'LAAT HULLE LOS!'

From that moment, everything happens quickly. The bushes opposite the station, as well as those bordering the office suddenly come alive, spewing Baboon Gang

136

members and their slaves. Maen bangs on the car window, shouting to Keesa, 'Get down!' Some of the members whip gags off the animals' mouths, some release the ravenous simians off their leashes, while others fire at the guards and the King. All members are masked, some in black balaclavas, others in baboon-facemasks fitted over their heads. The King lifts his rifle and fires back at the gunmen across the road. He manages to hit two of them. He knows they must primarily be after the vehicles; they are avoiding firing directly at them.

Four large baboons are hurtling towards him now, letting out high-pitched shrieks as they do. From his right he hears a human scream ; one of the guards has been attacked by a simian that scampered across from the office side. The tenacious creature has locked its jaws around his thigh. The guard is trying to take aim to shoot it but cannot do so without risking shooting himself. He begins smashing the creature hanging off his leg with the butt end of his rifle. Maen drops his weapon to his side, flicks his hood back, exposing his head, fills his lungs to capacity as he does so, and gives out a mortifying roar. Keesa feels the car shaking from it. The four baboons coming towards him all buckle to the ground; the bones in their legs have shattered. They writhe and complain in screeches, grabbing at their limbs. The other three guards are firing at baboons, which keep being released from behind the bushes, or at gang members, who remain hidden most of the time.

Keesa knows she is going against instructions but slowly gets up onto the seat to peek over the bottom edge of the rear car window. Toekoums is crouching on the car floor, making that growling sound again. 'Prepare yourself, youngling,' he says, in a voice that sounds older, disjointed from his usual kitten one, with his gaze still fixed on something that is not there.

Keesa watches as two guards stand firing into the bushes by the office. Both are attacked by a group of baboons just released. Some of the simians run and take flying leaps up towards the guard's weapon, knocking it to the ground, or grabbing it, beginning a tussle for it with the guard. She looks back to see Maen preparing to take on a freshly released group of baboons from the road bushes. She turns back, realising that the left side of the car she is in has just become an easy target. The guards have been pinned down onto the ground now, the baboons screaming their victory. Now three more massive simians are released, run out from the bushes by the office, pause briefly, surveying the scene before them. One of them, carrying a thick iron pipe in its hand, spots Keesa's eyes and throws out a champing sound in her direction. The other two look at their inmate, then look towards Keesa. Toekoums halts his low growl, jolts out of his trance state. He looks up to where Keesa is, and swiftly leaps up onto the backseat, yelling 'KEESA!' as he does so. Something about his tone causes Keesa to tear her eyes away from the three simians with their sights on her. She looks into the kitten's urgent eyes. 'The message is coming through clearly! You must find your roar! Now! Before it's too late!'

Keesa turns back to see the three hefty baboons galloping their way towards her window. She kneels on the seat, facing them. She thinks of the light coming to her through the water, remembers what it felt like seeping into her bones, her heart. The biggest of the three simians reaches the window and smashes it open with the pipe. Keesa imagines herself inhaling the sunlight blasted to her by the Lion of Light as she draws in a breath. What she takes into her lungs feels like something other than air. It is like a gas, highly flammable and so pressurised it makes her lungs ache. As the maniacal simian lunges forward to grab at Keesa's neck, she releases the breath. The sound it makes is a booming roar. The baboon directly in front of her is the hardest hit. It falls onto its back; everything in its head has exploded. There is blood, tissue and organ oozing out of every opening in its skull, steam lifting off the matter as it wells out. The other two simians have collapsed, clutching at their stomachs, which are gradually inflating like balloons. They begin slowly slipping out of consciousness. The group of baboons that had taken the two guards to the ground look at their dead and debilitated inmates in shock. Their grips on the guards loosen and they look towards the road, then at the bushes. They know if they try make a run for it, their punishment by gang members will be severe.

One more roar from Maen at full pitch and the baboons flying towards him and the other three guards all founder with their leg bones broken. The group of simians near Keesa, now thoroughly unnerved, look ready to make a dash back into the bushes and face what awaits them as cowards. Then there is a shout from the bushes across the road, 'Vok dit! Ons kry karre iewers anders. Dit kos te veel bobbejane! Laat waai!' A piercing signal is sounded out, followed by the rev of a truck starting up that comes from behind the Gengun building. Now another voice bellows from behind the foliage bordering the office, 'Ja, vokken amagqwirha are killing our stock. Hambani!'

With that, the baboon gang members begin a retreat, recalling any animals left alive, which are not many, with an ominous orchestration of whistles. Maen quickly looks into the car to make sure Keesa is unharmed. The truck is pulled around to the road, and pauses a short distance away, facing the direction that Maen's vehicles had come from. Gang members dragging baboons on leashes sprint towards it, hurriedly slam open the back hatch, and start loading into it. A few stand with their weapons aimed at Maen and the rest of his group, but do not open fire. All of Maen's guards are on their feet now and one of them grabs reinforcements of arms from their car. They lift their weapons and take aim at the gang members.

'Don't fire!' Maen commands. Scanning the animal casualties scattered before him, he says in a troubled voice, 'I think we've done enough damage as it is. We don't need to anger them now.' He pulls his hood back over his head. The gang has packed into the truck; it pulls off, quickly building up to a high speed. A few straggling baboons are attempting to escape into the veldt, but are quickly nabbed with lassoes and nets, and dragged some distance, yelping, before they are hauled back onto the caged vehicle that leaves a flurry of dust in its wake.

Maen opens the rear car door.

'Are you all right, Keesa?'

The girl twists her head towards him, 'I'm fine.'

'You're not hurt?'

'No.'

'I'm coming now. There is something I have to do, it won't take long.'

Toekoums emerges tentatively from under the seat. Keesa hears the truck leaving. She is staring at the limp, leaking baboons through the shattered window. Toekoums springs up onto the armrest of the car-door, and peers out at the carnage. 'Well done, Keesa, you did it,' he says cautiously.

She turns her head and looks at the kitten. 'Yes,' she says, 'I did it.'

Maen goes to one of the baboons he injured now. As it sees him approaching, it begins a yelping sound that escalates into a series of short screams. It is trying to run away from him but, without the use of its legs, all it can do is drag itself along the ground with its hands, the rest of its body a dead weight. The other injured simians join in these shrieks, also inching their debilitated bodies away. The baboon that Maen approaches cowers into itself as he kneels down beside it and places his hands over its knees. A low roar, like a very loud purring, sounds from deep in his throat. As soon as the simians hear this sound, they look back towards their friend. The animal that Maen is with closes its eyes, and seems to go into semi-sleep state. Less than a minute goes by. Maen lifts his hands off the creature. It awakens, gets up off the ground, a bit unsteady at first, backs off from Maen, almost loses its balance, then finds its feet. It runs a little distance away, stops, and looks back at its friends. The other baboons look from their friend to Maen and back, confused by what took place. Keesa watches, absorbed. Maen repeats the process on all the injured animals. Once he has finished, all the healed simians stand in a huddle across the road. They look lost. After being slaves to the Baboon Gang for so long, the freedom of the veldt has become foreign to them. They look towards the station.

The guards begin loading back into their vehicle, two of them still on lookout, weapons visible. Maen turns to get into his car. Keesa notices the little girl who was playing in the shop earlier scooting out from around the side of the office, her eyes fixed on her doll. She runs to where the worn Barbie lies abandoned on the ground, picks it up and hitches it on her hip, imitating what a mother looks like carrying a baby. As she turns to run back inside, she catches sight of the dead baboons. She jerks a few steps back, transfixed by the bodies. Then she notices Keesa. They eye each other with the curiosity of two young girls. Keesa knows in that moment that she will never feel like a normal girl again.

The back door of the office opens; the owner appears and hurriedly makes his way out to his daughter. He scoops her up, saying, 'How many times must I tell you not to come out front when there are customers here?' His eyes meet those of Maen, who stands between Keesa and him.

Maen speaks in a blunt tone. 'I apologise for the mess. I would bury the casualties, but I cannot afford to remain in an environment that is unsafe for my passengers, you understand.'

'What the hell kind of creature are you?' the owner sneers.

'I should ask you the same thing. I presume you are the one who gave the Gang permission to lie in wait,' Maen returns.

The owner cocks his head back. 'What can I say, that was the only way I could get the deal with them. Ammunition is scarce these days. I had to take my chance while it was there. If I don't have petrol or arms, my family doesn't eat.'

Maen keeps his eyes fixed on the owner as he makes his way back to his side of the car and gets in. The owner backs into his office, steers his daughter towards the back room, turns and locks the front door. Maen starts the motor.

'What about them?' Keesa asks, indicating the three baboons to the left of the car, 'Can't you fix them too?'

Maen drops his head for a moment, then turns to the girl, 'I'm sorry Keesa but I can only repair damage; I can't bring creatures back from death.' He turns the ignition and pulls out of the station, the guard vehicle following behind. Tears well in the girl's eyes. She gets up onto the seat and watches as the walking baboons move hesitantly towards their dead friends. As they grow smaller with distance, she can make out two of them starting to drag one of the bodies away from the station.

'I didn't mean to kill them.'

Maen's voice holds a tightness that Keesa has not heard in him before. 'You had no choice. They would have killed you. I should have been the one to fend them off. If I wasn't taking care of the baboons on the other side of the car, I could have.' More alarming to Maen in this moment than the ambush that had just occurred, is the realisation that he has come to genuinely care for the girl. Anger edges into his voice as it rises. "You must be more careful, Keesa! I told you to keep down! You're too young for this...to do what you had to do. I didn't even know that to be one of your powers. We need time to train so I can show you how to work that power to injure, rather than kill. This is all wrong. It's not how it's meant to go!'

Keesa starts to cry, screaming, 'I'm sorry! I'm sorry! I'M SORRY!'

Maen stops the car, unnerved by the effect his words have had. It dawns on him that he is sorely lacking when it comes to dealing with children. He gets out the car, indicates to the guard car to wait, climbs into the back seat, and takes Keesa into his arms. 'You have nothing to be sorry about, Keesa. I wasn't thinking. I will make everything fine, you'll see. Well done for what you did. You were a brave girl.' He feels unaccustomed to be holding an elfin frame such as Keesa's, which stiffens at first, but slowly thaws into his arms.

Once Keesa has calmed down, he readies the makeshift bed on the backseat for her—his coat folded up for a pillow, and the car blanket. She curls up with Toekoums at the crook of her tummy.

'You okay now?' Maen asks, brushing the hair out of her eyes. She is already half-asleep.

141

'I miss my mom and dad.'

That the girl has not said this once before now shows such courage it dumbfounds him. 'I'm sure you do, Keesa. As soon as I have you safe at the Chamber, I will go fetch them and bring them to you.'

'Kay, thanks.' Keesa falls into and out of sleep for a moment, opens her eyes halfway, and looks up to Maen. 'Can you put music on again? I like your music.'

'Sure.' Maen smiles. Back in his seat, he presses play on the car stereo and pulls off again. His road compilation resumes. He remembers compiling it, what seems like centuries ago now. It was Colter and his first road trip. It took weeks to convince his parents to grant them permission and they weren't allowed to travel far. Nonetheless, it's one of the sweetest memories of freedom that he can recall. After what Keesa did in the Gengun, he is almost convinced that Colter is her father. The manner in which royal Light power manifests is unpredictable but always follows the genetics of the bloodline. Coincidence perhaps? Let it lie for now, he thinks. We are almost home. His body is aching for sleep, especially after using his abilities repeatedly at the Gengun. His mind is wide awake, though, charged as it is with the protection of a modest, exceptional girl on the backseat. *Lucinda Williams: What If* lights up on the stereo display. A woman's voice floats out of the speakers, couched in anodyne guitar chords. The road is dark and resting.

CHAPTER 12

Chamber Day

16/12/2050

Keesa is stirred from slumber by the bracing smell of sea air and a gentle swishing sound. For a moment, she thinks she is on holiday at her aunt's house. She opens her eyes to delicate white chiffon suspended around the four-poster bed she lies in, lifting and falling with the breeze. She sits up. The last thing she remembers is falling into a heavy sleep on the back seat of the car. This must be the Chamber of Light. The bedsheets are made of cream silk, covered by an ivory mohair blanket. She looks down at her nightgown, made of eggshell-coloured cotton with blue stitching. It's pretty, she thinks, and smoothes the creases out with her hand from its twisting during her sleep, taking pleasure in its buttery softness.

The expansive sound of seagulls crying out over ocean draws Keesa's eyes to the square of light filtering through the gauze. She flips her legs over the side of the bed and draws the chiffon aside. Straight ahead of her is a window, wide open. Toekoums sits in the corner of the windowsill, curled up with his front paws tucked under, his body still as a painting, only his head twitching from place to place as he detects movement.

'Morning, Toekoums,' Keesa says as she gets off the bed and walks, revived, towards the nippy sea-breeze.

Toekoums startles a little, sits up. 'Morning Keesa, I didn't know you were awake.'

'Too busy dreaming of seagulls in your tummy.'

'More like they'd have me in their tummy.'

'Well, you can always dream.'

'I think small, fat birds will be my favourite.'

Keesa chuckles. She stands on tiptoe and takes in the view over the windowsill. The ocean sweeps out as far as she can see, dappled with a few fishing boats and the occasional sea-creature flipping out of water and back under in a glistening flash.

'This is the best window I've ever seen.' Keesa whispers. She turns and looks at the rest of the room. It is large and uncluttered, with walls and floor of sand-coloured stone. Someone has placed a small bunch of flowers in a violet cut-glass vase on the side table next to the bed. There is a dressing table against the wall opposite the window. It looks old, the original white paint with gold detail faded and peeling in places. But to Keesa, it is perfect. She goes to it, runs her fingers along its borders, sniffs it. The faintest whiff of perfume lives in its cracks. The only other piece of furniture in the room is a large, oak cupboard. Looking inside, Keesa finds three dresses hanging and a few other items of clothing roughly her size. Perhaps from the same Chamber worker's child? Keesa wonders if the child is cross about this.

There is a soft knock on the door. She goes to open it. It is a young girl, a little older than her, with strawberry blonde hair. 'Your ladyship,' she says, and curtseys to Keesa.

Keesa nods and smiles at the girl, 'What is your name?'

'June, my lady.'

'Hello June, I hope it's not your clothes I'm wearing.'

June looks blank for a moment, then clicks. 'Oh, no, some of them are from Peta, and some Queen Elke had kept for in case.'

'Perhaps I can meet Peta later and say thank-you.'

'I will take you to her myself, my ladyship. Now, I have been asked to help you with readying yourself for the day and showing you to where King Maen is expecting you.'

'Thank you. Do you think I'll be able to borrow a swimming costume from someone?'

June smiles.

144

As Keesa bathes, she becomes aware of a tingling in her tailbone. The area feels odd as it presses up against the bathtub. As she feels it with her hand, she is alarmed to find that a bump has formed there and, even though it feels numb and compacted to her touch, gooseflesh creeps across her skull as she does so. She wonders if something went wrong when Queen Elke struck her there at the close of the transmission. Perhaps it will go down if she just leaves it, she thinks as she dresses. She chooses a short, functional frock, terrified of messing the smarter ones up. She registers another sensation now and approaches the mirror, lifting her hair to reveal her ears. They are feeling hot, especially the uppermost tips. They look slightly red. Keesa dismisses her concerns as June appears in the doorway again. She shows her to the dining hall, a sizeable room that opens out onto a balcony overlooking the sea. An unfussy breakfast has been set out. Maen's eyes light up as she comes down. He stands next to the table, hams a sweeping gesture with his arms that exults in the reach of the dining hall, and promptly asks the kitchen assistants to help them take the food down to his favourite garden bench to eat there. He finds it saddening to eat in cavernous, unfilled spaces.

After breakfast, Maen shows her more of the Chamber. The lounge, with its bay windows pouring in light with a buoyancy that only sunlight reflected off the ocean can have. The study, with its smell of the paper of books. Keesa already has an entire day planned in her head to climb up and down the rolling ladder, exploring the library, a rare luxury after the burnings. The snooker room, with its table of green felt like a small lawn and shiny balls in deep shades of red, yellow, pink, so attractive that Keesa eye's keep getting drawn back to them. Queen Elke's old bedroom, with its gorgeous drapes. Since her departure from the Chamber, her room has been used as the place where the children of the Chamber workers are assembled for story-time before bed every evening.

There is an entire wing dedicated to the workers of the Chamber, who feel more like a big family to Keesa than how servants were depicted in tales she has read. There are groups of children in the passages as Keesa is shown through. She lets go of Maen's hand. Some of the children play catch; others are involved in a pretend game that features a fisherman and some kind of sea-monster. A group of adolescent girls talk incessantly, animating their words with hand gestures that intrigue Keesa. The teen boys strut along the edges of the passage, practising cricket shots with phantom bats and balls, or talking in low tones, followed by harsh bursts of laughter. The children and teens pause their games and banter, curtseying and bowing to the King and her as they pass. She meets their eyes, even though she feels hot shyness rising in her cheeks, smiling prudently when it feels welcome, wondering if she'll get to play with them like an ordinary girl someday, one of the gang. She had only felt part of the group at her village school intermittently, always feeling a little out, with things to hide. As they are leaving the wing, Keesa spots June among her friends.

'Hi, June,' Keesa says, the usual anticipation of rejection seizing her stomach on making contact with an older girl.

'Your...' June starts. Maen voicelessly mouths 'Keesa' in June's direction without the girl seeing it. 'Hi, Keesa,' June says, 'this is Peta.'

'Oh,' Keesa is glad to have found her, 'I wanted to say thanks for lending me your clothes.'

'It's a pleasure,' Peta replies, and she and her friends giggle a little at the unfamiliarity of speaking to a royal so young.

'I'll get them back to you soon as I've got mine from my home,' Keesa adds.

'No problem,' Peta returns and adds, pointing towards Toekoums, 'Cute kitten.'

'Thanks.'

'Cool.'

'Cool,' Keesa echoes, the word feeling strange off her tongue. She can tell, though, that the girls are not derisive of her, so that is good. Toekoums, on the hand, is blinking at her blankly.

There is a tranquillity in the people who work here and their children, among these walls. It seems to float on the air and plants in those who breathe it. As they leave that wing, Maen says, 'One more room, then I'll take you down to the water for a swim.' Keesa nods with a bright face at this. 'I'll be leaving early tomorrow morning. Once I am back from my trip, we will begin your training immediately.'

Keesa's step slows. 'You're leaving to fetch my parents?'

'Yes.'

146

'Shouldn't I come with? What if something happens to you, or something bad happens here?'

Maen kneels down, cups her shoulders. 'This is the safest place for you to be, Keesa. I will have every guard on high alert and a group of them will be assigned to your side permanently. I cannot risk you travelling again yet. I must inform your parents of your whereabouts; it is not right that they should be worrying.'

'Yes. Shame, my dad worries a lot about me.' Maen sees her eyes growing dewy.

'I think you'll like this next room, your Ladyship.'

The King is right. By far, Keesa's favourite room is one of the many guest bedrooms, this smaller one converted into what Maen calls his music room. There are piles of cd's everywhere and a sizeable collection of vinyl stacked up against one wall, sheets of plastic lodged between them and the stone. There is also a laptop with a mound of flash and external hard drives positioned next to it. The girl instantly senses a wonderland before her. She freezes, her hands propped in the air, as if poised to grab at this jackpot, repeating the phrase, 'oh, my word,' over and over. Her reaction is reward enough to take Maen through the long journey awaiting him the following day.

'So, I think this should keep you busy a while, after your swim?' he asks.

She stops herself venturing into this record of time, relishing the storing up of hours of discovery. Another thing that has invariably separated her from many of the other girls at her school—her unusual enjoyment of delayed gratification. 'Yes, it will,' she says, her eyes still on the stash. 'Would you mind if I made it tidier?'

'At last, someone who wants to show my treasure some love,' Maen beams.

Keesa's swim in the ocean is free and gleeful. The smell of salt right under her nose as she dives in and out of the waves feels to clear away the exploding baboons, the panicking goat and the gulping bird from her mind's eye, even if only for a moment. A group of whales and dolphins hail her arrival from a distance with outbursts of water and jumps. She waves to them, convinced that the largest whale is the one who has been guiding her from the depths.

That afternoon she begins to order Maen's music room. She finds an old CD with the scribbled title *Chill Comp* on it. She is taken by some tracks on it. The generators are on at the time—preparations for dinner are underway. A song with banjo, fiddle and harmonies like a balm plays now as she works. *I Draw Slow: My Portion* the track list says.

Later she puts on another CD, also labelled in someone's hand. She is curious about the title, *Groove*. This one, with its beckoning rhythms, wakes Toekoums from a nap in the corner and gradually draws a small horde of the Chamber-worker children to the door, which Keesa had left slightly open. She opens it so they can all hear better, grinning as they take stabs at stepping to the beat. She inches the volume up slowly on *Sun-El Musician, Ami Faku: Into Ingawe* until the passage is filled with young, pulsing bodies practising dance moves with assured clumsiness here, deft grace there. The DJ herself takes time out of her tidying to bob modestly with her followers. The party is shut down by a few of the parents, who herd the gathering to the bathrooms for wash time. Some of them throw smiles and signs of camaraderie back towards Keesa as they leave, filling her with a sense of being in the right place.

That evening, Keesa is allowed to go listen to story-time in the Light Queen's former bedroom, although she is asked by the Chamber-worker parents to sit on a chair separate from the other youngsters. Keesa is reluctant but they insist, saying that Elke would not approve of a Light dignitary sitting on the floor with the other children.

'A Light whattie?' Keesa asks Maen in a whisper.

'I think it best if you abide by their wishes for now. Change takes time,' he says quietly. Keesa obeys, but listens to the tale for that evening with only half an ear, her eyes continually trailing to the group sitting cross-legged next to her, as theirs do to hers, like watery, translucent magnets.

Unoccupied Chair

Kaleb thinks he hears something in the garden, shoves his chair back and goes to the front door. Just a couple of birds nipping around the garden in the hope of finding one last worm before nightfall. He lingers for a minute, his eyes scouring the expanse in front of the fence for a dot in the distance that could turn out to be Keesa making her way home. A few chirps from the foraging birds, their wings whirring as they up and leave. Kaleb raps his fingers on the door-frame a few times, makes his way back to the kitchen table, and sinks into his chair again. Aedan has never seen him like this before, even prior to one of their road trips. His eyes are dark and fervent. He has always had moments of moodiness in the past but now he seems to have come unstuck in some way.

Aedan remains seated, forearms resting on the table, her knife and fork suspended over her plate of potatoes and vegetables. She glances at the full plate of food set in front of the chair that Keesa always sits in. It is cold and drooping now.

'You've hardly eaten, Kaleb. You need something fresh. All that dry food on your trips is not good for you.'

'I'm not hungry.' He stares at his plate, starts spinning the knife next to it in quick, tight circles on the table with his thumb and forefinger. Aedan tries another bite, her gut becoming tenser with each rotation of the knife. His fingers flick faster and faster, until he slams his hand down on the table.

'I can't believe you just let her go!' Kaleb fixes his eyes on Aedan. He has been clamped and avoidant since their argument earlier. Aedan drops her fork into her plate.

'Kaleb, we have gone over this a million times. What choice did I have? Drag her home, and keep her locked her in her room till you came home two days later? The chances are she would have run even further after that. You know how she feels about being confined.'

'I know, I just...the thought of her out there on her own...I'm going to search the area again.' He starts up out of his chair and goes to get his jacket.

'We've been searching for two days. At least eat something before you go. Here, I'll come with you.' In his haste, Kaleb has twisted his jacket into a knot and is struggling to get it on. Aedan goes to him, starts disentangling the jacket arm. Her hand brushes his shoulder and an electric spark cracks at the point of contact. Aedan yanks her hand away, breathing in sharply.

Kaleb swings round to her, 'Are you okay?'

'It's fine.'

'Must be a storm on the way,' Kaleb mumbles and pulls his jacket on. He sees that Aedan is close to tears. 'Look, I'm sorry for being short with you. Keesa running away is not your fault. Let's go look again; we're bound to find her soon.'

As much as Kaleb is beginning to doubt that, he knows that Aedan does not deserve his wrath. He has become rusty at controlling his powers when his emotions get the better of him. Aedan has started clearing the supper plates away, covering each as a saving measure. Kaleb turns around, pretends to ready the small cooler box. He thrusts his fears out of his body, and grounds his current into the kitchen floor. Then he approaches Aedan from behind and embraces her, pressing a kiss into the side of her neck. Aedan is soothed, lifts her hand and runs it over the side of his head.

The scrape of the front gate opening takes their attention. Footsteps on the stones, and the tripping of an animal behind. Elijah appears in the doorway, Nefer at his side. Aedan knew it wasn't Keesa's walk. 'Elijah, come in. Are you hungry? There's supper if you like.' Nefer paws to Keesa's room. Elijah calls to him; Aedan indicates there is no need to restrain him.

'I'm good, thanks, Mrs Cross. Is Keesa back?'

'I'm afraid not, Eli,' Aedan says. Nefer returns to the kitchen after his quick once-over of the house. He settles next to his master, looks at Keesa's parents, lets out a few whines.

Elijah pats his sleek head. 'I...I came to tell you both something. When you asked about Keesa the other day...well...she made me promise not to tell but...I'm worried about her now...so...'

Elijah has their full attention now. Aedan urges him on, 'Anything you can tell us would be a help, Elijah.'

'I don't know where she is but, I have a feeling who she may be with.'

'Yes, go on.' Kaleb is struggling to keep his fear at bay again.

'Well, we kind of met this man about a month ago.'

'Met a man? Where?' A horror slideshow of images begins flashing through Kaleb's mind.

'Actually he sort of ran into us, on my grandfather's farm. Said he was looking for land to grow olives. He played cricket with us.'

'Cricket?' Now Aedan's imagination is becoming nauseating.

'He didn't seem like a bad man. It's just...'

'Just what, Elijah? You need to tell us.' Kaleb can feel current starting to whirr in his ears.

'Well, I know this is going to sound funny but...he's kind of half-man half-lion.'

His statement is met with silence. Elijah looks from one parent to the other. Aedan looks bewildered, while Kaleb seems to have frozen, apart from his eyes, which have opened wider and turned a darker colour.

'I'm sorry? I don't think I understand, are you saying—' Aedan fumbles to find words; alternating between thinking this might be a jumbled dream, or that Elijah might have lost his mind.

'What did he say his name is?' Kaleb is looking at Elijah with piercing intent now. The boy notices that the air in the room feels tighter, as if it could snap.

'He said we could call him Lion. I don't think that's his real name, though.'

'No, I don't believe it is. Thank-you, Elijah.' He goes to finish packing the cooler box. 'Aedan, could you throw some clothes into a bag? We must leave now. The journey will take us the better part of the night.'

'But, where are we going? Are you telling me you might know this creature that Elijah is speaking of?'

151

Kaleb continues grabbing his travel bags from around the house, stuffing various items into them, his worn pair of binoculars, walking boots, his gun. Aedan watches, stuck to the ground beneath her.

'Mr Cross, whereever you're going, can I come with? I wish I'd gone after Keesa that day and...maybe I can be of some help?'

Kaleb halts for a moment, looks at Elijah, 'Yes, fine, you can come. And bring Nefer, it's always good to have a dog when we refuel.'

'Kaleb—' Aedan is exasperated now.

'Aedan, there is no time to explain now. You'll understand soon enough. For now, I need you to trust me on this. I don't want you here on your own anymore. I can't lose you. I know you think I'm overprotective but, this time it's different. There are two places Keesa could be; I'm hoping it's the first. You're coming with me. The sooner we're packed, the sooner we can go.'

Again, the questions unanswered, thinks Aedan. If I had insisted on answers years ago, would Keesa be safe with us now? Elijah and Nefer look to Aedan expectantly; the boy apprehensive about going on the journey without her. She knows this is not the time to challenge her husband. Once again, the questions are swallowed.

'I'll be quick,' she says.

The packing goes swiftly. Elijah runs back to his grandfather's farm to fetch some clothes and to tell him that he is going. Kaleb and Aedan sit in the truck now, ready to leave. He turns to her, leans over and kisses her willing lips. He starts the car. As they drive towards Brick's farm, Kaleb is convinced he hears a fluttering of heavy wings, looks up. There it is again, perched on the branch of a low tree, that large eagle, watching. He presses the accelerator down lower. Once they have picked Elijah and Nefer up, they pass the spot again. For a moment, Kaleb is convinced the eagle catches his eye; then it takes to the air, headed in the same direction they are. Kaleb tries to shake an uncomfortable feeling. It's nothing, he thinks, I am reading too much into nothing.

Something about what they are doing feels fresh to Aedan, like a sheer cliff face, dangerous, yet bracing at the same time. The fingers of her left hand are tingling. In the waning light, she can make out their slightly reddened hue.

Perhaps she was rough with the packing? Then she recalls the moment of static when she touched Kaleb earlier. She opens the passenger window and allows her hand to dangle in the cooling, moving night air. Her faith in her husband comes from a place of no words. Despite the disquieting lack of sense that has bulged out from the moment she brinked over that ridge and witnessed Keesa's doing, Aedan is content in this moment. The love of her husband, the resuscitative air gusting into the car window and the prospect of finding her girl. It is enough.

CHAPTER 18

Return

17/12/2050

The King and Keesa both sleep early and soundly that night, clusters of guards posted at each of their doors. The next morning, Keesa is washing and dressing in between taking eyefuls of the view from her window—sky inching from black to dim mushrooming light to hanging with low clouds. Maen knocks on her door as she is finishing and tells June to make her way to the school lesson for the day, lest she be late.

'I will take you down now to meet the men who will be your personal bodyguards while I am away.'

'Okay,' Keesa says, adjusting the sleeves of the shirt she is wearing in the dresser mirror, and smoothing her hair down. Maen watches her prettiness. He will miss her quiet, unassuming presence while he is away. There is a knock on the door, left slightly ajar. It is Bryce.

'Forgive the intrusion, Sire, but a party of people have arrived at the Chamber requesting your presence. They are waiting in the reception room.'

'Is this important, Bryce? Can it not wait until I have gotten back from my trip?'

'I don't believe it can, Your Highness.'

'All right, then, I'll see to them on my way out.'

He holds out his hand for Keesa. They walk down together, Maen noticing an uncharacteristic hush among the workers going about their tasks. Bryce opens the door to the reception room. As he enters, Maen leads Keesa behind himself

154

in a shielding gesture. The small group stands at one of the large windows, taking in the seascape. There is a large dog, a young boy, a woman and a man. An air of apprehension weighs around them. They turn as they hear Maen enter. The dog growls; the boy quells him with a hand on his head. The man's face has aged very little. It has had more sun, and the eyes look more reflective than before but they still have that look of electric determination.

'Colter,' Maen murmurs. The man's troubled air clears for a moment, and warmth surges involuntarily from him to the King. He notices a small hand in Maen's; Keesa edges her head around Maen's side, peeking to see where the growl came from. The man's eyes harden again.

'Dad!' she cries, lets go of Maen's hand, and runs into Kaleb's arms. Kaleb squeezes her frame; an urge to never let go engulfs him. After their greeting, Keesa stands close to him, looking warily at her mother.

'Hi Mom,' she ventures cautiously. Aedan bends down, arms outstretched.

'Come here, my angel,' Aedan's voice breaks; she pulls her daughter into her chest.

Keesa goes to stand in front of Elijah, looking down at her hands as the right one squeezes the tip of each left finger. Her sightline shoots up to take in Elijah's expression for an instant, then retracts to her fidgeting hands.

'Hey, Elijah.'

'Hey, Keesa.'

Elijah goes to her side, puts his arm around her shoulder and sturdily pats her back twice. She steals another look at his eyes, smiling through her frown now. Toekoums has padded into the room and is sitting next to Nefer, whose tail is wagging. Maen pauses at the door, observing the greetings, feeling as though some comfort that he had unknowingly begun to settle into is being pulled out from under him, leaving a cold floor and yet another room of himself on one side, and an entwinement of people on the other.

Keesa senses an odd silence in the room. 'Dad, Mom, this is my friend...'

'Maen.' Keesa's head swings in the direction of her father's voice. Kaleb and the King move towards one another. Everyone else in the room can sense a thickening in the air between the two men.

155

'It's been a long time, Colter,' Maen says. The men embrace. The rain breaks from the clouds swollen like udders outside.

'What did King Maen call you, Dad?'

'He called me Colter, Keesa. I never planned on telling you this,' he aims this at Aedan as well, whose face is turning a shade of red, 'but Colter is my real name. This is King Maen of Day. He is my brother. Maen, please meet my wife, Aedan.'

Maen goes to Aedan and bows to her, kissing her hand as he does so. 'An honour to make your acquaintance, my lady.'

'King Maen,' Aedan avoids Colter's eyes for the moment but her face is scarlet now.

'And I'm glad to see you again, Elijah,' Maen smiles at the boy.

'Yes, Lio—I mean, King.' Nefer growls low in his throat again. 'Sorry about Nefer.'

'No offence taken, he's consistent, I respect that.'

Keesa and Aedan are both fixed on Colter.

'So, if you are King Maen's brother, doesn't that make you a prince?' Keesa blurts.

'It does. I am Prince Colter of Rising Star, of the Aduro royal Family of Light.'

'But then why aren't you a prince?'

The words slice through Colter's heart. He feels himself fall in her eyes.

'It's complicated.'

Aedan's voice is strung tight when she speaks. 'Could I have a word with you, Kaleb?'

Colter looks at the reproachful questions in the eyes before him. 'I think it best if we all sit down and talk.'

The rain has subsided, and occasional chutes of sun arm out of the clouds now, scanning the slate sea. They all sit in the lounge. Maen asked the kitchen workers to bring in tea, coffee and some simple platters of food. Nefer is the only one wolfing down whatever is passed his way, after which he regards the humans picking gingerly at the spread in bafflement. Aedan is being given a brief account by Colter of who the Family of Light is and what they are capable of. She has hardly moved through this, as though holding her body still will somehow keep what she thought was reality intact. Keesa is slowly digesting the fact of her Father's royal blood. She watches her mother's uncharacteristic stiffness, waiting for her to move, crack, and disintegrate onto the floor. There is a moment of silence after Colter finishes. A few stray spatters of rain tap against the window. Nefer adjusts his subtle begging stance in the hope that someone will notice. Elijah looks almost as shell-shocked as Aedan.

'So what powers do you have?' Aedan asks Colter.

'I can generate electric current and release it through my body.'

'Of course.' It's the first time Keesa has heard sarcasm in her mother's voice.

'Why didn't you tell us everything before?' Keesa asks.

'I considered it many times,' Colter answers, 'but I didn't want to expose you two to the dangers that go with carrying my secret.'

'I'm afraid it's also partly my fault, Keesa.' Aedan's throat sounds dry. 'I knew there were things your Father was hiding. I let it be because I was fearful that if I asked too many questions, he would leave. Perhaps I wasn't so far off the mark after all.'

'Why did you leave your family?' Keesa asks, her eyes on Colter. The tone of disenchantment in her voice is distressing to him. The events that punctuated the day he left are still clear in his mind. He has avoided pondering them over the years, and now they rise, like disinterred dreams.

The Spectator

07/10/2041

The Lion of Light's death has splintered the family. The Chamber is in the process of being packed up, all traces being erased. The current site, along an unpopulated stretch of coast to the east of Plettenberg Bay, is becoming too busy and risky. A new setting will have to be established. Their scouts have brought word of the meningitis bacterium sweeping across the land. For a while, the family and all the Chamber workers will have to find a temporary hiding place further north until the dust has settled. Maen is thinking a mountainous area might be safest for now. Elke has begun to close shut; even her embrace feels less maternal to her sons; she is holding a hardness in her muscles that hadn't been there before.

Maen had been well-behaved as a boy, although with spark. Recently, Colter had been sensing the exuberance of romantic love in his eyes, even though he denies it when questioned. After their father's death, Colter watches Maen retreat into silence and into the righteousness and comfort of abiding by royal rules, intent on being the good son. Colter feels winded by his father's murder and carries a rage that he strangles. His palms are always sweaty. Then it begins. The hunches, omens, the thoughts that dog their way into his head. To him, his family's untimely death is inevitable, given their lust for revenge and their reluctance to accept the new code from the oceanic council, which condemns reprisals.

That morning he sees his mother leaving with a large group of security guards and guesses her intent. He begs her not to attempt killing the Dark Queen.

'Don't you see that you're carrying on the cycle if you kill her now? Not to mention that you risk the Force of Light in doing it. If you are in turn killed, there will be no Sun-bearer left on the planet. It could throw the balance of the Forces in favour of the Dark forever.'

'She deserves what is coming to her.'

'Can you not reason with her? Mother, please, I don't want to lose my family.'

Elke's frame gives out some of its tautness with this raw plea from her son. 'All right, Colter, I will attempt negotiation. I should be back by nightfall tomorrow. I would advise that you and your brother do not leave the Chamber in that time.'

Colter takes the car set aside for Maen's and his needs and follows Elke and her guards, keeping a wide berth between them. If his mother is going to be in danger, he wants to protect her. Colter has always been good with stealth; he is the most talented in the family at identity shields. He can render himself virtually invisible simply by disguising his energy field. His mother's party stops in an area quite green with bushes and trees, close to where the Dark Chamber is alleged to be. He tracks them on foot as they close in to the area where Queen Signa and King Dallon are taking an afternoon walk. One of the Light guards spots Colter, indicates with a hand gesture for the Prince to keep down. Colter hides behind a bush, feeling current gathering inside him. The ambush is swift; the Dark guards are thoroughly outnumbered. A sinking feeling seeps down Colter's body. His mother is not making any overtures to bargain. Despite the fact that Signa's powers are based in her medical genius, she still manages to put up quite a fight against the sizeable contingent of Light guards that beset her. Colter waits for his mother to change her tack; his ears strain to hear her voice appealing to the Dark Queen for peace. When his mother's voice does sound, it is toneless.

'Hold them steady,' Elke orders, lifts her upturned hands to face the trapped royals, and projects scalding shafts of fire onto them, beginning with the Queen. Signa makes no sound and it seems to Colter she tries to hold herself still— perhaps in an effort to deny Elke any additional satisfaction. Her body disobeys this painless performance and begins to writhe like a scarecrow being wrenched around by a gale. In the last moment, Colter glimpses a kind of innocence in her eyes, which betray the surprise of death come for her. Elke finishes with the King, by this time terrified and blubbering. His cries remind Colter of a squealing pig stuck with a knife, unaccepting of its fate. In the silence that follows, it is as though the braying replays itself in an awful, looping echo in his head.

Some of the current in Colter's body overflows now and sparks with the air as it escapes. Queen Elke whips around upon hearing it and her eyes find Colter's. For a few seconds, it is almost as though she doesn't recognise him, as possessed as she is with retribution. In that moment, Colter feels something dislocate inside himself, as though his life has been irrevocably interrupted. Then Elke sees her son, sees her act.

'Colter...' Words falter in her mouth.

'You are not my mother. She is not a murderer.' Colter speaks these words softly but they carry in the crisp air. Elke feels the words right next to her now, out of place, and ugly. Colter turns and begins walking to his car. A few of the guards

159

move to block him, bring him back to the Queen. Security protocol stipulates that the royal heirs should not travel unaccompanied under any circumstances.

'Let him be,' Elke instructs. She trusts he will return to her. This is just a mood, he will come round. After all, he is young.

Colter starts the car and drives in the opposite direction from which he came. He runs away from putting on a public, false face, from losing any more of his loved ones to a fight he believes is futile. He makes the decision he can most easily cope with at the time. He will accept the imminence of his family's death and attempt to create a life for himself, disguised as a normal human. It will be simpler. The pain of their deaths will be less if he is no longer part of their lives.

Maen's face flushes livid as Elke informs him of what she did and that Colter has gone. She has never seen him so angry before, yet he contains it.

'I may be disappointed but, you are still my mother and my Queen. I will stand by you no matter what. You do realise that drastic measures will need to be taken for our security now.'

Elke and Maen leave the Chamber the next day, the Queen for her hideout in the desert, Maen and the rest of the Chamber workers for an unknown destination. It is the last time either of them will see their family home. They are not the only ones fleeing to the rural areas. They are careful not to come into contact with anyone else along the way. Maen will need to rebuild a new Chamber of Light on his own eventually; a daunting prospect but one that he embraces without question. It will help keep his mind off the distance between himself and his family and his longing for Regan, his poring over what happened. Within a day, the Light family are scattered, each cocooned in their own identity shield, with any means of communication crumbling around them with alarming speed.

Sleeping Dogs Wake

17/12/2050

Colter leaves some of the graphic detail out in his telling. He does not want to plant such images in Keesa's mind. Aedan draws the girl closer to her side, rubs her back as she looks at Colter, her trust of him thinning. If he left his family once, he could do it again.

'Are you still cross with your mom?' Keesa asks, a chain of logic tallying up in her head.

Colter looks at Maen before he answers. The King is standing by the window; his ears half folded back, his tail twitching every so often. 'It was a long time ago; I was young. I wouldn't call it cross.'

'What exactly would you call it?' Maen asks tightly.

Colter's eyes flash towards the King, 'Say what you want to say, Maen.'

Maen squares his brother. 'I know she did wrong but, she is still our mother and our Queen, you should have stood by her, no matter what.'

'What she did places her on a par with a lowly ruffian.' These words that have been lodged in Colter for years sound almost obscene to him as they leave his mouth.

Maen notices Keesa's face paling; he checks his temper. 'Her judgement was clouded by anger. She is, after all, still human. A critical quality in a Light royal is the ability to forgive. Clearly, you discarded any observation of the Light code with your abdication.'

'Indeed, it is our mother—by all measures, the embodiment of Light principles as our Queen—who should have found it in herself to forgive the Dark Queen!' Colter retorts.

Aedan has also noticed Keesa's blanched pallor. 'I think you two can have this conversation in private,' she says pointedly.

'Certainly,' says Maen, as the two brothers rein themselves in.

'How about you go show Elijah around while we talk, angel?' Aedan asks the girl cautiously.

Keesa looks from adult to adult. 'Okay, want to see, Eli?'

'Sure,' says the boy, glad for a chance to remove himself from the discord in the room.

'How about some fresh air?' Maen proposes, 'We could take tea in the breakfast room.'

———•••———

The three of them look out towards the sea. Colter has pulled a chair out from the long table and sits on it now at the edge of the red porch. He looks awkward in the space, like someone in a station between destinations. It makes Maen sad to see him like this. It is always his first instinct to reach out to him, find a way to peace. But the wall around Colter now is as thick as the identity shield he has shrouded himself in for a decade. Maen stands close to his brother, as though his proximity might convey some of the love he feels for him, despite Colter's reticence. Aedan sits on the steps of the veranda, relieved to breathe in salt water carried on a stiff breeze off the waves. She sifts through the dusty half-soil, half-sea-sand that meets the bottom step, lifting seashells that catch her eye.

Maen breaks the ice. 'I must apologise for the manner in which events unfolded and any distress the two of you no doubt suffered as a result of Keesa disappearing. It was unavoidable.' Silence, the pause of water peeling, then pounding in on itself. Colter dips his head in acknowledgement of Maen's words. The King presses on. 'Are you aware of Keesa's powers?'

Aedan looks up from scrutinising shells. 'No.'

Colter leans his torso forward, clasps his hands, and fixes his gaze on their rough, dry texture, avoiding Aedan's eyes. 'I have an idea.' Aedan throws Colter a look of deepening disappointment. Yet another thing he chose not to tell her about.

'This may be difficult for the two of you to hear but I would hope that you will take some pride in the fact that Keesa has been chosen as the next Sun-bearer, with the approval of the Queen, our mother.'

162

'What?' Aedan drops the pretty shell she has been wiping, black with purple streaks. Colter jerks his upper body up, his mouth half-open. Aedan is light-headed with the unravelling of the familiar. She senses herself fading in the picture of Keesa's life.

'That is unacceptable! I won't have it!' Colter stammers, getting up.

'I understand your fears as parents but, I must tell you that the wheels are already in motion.'

'Even if I assented to this, she is way too young and inexperienced to take it on and you know it, Maen.'

'Granted, the timing is unfortunate; I would also rather that this were taking place at the usual age of 16 years, but Keesa is the most potent candidate for training I have ever seen.'

'There will be no training. For Keesa to undergo the download from Mother is inconceivable for a 10-year-old.'

'I'm afraid it is too late. The transmission was completed two days ago.'

Colter's eyes spark cobalt-blue and strands of his inky hair start to lift into the air with static. 'You took her to Mother?'

A Mohican of hackles rises in the King's mane. He is not intimidated by his brother's powers. 'I did.'

'How dare you!' Colter knocks the chair he was sitting on out from between his brother and himself; sparks of electricity screech out from his hands, and ricochet off the chair, the floor and Maen's feet. The King does not flinch.

Aedan leaps up towards her husband, 'Kaleb, fighting is not the answer here, it will only make things—' Her hand is catapulted back with the shock of current as she tries to grab at his arm. 'Eina!' she cries, tucking her arm into her chest.

'Damn it! I'm sorry, Aedan,' Colter goes to see how her arm is, pulls back from touching her again. 'You okay?'

'It's fine,' Aedan says. 'What is not fine is that decisions have been taken regarding Keesa without our consent.' She throws this in Maen's direction.

'I admit, I should have consulted with you. There was no time. Colter, do you care nothing for the fate of our family? Or our dying mother's wishes?'

Colter presses his lips together, looks out to the water rolling onto shore, constant and oblivious. 'How is she doing?' he asks.

'She has weeks left, at most.'

Colter slumps against the table edge; his head dips.

'You know that what you did broke her heart.'

'What does it help to tell me that now, Maen? Of course I am aware that my leaving had an effect. It was not an easy choice to make.'

'On the contrary, I think it was the easy choice. You abandoned your loved ones when they needed you most, instead of facing the fact that life is messy, that not everything can be played by the rules.'

'That's rich, coming from you.'

'It has taken me some time to accept it myself.'

'I never meant to be gone for so long. As time wore on it just became harder to consider returning. As Keesa grew, so did my fear for her safety.'

'You deprived her of her heritage. The least you can do now is give her your blessing and become a teacher in her training, rather than an obstacle to it.'

Colter pauses, allows some of the hardness to leave his voice. 'Aedan and I still need to discuss this further but, I will take it under consideration.'

Maen is grateful for the respite. 'This is good to hear, Colter. Her gifts are developing at a rate I have never witnessed before.'

'What powers has she shown?'

'One of her strongest is in sound. Seems to be a combination between a roar like mine and Mother's fire power.'

'She has used it already?'

'I'm afraid she had to. We stopped at a Gengun on the way here and were ambushed.'

'You placed my child in the way of danger?'

'If we don't take her through this process, all of us will be in grave danger.'

'Are you telling me she has already used her powers to kill?'

'A few baboons, yes.'

'Keesa killed more animals?' Aedan asks, her hand over her mouth.

Colter lets out a cry of frustration. 'Can't you see? By accepting Mother's deed, you accepted the cycle of violence and now you have already started Keesa on that path—an innocent child!'

'She had no choice! She had to defend herself!'

'Where were you? You should have been defending her!'

'I was, on the other side of the car. You should be proud that she harnessed her powers at that moment, without any training.'

'Can you hear yourself? I should be proud that my child has murdered innocent animals?'

'Those baboons were brainwashed, starved and lethal.'

'That's not the point! How can you not get it? The cycle of blood and death will always follow our family, until we refuse to participate in it!'

'Just as idealistic as ever! You are the one who abdicated the real running of this family. If we had to follow your heady idea of operating through nothing but peace and love, we would be extinct by now. Where do you think that would leave the Light Force?'

'You mean the Light mafia.'

'Unfortunately there are times when we have to do what needs to be done. Once I begin her training, she will learn the skill of only injuring a creature rather than killing it. And healing it afterwards, where possible.'

Keesa and Elijah approach the arched doorway to the breakfast room. Her bodyguards wait in the connecting room. As always, Elijah's company has calmed her. She knows that they will find their way past what happened that day at the top of the hill. Nefer is lagging behind, gripped with the task of recording the million scents on the property, and marking the ground outside the walls at every possible juncture. Keesa freezes as she hears Colter raising his voice to Maen.

'That has decided me. I forbid that Keesa undergo training of any sort. Her powers are liable to either get her killed or turn her into a killer. I won't have it!'

Elijah takes Keesa's hand. His hands are always warm, even on a cold day. She likes that about him. They walk out onto the gusty porch. The clouds are banking up again, darker than before.

'Keesa; you're back,' Aedan spots her before the brothers do. 'How was your tour, Elijah?' Keesa can tell she is trying to smooth out the situation.

'It was great thanks, Mrs Cross.' An unnatural pause. Keesa instantly senses a change in the way her parents are looking at her, like a possession to be delicately kept in check. She lets go of her friend's hand and approaches the royal brothers.

'You know what happened at the Gengun?' she asks her father. Her knees feel weak. She is fearful of his reaction and can feel the electric current humming in his body, from where she stands.

'I do.' Colter is inclined to sweep her up and leave the Chamber immediately, but her extrication would not be simple and may cost him her trust altogether.

'So you're cross with me, like you're cross with your mother?'

'I told you, Keesa, I'm not cross.' His face is rigid.

'I think your mom is a nice lady. She was kind to me.'

'I'm concerned for your safety.'

'She is sad about what she did.'

166

'My mother should have known better than to transmit her powers into you, given how young you are.'

'Did you know that I had powers?'

Colter takes a breath, lets it out his nostrils, his chin jutting forward.

'I would like to know too, Kaleb. Exactly what did you know?' Aedan asks.

'I picked up when she began emitting her royal frequency signal,' Colter gives.

Anger rises red in Keesa's cheeks. 'So you knew that I had powers but you didn't teach me how to control them?'

'Yes, but only to protect you from the dangers of using them. And look! My fears were confirmed from the sounds of what you did to that goat. The Dark Force has clearly already begun to manipulate you.'

Maen looks at Keesa, 'Was that the day I picked you up? We still haven't spoken about what happened.'

'Yes, I felt funny when I did it. Like it wasn't me.'

'I rest my case,' Colter snaps.

'It is you who should be judged,' Maen responds. 'You intentionally stunted Keesa's growth as a royal. Otherwise, she might have proven too strong for Dark influences at that moment.'

'If aiding in the development of her powers would mean encouraging the growth of a deadly weapon in a girl's body, then the reason behind my reservations speaks for itself.'

'Are you cross because I want my powers and you don't want yours?'

Aedan intercepts now, 'Keesa! That is no way to talk to your father.'

Nefer trots in now, tail and ears pricked up. He starts giving out brusque barks in Colter and Maen's direction. Elijah restrains him but the dog is wary of the change in the brother's energies.

Colter glares at Nefer. 'I can defend myself, thank you, Aedan.' He turns to Keesa. 'I never said I didn't want my powers.'

Maen interjects, 'Colter, Keesa is your blood—reason enough that you would wish her to fulfil her royal destiny. I am presuming that Aedan is Keesa's mother and that you are her father?'

A strange silence. Aedan and Colter throw each other a trapped look. Aedan's eyes trail from her husband to Keesa. She drops her head in her hands, saying in a sickened tone, low enough to be out of Keesa's hearing, 'I told you we should have had this conversation long ago.'

'Perhaps we should talk to Keesa in private for a minute?' Colter puts to Maen.

Keesa regards Colter shifting his weight with a stumped expression on his face. 'No. I don't want to talk in private.'

Aedan moves to the girl and puts a hand on each of her petite shoulders. 'Keesa, there is something we need to tell you that's not going to be easy for you to hear. Come sit down.'

Keesa's eyes have widened and her body has gone stiff. She shakes her head tightly, remains standing, her legs like stuck planks. Maen goes to stand at the edge of the stairs while Aedan kneels down next to the girl. Colter makes an effort to neutralise the current running through him and cautiously places a hand on Aedan's shoulder. He senses a lack of yield to his touch; a partial but perceptible closing off has begun. To build a life on hidden identity is to build on clay feet.

'Before I say anything, I want you to know that, no matter how you came to us, you are a gift in our lives and we love you, little angel.' Aedan struggles to keep her voice steady. Keesa feels her blood draining down towards the hard floor and a leaden coldness comes over her.

'Your father and I, I mean, Kal—Colter and I are not your real parents.'

All the eyes on her, the red surface, Nefer whining behind her, all of it begins to spin, turning the chill on Keesa's skin hot. She removes her hand from Aedan's, takes two teetering steps back, connects with the breakfast table bench, and thumps down onto it.

'Are you okay?' Aedan asks, as she and Colter go to either side of her. Keesa closes

168

her eyes. More than anything at this moment, she wants to be under the waves, in the quiet water. She tries to force herself there, remember her way back. Nothing. She can still hear Nefer restless, feel hands on her body. She opens her eyes. It is comforting to see Maen's figure silhouetted against the glare coming off the ocean; the clouds thinning again. She can't see his face but can feel that he is with her. It occurs to her, though, that she might be fooling herself. Perhaps Maen's real interest is simply to use whatever means at his disposal to ensure the continuation of his bloodline. How to know his kindness is not merely an act?

'Can I sit alone, please,' she asks in a flat tone. Aedan and Colter hesitantly move to sit some distance away.

'Would you like to ask anything?' Aedan says after some moments of turgid quiet.

Keesa looks from Colter to Aedan. They look smaller to her and somehow wispy, as though at any moment they might evaporate completely.

'Who are my real parents?'

'I'm afraid we have no idea of that,' Colter admits.

'If I'm not your daughter, how come I'm living with you?'

'Aedan found you before I met her.'

'It was one evening just after sunset. I lived in the house alone. I heard a sound outside, got my shotgun from under the bed, and opened the door. There was no one there but then I heard the sound of a baby's voice. I looked down and saw a blanket on the step. I looked inside its folds and, there you were. You were tiny, couldn't have been more than a day old.'

Colter continues the thread, 'I met Aedan a few weeks later. After I left the Chamber, I travelled for some time before I came upon Hale. Aedan had her cheese stall out. I noticed the little baby with her. Once I knew there was no father in the picture, I decided to stay in Hale. I said that my family had been wiped out by the bacterium. Over time, Aedan and I fell in love. We went on to raise you as though you were our own child.'

They study Keesa's face for any clue as to what she is feeling. Her countenance is closed, looking from the ocean down to a loose thread in her denim skirt that she has been fiddling with while listening. She addresses Colter.

'How come you and the other royal people could pick up my signal but I couldn't pick yours up?'

'All royal family members are taught from a certain age how to place identity shields around themselves to avoid being tracked by the Dark Force.' Colter answers.

'As a future Sun-bearer, you will have to be taught that skill far sooner than usual. The Dark Force is likely attempting to locate you as we speak,' Maen adds.

Aedan bursts up and squares Maen, annoyed, 'Keesa has had quite enough scary situations and prospects thrust upon her in the last couple of days. Perhaps it is time to give her a break.'

Maen keeps his calm but speaks with weight, 'It is critical that she begin her training immediately.'

Aedan's voice rises, 'She's just a little girl, for God's sake!'

The adults lock horns now, Colter at Aedan's side with their backs to Keesa. Toekoums hops up onto the bench closest to the girl. Colter's voice is strident and has the broken pace of resentment. 'This is so typical of royalty. You think you can just swoop in and take her away but it's not your right. As the only father she has known, I explicitly forbid her to begin her training.'

Keesa rises to her feet. When she speaks, her voice carries the hint of her roar. 'You're all talking about me as if I'm not here. You think you can tell me what I can and can't do yet none of you are even my parents. I want to do the training. If I'm meant to be the next Sun-bearer, then I will.'

Colter and Aedan stare at Keesa as they would a stranger. Colter struggles to control the urge to grab her shoulders and rattle sense into her. He can feel sparks spitting off his hands. 'My girl, you may have powers but you do not speak to me or your mother like that. You will come home with us tomorrow and go to school and help your mother in the dairy and grow up like a normal girl.'

'You can't force me.'

'Don't push me, my girl.'

Nefer starts to bark again, this time at Keesa. An uncomfortable heat begins flowering into Colter's body. A strange sensation, as though it is originating in his organs and pushing out into his body space, like blossoming coals.

'I'm not your girl! You've been lying to me all my life!'

Colter has broken into a sweat now; his current is waning. He grabs at his heart, and begins doubling over. Maen senses what is happening, 'Keesa! Control your power! Pull it into yourself!'

Colter drops to the ground, moaning in pain now. 'KEESA! Listen to the King! What you are doing is hurting your father!' screams Aedan.

What Aedan is saying filters through a low hum in Keesa's ears and the penny drops. She looks up at Maen, the anger in her face replaced in an instant by panic. Maen approaches her, places one hand on the base of her spine, and the other on the top of her head. 'Close your eyes; focus on drawing it in and letting it flow along your spine,' he says in a collected tone, 'I will let you know when to let it out in a roar.' Keesa forces the anxiety down, lets her eyelids drop, and follows his guidance. Maen's body is starting to tremble; he bends his head forward, arches his neck. A central strip of hair stands upright on his head. 'Aedan, take the chair that Colter was sitting on and throw it onto the ground out front,' Maen instructs, still managing to sound unflustered. Toekoums nips off the bench, shoots to Aedan's side and nudges her with his paw. 'Steady now, almost there,' Maen says to Keesa, whose limbs are also beginning to shake.

Aedan swings her head from her aimless attempt to tend to Colter, to the kitten, then to the King. 'What? The chair that...out front...' Her voice is hysterical now, as Colter's moans grow in intensity.

'Take the chair and throw it out front! NOW!' Maen shouts. Nefer is barking ferociously now, Elijah is only just managing to hold him back with both arms.

Keesa's guards appear in the archway; one of them shouts to Maen, 'What can we do, Your Highness?'

Aedan lurches up, takes steps to grab the wooden chair inlaid with steel lying on its side on the patio floor, trips, and hits the ground. 'Stay back!' Maen yells at the guards, 'Just one of you help the lady throw that chair out front!' The head guard moves swiftly, lifts the chair, and flings it towards the patch of ground beyond the steps. As it hits the ground, Maen yells, 'Out of the way now and everyone, get down! Guards, shield everyone!' Aedan is getting up again; the head guard grabs her and forces her back to the ground, lying full over her to

171

protect her. The other guards follow suit with Colter, Elijah, and the animals. It takes two of them to keep Nefer down, one of them holding his jaw closed to avoid his bite. Maen disengages his hands from Keesa's body. 'Now Keesa! Open your eyes and throw your roar towards that chair, and only that chair!' he shouts, pointing to it. Keesa snaps her eyes open; they have turned a hot green; they locate the chair swiftly. She draws in a breath, and directs an ear-shattering roar towards the chair, which explodes instantly with enormous force. There are no flying pieces, as with Maen's practise targets. Instead, a cloud of smoke hangs over where it was, which slowly starts to twirl upwards with the sea breeze.

'Thank-you, guards; you can pull back now,' Maen says. As the guards clear the space, Maen drops to Colter's side, lays hands on him and begins repairing any damage done. The healing is quick; Colter's royal constitution is more resistant than humans to high-born powers and the fact that his current was strong when it happened also prevented extensive damage. Tears are streaming down Aedan's face as she watches. Every now and then, she darts her eyes towards Keesa, viewing her with horror and new-found distrust. Nefer is pacing and whining, footing towards the rising smoke to sniff it out, gingerly backing off with his tail between his legs. Keesa surveys the scene with a harrowed expression.

Elijah goes to her, touches her arm. 'You okay, Kees?'

She looks at him, looks back at Colter, who is coming round now, and nods her head in a stilted manner. Colter sits up; the colour in his face is good; he looks far stronger than Keesa does.

'Thank-you, Maen,' he says, his voice still taut.

'Anytime, Colt,' his brother replies, giving his back a pat.

Colter gets up, moves towards Keesa. She backs off a little unsteadily, 'I didn't mean to...I'm sorry...'

'I'm not angry, Keesa,' Colter offers, 'I know it wasn't your fault. But, can you see how—'

'Oh my God,' involuntary words slip out of Aedan's mouth as she gazes in the direction of what used to be a chair. The others turn. Most of the smoke has cleared, revealing a crater spanning a few metres. Maen and Elijah edge forward to peer at the remains of the chair, bits of melted, twisted steel still steaming, as flakes of black ash shift and settle around it with the wind.

'Her powers are growing all the time,' Maen remarks.

Colter approaches Keesa again, 'That's it, we need to get you home, you must see reason—'

Keesa lifts her hand, palm out facing Colter. He stops in his tracks. She drops her hand slowly, disconsolate. 'I don't want to talk anymore. I'm going to tidy the music room.' With that, she turns and walks inside the Chamber. Elijah follows and her bodyguards trail her as she goes up the sweeping staircase.

Despite the disagreement still hanging in the air between them, it pains Maen to watch Colter rejected by the girl he regards as his daughter. He turns to Maen, his face creased with disbelief and hurt, 'We leave first thing in the morning with her.'

Maen addresses him gently, 'Colter, can you not see? She is the one who took the step to set her destiny in motion—she drew the kitten into her life as an aide. She is living out her royal path, whether you give her permission or not. I think it would be better for Keesa to live in the protection of the Chamber. You could all move in. This is your home, Colter. Elijah and his dog and goats are welcome too.'

Colter takes in his brother's words; his face remains obdurate. 'I would appreciate if you could point me to the Chamber worker who can show us to a room for the night.'

CHAPTER 19

Friable Reunion

17/12/2050

Keesa spends the remainder of the day in the music room with Elijah. It is a relief to be in the company of someone she can be quiet with. Toward evening, Maen finds the two of them asleep on the sofa there, Keesa snuggled into the arm of the couch with a blanket over her and Elijah further down. Maen sends for Colter, who carries the sleeping girl to her bed. Toekoums patters into the room and curls up close to Keesa's feet. Aedan sees that Elijah is settled in his room with Nefer before she joins Colter and Maen for dinner.

—•••—

Dinner is short and, for the most part, laboured. The subject of Keesa is avoided. The Chamber workers have clearly missed Colter and the warm rapport between them is plain to see. The workers tending to the dinner seem more excited than any of the diners do about the ritual of the dining-room finally being used again, as well as the exquisite sets of crockery and cutlery that Queen Elke had originally received from her mother. Maen would invariably take his food to his bedroom or the library, or sit with the Chamber workers in the kitchen. There is something comforting in a meal that begins at a specified time in the dining hall and is served on plates pleasing to the eye.

'Mother misses you a great deal, you know,' Maen says as the plates are being cleared. Colter looks down at his warped reflection in his unused desert spoon.

'What's the place that she's living in like?' he asks, fighting his tightening throat.

'It's bleak. Or simple, I should say. But then you know Mom.'

174

'Oh yes, the most important things in life are the simple things.' The brothers chuckle.

'There was only so much simplicity I could take,' Maen recalls, 'those breakfasts of spelt flakes soaked in water still visit me in my nightmares.'

The two of them laugh out loud. Aedan can't remember the last time she saw Colter do that.

'Shame, Mom and her health regimes...'

'We could go visit her...all of us...soon, if you like?' Maen suggests.

'It would be good for Aedan to meet her.' Colter says. His eyes meet Aedan's. She softens to him; something in her lips. In that moment, it feels good to be home.

Aedan retires soon after this. As she makes her way out, the brother's voices waft up the stairs. The series of shocks that punctuated the day has had a thawing effect on the wall between them. This brings Aedan a measure of comfort and she falls into sleep surprisingly easily. The brothers stay up another hour, then also head for bed. Groups of guards keep watch outside the royal rooms. The Chamber is quiet with the rise and fall of sleeping breaths and, for the first time in many years, the tenuous contentment of a family reunited.

The Thorn

The clouds have cleared away, leaving the night sky fresh, silver light from the waxing moon bobbing in the water and scoping its way through windows and folds of curtains in the Chamber, like little searchlights. Not more than two hours after midnight, after some heavy sleep, Keesa opens her eyes. She feels the silk sheets and hears the waves and, for a moment, curls her toes, happy to be in her Chamber bed. But thoughts quickly elbow their way in, as she recalls the afternoon, Colter's moans, the adults talking at each other with anger and laying claim to her person. In a disquieting way, the fact her parents did not conceive her makes sense. She sees now that she's always been searching for something throughout her childhood, in the skeletons, the rocks, the inside of animals. Something that she knew was hers alone, that did not attach to her mother or her father, as arteries attach to organs and parental mannerisms repeat in their children. In the Chamber, she'd found a place she felt calm in, closer to the thing she was searching for, a place where she felt she might belong. Now she finds herself wondering who she can trust and where her home is. Whether she belongs anywhere other than walking in the veldt with the rocks.

The words of Queen Signa standing next to her surgical table keep sounding in her ears now: 'Beware the attachments that prevent your rise to power.' Perhaps it is her she should be trusting. Keesa starts dipping in and out of sleep again in a disorienting way, as though she is on a boat in heaving waters, and each plunge into or emergence out of slumber leaves her feeling heavy and queasy. The Dark Queen's voice begins rising and falling too, until it is difficult for Keesa to distinguish if it is part of her dreams or is sounding out in the air of her Chamber bedroom. A disquieting confusion is swimming in her head as, even in her dreams now, she is still lying in this same bed, unable to lift herself out of it. She can hear the guards shuffling outside her door every now and then, at times bits of sentences, spoken in low tones. She is aware of the warm ball on the covers at her feet, and tries over and over to call 'Toekoums!' and wake up her little companion. Just to talk to him for a while would calm her thoughts. But her voice gets stuck in her lungs, and feels to start drowning in them, until it is as though her very breath is being swallowed. Queen Signa's voice speaks markedly to her for an instant, as though her lips are right by the girl's ear: 'Get the heart of the kitten and you shall become my pupil. All my power and knowledge, yours.'

Keesa snaps wide-awake, having pulled herself out of the muddled sea-sickness of before. Or was she pushed? It's hard to tell. She is perfectly placid now. Everything is clear to her. Slowly she sits up in the bed and untwines herself from the covers, making sure not to wake the kitten. She sets her feet down on the cool stone floor and begins noiselessly padding her way to the dressing table. It is pleasing to feel contained in what is expected of her. No questions, no doubts, simply her instructions. Her orders fill the air around her, like warm liquid. Her feet know where to go; even the floor seems to support her course of action. She surveys the collection of lady's toilette objects from a bygone time laid out on the dressing table, and awaits instruction on which instrument to choose. She lifts the fine, silver-encased lady's comb, with its handle tapering to a point as sharp as a pin. Then she takes the ornate pair of scissors, the reflection of moonlight through the window in the mirror illuminating her elegant movements.

She sits down gently on the bed, one leg in a cross-legged position and the other hanging down the side, so that the small feline is directly in front of her. Keesa stealthily tucks the objects under her left thigh. She turns the kitten onto its back, feigning affection, and strokes his tummy gently. She takes advantage of his drowsy state—the only time that he will allow her to touch his sensitive inner torso. Toekoums begins to purr, half-in and half-out of sleep. Keesa waits until his lids have lowered shut again, then reaches for the comb and poises it in one quick movement above the kitten, just to the left of where his heart is positioned in his diminutive form. One clean puncture and she can use the scissors to cut from there.

Something about the pause in Keesa's petting and the realisation that it is not morning, prompts Toekoums to open his eyes. The sight of the silver barb aimed at his chest and Keesa's serene face looming behind, brings him fully awake with a start. He immediately attempts to flip himself over and escape. Keesa lets go of the comb and pounces her hands around his torso. Then she holds him steady with her left hand—quite easily, given how small he is— and aims the comb once again with her right. He begins struggling, his legs thumping repeatedly against her determined grip. He tries to cry out but Keesa presses down on his throat with her thumb, blocking his voice from air. Even though he knows what she is doing, that she must be in one of her states again, he refrains from sinking his claws into her. He is her helper; it is his foremost duty to protect her life, no matter what and to never put his life before hers. Toekoums' eyes are beginning to bulge slightly, and his twig legs are kicking slower and in spurts now. Keesa realises he must be suffocating. That will not do, she needs him alive until she has taken his heart. She lifts her thumb off his windpipe. The kitten lies still for a moment, eyes rolling back in his head. Keesa is struck by how soft his front paws are, resting on her hand. She jiggles his body, like a cat goading a mouse back to mobility to taunt it more. Toekoums splutters gradually back to life, his limbs lagging in receiving impulses from his brain to bolt. Keesa sees this and takes the opportunity to once again raise the lady's thorn with both hands.

Sounds of the guard's voices outside the door escalate slightly; it is three in the morning, they are changing shifts. Keesa's head jolts up, aware that they have free access to the room. The kitten catches sight of this distraction, and finally his brain and body reconnect. He scrambles to his feet, digging his claws into the bedspread to leverage his little body and springs off the bed. Keesa is up and after the feline in a flash. There is no irritation, she simply pursues him. Toekoums jumps up onto the windowsill, slips through where the window sits ajar, and begins making his watchful way along the Chamber wall guttering to the left of the window. Keesa places her hands on the sill, hoists herself up and stands on it to her full height. She opens the window wide, juts her head out and peers around the side of the building to where Toekoums is balancing on the piping, putting one hesitant paw in front of the other. The drop is sheer and so high that not one of the guards down below has noticed the dot of a kitten scaling along, or the girl in the cream nightdress looking on. Toekoums has not made it very far along; the section he is approaching now has been rusted by the sea air, it looks precarious. Keesa reaches her hand towards his tail; if she can just grab it, she can yank him back in, and execute. She seizes at the tail; Toekoums flicks it upwards, whipping his head back in fright. He lets out a meow, reverting in his panic to his feline voice. Keesa's eyes still have that cool, determined look.

The kitten forces his voice, keeping it low. He is concerned that, if the guards get whiff of the influence of the Dark Force over her, they will attempt to restrain her. This could be fatal, given that she is perched on a high ledge. 'Keesa, it's me, Toekoums, your helper!'

His words hang like an undone jigsaw in Keesa's ears. She can sense each word separately but, they make no unified sense. She is unaffected by his appeal; her eyes remain deadpan as she steadies herself to try snatch at his tail again, verging her body further out, dangling dangerously off the edge now. She becomes aware of a soft beating sound in the night sky.

'Keesa, please, can't you see who I am? It's Toekoums, wake up!'

Upon hearing his name a second time, the words slowly start to cohere for Keesa. Toekoums' head turns sharply but slightly; his eyes registering something behind her. She turns to see moonlight catching on two great wings making their way towards her. She surfaces abruptly from her state, losing her balance as she does.

'KEESA!' the kitten cries, alerting some of the guards to the strange scene on the ledge.

She is falling into the silvery night air. The moment is filled with terror, an exhilarating inbreath of freedom, and a wrenching sense that she will not fulfil her duty as Sun-bearer. Then Valtere is there, enclosing her petite midriff in his huge talons. He makes sure his grip is secure but not so tight that he could injure the girl. Toekoums sees the guards lifting their weapons. 'Don't shoot! Don't shoot! The bird has Keesa! You might hit Keesa!'

The guards lower their guns, scrutinising the dim window where the voice is coming from. Toekoums watches as the majestic eagle swoops away with speed over glittering waves. The guards exchange quick words and a few of them run into the Chamber. Candlelight illuminates one window after another. Toekoums carefully reverses back along the guttering to the windowsill. The comb lies on the floor. The unmade bed. A pair of scissors glinting on top of the silk. Toekoums stays on the sill, sits, nonplussed. He waits for the people and their questions.

The Chamber is well behind the flying pair. Keesa stops struggling now. She has been shouting to the bird to let her go, and attempted prying its talons off her for some time. She has tried using her powers but, nothing comes. Now she feels sleep finally washing over her.

'That's better. It's no use. I'm too strong for you. Do not fear; I will deliver you safely.'

Again, more questions. Too many questions to ask. But the blackness of sleep overcomes her now. She is half-aware that in the midst of this most arresting situation, the bird's voice comforts her. And then she is out, her little body drooping off his mighty tarsals like a kitten's that he would have for dinner. Valtere's winging feels like the motion of waves and, in her dreams, she floats along the currents of the ocean. No whale, no shore, just her and the vast mass of heaving liquid.

CHAPTER 20

Awakening

18/12/2050

Regan opens her eyes. Before her is a vast space filled with blackness, apart from rosy light that touches a strange collection of rectangles hanging along the left side of the emptiness. She becomes aware of something hard pushing against the side of her head. Then the smell, close to her nostrils—formaldehyde. She jerks herself out of what she thought was a dream, and pulls her body upright, the fluid in her inner ears smarting at the sudden movement. With a bilious feeling, she recognises where she is. The thing that was pressing against her cheekbone is a steel laboratory table that used to support cadavers; the floating rectangles are the rows of the other tables, stretching out ahead of her. The smell of formaldehyde is in the steel—lodged in tiny grooves made from slips of surgical instruments. The soft illumination of the space is flickered by a few candles. Who lit them?

She takes a quick look around; is that person still here? She has no recollection of coming to the Initium laboratory. Fogged, she tugs at whatever threads of reality she can recall of the previous day. Casting her mind back makes her head ache. She remembers seeing Valtere off to fetch Keesa outside her patio door just before daybreak. It had been a difficult day, trying to keep a million thoughts at bay. She had managed to control the urge to gather visions all afternoon. She wanted to set her mind at ease about the effect that her plan for the Dark order would have and what role Keesa could play in it. By the time night fell, she'd given in, and begun the gatherings. She recalls slumping into bed at around eleven that night, after having lost count of how many she had drawn, their contents roiling around her head, blurring into one another, her brain short-circuiting from trying to make sense of them. After that, a blank space. Could she have been sucked into one of her visions without knowing? She knows that she featured in at least three of them.

Something moves in the back corner of the laboratory, followed by a feeble champing sound. Regan starts, yet there is something familiar about the sound; she has the sense that it had been entering her dreams just before she woke. She gets up off the slab and goes to fetch one of the candles on the side-desk. She takes the tallest one from the group of three—they are all burning low—and moves warily towards the rear corner. Bit by bit, the dim light picks up a huddle of roughly constructed cages squeezed into the small space at the back of the laboratory. She can make out the baboon now, its champing sounds building as she nears it. Something is wrong with it; she cannot place what. She approaches the cage door, holding the candle up. The baboon senses that she is there but is growing increasingly confused, the closer she comes. Its eyes are trying to find her but, something keeps throwing it off-course, confusing it. It lifts its hands to cover its eyes, shaking its head in bewilderment. Its eyes look blind yet not blind; it's as though just at the point of registering the shape in front of it, it loses its ability to recognise it.

Regan knows this is not a vision she has been sucked into and neither is it someone else's work. She is the one who lit the candles. She is the one who administered the new mutation of meningitis bacterium to this creature. She walks by the other cages—a scrub hare, a yellow mongoose, a steenbok, and a family of mice. They all recoil as the candle is shone in their direction, then panic as they try to decide which direction to turn to avoid it. Eventually, they just stay put, frozen in their failure to grasp the shape in front of them and the light that bounces off it. Regan witnesses the despondency that droops their muscles, how the alienation of the state renders them alone, and quietly mad from it.

She almost drops the candle in fright as a strange clicking noise sounds close by, followed by a compressed, chattering laugh, like a possessed jack-in-the-box. Regan's eyes shift to where the sound emanates from. There is a large box of some kind next to the cages. She didn't notice before as it is shrouded in a swathe of black cloth, pipes leading out from under it, trailing their way to connect to the taps of one of the laboratory basins nearby. She places the candle down on the nearest steel table and, standing as far away from the shape as possible, reaches out and whips the cloth onto the floor.

The box is a sizeable tank filled with what looks like salt water with a dark-green hue. Suspended in the water is a fully-grown dolphin. It takes up most of the space in the well kept tank. Rocks inside look to have colour growing on them. One of the pipes propped into the surface has bubbles coming out of it and is in turn connected to a small machine, with a cord that leads up into the roof. Regan recalls her mother informing her that she had set up solar panels to permanently supply the laboratory with power, what with fuel supplies always being scarce. The dolphin's skin has no sheen and bits of it are peeling away, revealing pink flesh. It jerks now, clearly aware of Regan's presence. Its movements are manic, yet wooden, muscles that have atrophied with so little use.

Regan has broken out in a cold sweat. Her stomach is empty and acidic but is nonetheless rising into her throat. She has to test; she lifts the candle closer to the trapped sea-creature. It tries to turn away from the light, swim in the other direction, bumps up against the rear side of the tank. Short waves slap against the walls; even though the sides are high, drops spatter on Regan's face. The glass is thick and the container is held in place by steel stabilisers, she is convinced it would tip over otherwise. At some point the dolphin gives up and floats, as though dead in the water. Regan remembers a time when she was a young girl and did not feel anything for the creatures and people her mother used for research. To her, they were then simply a necessary part of the Dark Plan. Now the eyes are the most unbearable part for Regan. The resignation in them is harrowing to witness. Yet, there is another feeling beneath her horror at this creature that is in hell because of what her hands carried out at her mother's bidding. It is irritation. She cannot prise her eyes away because it is everything she does not want to see. The dolphin seems frightened of her, yet in the same instance craves contact. As though there is some part of it that believes that she might be different this time, that she might show affection, respect. That the world might be a place of love.

Regan runs to one of the basins and throws up. It doesn't relieve her; there doesn't seem to be much in there to come up. This situation does not offer the possibility of relief. Redemption is like a laughing ghost hovering somewhere out in the veldt. But she will do what she can. This is the last of this. Regan gathers all her strength and focuses on what the first thing she can do is and then, the next. She begins by lighting more candles and consulting the manuals, as she had watched herself do in the vision. This time her mother will not get to her.

———◆◆◆———

Upon checking the freezer in the front right corner of the Initium lab, Regan finds vials containing the entire array of meningitis bacteria in solution; she must have siphoned trace amounts from the reserves in the main laboratory and cultured them here, under orders. What is also clear is that the new, offshoot strain is being actively worked with. She carries out the necessary procedures, for what feels like a number of hours. The Initium laboratory is fitted with all the equipment essential to microbiological research, as is the main laboratory. Finishing up, Regan places all the syringes back into the solution of disinfectant. It is peculiar to notice the trail of her own handiwork in the laboratory, a familiar, yet unsettling signature that she doesn't remember leaving. Her particular sterilisation methods, her rigmarole of decontamination. She created them when she was still working under her mother—one had to be inventive, given the isolation of the Chamber; access to the quickest solutions was often unavailable. Regan has administered doses of an antidote to all the creatures in the laboratory. It should take 24 hours or so to take effect. The dolphin was tricky; she had to balance on one of the laboratory stools to get her arm over the side of the tank. Fortunately, she found a syringe thick enough to perforate the dolphin's thick exterior; she must have acquired it for this purpose. It bucked at the invasion, however, and Regan struggled to keep her balance, gritting her teeth in fear of the tank smashing to the ground and beaching the dolphin on the hardwood floor. Her arm is still aching from straining to hold the needle lodged in.

She gives the animals food and water, consulting the recent manuals full of her handwriting to see what is required. It is all substitute, dry versions that pale in their nutritional content, compared to the live or fresh alternatives. In a matter of weeks, forms of malnutrition would begin setting in if these creatures were kept under these conditions. All she needs is to see definite signs that the antidote is working and, she will set them free. Regan can see from the entry dates in the manuals that Valtere was correct. She set the experiment up in July. The dolphin is the most recent addition; brought in from the east coast in mid-November. Clearly, her mother's attempt to transfer the new bacterium into oceanic life, which had proven resilient to the first round. The large sea-mammals were her most prized targets there, crucial as they are to the Chamber of Light. How could she have carried out transportation of the dolphin on her own? Regan is becoming increasingly jumpy at the prospect that she must have had others assisting her. Her mother's tendrils reached far across the country; she went to great lengths to secure her various suppliers. The Genguns are proof enough of it. They wouldn't exist if it weren't for Signa's visits to her key henchmen in the cities at the outbreak of the illness. They and their families were the privileged few outside the Chamber who received antidote injections. They had gone on to establish their respective Gengun strongholds.

There is also evidence in the writing of some plan that her mother was overseeing work on. These scribblings, however, are the most unclear part of the records. From what she can make out though, the project aims to render the Light Force more vulnerable than ever. There is no information on who is overseeing this mission. Regan's head grows dizzy with this spilling Pandora's Box she has woken up to.

For a woman who stood for the Dark code—a code that nurtured its young into embracing the emptiness within and the random nature of life—Queen Signa certainly left little to random chance when it came to securing the future of her empire. Her legacy is like a sour, viscous glue that Regan keeps trying to pull off her person but the more she wipes at her hands, the drier and tougher the adhesive becomes. But act by act, she can change that.

She readies herself to leave, turns to the inmates, 'You're going to be all right. I'm coming back for you.' Their eyes search for a moment for this gentle tone of voice, then slump back to hollowness. The dolphin lifts its beak out of the water and lets out a few faint clicks, then sinks back down into its transparent prison. Regan's throat tightens; this communication seems to register her gesture and break the celled solitudes in the room.

She makes her way to the door, blowing out candles as she goes, till only the anchor one is burning. She turns the door handle, her lungs aching for fresh air. The door is stuck. She yanks at it. The door is locked. She suddenly feels too hot. Squinting into the lock, it appears that there is no key in there. Who could have done this? Perhaps the people who have been assisting her—but why? She looks up at the high row of windows lining the walls, painted black. It takes some time but, she manages to lug the tall ladder from the back of the laboratory and prop it up against the wall. Her limbs have become shaky; she is aware that she can't have eaten for some time. What if her mother has found some way of manifesting and it was her phantom dust that locked the door from the outside? Regan is holding wild claustrophobia in check now. Not another night in this haunted room.

The ladder is not the steadiest; she treads the rungs carefully. It would not do for the Queen of Night to end her time in a heap on this dank floor. She feels for the window handle, where it should be. In places the paint on the windows has fine cracks, she can tell it must be close to daybreak from the weak grey colour filling them. She knows the first shift guards might be close; they circle the perimeter of the grounds every morning. As her eyes adjust to the light, she can make out that the handles have been broken off. She squeezes her eyelids together; they are twitchy from sleep deprivation, checks again. 'Damn it!' she says under her breath. She can feel the animals becoming agitated at her fretting. Down the ladder again. She grabs a paperweight from the side desk, ascends again. Three whacks and she manages to smash it open. The animals startle, begin letting out distressed sounds, and she can hear the water lapping again as she takes a deep breath of veldt air. At this point, all she can focus on is getting out—whichever Chamber workers can assist her, she will deal with later.

She throws her voice out the window, 'Guards! Help! SOMEONE HELP ME!' The sound of feet crunching on stones, then two guards appear beneath the window, their weapons pointed at her. They had heard the glass being broken. 'It is me, your Queen!' Regan quickly cries, upon which they drop their aim. 'Open the laboratory door; use whatever force necessary,' she orders, pointing to the passage that runs by the entrance.

Back down the ladder; Regan calls out to the animals on her way to the door, "It's okay, it's going to be okay.' At the entrance now, the anchor candle's flame wobbling with her speed. She steps back again; the door will probably be forced open any moment. Instead, she hears the key being placed in the lock and turned. A peculiar feeling of déjà vu comes over her, as though the door is going to open and some spectre of her mother is going to be standing there. The door opens. Regan blinks against the morning light, the two guards silhouetted. 'I thought there was no key. When I looked earlier—' She can see the guards' faces now. Trent and Kasib. They look at her with perplexed expressions. 'Never mind,' Regan brushes her words away. Trent hands the keys to her; the guards step aside and Regan walks out. The guards begin making their way into the laboratory. Regan spins around, 'No, no, you two should get back to your shift,' and shows them away from the door.

'But, Your Majesty, we should—' Trent begins.

'I insist! All is in order here.' Again, the puzzled looks. Regan flicks the guards away with her hand. *Am I losing my mind?* she thinks. They begin leaving; Regan blurts to them, 'Just one more thing: did you see who locked it?'

They exchange a quick look, hesitate. 'We believe it was Ford, Your Highness.'

'I see,' Regan responds, 'and...has this happened before?' She feels naked asking this last question, like a little girl again. Now the guards look confused.

Kasib speaks, 'No, Your Majesty, you usually keep the keys yourself and lock it from the inside.'

A cold feeling scuttles up the back of Regan's neck. 'Of course, yes,' she says, scrambling for some composure. Again, she indicates for them to go. She doesn't have the stomach to disinter any more unattractive facts. She locks the laboratory door and makes her way back to the Chamber, stumbling a few times, dazed and disgusted. It feels to have been a lifetime since she was in the safety of her room. She requests a plate of food; eats it in her room at her writing desk. As hungry as she is, the act is more of putting food down her throat, than eating. The animal's eyes still shift before her, searching towards, then reverting away. Sitting wilted and ashen on her chaise longue, she asks for a bath to be drawn for her by one of her handmaids. The light gradually warms the room as the maid prepares the toilette. It is seldom that Regan will ask for help like this.

Finally, alone in her boudoir that smells so comfortingly female, she lowers herself into the bath. She holds back the sobs. Tears stream as she washes, dries, and enrobes herself. She leaves the curtains open, still hankering for sunlight after her murky night. She curls up under the covers, and, drifting now, feels herself floating somewhere near the captives again. This time, she reaches out and comforts them with her hand. The inside of the laboratory is light now and she senses someone behind her. She turns to look but, before she can tell who it is, heavy sleep envelops her and holds her in a cocoon of blank dreamlessness all day.

A Girl's Room

18/12/2050

The anticipation of meeting her daughter floods Regan as she wakes but unwanted questions mar her excitement. She requests Ford's presence as soon as she is up and dressed but, is told that he is on a scouting mission and will only be back the following afternoon. She shoves her concerns aside with effort and makes her way to her girlhood bedroom.

Even after all these years, it still has that smell. Regan goes to the dresser; all the crystal canisters still grouped prettily on it. Some of the containers are half-full, others lined with a residue. She picks one up, sniffs at it. The fragrance is deeper, sweeter but still present. Mixing perfumes had been one of her favourite pastimes as a girl—the one way in which she could practise chemistry skills before she was allowed to embark on medical concoctions. Although it was a frivolous endeavour compared with her mother's work, she could still pretend to be working with fluids and formulae and emulate the Dark Queen in her own, small way.

Regan decided it apt that this be the room she readies for Keesa, the only other one in the Chamber she left untouched after her parent's murder. She had stayed in it until age 16, when assigned her current bedchamber. Her mother had instructed her to keep it as was for her own daughter to use one day. At the time, Regan had allowed her ears to hear sentimentality; later she realised it was merely a ploy to encourage continuation of the Dark bloodline. She had ordered the room cleaned this morning, telling the servants that a young cousin of hers was coming to visit. She would have preferred to keep Keesa's arrival secret but is too concerned about the girl's security. She has already informed the Dark guards that, once the girl arrives, they are to consider her safety their top priority.

Stopover

The exhaustion has gone but her hip and cheekbones are aching from the hardness beneath them. A sound in the distance has a familiar ring to it, evokes the sense of a vast space. Keesa opens her eyes. A varnished, black stone floor. A wrought iron bench. The floor digs into her bones; she is lying on her side. The bagpipe skirl and merriment wafts about her, swelling and fading. Then the stroke of a bell, so loud it is as though it strikes her skull. The floor beneath her head shudders. She sits up. The clock tower. The procession. It sounds closer this time. Keesa scrambles to her feet. The dawn is further on than last time; she climbs onto the bench lining the east-facing side of the quadrant and leans over the edge of the railing, squinting through the dust and sun's rays to take in the moving crowd.

The procession is much closer. The celebrating people are still taken with their dancing and cries of delight. She can clearly make out the faces of the dignitaries but doesn't recognise any of them. And there she is again. The figure at the centre of it all, like an unmoving eye of a storm. The Queen. A crown encrusted with rubies and sapphires sits on her head. Her dark hair covers her ears and is swept back in a fetching, loose knot behind her head. Her burgundy lips are like earnest gems. Her expression is one of deep resolve, the acceptance of a weighty mantle of great consequence. It is her eyes that Keesa feels to know—green eyes that flash with power but also disclose sadness. The sun's rays from behind momentarily glint off something next to this Queen. Keesa rubs the swirling dust from her eyelashes, strains to make out the object. It is a cage of silver, shaped like a birdcage, only slightly bigger. Inside is a cat with red-brown fur and tufted ears. It seems to sense her gaze, and jerks its head in her direction. Even though it is a cat, she is certain she makes out its mouth forming the word 'Keesa' with disturbing urgency. Keesa's eyes trail to something hanging off the wrist of the Queen. She squints her eyes smaller, leans further over the railing. It is the pendant of Toekoums, its chain wrapped around her fair wrist to secure it. She takes in the Queen's face again. She recognises her. It is a grown version of herself.

Keesa wakes up. Brown blanket. Hard ground underneath pressing against her bones. Bird watching her. Eagle. She lifts her head; sits up in stages. Her right arm has gone dead; she is not used to sleeping on bare earth. She lets it rest on her crossed knee, waiting for the tingling to start. The sun is a way over the horizon; it must be around eleven in the morning. Despite the ascetic sleeping place, she can instantly feel that her energy has returned. The chair incident had left her sapped. She recalls being taken over by the orders in her bedroom in the Light Chamber. The memory is blurred, a bit like a dream had in the throes of a fever. She remembers waking up from it; knows she had somehow threatened Toekoums.

'Where are we?' her voice is parched. Valtere walks over, bends his upper body towards her, lifts his beak up and exposes the water sac hanging around his neck. Keesa removes the cap and takes a swig, her half-alive arm moving disobediently, like a baby's. Once she has quenched her thirst, the eagle steps back.

'I cannot disclose that. I had to stop to rest. We have some hours of travel left and then, you will be in a safe place.'

'Where are you taking me?'

'I am not at liberty to answer that.'

Keesa can feel that her powers have returned—even increased in strength, judging by the pulsation in the centre of her palms. She could decimate the eagle in a second, considers it for a moment. Valtere's head cocks back and his wings shoot outward at half-mast, readying himself for flight. He has sensed her intent. But where will it get her? They are in the middle of nowhere; at a glance, Keesa can see nothing but veldt and brush. She is not sure she would survive on her own, let alone find her way back to the Light Chamber.

'All right. Let's go then,' she says.

The eagle slowly relaxes his wings. 'You should eat something before we head off.'

He approaches her again, this time more gingerly, exposing a pouch strapped around his thigh. Keesa removes it, and begins wolfing down its contents: nuts, berries, a thick piece of rye bread cut in half and sandwiched together with butter. She pauses, slows her chewing down, offers Valtere the food in the pouch.

'I have eaten already, thank-you Keesa.' He knows her name. She resumes her devouring. Her appetite is massive.

'What's that around your neck?' Keesa is intrigued by the rock slung from a thick leather halter. She has never seen anything like it in all her expeditions in

189

the veldt. It seems to incorporate at least 10 different colours, with many facets that appear to have been lined up by a human hand.

'That is not your concern.'

Keesa thinks better of pushing the eagle with too many questions. She finishes off what's left in the pouch.

'Rest assured you will be given a tastier meal when we reach our destination.'

'This was fine.'

His eyes seem to smile at her. 'We should get going. Here, get into the blanket, and wrap yourself up in it with the ends pointing upwards.'

Keesa hesitates.

'It will not be so uncomfortable for you this way,' Valtere adds.

Keesa scratches the tips of her ears, they are itching again, gets onto her feet, and does as the eagle says. She first spreads the blanket out on the ground, then curls up in it, stretching her arms upwards with the ends of the blanket in her fists. Valtere spreads his wings, clasps the corners together in his claws and lifts off into the morning air. Keesa manages to peek over the edge of her brown hammock and watches the land sink lower and lower beneath them. She is struck by what a beautiful void the empty sky is. For now, she lets go of the Chamber of Light, of her parents, of the King who would be her teacher. She settles into her capsule, her little piece of neutrality, being winged into the unknown, where answers are promised her.

CHAPTER 21

A Bed Made

18/12/2050

Regan smoothes the sheets in Keesa's room down, sniffs their clean scent; it has traces of rosemary and orange. What if Keesa doesn't like the Dark Chamber? It is hardly the most attractive of abodes. Regan had ordered the clearing of the knotted growth over her bedroom windows a few months after her parent's deaths, to make her enclosed garden possible. She will do the same for the Princess suite but, for now, it is better that Keesa be kept well hidden.

Regan makes her way back to her room, checking the grandfather clock in the passage on her way. A quarter to two. The girl is close now, she senses. She is thankful that she managed to get some sleep the night before. Her body is straining from the past few days—an overload of information that has stunned her nervous system. She is coping on adrenalin, with exhaustion lying in wait beneath. She is concerned for Keesa's condition, given the unconventional journey here. Once in her bedroom, Regan chooses what she will wear for Keesa's arrival. She is clear about what she wishes to ask of Keesa yet, a pinching voice in her head questions her motives. A light-grey full-length dress of mottled yarn, laced with wine-red thread. She wants her daughter in her life; that is a certainty. However, will she ever escape her decision to order the infant's death? It may have spared her daughter a life of abuse at the hands of the Dark Court, yet, it nonetheless ensured her rise to the crown. Her cloak in charcoal with rosewood detail resting on her shoulders.

And now, is hauling the girl to her quarters again laden with incongruous motives? Regan slips into the elegant dress, adjusts it to hang in a becoming way. Yes, she wants to make up for her irredeemable choice all those years ago, by restoring the girl's royal status now. Yet, how much of this is to augment her own power as Queen of Night? Or her way of exacting revenge upon Maen for his latest rejection? Why should he draw the benefits from their child, when she was the one who brought her into the world?

She arranges the cloak around her shoulders, checks herself in the mirror, checks her nerves. She may be her mother but, she is also her Queen. Signa's callousness may have hurt Regan but her strength was a comfort and a safety to the young Princess. Despite the engineered warping of the Dark code by Signa and her forerunners, Keesa must know that she has a heritage, that there is great power in the Dark Force, and that it is her right to draw from it.

———•••———

She stands at the French doors. Saturated storm clouds are slowly blocking out the sun. Odd, thinks Regan but brushes it away. At last, Valtere sails in over the foliage-enveloped wall, with the priceless knapsack in his grip. Regan indicates to him to place it on the rug at the foot of her bed. As the eagle hovers, she gently cushions the landing of the blanket parcel with her hands. And there she is. The Queen can feel the hardness of little hips through the fleece. A shock of unexpected pleasure races through Regan's hands. She hears a reflex exclamation of fear from inside the folds. Regan strains to keep a grip on her queenly composure. Once the blanket is resting safely the floor, she takes the corners from Valtere's talons. The bird is relieved to go to his perch, rest his wings. He looks on, concerned to see the girl's condition.

Slowly, carefully, Regan lowers the corners of the blanket to the ground. Keesa sits hugging her bent knees. She looks up to take in the graceful woman before her. The girl's legs lift her from the ground; her face wincing with the pain of unfolding them. Despite her fear, her body knows what to do. She takes two steps forward, and curtseys before Regan, pausing with her head bowed. The Queen is taken by surprise; she didn't think the gestures would transfer to one who is not full-blood Dark. She touches the top of the girl's head. Keesa steps back. Regan is thrown to see what is clearly proof of the union between herself and the King of Day. She has her father's nose and jawbone but has her mother's eyes, only brighter and the shape of her lips, and dark, thick hair. Keesa's ears start itching again, keener than ever before. She gazes up at Regan, scratching the apex of her left ear, then her right. A startling rush of love courses through the Queen's chest.

'You have itchy ears?' Regan asks, a smile evaporating the anxiety from her face.

'Sometimes,' Keesa answers.

'I will see if I can find something to soothe it.' So much for her planned, formal introduction to the girl.

There is something about this woman's voice that puts Keesa at ease. 'Who are you?'

'I am Queen Regan of Night. Welcome to the Chamber of Dark, Keesa.'

'Thank-you.' Keesa surveys the room, the open doors and garden. 'It's not so dark.'

Regan laughs. 'My room has the most light.'

Valtere has not heard the sound of cheer in Regan's throat since she was a teenager. 'Forgive me, Your Majesty, but should I alert the guards?'

'Yes, Valtere, thank-you for bringing her here. Once you have relayed my instruction, you must replenish and rest.'

'Yes, Your Highness, just one last thing.' Valtere dips his head, allowing the amalgam to swing from side to side. Regan goes to him, and removes the rock necklace. The eagle takes off out the doors.

'Would you mind if I put this around your neck for while you are here?' Regan asks. The rock is a product of hours passed in the main laboratory. A great deal of trial and error resulted in her ability to chemically bond certain crystalline structures together. This particular combination serves to scramble a royal signal temporarily, as long as it is close to the particular royal—a useful tool for camouflage.

'What is it?'

'It will help protect you in the Chamber.'

'Protect me from what?'

'Let's just say it would be best if you wore it. All right?'

'You're the Queen. I should say yes.'

'Yes.'

Keesa bows her head and Regan drapes it around her neck. It doesn't hurt anyway, thinks Keesa.

'I hope the journey here was not too taxing for you; I'm afraid time did not allow for usual transport. There are not many subjects I would trust with your safety.'

'It was a bit uncomfortable but I slept for some of it.'

'Let me take you to your room. I'm sure you would like to get clean and have something to eat. Once you are more rested, I can tell you why I have brought you here.'

'My room? So you're not going to put me in a jail?'

Regan studies the girl's face. 'Things are not always as they seem, Keesa. And the Light royals are not always right.'

Keesa thought she would feel more scared of the Queen of Night. She certainly does not trust her yet but, for now, she feels out of harm's way. When they walk across the passage, however, a shadow seems to lurk behind them, even given the rayless light once they have left the Queen's bedroom. Keesa turns to look. The dimness discloses nothing.

The guards are stationed outside the door; Regan introduces them. As she ushers Keesa through to her chamber, she holds her hands a short distance away from the girl's shoulders; the Force flows from her hands. Before anyone around has had a chance to notice, the shield of invisibility is bolstered. Inside the girl's bedroom, three chambermaids stand in a row in front of what is meant to be a window. Any light from outside is crowded out by tortile branches. Quiet panic rises in Keesa's throat. The many candles in the room help though, and the crisp scent.

'Keesa, this is Sabrin, Alyx, and Clara. Ladies, assist Keesa with any need she may have and bring her to the ballroom within the hour.'

'Is there going to be a ball?' Keesa asks.

'No, that is where we will talk. If you require more time to rest, alert one of the chambermaids.'

Keesa notices that Regan's demeanour has hardened since they left her room. She speaks in a toneless voice that has cruelty in it by the mere fact of its indifference. Once the Queen has left the bedchamber, Keesa feels more alone than ever. The maids do not look her in the eyes, they seem unused to having charge of a little girl. They approach her cautiously, as though she might break or do

194

something alarming. Keesa constructs sentences to say to them in her head as they voicelessly show her where to undress, what to use in the bath. She takes a breath to speak on a few occasions but each time she can hear her words hanging like a duck among swans. She lets the breath out, unused.

Keesa has a plate of food and drink that have been set on a dwarfish table and chair against one wall. Her toes curl with the relief of consuming meat, vegetables and potatoes, all prepared with care. The crystal glass holds fresh orange juice—a treat in these parts. Furniture and objects in the room show the mark of wealth. Two delicate bedside lamps, comprising a candle encircled by violet agate beads. A black, lacquered dressing table inlaid with jasper. She is shown behind a screen, hand-painted with thick oil paints and undresses, her clothes whipped away by waiting hands curling around its side. The bathtub is made of pure black onyx. Immersing herself in the water is like being swallowed by a wave of night sky. She traces her hand over the pitch curves, enjoying the comfort of nothingness it evokes. But soaping her body in the bath on her own makes her miss Toekoums.

Afterwards, Alyx holds a simple nightdress out for Keesa to slip into. Keesa eyes the vials on the dresser as she is having her hair brushed by Clara. She is craving to sniff each one individually but is too shy to perform such a sensory act in front of the robotic handmaidens. Alyx turns down the sheets of the inviting bed. Keesa would rather not sleep but, her mind is feeling woozy with all the newness and travelling. She climbs in.

'We will wake you in just under an hour, your Ladyship.'

Ladyship? Keesa is already descending into dreams. A picture from one of the old books Aedan used to read to her surfaces. An old wooden schooner with an emblematic woman carved and painted at its helm. Then she is out.

The short sleep has done Keesa good; she feels her power vigorous again. Sabrin does the buttons up at the back of the dress readied for her, the clean cotton agreeable against her skin. It hangs from a yoke to just below her knees, its colour Italian rose, the borders stitched with black thread. She steps into a pair of black satin pumps with velvet trimmings. Sabrin stands behind Keesa as she inspects her image in the mirror and gives one approving nod, devoid of warmth. It pleases Keesa to receive this acknowledgement. She likes herself in the dress; the colours suit her.

Bats

18/12/2050

Regan requests that one of the guards outside the ballroom door fetch her dagger from the arms room. She knows that Maen is likely on his way now with his guards. She must equip herself for any eventuality. She places it behind a large vase on the refreshment table. There is a knock at the door.

'Enter,' Regan bids.

Sabrin comes in, 'Lady Keesa, Your Highness.' She stands aside. Keesa enters and pauses.

'That will be all, thank-you,' Regan directs; the three in attendance retract, closing the door.

'The dress fits perfectly. You look very pretty,' Regan remarks.

'Thank-you, Your Majesty.'

'It used to be mine.'

Keesa's eyes alternate between Regan's commanding figure and the expanse of the room. Her gaze keeps getting drawn back to the four huge candle-chandeliers, with their smoky quartz crystal tears hanging, lit from above by the throng of flames. The ceiling is a glossy black.

'Beautiful, aren't they? Come, let us sit.' Regan holds out her hand. Keesa steps forward and, a little warily, places her hand in the Queen's. Regan feels a humming in the girl's palms. The two of them eye each other but hold their grasp. Regan leads them to a couch covered in light grey silk, a few simple cushions scattered on it. Keesa sits close to one of its arms, on the edge, as though sitting on a fence. Regan feels all the words she will have to say to her looming in her mouth, like a horde of runaway bats.

'Can I get you something to drink?'

'No, thank-you.'

Regan rises again. This is harder than she thought.

'Keesa, there is something you should know.' She stops her pacing and looks directly at Keesa. 'Your parents are not your real parents.'

'I know.'

Regan lets out her breath. One step. Worst still to come. 'I see.'

She goes to sit on the couch, paling.

'Keesa, what I'm going to tell you now...' Regan trails off. There is no satisfactory prelude for what she has to say. She faces the girl, reaches her hand towards Keesa's small one, stops herself, lays it on the silk between them. Keesa looks at her uneasily. She notices a necklace Regan is wearing, a simple red stone strung on a strip of dark leather. Funny for a Queen, she thinks. Regan locks the girl's eyes.

'I am your Mother, Keesa.'

The words she has said, the sound of her voice and the deep green of her eyes cohere for Keesa. It shouldn't but it makes uncanny sense. Yet this is the Queen of Night. Everything Keesa has been told demands that she not trust her.

'Why didn't you keep me?'

'It was complicated. If I had kept you, you would have been killed, or worse. We both would have lived a life of torture. My mother would have made sure of that.'

'Why?'

Regan draws a breath, lets it out. All these leaps. She is patently aware that what she says now could destroy her stature and endanger her life, not to mention Keesa's.

'Because of who your father is.'

'Who is he?'

'King Maen of Day.'

And there it is again. Sounds that fit. Everything adds up in an instant. The inexplicable longing. The sense of difference between her and Aedan, as if she was always a few steps too far from her. The pieces of the jigsaw click together. Keesa nods. Known facts and an uncertain future pull at each other in her. A wave of excitement, an undertow of mistrust. Her palms are throbbing now.

'So am I Dark and Light at the same time?'

'Yes, Keesa, you are a halfling. But, as far as I am concerned, you are no less a Princess.'

A Princess. Keesa thinks of the ladies in the books with golden hair and white dresses, getting into coaches to go to balls. She thinks of her hand clasping a knife, digging at the flesh of a struggling animal, of her lungs thrusting out heat, of the sizzling remains of baboons. She looks around the unfilled ballroom now, its windows crowded in by the darkness of overgrowth.

'But which Chamber do I belong to?'

'That will be for you to decide.'

'Why didn't King Maen say anything?'

'I'm afraid he doesn't know.'

Their talk continues; disclosures made. Regan's mind is whirring now. How could Valtere not have picked up who her adoptive father is? A shield. Maen had once said, Colter had a knack with creating potent shields. The younger Prince had been kept well hidden in the Light Chamber. Valtere had never seen him. She can't decide whether this information counts in her favour or not.

Regan tells of her marriage proposals to Maen. There is resolve in the Queen's voice. The girl can hear she has groped her way through to it. But pulses of something else escape from her eyes, from the way she pushes her bottom lip out slightly and tucks the top one in.

'You realise that it is against Dark Law for me to love anyone?' Regan points out.

'Yes, Queen Elke told me about some of your rules.'

'You have met Queen Elke?'

Keesa nods. Maen has not wasted any time, thinks Regan. They must have lofty plans for her.

'So, after Queen Signa was dead, why didn't you come get me?'

The question that Regan does not want to hear. The answer wedges in her throat.

'I couldn't pick up your identity. I had placed a shield of invisibility around you before I gave you to Valtere to take away. And I didn't come and get you because I thought that you were dead. I had ordered my eagle to kill you.'

Keesa flinches. Regan's words hit something lodged in her that feels like black sludge, a sticky sadness she has carried around but never understood, ever since she can remember. She doesn't want it dredging up now. She looks down at her hands.

'Why didn't you just give me away?'

'I knew that as you grew, you would start doing things that didn't make sense to you, which felt as if it wasn't really you doing them.'

'You mean like bad things?'

'Yes. Our Dark ancestors can control us if they want to. I was afraid of what you might be forced to do.' Regan notices Keesa's cheeks have turned red and her face has become stoic. 'Do you have any knowledge of what I'm talking about?'

'A bit,' Keesa folds her arms into her middle, covering her hands. 'Why couldn't you run away with me?'

'A part of me wanted nothing more than to flee with you but, I was Princess of Night. I was the only one who could take over the Dark throne when required. I could not turn my back on my family, on the Dark Force. I did what I thought was my duty. That doesn't mean I didn't hate myself every day for the decision. I'm not sure it's possible to ever get past a regret like that. It just becomes a part of you.'

'Why didn't your eagle kill me?'

'He thought I might later regret the command. He was right.'

'He's a kind bird.'

Keesa looks up at the chandeliers illuminating the room, the flames now wavering, now still.

'I'm afraid that I'm going to lose you again, Keesa. Last time it was to my mother and her Dark vision. And to my Queenhood. This time it will be to Maen and the Light Chamber.'

The girl's eyes trail to the collection of musical instruments in the far corner of the room. A harp, triangles suspended from a wrought-iron holding rod, a mahogany grand piano, a cello, and a cluster of brass.

'I know that what I have told you cannot be easy to have heard. Are you all right?' Regan enquires. An embedded voice in Keesa says *Turn your back on her the way she did you.*

'Do you wish I was dead?' Keesa asks.

Regan kneels before her daughter, takes her young hands in hers. Her small fingers are cold but the palms are warm as embers.

'Keesa, I never wished you dead. I loved you from the moment I felt you inside me. I hate that I have lost all those years with you. My greatest wish now is to be a mother to you, if you will allow me.'

Suddenly, Keesa feels tired again. All these adults with their bad deeds, regrets and hearts that open and close like rules adhered to on the surface, but broken beneath.

'Everyone at the Light Chamber told me to be careful of you. You didn't want me before; now you say you do. King Maen wants me at the Chamber and Colter wants to take me back to Hale. I don't even know if you will let me leave the Dark Chamber. I'm just a girl. I can't answer you.'

Even as Keesa says these words, the comfort of Regan's hands around hers feels right, in a way that is indifferent to words of warning, or to past acts. Regan pulls back, stands up. As much as she might have wanted a different response, she is impressed by the girl's ability to detach.

'Of course; I understand. You have had to absorb a great deal recently. How about we stop talking about all this for a while. Do you need to rest again?'

'No. Could I maybe look at those music things though?'

Regan follows Keesa's eyes to the corner of instruments. An image from when she was 15 flies into her head. Maen giving her a disc of music and instructing her about which album to listen to first, what mood to be in for which artist.

'Of course you can. And how about some tea?'

'Yes please.'

Keesa makes her way over to the small orchestra area. Regan watches her. She senses the girl has stifled a reaction to the fact of her beginnings. Everything in its time. For now, tea, and something tasty to fortify her daughter. Regan goes to the kitchen to choose the best accompaniment, nodding to the guards outside the ballroom door as she does. The simple act of preparing a tray for Keesa fills Regan with such contentment that she has trouble containing the smile that threatens to break on her face. When she reenters the ballroom carrying the small spread, she is struck by Keesa's slight figure quietly absorbed in striking the triangles, exacting a set of three tings, the notes unadorned and clearing. It is like watching herself at that age mixing her perfumes, the scents rising unambiguous into the air. More hurdles lie ahead and some hang, partially undraped but, for now, to Regan, this moment is a good one.

CHAPTER 22

A Princess's Birthday

07/08/2034

He is 20 minutes late. Regan is not the most patient of girls. When she sees the dust being beaten up by the hooves of his horse though, her annoyance lifts. It is one day each fortnight she always looks forward to.

'You're late,' says Valtere as Prince Maen dismounts.

'I had to find a suitable moment to leave,' the Prince-cub apologises.

'Yes, I'm sure you did.' Maen is convinced the eagle cocks his feathery eyebrow. Valtere always finds some way of expressing his objection to their friendship, even after eight years of their meetings. The bird flaps a short distance away to keep lookout from the top of a koppie. Maen removes a carrier bag from the saddle, and ties the horse loosely to a tree, giving it some water. He walks to the Princess. She stands with her hands clasped behind her back, looking fair in her smock of grey and pillar-box red. Her face has that usual unswerving look about it, but he can see that her lips are hinting upwards.

'Happy 13th birthday, Princess Regan,' he says, and takes something small from his bag. Regan is surprised. For the first time, he has wrapped her present—awkwardly, in a sheet of gold-coloured writing paper. The gift is a small, rough ruby slung onto a soft strip of leather. She holds it between her fingers, allowing the paper to waft to the ground, her face suddenly solemn.

'You don't like it,' Maen says, his face dropping.

Regan looks at him with newness. 'I love it,' she says, 'Can you tie it for me?'

Maen does so, noticing that the milky back of her neck gives off a smell like freesias as she pulls her hair off it. 'There's a whole cupboard full of jewels at the Chamber. It was one of the only things I could find that was a colour you like. Most of the other things are blue and gold.'

'You stole from the Light Chamber for me? That's so cool, Maen. You broke the rules!'

'Not really stole; the jewels in that cupboard are for me. There, it's tied.' She turns around. 'It suits you.'

'Boys wear jewels like this in your family?'

'No, they're supposed to be for my wife one day.'

Regan looks at him again with that look he's never seen from her before.

'But it's no big deal, just a little stone.'

'Oh, of course, no big deal,' Regan returns with studied casualness, blushing nonetheless. 'Thanks for my present, Maen.'

'It's my pleasure, birthday girl.' With that, Maen goes to hug her. Regan takes a step back, unused to accepting physical affection.

Maen draws back, his tail whips. 'Since I'm learning about breaking rules from you, I think it's time you learnt how to hug. You're meant to open your arms, and then put them around me as well.'

'Why?'

'Because it feels nice.'

'I'm not supposed to.'

'It is considered courteous to return the gesture of a Prince.'

There is something about his sanctioning royal law that makes her feel safe. Despite the fact that that she often balks at it, royal law has infused her life, like an ever-present scaffold that holds everything else in. She tentatively lifts her arms and opens them like a girl at her first ballet lesson learning first and second positions. Maen smiles, makes an effort to stop himself from laughing. Her face is stern; she looks a little like a frightened animal. He senses that any sudden moves or bursts of laughter will shatter her trust. He moves forward again, and places his hands around her waist. Regan cautiously allows him to hug her, awkwardly returning it, not knowing quite where to place her arms. She likes it. She is aware of his heart close to hers; both are beating rapidly. His furry ears pressing against hers. It is as though some incalculable need in her is being answered. She pulls away gently, knows she must break this thing that feels too pleasurable.

'Did you bring it?' she asks.

'Of course I did.'

'Oh, exciting!'

Regan lays her cloak down on the sand, swishing her hands across her cheeks every now and then, as though that will take the heat away. Maen takes an old laptop computer out of the bag, sets it down on the fabric, and starts it up.

'How long do we have?' he asks.

'I told my driver that he is to wait until signalled by Valtere to come fetch me, or I would tell my Mother that he kidnapped me for the afternoon.'

'I don't like it when you do that.'

'Would you rather I didn't come?'

'No, of course not.'

'Anyway, we'll have our own cars sometime, then we won't have to rely on the Guards to get us here.'

Maen has an arrangement with two of his closest guards who have family in the area to drive him to the nearby town, Willowmore, on these occasions. They always transport a Chamber horse with them, which he then rides to meet Regan, while the guards do their visiting. The Lion of Light has always been in favour of his boys getting horseback experience. Maen has told the guards that he uses these rides for development of certain aspects of his powers, and that they are never to be spoken of to anyone.

204

Regan spreads the cloak as wide as possible. 'I wish you could see what it's like to watch a movie in a cinema,' Maen says, hitching his cloak onto the branches of the tree to shade the screen better.

'How many times did you go again?'

'Only twice, with my mom. But that was long ago. We'll never be allowed that again.'

'You're lucky you can at least watch movies now and then, though. Let's go to the city again sometime; we can go to the cinema together.'

'It's too risky. You know that. And after last time—'

'But we'll be more careful this time!'

'Regan, we have an obligation to our families to keep ourselves hidden. If something were to happen to you I would never forgive myself.'

'You wouldn't have to. You'd be dead. My Mom would see to that.'

Maen freezes, shoots Regan a deadpan look. 'I'm joking! Geez, you're so serious.' Maen checks the position of the shade-patch. 'Anyway, you could do your magic thing and save me.'

'My powers should not be treated lightly like a toy gun. That's what my Dad says.'

'Oh all right, Your Highness, we'll NEVER go to the city, we'll NEVER go to the cinema,' Regan uses sweeping gestures of obeisance for dramatic effect. 'Okay, now, boy-cub, can we please watch?'

They settle down on her cloak in the shade of the low tree, both lying on their fronts, with the computer propped before them. The edifying music that accompanies the titles is something that Regan has only heard about from Maen; he punctuates the surges in the theme with his hands like a conductor. He remembers seeing it once when he was a child; one of the Chamber worker boys had a badly damaged copy that he showed on the school DVD player. Maen had managed recently to convince one of the scouts to buy him this copy of *Star Wars, Episode IV: A New Hope* at a second-hand store in Port Elizabeth. Their time together, as always, goes too quickly.

---•••---

Valtere wings back as the sky is golding towards sunset. 'We must return to the Dark Chamber now; your mother will be finished her work for the day soon.'

'You mean Darth Vader?' Regan says with a straight face, looks at Maen, the two of them laugh.

'I beg your pardon?' The young royals are still chuckling.

'You should know by now, Princess, that your mother is not one to joke about. You need to gather yourself for the return.'

Regan's ebullience stops short. 'Valtere, I will have you know that I am the one who gives the orders here. I should mete out punishment for your insubordination.'

'Perhaps a wiser route would be to show Valtere respect, given that he has your safety in mind, and that he will be with you for the rest of your life,' Maen points out to the Princess.

'He's not supposed to be my friend; he is supposed to do as he is told.'

Maen turns to Regan; she is surprised to see anger in his face. 'Regan! Someone does not have to be your friend in order for you to treat them with kindness and respect. You act like this is all just a game, and you are playing the Dark Princess. Do you really want to copy your mother's ways?'

'My mother is a very clever woman who works hard for me and my family.'

'I have no doubt that she is clever. What is it that she is working so hard at?'

Valtere flaps his wings pointedly. The royals rein themselves in.

Maen speaks again, his eyes to the ground. 'I apologise. You don't need to answer that question.'

'Yes. Maybe it's better if we don't talk about those things.'

Regan addresses her eagle, 'Thank-you Valtere, you may fetch the driver now, I will wait here.'

206

The bird gives a quick bow with his head, then directs words to Maen, 'Please ensure you make your way within the minute, Prince Maen. Farewell.' The prince notices a lessening in the eagle's acerbity when addressing him. They watch as he swoops across the section of veldt enclosed on all sides by koppies that has come to feel like their personal territory. Regan's chest has gone tight. She traces her shoe through the sand.

'I didn't mean to spoil your birthday, Regan.'

'You made it happy. Maybe I shouldn't be so mean to Valtere. The game is all I've got in the Chamber. You know we're taught not to have friends.'

'I'm your friend. You could give some of what I say a try, and see what happens.'

'Yes.'

'Just be careful not to show it in the Chamber.'

'I know.'

'May the Force be with you, Princess.'

Regan smiles, 'Which one?'

Maen smiles back, kisses her hand. The sound of hooves galloping away has become coupled for her with a sliding down. Time slows. The sound of birds tweeting seems indifferent, whereas on the journey here their song bursts seemed to spur her life on. All of this, she knows, she ought not to feel. She draws a breath, closes her eyes, and begins the routine of cooling the fervour. She lifts her cloak, shakes off the orange dust. The car approaches. She blunts her face, gets in, orders the driver to take her home. As the car winds through the rough ribbons of road, she thinks of what he said, and wonders how long they can play their game.

Inheritance

18/12/2050

Regan sits with Keesa on the piano stool. Keesa faces the rows of sounds, black lifting over cream, pressing softly on individual keys.

'So, can normal people be ordered?'

'No, the deceased Dark spirits can only order their direct offspring. What things do you remember from it?'

The girl gets up, goes over to the harp, runs her hand down its glossy, black arch, paint peeling off in places to reveal cherry wood beneath. 'Like what you were talking about—bad things.' A veil of strings separates her and Regan now. 'You're going to be cross with me.' She plucks a string.

The Queen rises, moves to peek around the instrument.

'You don't have to be afraid of telling me those things, Keesa. I'm not going to be cross. You already know that I have done bad things too.'

Keesa looks at Regan. 'I did awful things to animals. I cut them open. They were alive. She told me to get their heart so that I could see, so that she could begin to teach me.'

'Do you know who she is?'

'She's tall, she's got short grey hair and blue eyes, and she's a surgeon.'

Regan's skin begins to crawl. 'This is what I was afraid of.'

'It's your mother, isn't it?'

Regan leans against the piano. 'It certainly sounds like it.' She glances around the room, despite the fact that she wouldn't see the dead Queen if she were there. Signa would very much like to be in on this conversation.

'Keesa, it seems that your Dark powers have elements of both my and my mother's talents. I have never heard of their expression at age 10. Sixteen is when it normally begins.'

What mother am I? she considers. *What poisoned gifts have I brought this child into the world with?* That same shadow that prowled in the passage earlier feels to be hovering close by Keesa once more. She snatches a look behind her: nothing again. She turns back to the Queen, who is real, who knows what she has done, recognises it, and allows it. Regan holds out her arms to Keesa, 'Don't be scared, you'll see, we can make it stop. I believe I know a way.'

She runs quickly on her tiptoes to the Queen, and curls up on her skirt, head in her lap. As soon as she is there, the shadow seems to withdraw. Keesa could swear she senses a gust of indignation, and perhaps jealousy as it departs. Regan folds her arms around the girl.

'If you like, I can coach you on how to have the visions without having to cut animals—ones that don't have my mother in them.'

Keesa looks up to her face and nods. 'That would be great.' She buries her head in Regan's warm belly again.

The Queen's hand finds the girl's back, and pats it, rocking her gently. Never has she felt so grateful to have hands and a voice that can soothe. 'There now', she says, 'there now.'

CHAPTER 23

Breakout

03/07/2038

They take turns driving so each has a chance to take catnaps in between. Time is tight. This is Regan's first road trip; Maen tries to time his shifts so that she gets to stare out the window at distinct sights. Regan hungrily digests the open expanse around the zooming car. She has taken short excursions with Maen to the nearest city a few times in the past, but nothing like this. Port Elizabeth is not the most appealing of cities; it has become a functional centre, no more. Regan exacts equal pleasure from stealing sideways glances at Maen as he drives, as she does taking in fantastic jutting rocks and hazy skylines. To be in a car with a boy, this boy, distance widening between the Dark Chamber and herself and music gliding into the cocoon they're in.

This breakout took a great deal of planning. It was timed to coincide with the annual assemblies of both Chambers, when both sets of parents would be away for a period of two days. Traditionally, the assemblies of the Light and Dark Chambers occurred simultaneously but in different places, so as to prevent the use of ambush tactics by one Chamber upon another during their sittings. Despite the increase in violations of rules of engagement between the houses over the last few decades, this aspect of the code is still upheld. The paradox of selective application of royal code has become accepted and expected. It is only the older guardians of each Force that decry the oscillation between respect for and flouting of these laws.

Today's destination for the two young royals is Cape Town. Even though it is far, Regan has heard so much about it from Maen that she has chosen it for this infrequent opportunity. They drive in Maen's new car, a four-wheel-drive—an early gift for his upcoming 18th birthday in December. Regan's 17th birthday approaches in August; she has been promised a car early next year. It has gradually become customary for young royals to master driving and acquire personal vehicles earlier than is normal. More than anything, this is for security purposes; they need to be able to exit areas quickly and independently should the worst-case scenario arise.

It suits them that their trip is during the winter months. The city is always that much quieter; they can move around unnoticed more easily. Maen has begun cropping his hair short. This helps with his wearing of caps to cover up his lion ears and the loose-fitting jeans he wears are perfect for keeping his lion tail tucked down into one of the legs. Hoodies and sunglasses serve both royals as camouflage wear. It takes them six hours to get to Cape Town.

They drive along a rugged stretch of coastal mountain with a near-sheer drop into the ocean. It is about four in the afternoon and they are fortunate, the sun has come out after hiding behind wispy clouds for the last hour's driving. The winter rays slant gently into the car; Regan hugs her knees to her chest, curls her toes in the sunny patch on the edge of the seat. Maen casts glances at her staring out to sea as he winds his way around the bends. She has that look of someone who is close to the end of a car trip. There is a certain repose that one is lulled into. He is seeing her in moods he has never witnessed her in before. He can feel something deepening inside him, something he would normally arrest. His resolve is down; it is as though the space between them is starting to blur.

The car descends a winding hill. The few people they see walk slowly, the better to soak up this bit of winter sun. A man walking a dog. A boy and girl a bit younger than Maen and Regan, each carrying a surfboard, their hair plastered wet in random patterns on their heads, their eyes red from the water. Maen parks in the almost empty parking lot. Down and up more paths, tarred and then sand. Over a set of giant granite boulders. And there it is. The place he wants to show her. A strip of beach cut off from the main beach alongside it by towering granite rock spheres. A gossamer spray of sea air effuses the shore. It could be the end of the world. A little piece of Eden, shimmering like a forgotten afterthought in the crassness of the planet. Regan has only once before seen a piece of sea as magnificent as this, in a vision. In it, the marine-scape might have been breathtaking, but the action was ugly. No matter, thinks Regan, her grandmother told her that the visions aren't necessarily the future. They make their way down to the powdery sand. Maen's feet feel as though they are home.

Regan skips ahead of him, 'It's the ocean! It's the ocean!'

He loves it when she becomes like a little girl again. She runs to a section of sand right at the end of the beach, not visible to any of the houses built up against the mountain. She tells him to turn around and quickly changes into a swimming costume. It hadn't been easy to acquire; one of her handmaidens found it for her in a store in Despatch on a recent buying trip. Given the strong association between the Light Family and the ocean, no Dark royal is encouraged to experience it, except for the purposes of gathering ammunition to use against the Light Chamber. The costume is a bikini, black with gold trim. Maen has changed into surfing trunks.

'You can turn around now!' Regan shouts. With that, she runs into the water and leaps into the oncoming waves, screeching as she resurfaces. The icy temperature jolting her system, combined with the sense of entering taboo territory is exhilarating. Her feet find the sand-bed and she stands knee-deep in the water, determined to stay in a bit longer. She turns to see Maen, his top off now, standing on the shore watching her. It is the first time they are seeing this much of each other's flesh. With his royal training, Maen cuts a strapping form. Regan is struck by his manly shoulders; he no longer looks like a boy. His chest is strong and square and carries his heart with courage. Her knees go weak; a wave knocks her from behind, she almost loses her balance. She digs her feet into the soft-course muddiness beneath and holds her ground, wiping wet strands of hair and salt water from her eyes. Maen takes in her quick recovery. Seeing the black costume clinging to her milky skin is all but stopping his heart. Her hair when wet appears ebony and, even from this distance, he can see her eyes have gone as bright as malachite from the innervating water. She has a body like a dancer's, strong and defined, softened by the fetching curves of her hips, her breasts.

He goes in after her, even though the feline in him starts a little at the water. They dive in and out of the waves a few minutes more. She touches his lion ears, curious of their texture when soaked. His hands find her waist under the water. Her hands drop to his shoulders, her lips part. He sees the darkness returning to her eyes. He starts pulling her closer to him. The water surrounding them begins churning, inexplicable, choppy waves. They both register the disturbance in the water. Regan wriggles out of his arms suddenly and starts wading back to shore. They towel off and sit on the sand in their little corner of the beach, watching the sunset.

'So…how many candidates have visited you lately?' Maen tries to make this sound like small talk.

'I think four since I last saw you.'

'Four?'

Regan observes the flash in his eyes, which he promptly covers, his jaw jutting slightly forward.

'My mother threw a dinner party and invited them all at once. I can see they all irritate her though. Actually, I think she would rather someone else be the one plying me with them. But she knows it has to happen. She doesn't like that stuff, though.'

'And you?'

'What?'

'Did they irritate you?'

'Some of them.'

'And the others?'

'Mm, not sure.'

'So you liked them?'

'They're okay. I'm not supposed to feel for them. Just choose one.'

'What do you mean? You're not meant to feel something, even for your future husband?'

'No.'

Maen goes quiet; his ears flat against his head.

'And you? How many have you seen since I last saw you?' the Princess asks.

'Two.'

'What were they like?'

'Like a lot of the other Light royal candidates.'

'What's that like?'

'Very well-mannered.'

'What else?'

'Serious.'

'Yes, I think that's a general royalty thing. So, do you like any of them?'

'Not rea—' Maen looks at Regan, 'Not sure.'

She pulls her upper lip in, pouts the bottom one out, smooths the sand next to her with her hand to form a palette.

'Are you supposed to feel something for the one you choose?' she asks, focusing on the shapes she is indenting with her finger.

'The rule is that I can only marry a candidate I love.'

Regan keeps her eyes on her sand etching. Maen looks at her. Her face has gone steely. She lifts her eyes to the horizon, Maen follows her gaze. The sun is a shimmering semicircle now. The orange exuding from it into the clear strip of sky above is so rich it is more like a movement than a colour, billowing out onto the cloud bank above, turning it deep ochre, lifting pink.

'Have you been working on your visions?' Maen thinks a change of topic is needed.

Regan nods. 'I'm getting stronger at them.'

'What have you seen?'

'I'm not at liberty to talk about them.'

'Of course. Is that what your mother told you to say?'

'Yes. To my chambermaids. They get curious.' She rubs out her drawing, suspends her finger over the new palette. It's a pleasant sensation—this being able to rub out what is there, start again. 'But maybe it's okay if I just tell you one. I saw you and your family.' Maen's ears prick upright. 'You were eating together—looked like breakfast. The light was jumpy, as if it was coming off the sea. You, your brother and your Dad were laughing about something—I think the food your Mom had given you? She looked sulky but I could see she was smiling a bit too. Then she said something about thanking her later when you don't die of heart attacks. Then Colter said no, instead you'd all die nauseous. Then you all laughed harder and Colter fell off his chair. It looked happy.'

Maen is staring at her now, the spine of his mane-hair standing up. Regan takes in the last sliver of sun slipping below the edge of the planet; the soft peal of the waves seeming to report it. The end of today.

'You have times like that with your parents, right?' Maen asks.

'Sometimes.'

He watches her pursing her lips. 'We should get going. Don't want to miss the beginning of the movie,' he says.

Regan puts a smile on and nods at him. He can see her eyes have gone misty, though. They resume their everyday disguises, gather their things and make their way back up the boulders. Maen hears a sound. Water being thrust out of a blowhole. A whale is trying to attract his attention. He turns; Regan is a little way ahead, she has not noticed. He takes in the mammoth tail flipping out of the dusky pink liquid. His instinct is to salute the guardian and go back to the water's edge. He pulls his hood lower over his forehead, turns and walks towards the Princess, stifling the unwholesome sense of treachery in his stomach. Another blast of water, this time fainter. He clenches his fists, rides the surprise of betrayal. He hopes that Regan's identity shield is strong enough. What happened in the water can sometimes affect the cohesion of his shield. If it weren't for that, the whale would never have picked up his signal. *Should have renewed it immediately after. Forgot. Wasn't thinking. That won't do*, he tells himself. *Now, of all times*. He reinforces it as they walk back to the parking lot.

The car has trapped the warmth of the sun, comforting after the beach that had cooled rapidly once it disappeared. Regan gets in first, watches the gloaming parking lot for people while Maen dusts the sand off his feet before climbing in. He closes his door, adjusts the mirror slightly, places the keys in the ignition. Regan speaks. Her voice is matter-of-fact, as it often is, but Maen hears a tone of disquiet in it that he has not heard before.

'Watching your family is like watching a movie. No, we don't have times like that. I avoid so much as laughing in my mother's presence. It would only be followed by questions.'

Maen takes his hand slowly off the ignition. The difference between their worlds is something they skate over too easily, and too often. It disarms their delusion, their playing at being two ordinary friends.

'Everything will be all right, Regan. You'll see.'

Hope surges in Regan's chest at the Prince speaking those words to her, yet her mother's voice scratches into her head, *We'll see*.

'Yes, everything will be all right...because we're getting to see *Terminator 2* at last!' Regan throws out. She smiles at Maen. There she is, like the skipping girl again. He smiles back but, he can see the raw fissure beneath. He starts the car and they make their way back up the now darkening hill.

The cinema they go to is old and somewhat run-down. Re-runs of classic movies are shown here every Wednesday. The two swallow the film in readily, starved as they are of the medium in its bigness. Later that night, Maen parks the car in an area that is not too built up, one he knows is safe. He chooses a cul-de-sac at the very top of a suburb close to town, which clads up the foot of the mountain. They use the back of his four-wheel-drive as a bed. They sleep in fits and starts, both concerned about security. They set out before sunrise the next day. As they drive, the morning develops blue skies, with a chill in the air. Their mood is at first subdued, the gravity of returning home from their little adventure weighing them down. But as they press on and, especially after a roadhouse breakfast with strong coffee, levity is kicked back into life.

With about two hours left before Regan's drop-off point, they stop for a short break to stretch their legs. Regan is sure Valtere must be anxious, even though she has arranged to meet him at the drop-off location where he will have her driver nearby, at the ready but out of sight. Regan is restless from confinement in the car and practises some court dancing on the gravel by the deserted road. Her formal dance lessons are some of her favourite times in the week. She is wearing a short denim skirt—something she would never dare at the Chamber and is basking in the freedom of flicking her legs this way and that, unhindered by a long, heavy skirt. Maen is finding it difficult to take his eyes off her thighs, her calves. Then she breaks out into dancing that she's seen the other girls doing illegally. Even though she is green at it, she is gifted with grace and rhythm and

216

makes a rousing picture. Maen's tail whips as he watches her from behind. Her hips swaying from side to side.

'Regan,' he says.

She keeps dancing with her back to him, saying in time with her steps, 'Yes, my Lord?'

He lunges in, grabbing her slim waist, spins her round and pulls her into his torso. She is taken off-guard. He looks into her eyes with a wildness she has never seen in him before. She can see his hunger; his eyes are blazing with it. Her lips part like velvet petals and, in her eyes, he sees her yield to him. They grow dark-green, almost black. It feels as though she could draw him into another time with them. He kisses her, hard and searing. She surrenders, then returns it, consumed. The ground beneath their feet tremors.

They pull their heads back. She says, 'We shouldn't be—'

'I know.' He breaks away from her abruptly.

'That's not what I—'

'We'd better get going; I don't want you to be late.'

He quickly makes his way back to the car, leaving her standing flustered for a moment. She smoothes her hair down, pulls her skirt as low as it can go and returns to her seat. On the way home, the conversation has dried. Suddenly they are on new territory so forbidden it is unfathomable. He drives. He has not so much as glanced at her since they left their stopping place.

'Was I the first boy to kiss you?' he asks suddenly.

She looks at him, his majestic profile. 'Yes,' she replies.

'Good,' he says, 'that's how it should be.'

She wants to ask what he means but his intensity is scaring her a little. She knows what can happen if his powers are unleashed.

'Was I yours?' she enquires instead.

'No,' he says. Regan's stomach seizes. She looks back at the road flying, flying towards her. 'I practised on a few of the court girls.'

'Practised? For what?'

'For you.'

Regan looks at him again. He keeps his eyes on the road. A hot bliss floods through her. She bites her lip, smiling.

That would not be the last time they kissed. After their road trip, their meetings became increasingly private and were moved to the site of the clay cube in a deserted piece of veldt close to Willowmore, where they could craft an unviewable space for themselves by throwing cloaks and cloth over the pillars. Maen would learn to stem his powers during their trysts so as not to leak into his desire for Regan. Valtere grew progressively concerned. Where most of the questions he would previously put to Regan would be answered, now they were met with silence, deep as a black river.

Tea and an Answer

18/12/2050

Regan grabs some fruit from the bowl on the kitchen table and makes her way back to the ballroom with a fresh pot of tea. She pours out two cups, places the tray on the low table next to the couch. She arranges the angora throws to make it cosier.

'Thank-you,' Keesa says as Regan hands her a cup.

'A pleasure.' Regan doubts that Keesa knows what this simple show of appreciation means to her. Every moment like this increases her yearning to rise to being a mother to her child. That dream is feeling closer, yet skittish. The girl watches the steam rising off her cup, her mind methodically turning over pebbles of new information, picking them up to look closer.

'So you're a doctor and you have visions but, don't you have a power to use like if someone's attacking you?'

'If I charge a knife with a particular intention and aim it at a living thing, it becomes what we call a scythe. If aimed at a Light royal, it will obstruct their powers. If I kill someone with it, it not only takes their earthly life-force but also splinters their soul into oblivion. They will never be able to reincarnate again, anywhere or any time.'

'My da—I mean, Prince Colter told me that when you die, there's nothing. You just go away.'

'Perhaps that's what he needs to believe. People have their reasons. What do you believe?'

'I feel like I go bigger than my body.'

Regan nods.

'Except after the orders. Then I feel small, bad,' Keesa adds.

'The order system is one of the things I want to change about the Dark Force.

Through my visions. If I can track one of the moments in time that the formula for them was uttered, I can change the rules so that the orders can no longer be forced on the royal concerned. Instead it can only be made as a request.'

'Why not just stop the orders completely?'

'It's not as simple as that, Keesa. If I did that, I would be replicating what those imposing the orders do now—taking choice away. I am Queen of Night. I need to respect the heritage that I came into this life with. My plan is to create more choice around the Force of Dark for the planet, not to vanquish it.'

Regan gets up and starts clearing the tea cups onto the tray. Keesa helps. They take everything to the refreshment table. The girl walks around it, tracing its undulating border beneath her fingers as Regan stacks the crockery. The girl freezes. She has spotted the knife, tucked away behind the large vase with its arrangement of agapanthus. She looks back to Regan, her eyes widening.

'I was concerned about the Light royals coming after you. I need to be able to defend myself if necessary,' Regan points out.

Keesa is drawn by the handle's design. She runs her hand over it.

'That will be yours one day,' Regan says.

'It's pretty,' Keesa remarks. A flicker in the window. Wind shrills in a channel that extends from under the door to cracks between the ageing farmstead roof. Keesa's eyes are drawn to the leaning flames above. A quick gust extinguishes a few. 'The weather goes funny sometimes when Colter is angry. He could be close.'

'Yes,' Regan says under her breath, stops what she is doing and kneels before the girl. 'Keesa, I brought you here today to ask you to come live with me in the Chamber of Dark. I will teach you everything I know about medicine. I will give you access to the Dark Chamber laboratories and manuals so that you can learn how to become a surgeon, without having to be taught by Signa. I will teach you how to hone your visionary skills, without harming creatures in the process. I am offering you the chance to take your rightful place as Princess of Dark. I am in the process of altering the Dark Force and it would mean everything to me for you to play a role in that reshaping. Ruling together, the possibilities of what we could achieve are immense.'

220

There is something irresistibly stirring and rewarding to Keesa to feel that, for the first time, someone has unreserved faith in her. She knows that Queen Elke will likely always look askance at her. As much as King Maen appears to have confidence in her, to a degree, he still seems to defer to the wishes of his mother and Prince Colter.

'King Maen has been good to me, offered me and my...other parents a home.'

'I know; this is not an easy decision for you. However, give some thought to why he sought you out. Queen Elke and he want you as a powerful contributor to the Light Force. I don't want to see you make the same mistake I made— trusting members of the Light Chamber to the point of idealising them. They are not all about love, take it from me.'

'And what about you?'

She takes Keesa's hands in hers. 'You came from my body, Keesa. I want to be your mother. I want to try right the past. My love for you is unquestionable. Yet I am Queen of Night. I will never be only about love. I am also about realism, autonomy, facing what needs to be faced and protection of your heart, of the Force that runs through it. I will grow you into your power, into the ascendant queen that you were born to be.'

Her words draw Keesa in like the tide sucking at her feet in the wet sand of a shoreline. Their palms are droning like the wings of a hive of bees. The air around them feels thick with raw potential that could condense into power, into sense, into the order that is to be.

Then Keesa's thoughts begin to filter into the moment. Elke's words clang in her skull. She retracts her hands from Regan's, casts her gaze down. She summons the breath to carry the answer she would rather not pronounce. She lifts her eyes to meet the Queen's.

'I can't say yes. I have made a promise to Queen Elke and King Maen that I can't break. I can't tell you what it is because they swore me to secrecy. I am sorry, Queen Regan.'

Those interminable days after Valtere took Keesa come swimming back into Regan now. The same pain that grew into her like a toxic mould as she lay at the doorway of the unoccupied temple, overwhelms her again now. Its spores multiply, shouldering their way into her pores, obstructing her ability to breathe.

Even as her soul feels to wilt, Regan hauls herself above the blight, straightens her spine, elevates her chin. The events that lead to Keesa's choice rest on her shoulders, not the girl's.

Keesa draws no satisfaction from rejecting her mother, as she thought she might. Watching the Queen wince at the answer to her proposal only serves to widen the split gaping inside Keesa, each half leaning one way, flailing wildly, then leaning the other.

Spotting from Above

The wind has picked up. Valtere cuts through its pockets and wheels on its billows, scouting for incoming visitors to the Chamber. The air is charged with electricity and pervaded by a quality of waiting, as it is when a storm hangs imminent. He spots a vehicle now, tipping into sight over the ridge of a hill, followed by a string of them. He boomerangs against the oncoming current of air, and heads back for the Chamber.

Beginning Snuffed

It occurs to Keesa that her safety is precarious as she stands before the Dark leader in her stronghold. 'Are you going to put me in a cell now?' Keesa asks.

The Queen's face has stiffened; her features have decoloured and dropped. 'According to Dark law, I should kill you now.'

Keesa glances at the knife still lying on the table, tries to calculate how long it would take her to rouse the fire in her hands. They start tingling at the thought.

'However, I am not going to.'

'Why not?'

'My love for Maen corrupted my Darkness. Or perhaps it's maternal instinct— although, as Dark Queen, I should be able to override that.'

Keesa pulls the fire into her centre, quells it.

'You know that, according to Light law, you should kill me now.'

Keesa nods. 'I don't want to.'

'I suppose it makes sense that you would show the same weakness as I— being incapable of killing those you have bonded with. Your Dark resolve is compromised by your capacity for Light, just as mine is.'

There is a knock on the door. Regan goes to open it and has a brief conversation with the guard outside. Keesa watches her close it again and turn the key in the lock. The fire starts to prickle her palms again; her body is fearful that she may never leave this Dark dwelling. She suddenly misses the predictable peace of her bedroom in Hale, Toekoums sitting on the windowsill cleaning his fur. Keesa notices Regan's cheeks are flushed as she foots swiftly back towards her.

'Valtere has spotted a group of vehicles making their way to the Dark Chamber. They are about 20 minutes away.'

'Are you going to let me go?'

It dismays Regan to see the girl's eyes flitting to the door as she asks this. 'The last thing I would do is keep you here against your will. However, given the choice you have made, there is one last thing I should do. I am the only one who has the power to lift your identity shield, since I cast it. From then on, it will be up to you to recast it yourself, or not.'

'But I don't know how to do that yet.'

'I'm sure that will be one of the first things you are taught at the Chamber of Light, if the Light royals choose to accept you once they see your true identity.'

'What will they see if you lift it?' Keesa has a bad feeling in her gut.

'The fact that you are the biological daughter of King Maen and I will immediately be evident to the three of us. All other royalty, including Prince Colter and Queen Elke, will be able to see that you are half-Dark, half-Light. The parent-child signal will be unreadable to them.'

Keesa thinks of Queen Elke's misgivings about entrusting her with the powers of a Sun-bearer. She considers Colter's desire to leash her capabilities. She pictures Maen's anger when he realises he allowed his mother to transmit the highest honour of the Light Force into one who has Darkness in her. Once Aedan gets wind of the fact that Queen Regan is her real mother, she might abandon her altogether. From what she saw at the Chamber of Light, who knows whether Colter and Aedan will even remain together? *Where will I belong then? And what will become of the Light Force with no Sun-bearer?*

'I don't want you to lift it,' Keesa blurts.

'You have chosen your side, Keesa. This is one of the consequences.'

Keesa takes a step towards her. 'Please, Queen Regan, I beg you not to lift it. It may destroy the Light family forever.'

Regan considers her words. 'All right, I won't lift the shield for now. I owe you that much for what I did. But, is this really what you want? You will be living a lie, just as I did for so long. Over time, it consumes you.'

'I am sure.'

Regan nods. 'And how will you resist the orders?'

'Toekoums can help me. I'll make sure I'm not alone much.'

'I hope that's enough. I am here if you need my help. What concerns me is that you will risk your life if you make contact. The Light royals will not take kindly to it. If what you want is a life in the Light Chamber, the best way forward for you will be to put me out of your mind and never visit me again.'

Keesa acknowledges her words.

'I was right, I have lost you once more. At least this time I have the comfort of knowing you will be well looked after.'

Keesa jerks forward and clasps her arms around Regan's waist. Regan drops to her level and they embrace. It is a cruel moment, a beginning snuffed. Regan doesn't know how she will let go of Keesa's small frame and face the life she has carved for herself. She pulls back.

'Come, let's get your things from the room; I'll accompany you out.'

They collect the clothes that Keesa came with. Regan puts everything into a leather bag, slings it over Keesa's shoulder. Then she takes the amalgam crystal from Keesa's neck, places it in a red velvet pouch and slips it into one of the side pockets of the bag. 'Just in case you should ever need it,' she says.

Regan goes to open the cupboard. Keesa looks down at her apparel. 'Shouldn't I give all this back to you?'

'I want you to keep it,' the queen says, adding other items from the cupboard to the bag, until it is full.

'Thank-you, Mother.'

'It is nothing, my beautiful girl.'

Regan offers her hand. The two of them walk to the front door and out into the brooding afternoon. Valtere meets them on the veranda. 'The vehicles are nearly here,' he says. A large contingent of Dark guards stand in wait around the front entrance. On instructions from the Queen, they have the white flag hanging out. Regan starts towards the gate.

'Please stay here,' Keesa stops, lets go of Regan's hand. 'I don't want you to get hurt.'

'I'll be fine.'

'Please.'

Keesa's face beseeches her. 'As you wish.' She looks at the girl earnestly. 'You are walking out of here armed with exceptionally volatile knowledge that I told you in trust. I can only hope you use that information wisely.'

'I understand.'

'Very well. Valtere, please see her to the gate. Goodbye, Keesa. I hope that you prosper in the Light Chamber.'

'Goodbye, Queen Regan,' Keesa says, as she sweeps a low curtsey. Being in full view of the guards, the two of them have resumed a formal stance. Keesa steps off the veranda and walks towards the gate, her petite pumps crunching the gravel. The eagle wings close to her, zigzagging to slow down to her pace. The oppressive blue-grey clouds spit lightning but the air is still dry. Tyres screech up to the gate, several Light guards disembark the first and second vehicles, immediately aiming their weapons at the mass of Dark guards with pointed guns. Keesa hears more cars pull up, doors opening and people getting out. Then Colter's voice, thick with rancour, rings out.

'As Prince Colter of the Light Chamber, I demand to see your Queen!'

'That won't be necessary.' On hearing Keesa's unagitated voice, accompanied by cries from Valtere, the Dark guards look to the girl, then on to Regan. The Queen nods once; they clear the gate area, now lining its sides, their guns still angling towards those of the enemy. Two guards open the gate of iron bars just enough for the girl to walk out, then close it immediately. Valtere settles on the railing. Regan can see the Light brothers now as well as other figures sitting in one of the cars. Her and Maen's eyes meet. He breaks their gaze, looks at his brother. Any progress forged in the restoration of their brotherly affection had been wiped the moment Keesa's abduction was discovered. Colter is fuming, steps forward.

'Are you that much of a coward that you can't even speak to us?' he throws out in Regan's direction. The Queen watches on in silence.

'I told her not to come out with me,' Keesa points out.

'Why?' Colter spins round to face her.

'Because I knew you'd want to stand and fight with her or do something to hurt her.'

'Perhaps that is what she deserves!'

'Can't we just leave it?'

Colter is stunned by her assurance. 'What do mean leave it? She kidnapped you against your will! There have to be consequences for that.'

'She's letting me go, isn't she?'

'Why did she bring you here in the first place?'

'She asked me to come stay here. I said no. Now, can't we just go?'

Colter takes one last look at Regan, backs off reluctantly. 'Damn right you said no. That's the last you'll ever see of this place.'

He walks to Maen and, out of earshot of the others, says in a low tone, 'I think you've done enough. Stay away from her, or you will be the one placing the Light Kingship at risk of being nullified for the foreseeable future. Do I make myself clear?'

'I won't be able to stay away forever, Colter. You know this is not the end of this,' Maen replies.

Colter turns from his brother sharply and barks at Keesa and the others, 'Get in the car now. We're going home.'

Keesa looks at Maen, then at Colter, 'But what about us all living together in the Chamber of Light?'

'You're coming home with us and that is the last I want to hear of it. Say your goodbyes,' Colter asserts.

Regan cannot hear exactly what is being said but it irks her that Keesa seems to be in trouble because of what occurred. Unable to face watching her daughter leave, she takes Maen's form in one last time, then goes inside. Colter charges to the car. Aedan looks at him with an expression of dread and gives Keesa a look of empathy, underlain with fear. She no longer feels safe with either of them but, they are the only family she has. She follows Colter to the car. Keesa catches sight of Elijah and Nefer on the back seat, and Toekoums watching her from where he sits on the inner boot lid. Part of her wants to backtrack to the gate, back to her mother. She goes to Maen, who kneels down to say goodbye to her. He feels carved out at having to part from the girl. They embrace.

'Please come visit me, King Maen,' Keesa whispers in his ear.

'Of course I will, Keesa. I just need to give Colter time to calm down. He's still your parent; I have to respect that. He'll come round, you'll see.'

Maen feels sick to see despair in Keesa's face. She goes to the car, gets in, and is gone in a cloud of veldt dust. Maen looks back at the Chamber. Empty doorway. He makes his way to his car, and gives the signal to the guards to follow him. He feels unhinged, and, for the first time, no longer has a sense that he is going home. Rather, the Chamber of Light feels more than ever like a place of lack, a place that the people who are closest to his heart are absent from.

Regan goes back to the ballroom, takes the teatray back to the kitchen. The emptiness of the Chamber now is so patent to her, it is deafening. She finds herself relieved to be informed that Ford has returned and is waiting to speak to her. Regardless of the odious answers he may have for her, the thought of being alone at this instant is unappealing.

'Do you know anything about the fact that I was locked into the Initium laboratory a few nights ago?' she asks him once they are alone in the lounge.

'You ordered me to lock you in from the outside, and to take the key with me. Forgive me, Your Majesty but I was concerned for your safety, knowing that I was leaving on my scouting mission; I regret to say I disobeyed your last order and rather gave the keys to Trent and Kasib. I thought since there are only the four of us guards who know the laboratory protocol, it was the most acceptable route to take under the circumstances.'

The gnawing feeling of susceptibility flares up again. 'Who is the fourth?'

Ford is growing increasingly uncomfortable. 'Livhu, Your Highness.'

'Have the four of you assisted me with the lab before?'

'We have been guarding the door while you work inside for a couple of months now. As well as assisting with cleaning the facilities and feeding the animals.'

'Anything else?'

'The transportation of the dolphin from the coast and acquiring the tank and all its equipment before that. Setting up the tank.'

It all makes sense now. 'You did the right thing by leaving the keys with the other two, Ford. I am grateful.'

The girl. Her mother wanted to get to the girl before she could.

'Please inform the other three that you will all be required to continue the maintenance work on the laboratory and its subjects as before. It is of the utmost importance that none of you disclose any information regarding these activities to anyone.'

'Yes, Your Majesty.' Ford leaves, looking somewhat mystified.

Regan wonders what it was that Signa was scheming for the girl upon her arrival at the Dark Chamber, with its Queen locked away unawares in the distant medical wing. The skin on Regan's skull crawls. 'No matter', she thinks, 'her plan didn't hatch. Keesa will be happy in the Light Chamber', she tells herself. 'It's what I wanted for her when she was born'. She wonders whether the girl will tell Maen the truth and, if so, what he will choose to do with the knowledge. *If my fate is to die at the hands of the Dark or Light army, then so be it,* she thinks. *There is a certain logic to it. The wronged princess rises to slay the Queen. I will have paid my debt.*

The clouds slowly unravel themselves as the day draws towards sunset; the lightning abates. The storm defers, leaving the air feeling close with the unrealised threat of thunder and rain.

CHAPTER 24

Girl Held

12/01/2051

The front garden. Seven pink flowers. One dying. Keesa strains her eyes, trying to count how many of its petals are browning and how many still hold their colour. The counting calms her, even if only temporarily. The shadow of the big tree is almost touching the house now. It must be close to five o' clock. This is Keesa's view of the outside now. The planks of wood that Colter nailed over the window still allow for her pinhole view, the size of a fist onto the world. The barring happened shortly after they got home. A few days after that, Colter caught Keesa making her way towards the gate to visit Elijah without asking permission. The locking of her bedroom door followed. She watches now as Aedan walks back from the dairy. Just before her body is obscured, her eyes flick in Keesa's direction. Her face is tight. Keesa lifts her arm and moves it slowly from left to right, allowing the sun patch leaking through the fastened wood to trace its warmth on her skin. This is another thing that pacifies her.

She slumps back down onto her bed, begins drifting off to the sounds of Aedan preparing an early supper in the kitchen. The rapping of a spoon on the edge of a pot hauls her back from troubled dreams. Back to dream fragments where she can't see properly or someone is talking to her but she can't make out what they are saying. The clinking of plates pulls her awake to this room that is now her prison, her homely cell. Then voices. Colter is home. Shortly after, the key turning in the lock. Keesa sits upright. Aedan pokes her head around the door. She finds it difficult looking the girl in the eye. Perched on her neat bed, the side of her face etched with the creases of her pillowcase, her hair sticking up on that side. A fragile smile towards Aedan.

'Would you like to come eat supper with us?' Aedan asks, attempts a smile herself but fails. The strangeness between them has worsened since they got home.

231

Keesa tilts her head, looking past Aedan to see the back of Colter's head. He is sitting in his usual chair at the kitchen table. She looks back to Aedan, 'No, thanks.' Toekoums pads quickly into the room and goes to sit next to Keesa's bed.

'All right then,' Aedan presents a plate filled with food from around the door. Keesa is surprised she keeps up the facade of asking every evening. Aedan places the plate on the white desk near the door. Keesa gets up. Aedan spins around, looks at the girl's hands. She brushes her long fringe away from her eyes, 'Well, eat it all, now,' and turns to go.

'Aedan,' Keesa stops her, 'how long are you and Colter going to keep me in this room?'

Aedan keeps her back to the girl. 'You will stay in there until such time as we can trust you not to wander off again without telling us,' Colter says from the table. Aedan moves towards the door.

'It's not just that, is it?' Keesa says to Aedan under her breath.

She turns to the girl. 'Your father knows what's best for you, Keesa.' She exits. The sound of the door locking brings up heat in Keesa's palms. She calms herself, waits for it to subside. She has not put up any resistance since the lockdown began. No shouting, no bad behaviour. It will only fuel Colter's temper. Toekoums watches her. The heat has gone. She goes to her food, takes the plate, places it on the floor, and sits next to it.

'Want to have supper with me?'

The kitten joins her. 'Aren't you hungry?' he asks.

'Not really.'

'It is important for your training that you eat properly.'

'What training? I don't believe it's ever going to happen. King Maen has forgotten about me and, in any case, at this rate I'll end up as another skeleton in the box under my bed.'

'Sulking is not becoming in a princess.'

Keesa looks down at the potatoes, goat's cheese wedged inside. Just how she likes them.

'I'm not sure how long I can take this, Toekoums.'

The kitten swallows a bit of potato. 'Beware of hurting the ones you love, Keesa.' He moves away from the plate, begins cleaning his fur. 'Now eat up; King Maen will come for you soon enough.'

Keesa leans against the wall, puts the plate on her lap and works her way through the meal. She remembers how she used to look forward to supper. Her mind wanders. If only she had a potion like Alice and could shrink enough to fit through the cracks in her prison bars. Twenty-one days. She will give the King a few more days. If he hasn't come by then, she will swill a potion of her own.

Righting

'All right, all of you get ready now,' Regan says. It still feels slightly odd to her to talk to the animals in a nurturing manner, but she is getting used to it. She stands poised to pull the blankets off their cage doors. Twenty large candles burn behind her on the floor and laboratory desk. After Keesa left, it took her a solid four days in the lab to culture additional antidote to the offshoot strain of the bacterium. Since then she visited the animals daily, injecting each with a dose that would last 24 hours. She changed their diet slightly, increased their intake of protein, and any foodstuff containing vitamins A, E and C. Mercifully, they all seemed to recover quickly and steadily. Nonetheless, she had kept their exposure to light to a minimum. Today is the first real test of their recuperation.

She pulls the first blanket back. The baboon shields its face. Regan's heart drops. 'It's okay, I'm right here,' she says.

Slowly, it lowers its leathery hands, exposing its eyes to the bright flames. The pupils constrict to small dots; it scans the gleaming columns, then looks at Regan, taking in her features, her clothes. Its eyesight has returned to normal. 'You're going to be okay,' she says, inwardly rejoicing. Each blanket she lifts in turn adds to the relief she feels at the animals' return to health. It does not take away the disquiet she feels witnessing their dejection, however. She opens each cage in turn to see if a period of moving around the laboratory might lift their spirits. Awfully, they all remain in their recesses, looking from Regan to the floor in front of their cage. She spends time petting each creature. She is more careful with the baboon than the others. To reach the dolphin's back, she balances two lab stools one on top of the other. The layer of oil on its skin is growing thinner yet. The petting seems to calm it; it lifts its beak above the surface of the water and clicks softly.

She leaves the blankets off as she exits this time. 'Just two more days, and then I'll set you free,' she says to them before she goes. Blank eyes observe her, disbelieving. Regan has already provisionally scheduled her four laboratory guards to conduct the freeing. She wishes she could go with, but travelling any significant distance is out of the question for her at present. She wonders if she will ever get to leave her cage in its envelope of buckled branches that she has grown so accustomed to. There is no experimenter to set her free. Lingering inculcation and the unkind, yet righteous turn of events are the only wardens keeping her in now.

Inching Shadows

15/01/2051

She can't afford to drift off this afternoon. By her count, today must be Thursday. It was about half an hour ago now that Aedan had walked across Keesa's square of view. That means he should be here any minute. Toekoums springs into the picture; he has startled a large moth out of its afternoon sleep, and is slowly debilitating the creature down to an afternoon snack. He exits her outlook following the insect, its one wing in tatters, wheeling in futile circles. A few minutes pass. Keesa watches the shadow of the tree inch towards the house. The maddening waste of time in observing a single rock on the ground being enveloped by the shadow of a leaf leaves her struggling to contain a scream fleeing her mouth. Save it, she thinks.

At last, she hears the engine of Elijah's grandfather's pick-up truck approaching. She knows its sound, its exhaust is a little spluttery. She sees it pull up. Elijah gets out, starts offloading the steel pails of goat's milk, carrying them one by one in the direction of the dairy. Aedan usually tells him to go help himself to some cool-drink out the fridge once he's done. He takes the last pail. Some minutes pass. Keesa wonders what they are talking about, and whether Aedan even speaks about the situation in the house at all. Finally, Elijah crosses towards the house, squinting in the direction of the cordon boards. Keesa jumps off her bed, moves to her bedroom door, places her ear against it. The two previous Thursdays Colter had been home. She had heard him and Elijah having clipped conversations in the kitchen. Today Colter is out. Sound of the fridge door opening, a bottle being removed. Pouring, boy gulps.

Keesa knocks softly on her door, then hisses, 'Eli!'

The gulping stops, a cup being placed on the table, then his voice on the other side of the door. 'Keesa? Are you okay?'

'No, I'm not; they've had me locked in my room for over three weeks now.'

'I thought they just barred the window; I was nervous to come round in case your Dad would get angry again.'

'There's no time to talk now; will you help me escape?'

'What if your Father finds out? He'll go crazy!'

'Eli, if you're my friend, you'll help me.'

A pause. 'Okay. How do we do it? There's no key in the door here.'

'I know, Colter keeps it on him; he told me. He's out for the day; I heard them talking this morning. I need you to go to your car, and drive it just out of sight; I'll follow and catch up with you there.'

'But where will we go?'

'I'll tell you when I get there; there's no time now, just go!'

'But how will you open your bedroom door?'

'Leave now; I don't want you to get hurt!'

She hears him making his way out of the kitchen, then runs and checks briefly that the coast is clear outside. She sees him crossing to the dairy to say goodbye to Aedan, who normally stays in the dairy working with the fresh milk for at least an hour after he goes. Keesa goes back to the bedroom door, stands in front of it, and aims her hands at the lock. She summons the heat now; it feels like liquid anger unleashing from recesses she has forced it into for three weeks, like a good girl. She concentrates all her energy on not causing an explosion; she can't afford the noise alerting Aedan to what she's doing. She releases a controlled, quiet roar. The sound almost gives her a fright, contained in this modest space. She has to resist the urge to scratch the tips of her ears, which have become very itchy, as has the bump at her coccyx. She sees a heavy, dark fluid beginning to drip down between the door and the wall next to it. The lock is melting.

After a few more moments, she ceases her roaring, drops her hands. She grabs a sweater from her cupboard, wraps her hands in it, and turns the door handle. There is slight resistance because of the stickiness of the liquefied lock, but the door gives; she pulls it open. She checks the front of the house briefly once more, then grabs the bag that she has prepared for this moment, extricating the amalgam crystal from its side pocket, and placing it around her neck before she steps across the doorway. She makes her way through the kitchen, and across the lawn, barefooted, slowly, and on tiptoes. Fortune smiles on her as she comes into the sightline of the dairy entrance: Aedan has her back to the doorway, and is concentrating on skimming the milk. Elijah has considerately left the gate open. She increases her speed now; she can see his car in the near distance, facing in the direction of Brick's farm. She breaks out into a run once she is sure she is out of earshot of Aedan. Finally, she climbs into the passenger seat of the old pick-up. Elijah looks nervous.

'If you're wanting to go to the Chamber of Light, I don't think I'll make it on the fuel I have.'

'We're going somewhere closer. Drive in the direction of the Dark Chamber. Do you remember where it is?'

'I have an idea.'

'Is your tank full?'

'Almost.'

'We'll make it, then. I will make sure it's replaced once we're there.'

'Are you sure you want to do this, Keesa?'

'Just drive, Elijah, please!'

The boy makes a U-turn, and slowly makes his way past Keesa's house. Keesa gives one last look as they pass. Toekoums is padding back from his hunting expedition, and catches sight of Keesa through the open car window. Shock comes over his face, and he freezes, his one paw suspended in the air. Keesa lifts her hand to him. It pains her to leave him, but this journey is one she needs to make alone. Far enough away from the farmstead now, Elijah puts his foot down, and heads off into the veldt. Keesa drinks in the light and the air like one who has been in a dungeon. She is still struggling to come back into herself; part of her had begun spiralling out into the realms of unreason in the confines of that airless bedroom.

'I owe you for this, Eli. You will be rewarded.'

'It's okay, Keesa. I'm your friend. I don't need a reward.'

He touches her arm with his hand. She looks at him and smiles. The comfort of tactility is overwhelming after nearly a month of isolation. Keesa graciously withdraws her arm, and turns to look at the orange and brown coursing past like a river of embers and earth. She doesn't want him to see her wet eyes. *So lucky*, she thinks, *to have a friend. I will reward him nonetheless. I will find a way to pay everyone back what I owe them one day.*

Trouble

15/01/2051

Forty minutes after Keesa's departure, Colter arrives home to find Aedan pale and unnerved, like a stomach-turning rerun of the girl's disappearance before. She had heard the pick-up careening into the desert, run out of the dairy and watched its dust trail lift lazily into the afternoon heat, unable to follow after. At times like this she wished they had a second vehicle.

This time Colter acts quickly. Keesa's signal is scrambled again; he can't pick up where she is. Within minutes he is packing the car. When they go looking for Elijah, Brick tells them that the boy had not returned with the truck when he was meant to. The old man looks shaken, and annoyed when they mention that Keesa is missing too.

'Trouble seems to have a way of finding that girl of yours,' he says. Colter keeps his words to himself. As they make their way back to their car, Brick looks at Nefer straining at the bit to go with them and adds, 'Take the dog with. If anyone will pick up the boy's scent, it's him.' Half an hour later they embark for the Chamber of Light, Toekoums and Nefer on the backseat. Colter is convinced that Keesa is hastening to Maen.

Empty Tank

15/01/2051

With just five kilometres to go, Brick's pick-up truck runs out of petrol. Although the light is quickly leaking from the day, Elijah luckily recognises how close they are. They leave the car to complete the journey on foot.

'I promise we'll come back for the truck as soon as we get there,' Keesa says.

'It's okay, I know I'll get it back,' Elijah replies. He glances towards Keesa, offers her his arm. She is walking strangely, trying to keep her stomach steady while moving her legs. Her countenance is tight and fatigued, as though she is holding her face on her body with effort. The responsibility of asking Elijah to drive her prevented her from letting go into sleep in the car. Since the lockdown, her appetite has been scant; her physical reserves are low. What with using her powers that morning, and their meagre supplies of food and water in the car, she is reaching exhaustion.

Once they are within a hundred metres of the Chamber, and have the gates in their sight, they are spotted by two Dark guards roaming the perimeter. They approach the children, guns hoisted. One of them studies her face more closely and says, 'Lady Keesa.'

Keesa nods. The guard can see she is about to topple, and lifts her up like a twig into his arms. His face swims in front of Keesa's eyes for a second, and then she is out.

'She has come to see Queen Regan,' Elijah says in a sapless voice. The other guard offers Elijah a piggy-back, which he gladly accepts. Despite the strange sensation of knowing he is being taken into the Dark headquarters, his fear is tempered by how tired and thirsty he is.

At six thirty, Regan has just completed her medical rounds of the Chamber for the afternoon. She is in the kitchen getting herself some water, when one of the kitchen staff coming in says to her, 'You have a visitor, Your Highness,' indicating the passage. The last time she remembers a visitor being announced to her was when candidates still came calling to suit her. When she glimpses the half-lit outline of the guard carrying her young, limp girl, her first thought is that her worst fear has come to roost.

'She has passed out; I think she might need medical attention—her friend too,' the guard informs her. Regan breathes. She sets Keesa up in the same room as before, and Elijah in a small guest room close by. She treats them both for mild dehydration, Keesa is also in drastic need of nutrients. She wakes them both up in turns to administer a rehydration solution and mashed food. Elijah introduces himself drowsily to the Queen as she tends him and tells her that Keesa came for her. She is impressed by his courteousness. On one occasion of ministering to the girl, Keesa starts talking to her.

'The truck, Elijah's truck, it's close by...we left it there...no petrol left.'

'Sshh, I'll send the guards to get it, don't worry.'

'And...I came here to ask you something.'

'Not now Keesa; we'll talk tomorrow. For now, you must rest.'

The girl goes quiet; her eyes start wheeling back into sleep, attempting to focus on Regan's face each time they surface. Regan savours the act of nursing her. She presumes that any peaceful moment she gets with the girl will be snatched away before long. The girl has slipped into slumber. Out of habit, Regan looks towards the door, listening out for anyone who might be in the passage. All clear. She turns back to Keesa, brushes her hair the colour of baking chocolate back from her forehead, and kisses it.

Unexpected Caller

15/01/2051

Six hours later, they arrive at the Chamber of Light; Colter had sped all the way in a silence that Aedan dared not impinge upon. On hearing that Keesa was not there, he didn't initially believe Maen but, once he registered his brother's tangible anxiety regarding her disappearance, he thought better of this. It took Aedan a full 10 minutes of persuading him that to leave for the Dark Chamber immediately was not feasible. Colter surmised this as Keesa's next most likely destination. They needed to rest, at least eat something. At 11, the three of them sit down to a late supper thrown together by the kitchen staff.

Dinner is stilted, the conversation sputters. Gradually though, Maen coaxes his brother out of his sultry mood; he has always been one of the only people able to do this. Despite himself and perhaps through his sheer weariness, Colter's sense of humour returns—fragile yet visible.

Towards the end of dinner, one of the Chamber workers goes to Maen's side and indicates that another visitor has arrived on the grounds. There is a tentative knock on the door of the dining-room; a few of the guards whose detail is to man the outer perimeter. They are aiming guns in the direction of a Dark guard, whose hands have been restrained behind his back. The royal brothers jerk up off their seats, Colter moving to place himself between the guards and Aedan.

'Forgive the interruption, King Maen, Prince Colter but we thought you would wish to attend to this immediately. He approached the Chamber without aggression.'

The Dark guard looks pale; it has clearly been a long and arduous journey. At the mention of the Prince's name, he looks over at Colter with some surprise.

'Yes, of course,' Maen says to his man, then addresses the visitor directly, 'what is your business here?'

'I represent Queen Regan of Night and come to bring a declaration of war by the Chamber of Dark upon the Chamber of Light.'

It feels to Maen as if the blood in his veins has frozen. He knew this was a possibility, but he had hoped she would decide against it. His voice feels swallowed away, his throat suddenly as dry as a desert. All eyes are on him.

'I see. An unfortunate decision for us all. Please take acknowledgement of the declaration back to your Queen. Guards, give him some water and food and send him on his way.'

The guards exchange looks and one of them hesitantly speaks to the King, 'Forgive me, sire, but do you not want us to lock him in one of the holding cells?'

'I will not detain enemy personnel unless it is necessary. He is unaccompanied and did not antagonise you. Our holding cells may be filling up soon enough. The rules of engagement between the Chambers state that the messenger of war is to be spared imprisonment. I will abide by them.'

The guards leave with the Dark traveller. 'As much as I believe your adherence to Chamber rules is admirable, I can only hope that the new queen shows the same compliance,' comments Colter.

'She will,' Maen responds, his ears and tail drooping.

'How can you be sure?' Colter is surprised at the certainty in his brother's voice, given the treacherous nature of previous Dark monarchs.

Maen attempts to shake himself out of the sinking sense of betrayal that has broken a sweat out under his fur, despite the lack of logical grounds for it. 'She has not attacked pre-emptively in 10 years. If her intent was to play against the rules, she would have sent an ambush team.' He nods twice, as if trying to convince himself of something and takes a deep breath. 'Well, this changes things. I will call a meeting of the guards. As of now, the Chamber is on high alert. A plan of attack must be tabled.'

Colter knows his brother well and can't ignore the feeling that he is reluctant to strike the first blow against the Dark Chamber, that the prospect of it seems to make him sad and tired. So much for his bravado in their arguing the month before.

'Colter, I know your intention was to return to Hale and remain there and I won't stop you if that is still your wish but, given this shift in circumstance, do you not think it would be prudent for us to locate Keesa and bring her to live in the safety of the Chamber?' Maen appeals.

Colter looks to his wife. 'He is right,' she says, takes his hand in hers.

'Yes,' Colter says, 'once we have her back, we will stay with her here until this blows over.' He knows only too well that could take years.

'As your brother, there is one other thing I need to ask. Will you take your place as Prince of Light now and join us in this fight for our Chamber?'

Colter draws in a breath, looks once again into his wife's eyes. They tell him what he already knows. He inclines his head, 'I will do it for Keesa. If anything were to happen to her because of this primitive feud, I could never forgive myself. And regardless, you shouldn't have to take on the next family crisis alone again.' The relief and appreciation on Maen's face is palpable.

The briefing meeting with the guards ends around midnight and both brothers retire to their rooms soon after. The perimeter of the Chamber is now heavily populated with armed sentinels; a system of shifts for them already established in the meeting. Word travels quickly among the Chamber workers and, after an initial buzz in the passages, everyone is settled in their beds. Many of the children react with excitement at the news of war between the Chambers, having never before experienced it in their lives. The adults are far less enthusiastic; many have broken sleep that night, with the dread of their lives once again being invaded by this vendetta. Maen's sleep is intermittent. In his dreams he is driving towards their hiding place. It is early morning, 11 years ago.

The Island Awaits

21/09/2039

They hadn't seen each other for an entire month. Just hours before it, Regan had called off their last fortnightly arrangement. Her mother had sprung a candidate screening on her at the last minute; the Chalon Dark family and their son were out from France and would only be in the vicinity for the day. In the last year, both Regan and Maen have had to cancel on a few occasions. It is becoming more difficult to stick to set times as the demand on their schedules by parents and royal obligation mounts.

It is a crisp morning, the dawning sun lifts the layer of dew off the ground and turns it into filmy steam. Maen is making his way to her from his car; draws his hood back from over his head, the light hitting his chestnut hair and ears. He is a tall, august man-in-the-making now, with a stride that unhinges Regan every time she sees him. He lifts her up, spins her around, then slowly lowers her back down. There is something about feeling her weight in his arms that he savours. She always feels lighter than she should.

'I missed you so much I thought I'd lose my mind,' he says, brushing his mouth over her cheeks, her eyes. As he reaches her lips, Regan pulls back.

'Maen, wait,' she says gently, 'We don't have much time today. I have to be back by 11 at the latest and, I have something I want to...say.'

Maen backs off. 'This sounds serious.' Images of war flicker across his mind. He had been hoping to avoid any Chamber talk today. It's been so long; all he can think of is having her.

'It's not going to be possible for me to see you for a while,' Regan lets fall.

Maen's brow furrows, 'Why not? Where are you going?'

'I cannot say...you understand?'

His frame drops slightly. 'Of course. We must protect each other, protect ourselves.' He lifts a lock of her hair, places it behind her shoulder, 'How long will you be gone for?'

'A year.'

'A year!' Regan nods; her eyes direct. He drops his hand, turns away. A month without her had felt like a year.

'Surely we can meet somewhere. Are you really going to be that far away? Wait... is this that isolation thing you're put through by the Chamber? What happens out there?'

'Maen,' Regan looks at him calmly.

'Yes, yes. I know. I can't ask. It's just...I can't imagine...I'll worry about you, that's all.' He notices her eyes have gone dark and still.

'I have something I would like to ask you.' She hopes he does not notice how she is shaking beneath the folds of her dress. A bird calls from a nearby hill. It occurs to her that it is going about its day without a thought, just doing. This moment is so clear to her it feels to cleave her life in two. Maen squares his body to face her. The change in her demeanour is unnerving him.

'Prince Maen of Day, will you marry me?'

His head jerks back slightly; his eyes widen. 'You want me for your husband?' Regan nods. She can see something opening in him. She has never seen his eyes like this—vivid, naked, as though this moment makes sense of it all to him. He pulls her into him, one hand on the small of her back, the other around the nape of her neck and kisses her with all the longing of the last month, all the waiting through the years for the next time he would see her, catch a glimpse of her black hair, her eyes that deepen, hear her velvet voice that soothes his ears, hear her breathing that makes him purr. He lifts her and takes her into their tented space. As he drives into her, untamed, Regan knows with all that she is that she is meant for him alone.

They fall into easeful sleep after. The bird calling from the hill outside dips in and out of Regan's dreams, in which she is lying on her back on something soft but supportive, wet sand, it feels like. Waves lap over her midriff and tug at her hair. She keeps her eyes closed. The water is cool and pleasant. She can feel the salt sinking into her skin, enlivening, mingling with her blood. She hears a sound, a blast of liquid through a small space, a happy trumpet. Something flutters in the dark warmth of her belly. Another wave. A bird calling. The bird from the hill.

Regan stirs from her sleep, cradled in the hook of Maen's arm, her cheek resting on his chest, slowly lifting and falling with his breath. She rouses him, tells him that they only have an hour left. They get up, silence between them now where there were kisses before. He avoids her eyes. She feels off-kilter, unsure of how to navigate this moment. She wants his voice to cut the stillness with an answer, certain and steady. He does not look certain; he looks closed. They take the cloth and blankets down off the pillars. The morning is serene in their nook, a perfect, calm day.

'Maen,' Regan's voice ripples the hush, 'you haven't given me your answer.'

Maen sets down the cloth he has folded, straightens himself up. His movements are steeped in dread, patent as stirrups on his body. For the first time since they woke, he forces himself to look directly at the Princess.

'I'm afraid I must decline your proposal.'

An awful sound cries out in Regan's being. A horrible scream that stops her breath dead. She finds herself wishing she was back in her dream by the water's edge, sunlight on her eyelids. Maen continues; perhaps he can explain. She'll see, she'll surely see.

'I wish this could be different. You know that a marriage between us is inconceivable. It will shatter my parents, not to mention yours. I shudder to think what your mother would do to you.'

'How princely of you to take me first and tell me after.'

'It just happened. I—'

'I took it as your answer.'

'I didn't mean it that way...you just...you do something to me that I can't—'

'Do something to you?'

'Yes.'

'So, I'm the Dark Force doing and you're the victim, Light and beyond reproach? Maen, all these years, your words, your actions, they have consequences, they mean something! Was this just a game to you? Play with me till you're done and then discard me?'

'I admit my timing was unfortunate just now.'

'Just because I am your Family's enemy, doesn't give you the right to bad behaviour.'

'I'm sorry. You're right.' He pauses, swallows his words, shakes his head. He suddenly feels hot.

'What?' Regan's patience with his muteness is growing thin.

'Nothing.'

'Just say what it is you want to say.'

'I'm starting to think that what we have been doing is a mistake.'

'A mistake? Both of us knew from the beginning that we were crossing a line.'

'Do you understand the ramifications of what you're asking of me?' Maen asks.

'Of course I do. How can you ask that?'

'You've been fairly flippant about our obligations to our families until now.'

'I'm not a little girl anymore, Maen. I believe that this could be the merger that brings peace between the families once and for all.'

'Merger? So you see this as a business deal?'

'Of course not! That's just a word to describe the families coming together.'

'Which is likely to end in the most gruesome bloodbath yet!'

'Not if we go about it in the right way.'

'There is no way to go about it! We agreed to keep our relationship a secret. That was the precondition.'

'Things change, Maen. People change. Worlds can change too, but that takes courage.'

'Are you calling me a coward?'

'How long did you plan on stringing out our arrangement?'

'I don't know! That's not really something you can plan in advance.'

'Well, for me, we have come to the point where we have to make a decision.'

'Why now?'

'Maen, I am 18. You will be 20 in December. How long do you think we can put off choosing our respective candidates? How many more lies can we tell our parents? I just happen to be lucky that my mother finds the subject of marriage mundane. All she wants to know is that I will produce an heir to the Dark throne, and, at this point, she still trusts that I will do that. But I can't fool her for much longer.'

'Perhaps I'm not ready to choose yet.'

'And why do you think that is? What are you looking for in the candidates?'

'Maybe I just don't want any of them at the moment.'

'Why not?'

'You and all your deep questions! Can't you just leave things well enough alone? Don't you enjoy what we have?'

'That's just it, Maen. I don't just want to have a thing with you. I can't stomach the thought of being with another man. The thought of living a life without you in it is deplorable to me.'

'Then let it be.'

'Maen, I'm not a teenager you can plant dreams in that starve to death before they see the light of day. I will never be satisfied merely being your little Dark mistress. We said that this could not last forever and, that moment has come for me. Either we move into an uncertain future together, risking what we have to in showing our bond to the world or it ends here, now.'

'This is ridiculous! When I came here this morning, everything was as it always has been. What happened?'

'I grew up, Maen. Something you are clearly reluctant to do.'

'I don't want to lose you, Regan.'

'I am showing you a way that you don't have to.'

'You're asking me to choose between my family and you.'

'That is how you see it. What is your decision, Maen?'

He pauses. 'You know I cannot agree to this, Regan. It goes against the oldest, most sacred laws of my world.'

And there it is. The jaws of the trap snap, slice into her like hungry iron teeth. She was a little girl when her mother began warning her of this. Her tutor had advised it, the Dark Code had stipulated it but still Regan, headstrong as ever, had chosen not to heed. Instead she chose to hoodwink herself into the hoax that love would conquer all. Her mother's smug voice sounds in her head now: 'I told you so.' Perhaps Signa had been right to deny her motherly love. It may have pained Regan but at least she could trust her mother to stick to her principles and show constancy. The snare that Maen has sprung may have been a gorgeous one but this pain is worse. It is a slow death.

'Then I will no longer be an adjunct to that world. Goodbye, Maen. I wish you well in your kingship.'

'Regan, stop being so final; I'll see you in two weeks, we'll talk more then. Give me time to think, and—'

'No-one will see me in two weeks. This decision should not be one that you have to think about.'

Maen finds that he cannot move. He knows that if he steps off the lattice now, the one thing in his life that shines will cease. 'Please be careful when you get home today, Regan. You're in no state...your mother will sniff out emotion in an instant.'

250

'I know how to handle my mother. I don't need your advice in regard to her.'

'Please Regan, you're going cold on me, this is not how I wanted to end. I didn't want it to end!'

He has never heard this tone from her before. A reporting of words. He can see the distance her mother has sculpted in her. 'You have made your choice, Maen. Staying together meant risking our thrones. I will admit that you were the only person I was prepared to do that for. But, we are done. You have pleased our parents with your decision today. Please leave.'

'But Regan—'

'Do you want me to signal to Valtere to call in guards? You know he has been itching to do that for years.'

'No, Princess, that will not be necessary.'

Maen goes to touch her hand but her steel eyes cut him short. He turns, steps off their ground, and walks to his car. Regan no longer sees veldt and peace and blossoming morning sun. Before her is destruction, splayed and spilling like an ill-fated wasteland, shrapnel dug into its recesses, final, and poisoning. The eagle is winging his way to her. Hurtling back to the Chamber in the car, she keeps her cloak over her head. The driver must not see her leaking eyes. Her one solace now is that the ship awaits her at the end of today. If she can just remain collected till then and stop the thought *What was I thinking?* from swimming round and round her head like some aimless, horrified fish. She was dreading the distance from the Prince before. Now, it will be her salvation.

CHAPTER 25

Return of the Messenger

16/01/2051

A new morning. There is a knock on the door. Her chambermaid informs her that Ford has arrived from his scouting journey with a message for her. She meets him in the lounge. He looks haggard.

'You have news for me, I am told?' Regan asks.

Ford's voice is hoarse from sleep deprivation, 'Yes, Your Majesty. King Maen of Day sends acknowledgment of the declaration of war upon the Chamber of Light.'

Regan pauses, stumped. 'What are you talking about? What declaration?'

'No disrespect, Your Highness, the declaration you ordered me to deliver to the Chamber of Light.'

The room begins whiting out in front of Regan's eyes. She maintains her stature, uses all her willpower to stop herself from fainting. She keeps her eyes open, focuses on where she knows Ford must still be standing. Within a few seconds, a pinhole of reality opens up again, his face at its centre.

'Are you all right, my Queen?'

'When did I ask you to do so?'

'I'm sorry...I don't understand...'

'Answer my question.'

252

'It was in the early hours of the morning, perhaps two o'clock, the night before last. You woke me from my sleep, told me to leave immediately, gave me your private vehicle. It had extra gallons of petrol in the trunk, so I didn't need to stop for fuel.'

'Have you spoken of this to anyone at all?'

'You said it was a matter of the highest secrecy and that you would have my head if I breathed a word of it. Your Majesty, forgive me, but I don't understand why you're asking these things.'

'Suffice it to say Queen Signa has been continuing her plan through me. Can I trust you to keep this secret?'

'My Queen, that is without question.'

'Thank-you, Ford.'

'I also thought you might like to know that Prince Colter was present in the room when I relayed the declaration.'

'I see. I appreciate your work. You may leave now.'

Even with the effort Regan had been exerting to fend off the orders, the revenant ogress had reared herself again.

Distance Crossed

16/01/2051

Birds are well into their morning activities of gathering and delivering. Their bursts of sweet song and flitting from bush to low tree is a calming flurry around the camp. Everyone has finished eating their breakfast of sandwiches prepared in the kitchen of the Light Chamber in the early morning hours. The guards sit in clusters around vehicles. Twenty minutes rest time, then back on the road. Maen goes to sit next to his brother on the bonnet of one of the cars that is partially shaded by a sweet-thorn tree. The light reaching the low koppies surrounding the camp is draining of its yellow, its stark whiteness a reminder that time is marching on.

It still feels to Maen as if each time he starts words with Colter, he is bridging a gulf of silence. 'You don't need to worry about Aedan, she is in good hands at the Light Chamber.'

Colter nods, watches a group of guards pitching cricket balls to each other, amused by Nefer and Toekoums, who take fielding positions. The animals have been assigned a personal protector, Nathan, who has experience in animal handling. The royal brothers are aware of the animals' strategic value in locating the children.

'She seems like a good woman,' Maen persists.

'You don't have to mince your words with me.'

'What do you mean?'

'You were always on my case about marrying the appropriate royal, placating Mom and Dad.'

'Perhaps I've changed.'

'You still put royal law before anything else. Turning Keesa's life upside down is proof of that.'

'We've been over this. She was already on this path. And yes, I can't say I feel no concern about you being with non-royalty. It's been up to me alone for some

254

time to ensure that our Light legacy is preserved. Nonetheless, I know what it feels like to love someone who is unacceptable to our parents.'

'You? I find that hard to believe. Who is she?'

'It was a long time ago. It doesn't matter now. What I'm trying to say is, you should do what is right for you rather than spend your whole life thinking back and wondering.'

Colter examines his brother's face, looks back to the play. 'I don't need your permission to do anything.'

'No, of course you don't.' Maen watches one of the guards hit a six; some of the others cheer him on. The ball comes close to hitting Toekoums. Nefer herds the feline out the way and Nathan lifts him onto the bonnet of a nearby four-by-four. Toekoums obeys and looks on, crabby at being such a tiny creature.

'No matter how she left, it's a good thing Elijah is with her. I doubt the journey was upon the boy's motivation; Keesa can be very convincing. He is a mannerly boy. She is lucky to have a friend looking out for her,' Maen comments.

'I think he has a crush on her.'

'He must like complicated girls.'

This gets a grudging smile out of Colter, 'That's putting it lightly.'

'Should we try get Mom through that cell phone once more before we go? I know she'd want to see you. Her receiving equipment runs on solar power; by now it might be working. I've seen a connection made that way before. Worth another try.'

The smile drops off Colter's lips. 'Yes, we had better. Her support for this would be preferable.'

The brothers' attention is taken by Nefer barking. They are both a little jittery and spring up, taking in the encircling low hills with quick glances. Nothing out of place. Then Nathan shouts to them, 'King Maen! Prince Colter!' pointing vigorously towards Toekoums on the bonnet of the vehicle. They make their swift way over.

'Look closer,' Nathan directs them as he tries to calm Nefer, who is now anxious. The kitten sits on his haunches, his head lifted slightly, his body paused, and his eyes almost closed but for a sliver at the bottom. His pendant is glowing green and in the blur inside, the shadows of a visage can be made out. Within a few seconds, Queen Elke snaps into focus in the sphere.

'Maen, thank goodness. I saw you tried to make a connection this morning. Is everything all right? How is...' Her words break off. She has noticed the dark-haired man next to the King.

'Colter?'

'Hello, Mother.'

The Queen lifts her hand to cover her mouth. 'My boy.'

The air in the camp becomes crisper, more electric. 'It's good to see you again.' Colter's voice is hoarse, he struggles to rein the welling in; this is not the time for it. Elke wipes away her tears and composes herself but she is thrown. Ninev fleets onto her shoulder, letting out a series of staccato chirps aimed first at Colter, then at Maen.

'Is there something we should know?' Maen asks.

'All right, Nintjie, I'll tell them,' Elke says resignedly. 'She says that the two of you are not to push me. She says...' Elke catches herself again. 'She says there is not much time left.'

Acidic reality courses through the brothers.

'She said something to me, didn't she?' Colter asks.

'Yes,' Elke replies, 'I'm afraid it's not very nice.'

'No, I didn't think it would be.'

'She's just angry, that's all. You know Ninev, she's always been one to get hot under the collar when it comes to me.'

'Mother, I—'

'Let's not do this now, Colter. So little time. Let me just get a better look at you.'

My word, you boys are handsome.' She takes a moment to relish seeing her sons standing side by side again. 'Well now, and how is little Keesa? Has she begun her training yet?'

Maen glances in Colter's direction, sees how he is struggling. 'Mother, we have much to tell you and time is of the essence. I need you to brace yourself. We are en route to the Dark Chamber. War has been declared on our Family. We must entreat your help with gaining access once we are there. However, if you are not up to it, you must say so.'

The momentary happiness that had vivified Elke's face recedes now.

'Yes, I noticed that the girl's signal has been shaded. Have you lost it too?'

The brothers nod.

'All right then, anything I can do to assist. Ninev will monitor my limits.'

'Thank-you, Mother,' Maen says, 'It's essential we get to the girl as soon as possible.'

'The girl is at the Dark Chamber?'

'We think so, yes.'

'Dear Lord.' Elke pales. She indicates to Ninev to bring her remedy for strength. 'What is your plan?'

The telling is concise and pointed. Both brothers would prefer to be gentler and slower with Elke but, it is uncertain how long Toekoums can keep the connection. The kitten remains mostly still throughout, apart from the occasional twitch of his whiskers or a paw, usually when Colter's current is gaining charge. Once they are done, Ninev orders the Queen to rest immediately; there is work to be done ahead.

The prince catches the heels of the bird's cheeping. 'Mother, I know you don't want to talk about the past but, there is something I have to say.'

Ninev gives Colter a stern eye, flips her tail, and wings out of view. Maen takes a few steps away. Elke looks at her surly second-born. *Always so serious*, she thinks.

'I'm sorry, Mother. I'm so sorry I left all of you like that.'

'I know you are, my boy. I'm sorry for what you saw. No son should witness that in his mother. But I have never held anger toward you. Let it lie now, Colter, leave it in the past. You've always worried too much.'

'Yes, Mother. Perhaps after all this I can come visit?'

'Now that would be wonderful, my prince. To have both my boys by my side once more. You two drive safe now and make sure the kitten gets some rest.'

Colter looks at his mother, so small and frail, like a rare bird caught in a circle cage. Unreachable, and going. Even as the sun grows brighter and hotter, storm clouds are brewing in the distance. The pendant's glowing ebbs. Toekoums opens his eyes. He is patently tired. Maen places him on the back seat of his Land Rover where the kitten falls straight into sleep. His little heart is racing arrhythmically. Maen tells Nathan to bring Nefer and ride in his car. The camp is packed up soon after; all evidence of their presence erased. Colter drives behind Maen, their cars flanked on all sides by guard vehicles.

Maen wrestles with his thoughts, which race through all possible scenarios that might transpire once they reach Dark headquarters. The one thought he keeps trying to push aside is of Regan. No matter what she has done, he does not want her to come to harm. This is unacceptable. He is King and must be prepared to do what needs to be done. He will be watched. The only way he will get through this is to make his heart as hard as the rocks in the veldt that her pretty young feet used to skip over.

Prelude

16/01/2051

Regan calls in her head of staff. All staff, apart from military personnel and a few select chambermaids, are to retire to their quarters immediately after lunch. Doors are to be kept bolted. Next, Regan informs Haaken, the head of her Dark army, of the news. 'There has been a misunderstanding. The Chamber of Light is under the mistaken impression that we have declared war between the Chambers. I will rectify the situation if they attempt an invasion. However, until then, we need to be on high alert. Tell your commanders that in the case of an attack, our army should take a defensive stance, yet assume positions of neutrality and fly the white flag.'

There is confusion on his face but he refrains from asking for clarification. A Dark subject does not question the word of the Queen.

'Oh, and one other thing,' she halts him with her voice as he exits. He turns to her. 'Under no circumstances are King Maen or Prince Colter to be harmed. They should be restrained by your men and brought to me. From there, I shall personally deal with them.'

'Understood, Your Majesty.'

The two brothers presenting a unified front is a formidable prospect. She wonders whether her guards will manage to fetter either of them, what with their powers. Regan fights the desire to flee the Chamber with her daughter, abdicate her throne and never look back. The vacuum she would leave in her wake, however, could open the way for undesirable alliances to form between those left in the Chamber and criminal bands. No matter Regan's disillusionment with the Dark code, she is still responsible for her subjects. She will not leave them open to attack or infiltration.

Ingress

'Do you think Nefer is ready?' Colter asks Nathan.

'I hope so,' he answers, giving the dog a long drink of water from a bowl. Colter is nervous; being this close to the Dark Chamber does not agree with him. Nathan picks a bundled up old jersey off the ground, 'I'll practise a bit more with him while we wait; do you have any more treats?' Colter hands him the rest of the nuts from his pocket and goes over to where Maen is sitting on the bonnet of his car, Toekoums next to him. The kitten is lying on his belly, his front paws tucked under his chest, sleeping lightly.

'If we find that Keesa isn't in the Chamber, can you promise me you'll instruct our men to use the white flag rule? You and I can negotiate an agreement with Queen Regan if she's holding her somewhere else, instead of sacrificing our men's lives.'

Maen shifts Toekoums away from where the sun is slanting through gaps between branches. The kitten begins to rouse.

'Go back to sleep,' he calms the feline with his hands, lifts them off as Toekoums drifts back into sleep. 'All right, I promise. But I think you're being your usual unrealistic self in thinking the Dark Army would even heed the white flag. Or that Queen Regan would be open to diplomacy at this late hour. She must be determined to get something to have declared war.'

'And you're convinced this is only about preventing us from having Keesa as part of the Force?' Colter asks.

'I don't know what else it could be.' Maen avoids his brother's eyes. He is growing impatient with the heat, the waiting. 'You're sounding amenable, suddenly. Changing your mind about her as Sun-bearer?'

'No, I was just estimating the Queen of Night's position on this.'

Colter looks at the angle of the sun and the laden storm clouds fast impinging on what is left of blue sky. The last thing they want is to be approaching the

Dark Chamber at night, with little knowledge of its layout. That would no doubt result in scores of casualties among the troops. He notices the pendant changing colour. 'I think she might be coming through.'

Maen starts up from sitting against the bonnet, 'Yes, I think you're right. Get Nathan and the dog. Let's get the show on the road.'

Colter signals to some nearby guards to get Nathan's attention. Toekoums wakens, and sits upright, his eyes still closed. Elke starts crackling into the pendant and, within a few seconds, her image is clear.

'Right boys, we'd best get going,' she says. Maen goes to talk briefly to the head of his army, checks that the walkie-talkies are working. Colter has rounded Nathan and Nefer up into the most inconspicuous vehicle they have and is waiting at the wheel. With care, Maen lifts Toekoums off the bonnet and climbs in. They leave the area, the Light army behind them preparing to make their way to the Chamber, taking the conventional, front-entrance approach.

Colter drives in the opposite direction to the army and veers into the veldt a short distance on, doubling back to approach the Chamber from the most sparsely guarded side, Elke pointing them in the right direction. She had sent a spy in to the Chamber all those years ago, in order to plan the attack on the Dark royal couple. She had committed the layout of the Dark Chamber and its surrounds to memory. Her body may be winding down to death but her brain is still sharp. She instructs Colter to stop. From this spot, they are about 15 minutes walking distance from the back left entrance to the Chamber. They all disembark, Maen slowly, still holding Toekoums in his hands. Elke is focusing on holding the connection; her eyes clap onto Nefer. Nathan goes down onto his haunches, holds Nefer's face in his hands.

'Okay boy, that's Elke,' he says, pointing to the pendant, 'listen to her, okay? And remember what we've been doing—hold gently. Gently, boy.' Nefer sits on his haunches and parts his jaws slightly.

'Mom, the kitten is stiff,' Maen comments as he hands a rigid Toekoums to Nathan.

'Toekoums, relax your body and remain open to my voice,' coaxes Elke.

The feline slumps into a loose state in Nathan's hands. 'Okay, Nefer, here we go,' Nathan lifts Toekoums to Nefer's mouth. Nefer jerks his head back, shuts his mouth, gives a questioning whine, and looks up to Nathan. 'It's okay, boy, go on, hold gently.'

The dog opens his mouth again. The guard places Toekoums delicately between Nefer's teeth, making sure the kitten's shoulder and hip bones are positioned directly beneath his bite, not the vulnerable, organ-filled cavities held together by furry skin. He positions the pendant between the front teeth, so that Elke looks out from inside the dog's mouth, just in front of the feline. Colter hands Nathan a piece of fabric cut from one of Keesa's denim over-dresses. Nathan holds it in front of Nefer's nostrils; the dog sniffs at it and looks towards the Chamber, straining to go. 'Keesa, find Keesa, boy. Go on!' the trainer commands. Nefer sets off, Elke's voice coaching him every now and then from the portal locked between his teeth.

They watch the dog disappear into the overgrown straw-coloured grass. Twenty minutes wait, and then Maen will give the signal for the army to advance. The two brothers begin loading their firearms. Standing in the heat, a gun in his hand, his mother guiding them towards the Dark Chamber, is making Colter light-headed. He climbs into the front seat for some shade. The storm clouds are banking up fast; it will not be long before they obscure the sun completely. Maen senses Colter's anxiety, and goes to sit in the passenger seat.

'Odd weather,' Maen comments, looking pointedly at his brother.

'Mm,' Colter deflects.

'How much practise have you had lately at managing your powers?'

Colter shoots him a curt look. 'Enough.'

'We'll bring her home safe, don't worry.' There is another he wants to keep safe. He wants Keesa back in the fold but he does not need an eye for an eye. However, he is not so sure that Colter's passive leaning will hold up in the face of a threat to the life of the girl he calls his daughter.

Cars in the Library

16/01/2051

Elijah looks slightly lost without Nefer near him, Keesa thinks. They have both bounced back after a great deal of sleep and a solid breakfast. The two of them have been shown to the Chamber library after they began to get restless in their rooms.

'So, I'm going to go talk with the Queen for a while now. You okay here?' Keesa asks.

'I'll be fine, thanks, there's lots to look at,' the boy replies, seeming a bit daunted by row upon row of books.

'I thought you might like this section,' Keesa runs her fingers over the section of tall volumes, each carrying a different animal as its title. Then the birds, insects, sea creatures.

'This one too,' Elijah stands before the history of technology. He is eyeing a volume entitled *Cars of the Twentieth Century*.

Sabrin appears in the doorway.

'Her Majesty will be ready for you shortly, Lady Keesa. Mister Elijah, the scouting guards told me to relay to you that your truck is on the Chamber grounds and is being re-fuelled.'

'Great, thank-you.' Keesa can see that he is relieved.

'You know that you can leave if you want to, Elijah. I could organise some guards to go with you, make sure you are safe.'

'You're not planning on staying here long, are you?'

'I suppose not,' Keesa says.

'You go have your talk. I'll wait here for you. We'll have to wait for this weather to blow over before we go anyway. I can't risk driving on gravel roads if it rains— they become like mush.'

'Kay, thanks, see you just now.'

Keesa follows the chambermaid two doors down the passage to the ballroom.

An Afternoon Snack

16/01/2051

'I'm hungry.' Frik looks over to Sibu. The two Dark guards are posted on the outskirts of the rear area of the Chamber. 'Don't you have something on you?'

Sibu looks at his fellow soldier without moving his head. 'Just nuts.'

'Bloody nuts. Jesus, what I'd do for a Tempo now.'

'Bar-One.'

'Oh God, let's not talk about it, actually.'

'You had lunch.'

'I know, just feel like an afternoon snack.'

Frik lets out a sigh. They scan the area before them. It's quieter than usual out here today. There would normally be some bustle in the distance around the back door to the kitchen—the comings and goings and conversations of the kitchen staff. The Chamber staff all retreated to their rooms hours ago.

'Ag, give me some nuts, please man?'

Sibu slings his rifle around his shoulder and gets the handkerchief of nuts from the side pocket above his knee.

'You're a star,' Frik throws a handful into his mouth.

'Don't finish them.'

The storm clouds are closing in and a wind is gusting up.

'Hey! What's that?' Sibu thumps Frik's arm, tipping the nuts to the ground. Frik focuses upwards and the two of them lift their rifles shoulder height. Something is moving at a brisk pace about 10 metres in front of them. It freezes at the sound of their voices and the cocking of their guns, turns to look at them, a small, furry creature hanging from its jaws.

265

Sibu lowers his rifle, 'Ah man, it's just a dog.'

Frik follows suit, 'Ja, with its afternoon snack—looks quite possessive of it, hey.'

The two guards chortle. 'Ja, the dogs that survived are tougher than before—no more Dogmor for them,' Sibu comments.

'True as, hey. Damn it! The nuts, man!'

'Well, pick them up!'

'I'm doing it! Just keep watch!'

Nefer senses that he has averted danger for now. He spots the kitchen door in the distance, puts his head down and sets towards it.

'Yes, that's it, that's the entrance we want. Good boy, Nefer, nearly there,' Elke encourages him from the pendant.

Crewless Kitchen

16/01/2051

'I don't see why you can't send a messenger to call off the war,' Valtere, perched on the edge of a chair, suggests to the Queen. The kitchen is empty, apart from the two of them. Regan prepares a tray for tea.

'It's too late now. Unless it comes from my lips, they are bound to think it's a bluff forerunning an ambush. I need some time with Keesa; it's not feasible for me to travel now.' Regan observes Valtere's worrying face. 'For now, all is under control. Keep a look out out front for me, but don't stray too far. I may need your assistance at short notice.'

The eagle assents and goes to the front gate area, winging high, his eyes scouring in the direction of the gravel leading to the Chamber, worn in with car tracks.

Approach

'Just hold for a sec,' Colter says directing his hands towards Maen and Nathan. He completes the seals quickly. The wind begins whipping through the veldt. Maen's tail swishes involuntarily every now and then. This weather has always made him edgy.

'Okay, Nathan,' Maen says, 'like I said, keep yourself scarce. Colter, remember, as quiet and low as possible. Follow my lead, sticking close to any bushes or trees. And wait until I've relayed the message on the talkie before we cross to the back entrance. Let's go.'

The two of them start off on foot on the same tack that Nefer trotted. Any streaks of remaining sunlight have been shouldered out by blackening clouds and the first rumbles of thunder sound out from them now. Maen's ears flatten against his head. He can feel Colter humming behind him.

Encroaching Storm

16/01/2051

Regan nips into Keesa's bedroom to fetch something from the cupboard while the water is on to boil. The air has chilled suddenly and, despite the sigmoid harness over all the windows, the low thunder rolls from above are accompanied by sharp flashes of light in each of the casements. Regan grabs a knit for Keesa. The water is piping hot on her return to the kitchen. She transfers it into the china and makes her way along the passage. She instructs the guards at the door to let no one in at all, apart from Valtere or Keesa's friend, if it is a matter of necessity. Keesa is hitched up on the arm of the couch, taking in the erratic, blinking windows. Regan joins her there, hands the girl the cropped jersey to put on, sets the tea tray down.

'How are you feeling now?'

'Much better, thanks,' Keesa sits down, facing the Queen. It strikes her that she feels safer here than in her home in Hale.

'Would you like some tea?'

'Not right now, thanks.'

Regan puts the teapot down. 'You said you wanted to ask me something?'

'Yes.' Keesa's stomach is jumpy. Her body is becoming tetchy from the unflagging state of limbo of not knowing where home is.

'Would you consider a truce between the Chambers if I was the one to put it forward to the Light royalty?'

With these words hanging in the air, Regan realises that, despite her resolve a month ago, she had been hoping that the girl had changed her mind and would ask to come live at the Dark Chamber. 'I thought you had made your choice.'

'I know but I still don't see why the two Chambers can't end the fight and start working together.'

'What brought this on?'

269

'Just a feeling that maybe I'm the one who is supposed to bring the change.'

Regan considers this. The girl may well be right. 'You know that I agree with your sentiments. However, after offering a way to peace between the families on two occasions and being rejected on both counts, I vowed I would never do it again.'

'But I would be the one offering it.'

'I know. I am surprised you would put yourself in that type of danger. You came all the way here just to ask me that?'

The girl nods unconvincingly. Another flash in the window. Keesa's eyes flit to it.

'Is something happening outside?' she asks.

'You've seen thunderstorms before, surely? Do they frighten you?'

'I've seen some. They don't scare me. I like them. It feels like there's something else happening too, though.'

As intuitive as my grandmother, Regan thinks. 'I'm afraid I must have taken orders in the last couple of days. The Light Chamber thinks that I have declared war on them. We are at risk of being attacked.'

'Yes. I can feel the Light royals coming towards us. It's not too late, Mother, this could be the perfect chance to call a truce.'

'I think it is time I finally accept who I am, Keesa, and the family I come from. You, however, can still decide to join the Dark. It is not too late for you either.'

'I have a duty. It prevents me from joining you here.'

The two of them look at each other, a comfortless impasse hanging between them again.

Talkie Whispers

16/01/2051

'Ryle? Come in?'

'Ryle here, Your Majesty,' the reply crackles through Maen's walkie-talkie.

'Advance to the front entrance. Do you read me? The front entrance.'

'Copy that, advancing to front entrance now. Over.'

'Do not contact me until I have opened communication again. Over and out.'

He switches off and shoves the outmoded device into his side-pocket. It might be an old model but at least it doesn't require a cell tower to operate.

'We'll have to wait until those two go before we move,' Maen whispers.

'Shouldn't take too long. Scouts will spot the army soon enough,' Colter replies, shifting his weight from one knee to the other. The two of them are crouching in a section of tall grass, a short distance from where Sibu and Frik are standing guard. Lightning flickers the Dark Chamber into clarity every now and then and, as the clouds rumble, a warm rain begins to spit.

A Meeting of Old Enemies

16/01/2051

Valtere throws out warning cries as he makes his way back to the Chamber, the fitful wind jerking him off-course every now and then. He spots the scouting vehicle scrambling beneath him now, headed for the gates. They must also have sighted the chain of Light Army vehicles making their way towards the Chamber at full speed. Within a minute of the scouting vehicle's arrival, word of the enemy's imminent approach is relayed to Haaken and, from there, circulates quickly through the ranks of guards and soldiers. Soon every guard has been recalled from around the grounds to amass behind the front gates, snipers peering over the walls next to it and alighting in any trees high enough to have a view of the road.

The Light troop pelts over the ridge in the distance, chewing the road up and spewing billows of dust into the cooling air. One Dark guard, carrying a large wooden pole with a plain white flag suspended from it, is let through the gate. He lifts it as the chain of vehicles approaches. The first four-by-four screeches to a halt within a few metres of the lone guard. Army cadres step out from it, clipping themselves quickly to the open car doors, guns poised over the frames.

Ryle disembarks, flanked by armed Light guards. He makes his way to the gate alone. It is opened, and Haaken steps out. The two men stand face-to-face, each has his weapon holstered at his hip.

'Haaken, it is has been a long time.'

'Ryle, that it has.'

'Why the white flag?'

'Orders from our Queen.'

'We believe she is holding a child by the name of Lady Keesa. We have orders from our King to collect her and return her to the Light Chamber.'

'You will need to personally request that from the Queen. She is presently unavailable.'

272

'We have come to settle a war and your Queen is unavailable?'

'I'm afraid so. I ask you to respect the white flag rule.'

'We shall wait for your Queen, then.'

The two men nod to one another.

Ryle turns to his army in their vehicles filed back along the road and addresses them.

'We await the Queen of Night. The white flag is out. Do not disarm.'

He throws Haaken a look and retreats to his vehicle, his message getting relayed from one Light car to the next as he does. The gate is opened slightly and Haaken goes back inside, some of the Dark guards shifting their weight from one foot to the other, checking their weapons, taking aim once again.

Preparing for a Truth

16/01/2051

Regan stands. 'I am going to lift the shield of invisibility from you now. As much as I would like to, it's not appropriate that I continue to protect your identity.'

Keesa's hands start tingling. 'Can't we wait a while longer? A few more years? Until I've found my feet?'

'It's time you take responsibility for the choice you are making, Keesa. You cannot build a reign as a Light royal on a lie. If I am with you when I remove it, I can protect you from any punishment by the Light family.'

She knows her mother is right. The terror is sheer. 'Okay. What do I do?'

'Come stand here.'

Regan moves to the open space in the centre of the ballroom. Keesa follows and stops in front of the Queen.

Scent

16/01/2051

Nefer looks back to see the two guards breaking into a run, crossing the patch of ground between them and the back wall of the Chamber and disappearing out of sight around its side. He corners the edge of the kitchen door cautiously, checking for any human movement.

'Yes, this is the right entrance, good boy. Now...' Elke's voice begins fading in and out, 'Oh, dear...think you might lose me...' And with that, the connection is lost. Nefer feels a shudder in Toekoums as he wakes up in the dog's mouth, followed by alarmed wriggling. He gently sets the kitten down on the floor. Toekoums turns on him, hackles up—as up as they can be given that he is soaked in Nefer's saliva—and hisses at the dog. Nefer backs off, taking a passive posture and cocks his head to one side. The kitten registers that they are in an unfamiliar kitchen, feels the pendant still warm from use and realises this must be the scullery of the Dark Chamber. Nefer sniffs at the air, whines softly.

'Keesa,' the kitten whispers, looking in the direction that Nefer's nose is pointed.

The two animals steal out of the kitchen into the passage. Luckily for them, the darkness of the corridors is even heavier than usual, what with the storm gaining momentum outside. Nefer leads them around three corners and comes to halt at the fourth, sensing the presence of humans. He peeks around it, sees four guards stationed outside a door. He looks back to the kitten, who can see by his straining legs that Nefer has located the whereabouts of the girl. Nefer turns his snout back to the passage and starts to wag his tail.

＊＊＊

Once the two guards are out of sight, the royal brothers foot it to the kitchen door, entering circumspectly, guns at the ready. They look towards the unlit passage beyond, then at each other. With Keesa's signal still obscured, they know they will be going forth blind to find her. With his feline nostrils, Maen is picking her scent up at moments now but he can't be sure. They both turn as the sound of quick claws on wood scratches out in the nearby corridor. A dog rounds the corner. Colter is aiming to kill. The kitten bounds in behind and Maen stays his brother's arm.

'Take us to her, boy,' Maen whispers to the canine, picks Toekoums up and places him in one of the generous side-pockets just above his knee. The brothers follow Nefer quietly down the first passage, the second. Despite the weapon cocked in them, Maen's hands are throbbing with power. His brother in front of him is unknowingly beginning to shed sparks of electricity. The wind whistles through the old farmstead and every now and then, the passages flitter a little brighter as lightning forks outside.

Unlocking

16/01/2051

She looks up to the Queen's face, which has taken on a single-mindedness. Her eyes have darkened and it feels to Keesa as if she is peering into her soul. Her hands are poised before her, aimed towards the girl. Keesa feels energy issuing from them, slightly volatile and restless at first, which then settles to a steady stream. Regan closes her eyes for a few seconds and draws air into her lungs, as though she is breathing herself back into the moment she first placed a shield around the fetus in her womb. Keesa feels the coursing from the Queen's hands shifting to higher gear now. The room feels to have less space in it; the girl's ears begin popping with the pressure.

Regan opens her eyes, draws her palms to her face, then swivels her hands, moving them towards Keesa, thumbs protruding. Keesa feels a sharp pressure on her forehead, just above and between her eyes and her stomach lurches. Her legs are screaming out to turn and run as fast as she can. She stops them, feeling nauseous with the effort of it. Regan gradually peels the shield away, her hands fanning out from the vertical midline of Keesa's body. To the girl, it is like having something that has become an integral part of her being in its familiarity torn away, an adjoined barnacle.

'It is undone,' Regan states, drops her hands, and steps back. There it is. A marking in Keesa's energy field. The girl's is a disc of red and gold, swirling in and out of itself, level with her heart.

As the brothers round the third corner, the shearing of Keesa's shield ripples out to them like an invisible bomb. Colter looks at his brother, who stares back at him. They are thrown, despite the fact that each of them had seen signs of it before.

'She is a halfling,' Colter says under his breath.

Maen nods, his face anxious. There is one thought in both of their heads: Elke. The consequences of this discovery are harsh. What with Elke's history with Dark royals, Keesa's prospects suddenly appear tenuous at best, at worst, grave.

'Do you see anything different about me?' Regan asks the girl.

'There's a round red thing moving in front of your chest.'

'To me yours is red and gold. Aside from your father, we are the only ones able to see these markings. It proves beyond doubt that we are mother and daughter.'

Keesa lets out an unmeditated laugh of pleasure. A smile breaks out on Regan's face. The storm, the misconceived war, the incalculable future, all fade. This moment is theirs, and it is good.

Colter has eyed the guards around the fourth corner, indicates the number to Maen. The two brothers lift their assault rifles, and Colter shoves Nefer out into full view of the guards. Nefer starts barking viciously at them, making his way towards the library. It was Elijah's scent that had set his tail wagging earlier; he is concerned for his master.

'Hey! Where's this dog from?' one of the guards shouts.

'Jesus, I don't know, let's take it out!' another answers, aiming his gun at the canine.

'Don't shoot! What if it belongs to the Queen? You know how the royals are about their pets!'

By now, Nefer has inched his way just past them. Elijah dashes into the passage.

'Fer! I knew it was you! Don't hurt him! He's with me!'

The dog goes to stand between the guards and the boy, still showing his teeth. With the guards' attention taken, Maen and Colter round the corner. 'Elijah, get out of the passage!' Colter shouts, as they each fire shots into the guards closest to them, a bullet in each leg. Elijah grabs Nefer by the collar and ducks back into the library. The two guards hit the ground, grabbing their limbs and howling with pain. The guard furthest from the Light brothers is retreating down the passage, his weapon aimed at the royals. Colter sends a brief current from his hands to those of the guard still standing by the door, who drops his weapon from the shock. Maen, in the meantime, has exploded the lock on the door to the ballroom with a quick, focused roar. Colter fires into the guard's leg as he is crawling towards his weapon. Maen takes aim at the guard backing off down the corridor, but as he about to squeeze the trigger, Nefer escapes from Elijah's grip on his collar, and attacks the guard, sinking his teeth through army gear and into thigh.

'Elijah! Get your dog out the way before I shoot!' Maen yells. Elijah watchfully enters the passage again, extricates Nefer's jaws from the guard's flesh, and yanks him back into the library. Maen shoots the lone guard making a limping scurry down the corridor in his good leg, then says, 'Colter, you need to put them all out; it's too risky; they could notify the others.'

Colter sees Maen's point, lifts his hands, and projects just enough current into all four guards for them to lose consciousness.

'Come on, Eli, you'll be safer with us,' Colter calls to the boy, who pokes his head out and joins the brothers, trailing Nefer behind him by the collar. Colter struggles to turn the door handle of the ballroom, which is now merely a short piece of iron—the rest of it lying on the floor in pieces.

Something large flies around the corner. 'Look out! Above your head!' Elijah yells to Maen. It is Valtere, suspended in the gloom, stirring up the clammy air with the flapping of his imposing wings. He settles on the ground, only to be charged at by the horsey Dane, nearly strangling himself on his collar. Maen blocks the dog's path to the eagle.

'Leave the bird be—injuring the Queen's helper is not going to aid us right now,' he cautions. Colter turns back to the door, leans on the handle, and manages to thrust it open.

CHAPTER 26

The Battle Within, the Battle Without

16/01/2051

The heavy wooden door swings back and bashes against the wall. The brothers both take a few steps inside, and halt. After the sombre passageway, and the expectation that they would enter some kind of holding cell, they are surprised by the sweeping ballroom with its greys and reds and orchestra, all swathed in the theatrical light of candelabras. Regan stands in the centre of the expanse, her sword raised in one hand, her other arm shielding Keesa, who stands behind her, looking out at the intruders. The pressure in the space shifts the moment Keesa, Regan and Maen all occupy it, as though molecules move at a higher speed; objects are more distinct, colours look syrupy. Elijah and Nefer slink unnoticed into the back corner of the room, taking cover behind a large armchair. Toekoums springs out of Maen's pocket and goes to join them, crouching on the arm of the lounger. Valtere follows, perching on a nearby table, keeping a watch on the animals. Maen carefully shuts the door again, still facing the Queen and her captive—the less attention drawn to this room, the better.

Colter sets his eyes on Regan, and paces briskly in her direction, gun still slung over his shoulder, his hands raised towards her heart, shards of current flaking off of them in anticipation.

'Colter, NO!' Maen overtakes his brother, intercepting his hands with the barrel of his weapon. The rifle lights up like a blue Christmas tree, Colter's current crawling over it. Maen cries out and drops it to the ground quickly enough to avoid the shock travelling further than his hand. As Colter turns his head to him, Maen's fear is confirmed; he can see that his sibling has one goal in mind. His eyes are roving, like a turbulent ocean, wanting to engulf, destroy. Colter's faces hardens into indignation; he turns back towards the Queen, and raises his hands once more. She hoists her sword, ready to fling it into Colter's chest.

'DON'T HURT HER!' Keesa screams, as she manages to wrestle out from Regan's insulating arm, and goes to stand in front of her, raising her hands dauntlessly towards Colter. Both the Prince and the Queen lower their hands.

Maen takes a few wary steps towards Keesa and Regan. 'Everyone calm down. Even though the state of war might dictate killing each other as a logical course of action,' he throws Regan a slighted look, 'it is not the answer here.'

'With all due respect, given that our arch enemy, the Queen of Night, declared war on us a day ago, and has detained the youngest member of our family against her will in this Chamber, I ask you, why are you both so quick to protect this untrustworthy woman?' Colter asks.

Silence descends in the room for a moment. Colter looks at Maen, who appears immobile. The King has noticed the slowly revolving discs hanging in front of Keesa and Regan's chests. He looks down to see a pure gold counterpart to theirs, rotating an inch away from his sternum.

Colter eyes his brother, 'What is it?'

Maen looks up into the girl's eyes and murmurs, 'Keesa, I had no idea.'

'Yes, we know that you're a halfling, Keesa. It's no wonder this Dark despot wants you for herself, but it doesn't give her the right.'

'No, Colter, there's something more,' the King says, shaken.

'What?' Colter's snap is met with blankness.

'Will someone please speak sense here?' the Prince persists, exasperated.

'Queen Regan is my mother.'

Keesa's voice rings with pride. Colter's words dry up. His mouth hangs half-open, trying to digest this fact. *Of course*, Maen thinks, *how could I not have realised? There was something about her from the beginning.*

'There's more,' Keesa continues, 'are you going to tell Colter or must I?'

Colter half-chokes words out, 'Tell me what? There's more?' Maen remains wordless.

'King Maen is my father.'

Colter's eyes widen, and see red. He looks at his brother, staggered. The King looks from Keesa's eyes to Regan's.

'It's true, Maen. She is ours.'

Maen's mind trawls through moments that were clues. The signifier on Keesa's forehead during the cricket game. The way her laugh reminded him of another young girl. He casts back to the day that must have been her conception. *If I had known*, he thinks. *I failed the woman I loved. I failed our child. Ten years lost.*

Colter's seething voice pulls Maen out of his head, 'No wonder your fixation on the etiquette of the Light Chamber. It was all compensation for the fact that you, Father's favourite, ascendant to the throne, had broken the most sacred of those laws! The good son is nothing but a treacherous coward.'

'I never knew about Keesa.'

'Well, you certainly must have known what you were doing when you created her.'

'Regan and I have not seen each other for many years.'

'Are you telling me this war has nothing to do with the fact that you and the Queen conceived a halfling together?'

'There isn't a war,' Keesa states.

'I'm sorry?' Colter scoffs, lifting his hands to the heavens in incredulity. 'Have I journeyed through the Looking Glass? Maen ordered our army to approach your front entrance minutes ago.'

'Keesa is right. I'm afraid that war was declared mistakenly on your Chamber. Your men would have been met with a white flag.' The Queen looks to Valtere.

'Your Majesty is correct. Both armies were awaiting word from you when I left there,' the eagle confirms.

'This is nothing short of a farce! How on earth does one 'mistakenly' declare war?' Colter barks.

'I was under orders at the time that I assigned the messenger his mission,' Regan answers.

'From who?'

'My mother.'

'She's dead.'

'That's how it works in the Dark Chamber. The ancestors can wield influence in spirit form over their offspring.'

'It's what's been happening to me with the goat, and Toekoums, and other things,' Keesa says.

'We had been told something of this, but mostly believed it to be a myth,' Maen remarks.

'Queen Regan wants to change the way the orders happen,' Keesa says.

'How do you propose to do that?' Colter asks the Queen sceptically.

'I have some ideas. It would best be achieved in conjunction with Keesa,' Regan replies.

'A convenient trump to play so as to manipulate her into joining your Chamber,' Colter comments.

Keesa cuts off his disdain, 'Nobody made me come here. I asked Elijah to bring me. I want to propose a truce between the Chambers.'

The brothers fall silent.

'Are you sure this was your idea, Keesa?' Maen asks.

'It was.' He can see she is telling the truth.

Memories of entreating his mother to call for peace between the families flit across Colter's mind now. 'And are you open to this, Queen Regan?' Colter puts it to her.

'I was not in favour at first,' her gaze flickers in Maen's direction, 'however, I consider the loosening of my mother's hold on the Dark Force to be of the utmost priority. A working relationship between the Chambers with Keesa as bridge may be the only answer left.'

'But have you not been continuing your Mother's legacy in the meantime?' Colter poses.

'No, I have gradually been changing the Dark Force to move away from my mother's tactics and philosophy.'

'And what exactly has happened to the bacterial mutation—are there any remnants of it left?' Maen enquires.

'I am in the process of eradicating them.'

'In the process? You've had a decade to do this—why only now?'

'It has come to my attention lately that there was still some work being carried out on a new strain.'

'By who?'

Regan pauses. 'I have been carrying it out, but—'

'So! The truth comes out! So much for your new plan!' Colter jabs.

'I was under orders at the time.'

'Yet again, the orders! It strikes me as an exceedingly useful blanket excuse to claim for any wrongdoing on your part,' the Prince smirks.

'Both Keesa and I would need to cultivate certain Light powers in order to carry out the nullification of the order system.'

'I struggle to comprehend how a Dark Queen such as yourself is capable of holding a Light frequency,' Colter comments.

'With all due respect, Colter, you hardly know the Queen,' Maen points out.

'Coming to the defence of your whore once more?'

284

Maen turns on his brother, his eyes turning bright green, his voice bordering on a roar, 'I would ask you to refrain from your vulgar remarks. You should know that is no way to refer to a woman, let alone a Queen.'

This shuts Colter up for the moment. An icy gust of wind slices through the room. Keesa cranes her head to look at the ceiling behind Regan's head. 'She's close,' she whispers to Regan. 'I'm here with you, we won't let it happen,' Regan assures her.

Maen addresses the Queen. 'Keesa has been chosen as the next Sun-bearer. What you are proposing to us is that you step into the role of mother to Keesa in some manner. We need some indication that your basic maternal instincts are intact.'

The Queen looks down at her girl with pride. 'That was the promise you spoke of?' Keesa nods.

Maen continues, 'My question is, how is it that Keesa came to end up on the doorstep of Aedan's house?'

Regan pauses. She cannot build her reign on a lie either, Dark Queen or not. 'Prior to her birth, I ordered my eagle to put her to death. He disobeyed my orders, and left her instead on a doorstep.'

Maen lowers his head and brings his hand to his brow. He had been coming close to entertaining their proposal. This does not bode well.

'And you still have the audacity to call yourself her mother!' Colter's vitriol is back in full force.

'I am the woman who brought her into this world,' Regan retorts.

'I will never give you the opportunity to exert your twisted form of maternal cultivation on Keesa,' the Prince spits out.

'That's not up to you. That's Keesa's choice to make.'

Colter is itching to lunge at her again, 'You don't deserve to live after what you did!'

'COLTER! ENOUGH!' Keesa screams. He is surprised by the power of her voice, and reels himself in. 'Queen Regan tried to have me killed because she knew I would die a worse death or live a life of torture at the hands of Queen

Signa. You are killing me every day keeping me locked up like a prisoner because you know that I will live the life that you are so angry with yourself for giving up. Your bitterness stops me from becoming the royal I was born to be.'

Colter stares at Keesa, resisting swallowing her words of truth. Maen senses that Regan's derisive sense of humour has minified; the Regan of past would surely have inserted a dig to Colter's detriment in this moment. Traces of her arrogance, her presumptuousness, seem also to have evaporated. Her face reminds him of how she used to look as a girl before she learnt how to smile or laugh. She has put herself back together, but a rip is still evident, like a watercolour imprinted in her fibre now.

'To speak to me with such a tone of disrespect is unacceptable, Keesa,' Colter says. 'I never set out to hurt you. I will admit, I have my regrets about cutting ties with my family the way I did. But jealous of you? I chose the life I have with Aedan for a reason. It's an uncomplicated one. It suits me.'

'No disrespect, but it's not the one I want,' Keesa returns, more contained now. 'I love our home, and am grateful for everything you and Aedan have done for me, but I am asking you to let me choose my path now.'

'You're 10 years old, Keesa.'

'Things are happening quickly. If we wait until I'm an adult, your family will no longer exist.'

Colter's chest closes up, a dark clam, retreating. 'It seems you have already made your mind up. Why even ask my permission?'

'Because I don't want to be your enemy. I don't want to lose you.'

Colter looks down, avoiding the girl's entreating eyes. Regan feels Keesa cringe; she places her hand between the girl's shoulder blades.

'Everything has its consequences, Keesa. You need to have patience,' Maen tries to assure her. As much as his brother has stirred his wrath, it gives him no joy to observe strain between him and the girl.

Keesa's voice is crestfallen now, 'Why must we all fight? Why can't we have peace and all be one family with the mother and father and uncles and aunts, like it's supposed to be?'

286

'I wish it was as straightforward as that, Keesa,' Maen replies. 'It is an impossibility for the two families to come together, let alone call a truce.'

Regan looks to Maen. 'Is it an impossibility, Maen? We have been here before. This time it is your daughter who is asking you.'

Colter stares at the Queen, dumbfounded by what has yielded from her mouth. He turns to his brother, 'You've considered a truce before? You didn't tell me? After all my pleading to end this feud?'

Disinclined to answer, Maen keeps his eyes on Regan, his brow furrowed, tail whipping. 'Regan has approached me a couple of times with the proposal, yes.'

'A couple of times?' Colter is becoming rankled again. 'Just what kind of proposal are we talking about here?'

Maen holds his words, stony-faced, focused on those dark eyes that still pull him in, willing or not.

Regan provides an answer, 'A merging of the houses. A marriage between King Maen and myself.'

Colter's voice is rising again, 'You have considered taking the Queen of Night for your wife?'

Maen clips his brother's mounting ferment, 'Now is not the time for this conversation. I couldn't tell you, it was the highest act of treason possible. And anyway, you were gone by then.'

'Did mother know?'

Maen pauses. 'Mother and Father both.'

Regan presses on. 'Maen, you must make a decision now. Truce or no truce, I will call off my army. However, I cannot predict what my mother might unleash on the Family of Light.'

The Queen and girl watch for his response. Maen picks up a glimmer of hope in Regan, only because he knows how truth makes its way out of her eyes. Colter's stare is boring into the side of Maen's head.

'I admire your courage, Keesa. My father's blood shows. I wish I could give you the answer you are looking for. The risks involved in agreeing to a truce still appear too great to me. Rules are rules. I know that they are not all ideal, but the fundamental ones are surely what has kept the families intact, and a balance of kinds in place.'

He hears Colter breathe a sigh. *I may have wanted a truce before*, the Prince thinks, *but not with the woman who ordered the murder of my girl.* Keesa looks at Maen in disbelief. The familiar sense of snuffing out the promise of some desired future slinks over the King.

'As you wish.' Regan says. That sense that she is withdrawing never fails to raise an untenable panic in Maen. 'I will inform my Army of a complete retreat.' *I am the dolphin trapped in a tank*, she thinks. *Stupid, stupid, blind belief.*

Keesa walks to stand in front of Maen; her mind scrabbling to find a way to convince him to reconsider. *If you had listened to me, none of this would have happened*, Regan imagines her mother hissing. She hears her mother. It's a small sound, in among others. Valtere adjusting his claws where he is perched. A thin whine from the dog. The wind pulling around the Chamber, rain freckling the ground. An almost imperceptible chuckle. Not that she had ever heard genuine laughter from her mother, only audible sneers. Regan begins turning her head to locate Signa's energy, then jerks it forward again. The skin on Keesa's back crawls. She can smell her from here. A non-odour, like the smell of cold. Or mucid reptilian scales. Regan raises her sword and begins tracking it from side to side with tight control, including the three royals in its range.

'What the... Maen, get Keesa out the way!' Colter shouts. Keesa is yanked and placed behind Maen. Colter lifts his hands once more towards Regan.

'Not yet, Colter!' Maen asserts, but readies himself for attack nonetheless.

'My powers... there's something wrong,' Colter's voice is edged with panic.

'Mine are not coming through either,' Maen echoes.

'Show the girl,' Regan commands in an even voice.

'Not a chance,' Colter responds, and adds in a low voice to Maen, 'I told you we couldn't trust her.'

'Let me through,' the girl says, trying to shove her way forward; Maen's arms restrain her.

'Keesa, keep still,' the King whispers, then addresses the Queen, 'Regan, please see reason, I know you care for the girl, let's work this out without hurting one another.'

'Enough words. Bring the girl into my view,' Regan says, in a voice like a chant.

'What, so you can finish the job you intended all along? Dream on!' Colter throws at her.

Keesa struggles against Maen's arms, 'You don't understand, I know what's happening, I can stop her, just let me through!' Maen and Colter exchange a glance; they have both learnt the hard way about underestimating Keesa. Maen slowly lets the girl come to stand between the two of them, each brother extending a hand to shield her. Keesa's eyes trace from the Queen's singular stare up to the ceiling. 'She's turned her sword into a scythe,' she says, testing for the tingling of fire in her hands. No response. 'Signa's made her do it.'

'A what?' Colter utters.

'Using her intention, her sword can now block our powers, or obliterate our souls forever if she stabs us with it.'

'Well now, there's a rosy thought,' Colter remarks.

'I thought that was a myth too,' Maen says uneasily.

'We can't just wait for her move. I'll get the sword, you protect Keesa,' Colter says in a low voice, and starts forward tentatively.

'Don't move! She'll kill you for sure,' Keesa cautions. Colter pauses; he needs Keesa in a safer place before he starts taking chances with his own life. 'Let me try bring her out of her ordered state,' Keesa adds quietly. Another snigger scratches out from Signa. Keesa feels the temperature of her blood beginning to rise. She glares at the Dark matriarch. Signa looks somehow older than before; soft blue veins web across her temples; her hair is cropped shorter, barely covering her head. Keep focus, Keesa thinks. She fixes her eyes to Regan's, which are glazed, as though her personality is folding away into her, leaving a space blank enough for doing, executing.

'Mother, she is hanging above you.'

Regan has not registered her words. 'If you will not join the Dark Chamber, there is only one course of action to take, little girl,' she intones. Keesa watches as Signa's mouth forms the words that Regan is speaking. The old monarch views her daughter, contempt oozing for this her puppet. Keesa is beginning to fume.

'Mother, listen to me, it's your daughter, Keesa. You are under orders. I need you to wake up.'

Signa's grey-white skin is pulled tighter over her protruding bones. Her eyes are recessed into sockets the colour of deep red bruises—yet are no less intense in their single-minded stare. One can hardly tell if she is a woman or a man, were it not for her queenly regalia of black. She snarls a smile at Keesa now; she does so enjoy the child's spunk.

'Mother, can't you see? She is using you once again to her own ends! Put the sword down and walk to me. We can defeat her together.'

Signa throws her head back, and a raw cackle hacks from her throat. Her eyes come back to Keesa.

'Clever girl.' Her lips form the words, but the sound finds its outlet in Regan's mouth. It is clear to Keesa that Signa feels no love for her daughter. She will make Regan pay for the shame she has brought to the Dark Force. Elijah is struggling to curtail Nefer now; the dog has dashed out from behind the armchair, and is straining towards Regan, barking savagely. Valtere has unfolded his broad wings, and directs sharp cries towards Nefer and the ghoul hovering above Regan. He cannot see her, but knows her energy only too well.

Something about witnessing Regan being operated like a dumb marionette dredges up unbearable sadness in Keesa. Stay focused, she thinks. Don't play into her hand. But as she shoves it down into her gut, it veers up in a turbid deluge, gathering impetus as all the pain, all the anger from the instant of separation from her mother so long ago rises to the surface of this moment.

'Mother, it is me, Keesa, your daughter, I want you to wake up! MOTHER! WAKE UP!'

Still no response. Keesa's heart drops. Signa's grip is tighter than ever.

Probably because she knows that if she kills me now, it will snuff out Elke's legacy for good, she thinks.

'This is not working; I'm going to take her out from behind,' Colter murmurs.

'Please, no, she'll snap out of it soon... Please don't kill her,' Keesa begs Colter. He pauses, regarding the girl. He will give her a few moments more; then he will do what needs to be done, even if it means she will hate him forever. At least she will have her life.

'Toekoums!' Elijah lets slip. The kitten has tumbled to the floor, and lies on his side, his body stiff. The pendant is lit green. Keesa looks to Elijah. He catches her eye.

'I think the Queen is coming through again,' he says in a pressing tone, still keeping a rein on Nefer.

'Bring Toekoums closer so I can see him,' Keesa asserts, keeping an eye on Signa's actions.

'Mother's in for a few shocks,' Colter remarks, glancing at Maen.

'Damnit,' Elijah says under his breath, as he picks the kitten up with one hand, while gripping Nefer's collar with the other. 'Nefer, sit.' The dog is becoming increasingly more frenzied with Regan's threat, as well as the sinister energy pendent above her—this is not the first time Nefer has sensed that same menace. Elijah edges towards the small table that the tea tray and its unused contents still stand on. Keesa watches as Signa and Regan's eyes take note of the creeping boy. It is evident, though, that Signa's energy must remain focused on Regan so as to maintain her ordered state. Were it not for this, Elijah would have been dealt with by the Dark Queen by now.

'Wretched kitten,' Signa mutters; it parrots from Regan's lips. The two of them turn back to their main targets. One moment more of their eyes trailing and Colter would have made a break for Regan. *Next gap*, he thinks, *and I make my move no matter what.*

Elijah carefully shifts the tray to one side with his elbow, and sets Toekoums down facing Keesa. The locket's light hums stronger, Elke's countenance bright in the centre of it. Even though Elke has never been able to see spirits with her naked eye, she senses the visitant in the room immediately. The Dark Queen's energy is blurred to her, however, and her intentions inscrutable. Elke instructs the girl.

'Keesa, go inside. I will protect you.'

Keesa's ears are itching madly, and the pressure underneath the bump on her coccyx is building to an ache. She looks back to the resolute stares of the enforced dyad before her, and the gleaming blade aimed forward.

'I can't. There's too much happening.'

'It's the only way! Trust me, Keesa!' Elke persists.

'Not now!' Keesa feels a wave of nausea heaving through her stomach. Signa is beckoning her with orders, trying to suck her in with Regan.

'MOTHER! Why can't you hear me? She's pulling me in too now! Mother! PLEASE!'

Keesa breathes in sharply, lets the breath out gradually, a liquid assurance filling the space around her body as she does so. Her feet are wanting to walk towards the point of the sword. A thought presents itself like a place of comfort, an obvious verdict. The blade belongs in my heart. Her left foot inches forward.

'KEESA! Don't do it!' Elke shouts. Nefer unleashes a string of ferocious gnashes, now towards Keesa. Maen and Colter each grip one of the girl's slender arms tighter with their outstretched arms now, forced to move closer to Queen Regan.

'KEESA! It is your grandmother, Queen Elke, telling you to stop!' the Light Queen exclaims again.

Nefer is practically foaming at the mouth now, pulling Elijah along behind him as he writhes towards Regan. Valtere is rapping out squawks, and suddenly takes to the air, swooping down towards Nefer. Even though he can see Regan is under orders, he cannot allow the canine to sink his teeth into her. Nefer yanks Elijah forward once more, and the eagle misses the dog, crashing instead straight into Elijah's head. The boy is caught unawares, and brings his hands up to his head in a reflex motion, allowing his grip on Nefer's collar to loosen. The dog leaps at the opportunity, and breaks out instantly into a gallop towards Regan.

'KEESA! GO INSIDE! OR IT WILL BE TOO LATE!' Elke screams.

Close enough now, Nefer takes a running jump, soaring through the air past the Queen of Night, snatching the sword clean out of her hand. A clang of steel on teeth rings out as he connects it; then his paws hitting the wooden floor, a scratch of claws as he carries on running to the far side of the ballroom, where he comes to a stop, and turns. He stands, hostile, the blade between his teeth, growling at Regan and in Signa's direction.

'KEESA, FOR LAST TIME, WAKE UP!' Elke bellows.

Keesa's body shudders; Regan's follows suit. The two of them come back into their eyes, and lock onto one another.

'Mother? Are you awake?' Keesa ventures. She notices Nefer from the corner of her eye.

'Oh dear God, no,' Regan says. 'What did I do?'

'It's okay, the dog stopped you.'

Regan glances towards Nefer, her sword balancing in his jaw.

'Keesa, I'm so sorry. I thought I was strong enough.'

Keesa becomes aware of a cold lack in her right arm; Colter has stepped away from her; his voice assaults the air now, 'You've used up all your chances, Queen of Night, I won't let you play with my daughter's life again!' With that, he lifts his hands towards Regan.

'No! COLTER! NO!' Maen screams, and starts towards his brother.

'MOTHER, RUN!' Keesa shouts, as she bolts towards Colter, her hands up. The power in them is weak, however, as it always is just after she has awoken from an ordered state. A thought like a dull mallet thuds into Regan's head. There's nowhere to run. She has no fear of death. Only of leaving Keesa once more, this time with Signa ready to fill the space, mouth watering. She takes stock of the distance between herself and her sword lodged in the dog's mouth, and starts to make a dash for it. Valtere wings towards Colter, senses the vehement electrical field around him, and has to angle off.

'COLTER, DON'T DO IT!' Elke yells, watching the scene with a chilling sense of déjà-vu. Keesa resorts to her bare hands, and goes to force Colter's arms to

293

aim elsewhere. Maen grabs Keesa and thrusts her to his left side, knowing that if she should touch Colter now, the shock would be severe. He turns towards Colter, fills his lungs to roar.

They are all too late. Colter catapults out a lethal surge of current, so bright in its blueness, that all in the room are blinded momentarily. A scream of pain is flung from Regan as the force hits her. The sound tears through Maen like a scraggy crow plunging its beak into his chest and wresting his heart out. The current holds Regan clean off the ground for a few seconds in a wild jerking dance. Then, as though the music is stopped suddenly, she thuds to the floor, face-up, arms splayed, eyes unmoving, her dress crisp and blackened.

Then quiet. Wind whips at the walls. A silent flare of lightning. A crack of thunder directly overhead. Rain starts to fall in earnest, the pattering on the roof somehow too innocent a sound for the scene.

Maen hastens to the fallen Queen's side, drops to his knees, feels for a pulse on the side of her throat. Valtere gives out a crushed sound, and goes to settle near her. Maen is repeating her name over and over, as though chanting it might call her back to the room. Her neck is as soft as ever, warm still, with life. But no beating beneath her cream skin. He looks up to his brother, his eyes craters of devastation. He looks at his girl.

'She is gone, Keesa.'

Keesa stares at Regan, unbelieving. What is in front of her is not possible. It is a string of misguided images wedged together. It is not how this was meant to turn out.

'Mommy.'

The sound of her own voice naming her now is abhorrent in its emptiness. Colter knew the aftermath would not be easy. He goes down onto his haunches next to the girl.

'She was going to kill you, Keesa.'

'She had come out of the orders.'

'I couldn't stand here and wait for her to follow Signa's command again. It would only have been a matter of time before—'

'Colter,' Maen's voice is swollen with fury, but restricted by grief and the impulse to be gentle in the presence of the body, 'there is nothing you can say.'

Keesa lurches forward and walks to Regan's side, her movements unhinged and odd. On her knees, she brushes the stray hairs from Regan's forehead.

'How come her skin didn't burn too?' she asks.

'Her royal blood. It makes her stronger. The body maintains its integrity.'

'Not strong enough.'

An outbreath of derogation sounds from above.

'She was never strong enough,' Signa snipes.

Something in Keesa snaps. Her skin begins prickling with heat. Her eyes rise slowly to meet the Dark Queen's. They are no longer the eyes of a young girl. There is something fierce in them, animal, unformed.

'This is all your fault,' she says to the monarch.

'So much the better,' Signa retorts. 'She was a waste of space in my womb, a disappointment to the Dark Force, and a whore to the Light. I only wish she had died by the scythe. Her traitor soul does not deserve to survive.'

'It is you who should die forever!'

'Have your turn at last words. I heard all their vile admissions earlier. I was prepared to look past your base beginnings, even had hopes that you might reject your Light infection. But you have proven yourself to be nothing but a half-breed stolen from my blood, tainted, like your mother. The time has come to terminate the whole abject lot of you.'

'You are not Queen. My mother is Queen of Night. I will be the next. And I will be your destruction.'

'Ungrateful imposter. You think you can be Sun-bearer and Queen of Dark. Not on my watch. Time to put out your light, little girl.'

With that, Signa stretches her hands towards the sword. The plate of steel squeaks against the dog's teeth as he begins straining to take steps backwards, growling at the force pulling at the sword. Keesa lifts her hands and aims them towards Signa, her eyes rabid.

'I feel her strength, Keesa. It has grown. You must go inside,' Elke says in voice that is growing weaker. Keesa flicks her gaze to Elke; turns back to Signa. Her attention is drawn back to another screech of steel—Nefer is fast losing his grip on the sword.

'What the... What is she doing?' Colter has noticed the teetering blade. He approaches the dog gingerly.

'She'll only kill you with it, Colter,' Keesa murmurs. 'Let me take care of her.'

The veins on Signa's head are bulging with her effort to draw the sword. The determination on her face is ugly. Maen pulls himself up, laggardly leaving the body, and goes to the girl's side. 'Keesa, let Colter and I do this; I want you out of this room and safe now.'

Colter continues edging forward. 'You and Colter can't even see her. How is that going to work? You should all move out the way,' Keesa says in a fixed tone, her eyes set on Signa.

The Prince is within reach of the blade, his fingers poised to snatch it out of the forbidding dog's jaws. In that moment, Signa's exertion pays off. The sword escapes Nefer's grate, and whips up into the air in the Dark Queen's direction, its handle coming to the resting place of Signa's right hand.

'Boys, I am telling you as your mother: listen to the girl right now, and get out of the way,' Elke instructs.

The brothers exchange a glance. Maen goes to lift the unmoving body of the Queen of Night. Once up in his arms, her head lolls back, succumbing to gravity. Colter goes to support it, uncomfortable regarding his brother in distress. Valtere squawks at him, outraged.

'Don't touch her,' Maen snarls, and adjusts his arm so as to support her head in its nook. Colter pulls away. The brothers heed their mother's bidding, uneagerly backing away from Keesa, their eyes returning to the sword in its weird place suspended in the air. Ninev can be heard through the pendant now, rapping out agitated strings of notes. The brothers look towards it to see her delicate yellow form flittering around the shoulders of the Light Queen. They exchange another look; both know to steel themselves for more than the harrowing scene before them.

Elke speaks. 'Keesa, this might be the last thing I say to you: Go inside now. You need to gather your strength from there for this.'

Signa smirks, pleased with her triumph of the will, and how it coincides aptly with the imminent death of her assassin. She aims the blade towards Keesa's chest, sucking up any last shred of vigour still lurking in her phantom sinews so as to fling the weapon accurately. Keesa's hands are throbbing now, but she senses that Signa's force is formidable. Regan had never mentioned Dark spirits moving objects. She takes a deep breath in, and focuses everything that is her on annihilating the monster above. In that moment, Signa finally ejects her avid intention into the sword, and sends it hurling towards Keesa.

'KEESA! REMEMBER YOUR PROMISE! GO INSIDE NOW!' Elke insists for the last time.

With the cursed missile catapulting towards her, Keesa forces a calculation of the energy in the sword, and of that in her lungs. The two do not match. The marvel of erasing the Light family flashes in Signa's toothy smile. Keesa decides to trust her Light grandmother, as Elke had trusted her. She closes her eyes, and sucks all the energy generated in her hands and lungs sharply down into the core of her being. She feels time suspending as she does so—her heartbeat slackens to a near standstill; her lungs empty themselves gradually of air. Everything goes quiet. The only sound she can hear now is the even rhythm of the new, slower cycle of breath that she activates, like the sound of the ocean as it heaves water into itself, and then expels it onto the shoreline.

She keeps her eyes shut, savouring the feeling of being adjourned out of the bedlam of uncovering parents, uncovering powers, Colter's hands facing her mother, the sooty dress. Only the ocean, temperate and subsuming. She forms a picture in her mind of what she will see when she opens her eyes. Pea-green and cerulean-blue moving in currents, and then the oat-coloured sand shifting below. She raises her eyelids.

Nothing. Black. She could be hanging in the sky, orbiting the planet. Her stomach flutters. Careful, she thinks. Concentrate. Lest she return to the room of horror without what she came for. No, she is certain there is water. She moves her hands. Yes, there it is; the soft pressure of liquid sifting between her fingers.

She shifts her feet slightly, feeling for the soaked seabed granules. Something else. Moist, ridged, and buoyant. Sea-moss?

The current changes, starts seeping towards the area behind her. A thin strip of light becomes visible a distance in front of her, an upside-down, shallow U shape. It grows thicker; shows itself a murky green. Bits of it are spilling closer towards her, throwing dull visibility on what surrounds her. She looks upwards, can make out a pattern of corrugations, like the impressions left in sodden sand once the tide has gone out. Then shiny, pointed arrows all in neat rows forming that U shape again. She looks down. Pinky-red. It moves; she almost loses balance. That's when she realises where she is. She is standing inside the whale's mouth, her feet gripping into its viscid, warm tongue, like a stubborn, upright fish. The curve of light ahead is the whale opening its massive jaws. Keesa's stomach reels again. There is nothing to fear, she thinks, you are safe inside yourself. Then the huge sea-creature clamps its great beak shut once more.

Darkness again. Keesa feels something like an implosion happening deep inside the body of the mammoth. Tremors shudder out of it, like a gentle earthquake beginning. And then the light. It seems to well out directly from the whale's structure—billowing out from the gums, twirling out of teeth, sheeting from the top palette, and rising like steam from the tongue. It is the light from behind her that feels most intense, as though the sun is shining on her back. Without knowing how she knows, she is suddenly aware that the whale is turning into a sun of sorts, and the light is exploding out from his centre.

Terror is threatening to overtake her; she arrests it with difficulty. Gradually, reluctantly, she turns to look behind her. What appears like a tidal wave of fire is ballooning out from the whale's throat, illuminating the arched, cerise palette, and the pair of tonsils being thrust forward with the force like two lumbering, meaty wind-socks. A scream breaks loose from Keesa's mouth, and her body relents to an uncontrollable urge to escape the fire. She launches herself up into the water filling the living cavern by bracing her knees, and pushing off from the tongue. She hangs in the centre of the mouth cavity and watches as the fire swamps the space. The fire changes as it comes within a few metres of her into something that looks like pure sunlight. The whale imparts three notes. Keesa looks on as both the salt liquid and blaze before her judder perceptibly with the sounds, as do her own bones. Then she closes her eyes once more as the imploding sun of the whale engulfs her.

Quiet again. The flooding light races and flurries in, in, into the million million minutiae that make up Keesa. Skin, muscle, bone, cell. Never has she felt so complete, so beginning. She hauls all this potency up, up into her lungs like beautiful inflating flowers of gold. Then she opens her eyes.

The scene crashes back in—the air in the ballroom slightly damp with the thunderstorm, a hint of live electricity still clinging in scent, Elke in the corner of Keesa's eye issuing her exigency from the locket, and an awareness of the royal brothers, her insensible mother, and the rest of the animals behind her. And most vividly, the rapier hurtling towards her, Signa grimacing behind it. Keesa fastens her eyes on the tip of the blade, opens her mouth, and lets out a volcanic roar. The sword about to pierce her chest explodes in mid-air, tinkling a small heap of steel onto the floor. The devastating spume continues on its path with virulence, ploughing into the old Dark Queen, blowing her backwards and upwards, surprise dropping her face and extinguishing the smile from her lips. The ceiling is blasted apart with the force of the roar, chandeliers shattering, candle flames quashed, shards of crystal smashing the walls.

Elke watches on as the decimation of Signa by fire 10 years ago is repeated by her granddaughter, amplified with sound. The itching, pressured feeling in Keesa's ears and coccyx is worse than ever, as though something is bursting through. The symbol on her forehead burns bright now—a sphere of light that contains a black counterpart in its centre. Signa hangs onto the split open roof for a moment with gaunt venom.

'You will regret this day, misbegotten mongrel, we will meet again!'

Her voice battles against the last of the torrent that issues from Keesa's mouth. The girl notices how old her hand looks as it clings to the cleft wooden beam. Signa's eyes are laced with hatred and anger, but it is deflation at another plan shattered that renders them listless in this moment. Keesa finds some gratification in glimpsing this.

The old Queen relinquishes her grip and is driven out into the storming sky, ragged and beaten. The wind howls in through the roof, bringing bouts of soft rain with it. Bated late afternoon light filters into the room from the gaping crack in the ceiling, and a flimsy glow still emanates from the pendant. It occurs to Elke that the girl has already repeated the pattern of revenge killing; two reigns of Sun-bearer branded by that is now a reality. *Today's was more of a banishment,* she

299

tells herself. But, yet again, she questions what chain she set off that calculated day in the veldt all those years ago. As her eyes get used to the light in the room, she observes again the symbol on Keesa's forehead, receding slightly now, and other changes that stir in her a somewhat unwilling affection for the girl.

'Well done, Keesa,' she says, 'I see you carry the markings of royalty now.'

'Thank-you, Queen Elke,' the girl replies, unsure of what she is referring to.

Stray Guard

16/01/2051

The guard that had almost made a run for it earlier comes to. He begins edging his way along the ground inch by inch down the labyrinthine stretch of passage that leads to the front door of the Chamber. Each hoist of his limp legs using his arms is punctuated by excruciating pain.

Exit Strategy

16/01/2051

The picture in the pendant is obscured for a few seconds. The connection is growing precarious. The kitten's eyeballs begin roaming beneath his shut eyelids; he is coming up into a midway state. Maen and Colter both come forward, concerned for their mother. The interference lifts, the kitten's eyes settle, and Elke reappears. Her life-force is plainly faltering.

'Mother, I would prefer not to ask you this now, but I am...not certain whether I will get the chance again. I know you can see Keesa's origins now, that she is the daughter of Queen Regan and myself.' He throws an involuntary look towards Regan's body. It feels hollow to say her name out loud in this room now. 'Given these circumstances, as well the fact that we, the Light family, require your permission for Keesa to become the next Sun-bearer, I must ask for your answer on this now.'

'I think you know how I feel about your union with Queen Regan. That Keesa is a result of it is not her fault. I could sense earlier that Regan had been leading the Dark Force on a different course from her mother.' The dwindling Queen pauses, catching her breath. She hesitates at her next words.

'I hereby grant permission for Keesa to become the next Sun-bearer.'

She sees reprieve on Maen and Keesa's faces, and addresses the girl candidly. 'I may be your grandmother, but do not think I give this permission out of familial sentiment. With the blood of the Dark Force in you, I do not trust you. I give permission because you are my last and only hope. You would not have been my first choice. Do not let me down, young Keesa.'

'I will not, Your Majesty,' Keesa says.

Elke turns to her youngest son, 'Colter, it saddens me that you allowed your rage to rule you when what was called for was understanding. Regan was not the peril in that moment. Signa was, and still is, I fear.'

Keesa looks at Colter, bristling. 'There are things she still needed to teach me. I'm not sure how to overcome Signa on my own.'

'I was only trying to protect you!' Colter is feeling the weight of his actions.

'We know this, Colter, but it is time you become more discerning about which battles are worth fighting, and which a good dose of diplomacy can resolve,' Elke points out.

Colter casts his eyes to the ground. This is not the way he wanted to say goodbye to his mother.

'Given the hazard that Signa poses to our future Sun-bearer, I will offer a solution here. My sense is that Keesa is correct in her estimation that it is only through a combined effort between her and Queen Regan that we have a chance of thwarting Signa's cumulating power as a spirit. There is a method of resuscitation that I don't believe you are aware of, as it has hardly ever been used. As the outgoing Queen of Light, I am able to transfer my life-force into another royal, as long as they have not been dead for over three hours. It has never been used on a Dark royal, but I am willing to give it a try now on Queen Regan.'

Maen and Keesa's faces relume; they scan each other. There is no question.

'We accept your gracious offer, Mother. However, it goes without saying that I would not want you to speed up your...departure for that reason.' Maen is working to control uprising emotion. For everyone here, he must show himself brave.

'I am ready to go, my boy. I can feel it is time. Colter?'

The Prince's voice is subdued. 'I cannot say I feel comfortable, but I will not stand in the way.'

'Take this action as my way of righting what I did to Signa. Colter, I hope you will think twice before making reactive choices in the future.'

Colter nods, but his eyes still harbour wariness.

Game Up

16/01/2051

The crawling guard had to stop a few times to rest so as not to black out. Now, at last, he has reached the front door. He manages to open it, and pull himself over its threshold. One of the soldiers towards the back ranks of the Dark Army—still accumulating behind the Chamber gates—notices a slumped body there. He alerts a few combatants, and they make their way towards it, forming a circle around him. The slouched guard just gets the words out of what is taking place inside, before he slips back into unconsciousness. One of the soldiers breaks away now, sprinting towards Haaken. He shunts his way through the bank of soldiers, all throwing him questioning looks. He whispers into the commander's ear. Haaken's eyes freeze, glance in Ryle's direction. He makes his way to the front gate, a path clearing before him as he strides. Ryle and his men begin retreating to behind their vehicles. Then Haaken's rough voice rings out through the muggy air.

'Take the white flag down! Queen Regan has been detained by King Maen and Prince Colter inside! Form your ranks! Shoot to kill!'

Ryle quickly signals his army into attack mode. Gunfire cracks open, quickly accelerating into a fusillade across the gate.

Passage

16/01/2051

'They must know we're here,' Maen says to Colter, as the volley of shots report through the ruptured ceiling.

'Well then, we'd best get started; it won't pay for the Dark Army to clap eyes on Queen Regan in her state,' Elke says.

The Prince panics, 'But Mother, surely there is more we should talk about—'

'Come now, Colter. You know I'm not one for goodbyes. Be kind to one another, all of you, and respect the word of your King. Now, lay Queen Regan's body closer to the pendant. Colter and shepherd boy, secure the door, we can't afford disturbance.'

Elijah and Colter drag one of the heavy couches in front of the door. Maen lifts the body of the Queen of Night once again, and sets her down on a blanket that Keesa has grabbed and spread on the floor.

'Give her room,' Elke says. Maen and Keesa kneel on either side of Regan's body. Maen fixes his gaze on his mother in an attitude of support. His heart is drumming, his throat tight. Ninev begins to sing a melodic tune, a divergence from her usual staccato. Nefer cocks his head at the bird's sound, whining in the back of his throat every now and then. Valtere is positioned on the floor above Regan's head; he starts swaying back and forth slightly on his thick claws. Colter stands back, placing his hand over his mouth. He cannot look directly at the pendant. Keesa's eyes settle momentarily on Regan's skin that has drained of colour. The blood seems to be present only in fast thinning circles now. Her gaze is drawn to the brothers. She knows she will probably always feel torn in this family.

Elke's eyes have brightened now. She flicks them quickly to her sons.

'Here we go. I hope this works. Till I see you again, my boys,' she says in a voice that seems to rise upwards.

'We love you, Mother,' Maen returns in a held voice.

'Till then, Mother,' Colter says.

305

Elke focuses her eyes on Regan. Her breathing becomes uneven. Short in-breath, long exhalation. A magnetic force forms between her and Regan, hoisting towards Elke as she breathes in, and bilging towards Regan as she exhales. Everyone in the room can feel it. Nefer lets out a bark at the bubble of energy. Elke's body and the room in the small house around her grow brighter and brighter, until it seems the sun is rising in it. Ninev flutters above the Queen's head. The magnetic field between the two Queens reaches its height, and feels to pull at the flesh of all the other occupants in the ballroom. A final pulling in of air into her lungs, a brief pause, and the last exhalation leaves Elke's body, moving promptly and surely into Regan's.

The Queen of Night remains motionless. Maen and Colter watch as Elke's gaze aims forward now, as though she is seeing something they cannot, her mouth venturing a smile of deliverance, but her eyes registering another task ahead. Her body goes stiff for second, her back arches. The projection in the pendant begins to flicker out, static interrupting it fitfully. The last image of their mother is of her body giving in, buckling off her chair, out of the oval that frames her. The smile has left her lips. In her unravelling she resembles a child letting go, falling into a sweet sleep. The pendant is black by the time she hits the floor.

Maen cannot allow himself to register what has just happened. He stems the churning within with difficulty, and turns to Regan's supine body. Keesa's eyes catch him as he does. The mere acknowledgement of his pain in them bolsters him slightly. The girl tries to connect with Colter. Despite the anger that she harbours toward him now, she is not oblivious to his loss. But he has turned to the wall, overcome, and is earthing the spill of current out of his body into the bricks. Maen takes Regan's chilled hand.

'Mother, come back to us, wake up,' Keesa says, touching Regan's shoulder. The din of shots and shouts from the ongoing battle at the gate of the Chamber is carried in louder than before on a gust of wind.

'Regan, wake up!' Maen urges. The Queen remains insensate.

'Damnit, we need more time,' Maen murmurs. He looks to Valtere. 'Would you go and inform Haaken that the Queen is not in danger, and to hold off from battle? I don't want more men to lose their lives.'

'Of course,' the eagle says, and flies out through the battered roof. The wind eases for a moment; a pocket of quiet descends upon the room. Elijah has picked Toekoums up with care, and holds him in his arms. The kitten is hardly aware of his surroundings, near delirious with exhaustion. Nefer gives a single, warning bark. His dog-ears are picking up a scuffle happening at the Chamber front door.

The Queen's eyes open, register Maen and Keesa's faces looking over her. Alarm flares across her countenance.

'What happened?' she asks.

Maen's heart leaps. 'We'll explain later; are you all right?'

'I think so. Was I unconscious now?'

'You were dead; Elke breathed life into you again,' Keesa blurts.

'What? Of course. Colter...' Regan strains her head around to see the Prince.

'Don't worry,' Maen places his hand on her shoulder, 'He's not going to try again.'

Regan rests her head back down bit by bit. It is pleasing to simply allow herself to trust Maen's word right now. Then her face clouds; she twists around the other way, senses Signa has left, feels the stiff breeze on her neck, notices the breach in the ceiling.

'And my mother?'

'She's gone,' Keesa states, 'for now, anyway.'

'Keesa repelled her with a roar,' Maen tells.

'That's a first. Clever girl, Keesa. Thank-you.'

She lifts her hand up and touches one of Keesa's ears.

'I thought you looked a bit too much like me,' the Queen says gently.

'What?' Keesa says, lifting her hands up to feel her newly sprouted feline ears, small versions of her fathers, and tawnier in hue. 'Oh! I thought something felt like it had come out... Why didn't you say?' she asks Maen.

'I didn't want to you to get a fright,' he replies, a smile bordering on pride turning his lips.

'When did they...?'

'During your roar. There's one other thing too,' his smile is broad now.

'What?' Keesa is thrown, starts feeling around her coccyx. Her lion cub tail whips up and whacks her hand.

'Argh!' she yelps. The tail twitches away a few times before she can grab it. The three of them grin at each other.

'You have come into your Princesshood, Keesa,' the Queen pronounces.

The sense of peace in the room is disrupted by mounting boot-steps approaching the door in the passage outside. Regan tries to get up.

'Slowly does it,' Maen slips his hand onto the small of her back, and helps steady her into sitting position. The warmth of his manful hand is too good. Think like a Queen, not a teenager, Regan instructs herself. Thuds and exclamations of tussle sound out between the two factions outside the door, then the sound of Valtere squawking.

'Please help me to stand, they are almost inside,' Regan appeals. More shouts outside the door. A brief pause, then heavy men begin bashing the door with their full body weight. Regan is woozy, and unsteady on her legs. Keesa offers her shoulder as support, while Maen stands in front of them, taking up a combat stance. The couch barring the door is edging forward. Regan notices the Prince standing near the door, tense, his hands on the ready to fend off an attack.

The door is forced open all the way. Haaken and Ryle enter first wielding machine guns, a pack of soldiers from either army following, still squaring off on each other behind their commanders. Ryle immediately dips his semi-automatic once face to face with the royal brothers, but remains vigilant. Haaken aims for Maen, and two of his men behind him for Colter.

'I am not under threat, Haaken, you can lower your weapon,' the Queen addresses her commander quickly.

Valtere screeches in above their heads, catches sight of the resurrected Queen, and goes to settle on the ground next to her. It is one of those rare occasions where the big bird looks happy. Haaken and his men decline their firearms.

'You, too, can withdraw, Ryle,' Maen instructs.

'I will come out and make an announcement shortly. Please go out and call a ceasefire immediately,' Regan bids.

'Tell our men to assemble and await my briefing,' Maen says.

The soldiers and their commanders hesitate a moment, size each other up, and file out, still wary of the situation. Elijah sits on the armchair, shell-shocked from the bizarre goings-on he has witnessed that afternoon. Nefer goes to his master's side, his tail lowered.

'Hey, Fer,' Elijah says. The dog's tail rises and gives a few feeble wags. He peers at the spent kitten in the boy's arms, and licks the feline's fur a few times. Regan conveys that she is feeling stronger, and nudges Keesa in the direction of the kitten. The girl pours some water into a tea saucer and takes it to him.

'Thank you so much Toekoums,' she says, stroking his forehead and holding the water to his mouth. The kitten rouses briefly, takes a few sips. His eyes look up to Keesa, take in her ears, widen slightly, then dip again contentedly.

'My pleasure, Princess,' he murmurs, and falls back into slumber.

'I appreciate all your help, too, Elijah,' Keesa says.

'No prob,' he replies, taking stock of her new appendages.

'Do I look funny?' the girl blushes.

'I always said you were a bit weird.' He smiles. A short laugh escapes her. She takes note of Colter about to leave the room, goes to him.

'Colter.' He turns. 'I'm sorry about your Mom.'

He nods stiffly, pauses. The girl has never seen him this breakable. 'I know what I did hurt you. It was not my intention. My only wish was to ensure your safety,' he says. His eyes dart momentarily to Regan, who watches the conversation.

'I know. I can protect myself now.'

'I think you were lucky today.'

'What happened to your mother?' Regan asks, looking at Colter.

'She is dead.' He glowers back at her.

'Oh no, I'm so sorry.' Her eyes sweep between the brothers; she touches Maen's shoulder. 'I wanted to thank her. I still don't understand why—'

'She gave her life-force to you?' Colter retorts.

'What do you mean? That she would still be alive if not for—'

'We all heard her saying it was her time. She was preparing to die today,' Maen interjects. He turns to Regan. 'Don't listen to him. She did it because she could sense that you and Keesa need each other to conquer Signa.'

Regan nods. 'I want you both to know that I am exceedingly thankful for what your Mother did. I am in your debt, King Maen.'

'I may regret causing Keesa pain, but I cannot say I agreed with my mother's sentiments. The best way to repay her kindness would be for you to keep well away from Keesa,' Colter snipes.

'You made your opinion quite clear to me, Colter,' Regan bristles. 'As I have said before, Keesa is entitled to make the decision as to where and with whom she will live for herself.'

'Allow me to resolve this here and now for all of you. As King of Day, I will abide by our late Queen of Light's dying wish. I hereby ordain that Keesa and Queen Regan of Night be allowed to consult on a regular basis, until such time as the influence of Queen Signa is brought under control. In order to render this working relationship feasible, I hereby agree to a truce between the Chambers. For practical purposes, I am extending an invitation to Queen Regan to live under the protection of the Chamber of Light for now. Given that the staff of both Chambers will no doubt need time to acclimatise, I would ask from all in this room not to divulge who Keesa's real parents are. We cannot afford violent or mutinous action. The announcement will be made at the right time.'

Colter is struck dumb. Relief and ebullience flush Keesa's face, but she checks it given everything that Colter has done for her over the years. 'Thank you, King Maen,' she responds.

'I would need to make the necessary arrangements here, but I accept your proposal gratefully, King Maen,' Regan says, sweeping a modest curtsey. Even given that she has just agreed to what could be a pathless journey into a hornet's nest, doubt is absent.

'Colter, my offer for you, Aedan and Elijah to reside in the Light Chamber still stands. I will need assurance from you that your unilateral violence today will not be repeated. However, the fact remains that you and Aedan brought Keesa up; you have a right to maintain a parental relationship of sorts with her. And regardless, it is high time that the family be reunited.'

Colter struggles to swallow the ire threatening to spew from his mouth. 'It seems you have your family all worked out already.'

Maen exhales, tired and troubled by Colter's recalcitrance. It had taken enough self-restraint to stop himself from expelling him outright given his hot-headed behaviour. But Maen knows that exiling his brother would have displeased Elke.

'At some point you are going to have to let go of your bitterness, and accept the inevitable changes afoot. Keesa is my daughter. Queen Regan is her mother. A strange family we may be, but a family we are. Where that leads us going forward, only time will tell.'

Colter drops his eyes to the floor. 'If you're finished, I will take my leave.'

Maen's spirits sink. He nods. Colter departs. Despite the King's recent desire to restore it, their fraternal bond seems more splintered now than ever. He turns back to Regan, attractive even in her pallid state. 'I will never afford him the opportunity to inflict that kind of viciousness on you again.' His eyes take in his girl too. 'I want you both to know that I will always protect you.'

Regan wonders at what has transpired in a matter of hours. Today she has been killed and restored, both in the name of Light. And now Maen stands before her using words that amount to an elixir. For so long she has lived with that which is unattainable whistling through the passages of her life, like a fickle mirage that jinks in and out of obscurity. An old, faithless friend, one she knew she could rely on never to deliver. His words are so gratifying to her now, it is difficult to trust them. She feels the blood rising to her cheeks nonetheless.

'The troops await us,' she says.

'Of course,' Maen replies. *Everything in its own time*, he thinks. 'I'm sure they can wait a fraction longer. You might be more comfortable in a more constituted dress.'

Regan glances down at the singed tatters. 'I believe I would.'

CHAPTER 27

A New Order

16/01/2051

Even given the ceasefire, Maen stands guard outside Regan's room as she changes. He catches a glimpse of her boudoir as she reappears in an understated, yet formal garment. A hint of her femaleness suffused in the room reaches his nostrils. For a second he is stopped in his tracks. Keesa notices an awkwardness in him, as though he has temporarily forgotten how to walk.

'Shall we proceed, King Maen?' Regan prompts him.

'Quite right,' he replies. They make their way along the draughty corridor, and emerge into the closing day.

The storm is tapering to reveal a cleansed twilight sky. A few dead bodies are scattered throughout the area. Regan and Maen announce the truce and imminent instatement of Keesa as Princess to both Chambers to a crowd gathered at the gates. A disoriented silence descends, then baffled murmurings, a few gasps of relief. They regard the girl. Keesa's tail snips. The air is thick with mistrust. She sees eyes narrowing, mouths whispering, some constrained, encouraging smiles.

Regan makes her way to the common stretch where the injured from both armies have been placed. She scrubs her hands clean in a washbowl. Her assistants are waiting for her with rubber surgical gloves, coat, head-wear and instruments. She begins with the first soldier in line and continues throughout the night, assisted by medics from either army, ordering casualties to be moved to the general laboratory shed once they have been stabilised. She transfers there in the early hours of the morning, and continues on till sunrise. Maen and Colter contemplate the Queen from the side-lines as they assist with moving the injured, coordinating supplies and burying the dead. Few words pass between the two brothers that night.

313

Uneasy Peace

The next afternoon, the long convoy departs for the Light Chamber. Small detours are made along the journey to release Regan's laboratory animals back into the wild. She is glad to watch the creatures set eyes on light bouncing off bush, an including sky above rather than a carceral ceiling, and orange ground extending. They dart out of their cages, some of them looking back uneasily to Regan. She might have been their captor, but they had grown to take security in her voice, her hands. But one more glance at the veldt before them, and they scamper off into it with speed, lest some human should tamper with their freedom once more.

The convoy veers off the route one final time to pick up Elke's body. The brothers go in. She has been laid out on her bed, her hands folded on her chest. Her hair has even been brushed; Maen knows it must have been an irregular act for the guards to perform. Ninev is perched on the headboard. She gives a dampened chirp as the brothers enter, and pause. One would not think she was a Queen, Maen thinks. Such a simple room, sensible bed, undramatic dress.

Once Elke is in the coffin, Keesa goes over to Colter, who eyes have been streaming throughout the carrying, and puts her arms around his waist. He caves, kneels and allows her to comfort him. As he pats her back over and over, Keesa hopes that this moment might be a harbinger of forgiveness on both their parts. With all the guards present, Regan must restrain from any display of emotion. She goes to stand next to Maen, an act that in itself might raise eyebrows. Ninev looks crumpled sitting next to Toekoums; even her feathers look somehow lacklustre. Valtere is perched on the bonnet of a nearby car, his penetrating eyes locked on Ninev. It is the first time they are this close to one another. As they ready to go, Maen addresses the small bokmakierie.

'I insist that you come with us, Nintjie. There is no reason for you to stay out here on your own.'

The bird assents with a diminished tweet, whirrs into the truck acting as a hearse, and settles on the coffin. Maen and Colter sit on either side of it. The cavalcade resumes the final leg of the journey.

———•••———

They have been driving an hour. Shadows are elongating as the sun verges the horizon. Keesa is slipping in and out of sleep, her head resting against Regan's side, Toekoums out for the count in the girl's lap. Valtere is dozing on the front passenger seat. The Queen pats Keesa's thigh every now and then, her arm enveloping the girl. She is tired, she should sleep too, but the levity of this moment prevents it.

Keesa feels her body becoming imbued with weightlessness. She senses she is somewhere else, somewhere far more pacific. Then the great flaming ball of the sun is before her, as though she has become an eye in the sable sky. She looks behind her, sees Earth in the distance. Elke floats between the two globes, beneath a central shaft of light that seems to connect them. The previous Light Queen is propping it up in its centre. Elke is a younger version of herself now. She bows her head down and to her left side, and slowly lifts her arms up in a V shape, her right shoulder elevating and protruding, preparing to support. The outgoing sunbearer allows the yoking chute to dip slightly in its middle as she sinks down away from it, carefully transfers it into the curve between Elke's arm, shoulder and neck, and begins to lift away into the star-infested vacuum. Elke's body begins to pulse with sunlight. The last thing that Keesa can make out is her eyes like two blue, glistering gems.

Keesa is jerked awake by the sound of the handbrake being yanked up, and the driver's voice.

'I believe you wished to take care of the transaction personally, Your Majesty?'

'Yes, thank-you,' Regan replies, then looks down to Keesa, 'I'm going to speak to the owner. We need fuel. I won't be long.'

Keesa looks out the window to see they are at a Gengun, bare bulbs blaring through the dusk, strung around the station with exposed wires like glum fairy lights. It's a different one to the last she had been in.

'Okay,' Keesa says, 'be careful.'

As Regan disembarks the vehicle, a small throng of Dark guards surround her. She makes her way through them to Maen, who is walking towards the ramshackle office at the back of the station, also flanked by his guards. He catches sight of her, pauses, indicates to his guards to hold back, as does the Queen.

'I think it might be best if I handle this,' Regan says in a low voice.

'But it's not safe, I—'

'Maen, hear me on this, I will get us a better deal.'

He studies her face. 'So the rumours are true, then. The Dark Chamber still has ties with the Genguns.' Regan's stomach turns at his look of disenchantment.

'They serve their purpose. It's a relationship of necessity, not choice. It can serve both of us, if you'll allow it.'

'This is a discussion for another time.' He indicates for her to go ahead. As she walks, her guards go to her side.

'Please wait here for me,' she instructs.

'I insist that—' Maen begins.

'The owners get jumpy around the guards. It will be quicker and easier if I'm alone.' Her guards hold back.

Maen holds his tongue, uneasy with the situation. He wonders what he has got himself into. Still, an unforthcoming relationship with Gengun owners will not serve the Light Chamber or Keesa. The King lets it lie for now. Valtere settles on a defunct motor oil vending machine close to the office window, and fixes his stare on the owner. The trade goes swiftly.

'Don't worry, Toekoums, soon we can stop,' Keesa says, as his nerves seem threadbare.

The kitten eyes the girl. 'Yes. You have done well.'

'Thank-you.'

'You have changed your course, though.'

'What do you mean?'

'It is not for me to say. Hearing it will cause fragmentation in you.'

'So, are you saying the change was a bad thing?'

316

'You know by now that good and bad are words, nothing more. They serve to assuage our conscience. The only real thing is what you want, intend, and act upon.'

Keesa nods, apprehension puckering her brow.

Toekoums continues, 'Fear will not help. Honour your choice as one made in a particular moment for a particular reason. Then move forward. It is all most of us can do.'

The car door opens, and Regan climbs back in. She observes the girl's trepidation.

'You can relax now, everything went fine,' she says, enfolding Keesa once more next to her on the seat in readiness for the final leg of travel.

'Yes,' Keesa says, and looks forward, her expression unchanged. Valtere is let in the passenger door by the driver, and perches on the front dashboard. The driver turns the ignition, and the car pulls off. Keesa pulls Toekoums towards herself with her tail. The kitten's tail whips automatically, unused to this new, feline aspect of his owner. Keesa dips her face towards him, allows a spent smile to break through. The kitten's eyes soften, and he begins cleaning his coat. The feeling of his little, furry frame knocking against her with repetitive motion is comforting. The last of the sunset is magnificent rose red. The sobering smell of fynbos soon fills the car. The mother and daughter both slowly put aside thoughts of the imbroglio ahead, and surrender to the rocking car, each other's warmth, and the joy taken in being transported together toward a new beginning.

CHAPTER 28

Procession

20/01/2051

Keesa stands before her mirror. Her chambermaids, June and Sabrin, are carrying out the final touches on her appearance. Keesa would normally have made a comment to them by now about the peculiarity of the two of them being coupled as handmaids, coming, as they do, from the Light and Dark Chambers respectively. But today feels sacrosanct; silence feels to be a prerequisite for the Princess-to-be. Indeed, the handmaids appear to prefer it. Each of them has taken great care with their part in the arrangement of the girl's exteriority. A great deal of silk-encased buttons had to be done up, a length of velvet strip threaded and tied at her back, jewellery clasps fastened, hair brushed and shaped into a loose knot. Sabrin is arranging the girl's fringe now, sweeping it carefully to the side with a small comb, more in keeping with a young lady than the jagged edges Keesa usually wears straight down. Sabrin stands back now, scanning Keesa up and down with her sharp eye. She gives her solemn nod of approval, as before, unruffled by prattle. Keesa can't help a little smile; she likes the handmaid's sober consistency. June approaches Keesa now with a small make-up case in the shape of a clam shell. She unclips it to expose a small palette of lip colour pastes made from crushed berries and red rose petals. She applies a tiny amount to the girl's lips, finishing it off with a daub of beeswax to set it. The two handmaids clear the mirror now; Keesa assesses her reflection.

What she sees is at once startling and agreeable. A cardinal-red, silk, fitted shirt, ruched on the bust. A white, velvet jacket that hugs her waist flatteringly. Her skirt of silk brocade fans out from her hips in gorgeous folds. The innermost section is white dotted sparsely with black, embroidered flecks in shapes resembling tiny crowns, with outer layers of ultramarine-blue. The skirt is edged with a thick, auric twine. The shade of the trim is answered by her feline ears, which somehow finish the raiment off in their upright confidence. Sabrin

318

holds a mirror so as to allow Keesa to observe a rear view. Her tail protrudes at the level of the skirt's flourish. Perhaps she is growing accustomed to her tail, but it, too, seems apt.

'I appreciate all your help,' Keesa addresses her two attending. 'Your teaming looks superb to me.'

There is a knock on the door. June goes to open it. It is Regan, a captivating sight in her queenly guise. She surveys her daughter, feeling the handmaids studying her reaction. Her facade of dispassion is impeccable.

'You look splendid, Lady Keesa. Your attendants have done a commendable job.'

Keesa does not need her to smile and fling her arms about her person. She enjoys the moments when her mother can express affection to her, but does not hanker after them. Everything has its place.

Another knock on the door. It is Aedan, cautiously peeking around it. She catches sight of the Queen.

'Oh, please excuse the interruption, I will come back,' she blurts.

'Not at all, please come in,' Regan says graciously, stepping aside that Aedan might view the girl. Aedan is wearing a modest navy-blue dress and low heels. Colter must have sourced them for her from the Chamber's wardrobe. She makes for a winsome picture that Keesa has never seen in her before. It pains her, though, to observe Aedan's plainness next to Regan.

Aedan consistently averts her eyes to Regan's feet, stealing quick once-overs at the full grandeur. She turns to regard the girl. 'Oh, Keesa,' her face twinkles. The girl can see she stops herself from hugging her, shy in front of Regan.

'Will that be all, my Lady?' Sabrin asks, conveying to June that their cue to leave has come.

'Yes, thank-you both,' Keesa replies.

Aedan begins following the handmaids out.

'Please do not leave, Lady Aedan,' Regan says, swishes to the door, and shuts it.

'No need to call me Lady,' Aedan brushes off.

'In my opinion, it is a fitting title for the woman who raised the Princess to be. Indeed, you have as much, if not more, right to be with her at this promising moment.'

The Queen's words take Aedan by surprise. Her blushing lack of answer attests to her agreement. Keesa feels the tension between them give a little. A necessary levelling has been told.

Regan turns to the girl. 'I'll see you out there,' she says, nods in Aedan's direction, and leaves.

Keesa approaches Aedan. 'You've been a good mother to me all this time; I am grateful. You and Colter will never be without a home, or the things you need to live. I will see to it.'

Aedan's eyes soften, and she brushes the tussock of one of Keesa's ears.

There is a hush in the room. Keesa keeps her eyes facing forward, even though she is itching to look around. It is the biggest gathering she has ever seen. The conference room is filled with all the workers of the Light Chamber, those Light dignitaries who live close enough to have made the journey in a day, and Regan's covey. Seawater slaps against the sides of the enormous glass receptacle. Its inhabitants were circling it as the guests arrived. Now they are suspended in an uneven row, their sleek forms bobbing slightly, their eyes focused on Keesa. She recognises the unmistakable eyes of the whale that she has visited in the depths.

King Maen and Queen Regan stand in front of the girl, their backs to the tank. There is small table between them, covered with a white velvet throw. Upon it sits a tiara of gold, a sapphire to the right of its band, a ruby to the left, and an exquisitely angled onyx in its centre. The bare tiara had been Elke's as a young Princess; the blue gem a gift meant for Maen's first girl. The red and black gems had been given to Regan by her grandmother as a reward for gathering her first vision.

Maen and Regan each lift a hand and place it on either arm of the tiara. Keesa kneels on the plush runner beneath her feet.

'Lady Keesa, by the power vested in me, King Maen of Day,' the King begins.

'And by the power vested in me, Queen Regan of Night,' the Queen continues.

'Let this tiara symbolise your instatement as Princess Keesa of the Alliance,' they intone together, and place the tiara on her inclined head. A trumpet blast leaps up towards the vaulted ceilings. Princess Keesa holds out her hands; the King and Queen each take one. She rises from her kneeling position, and turns to face the gathering. As she begins advancing down the central aisle, Maen and Regan following her, each row of attendants bow and curtsey. A gold-plated carriage waits for her outside the front door, drawn by two horses. Keesa is unnerved as she sees it; it is exactly like the one that featured in her dream. The footman assists her up onto the seat. June approaches the side of the carriage carrying Toekoums in her arms. He springs onto the seat next to Keesa.

The procession begins there, and slowly winds its way around the Chamber grounds. King Maen and Queen Regan ride on horseback, one on either side of it, and the Light dignitaries pace alongside them. The rest of the gathering, joined by all the Chamber children, use this singular opportunity to celebrate. The music is fitful and imprecise, but it serves as ample reason for arms to be hurled about and twirls to be spun. Members of the Dark Chamber do not attempt such animation. If they were on home ground, they would engage in a courtly rendition of dance. The Princess maintains a reserved composure. It is a propitious day, but the road ahead is a briary one. Outright celebration feels premature and inappropriate, despite being drawn around a castle in a golden carriage, surrounded by a throng.

Deliverance

20/01/2051

Once it is all over, Regan calls her cabal of guards. They know what has to be done. They have the truck close by. They ride it down to the water's edge. The hatch door of the truck is opened, and Regan climbs in. Her eyes take a minute to accustom to the dimness inside.

'It's okay, it's just me,' she says. The dolphin is more restless than normal. The sounds of the others must have carried from the conference room. It jerks the water into confusion, lifts its beak abruptly over the surface, and gives out a high screech. She moves closer to the container, presses her hand against the glass.

'I owe you,' she says. The dolphin pauses. It looks forward, yet it feels to Regan as if its black eye takes her in. She calls the guards. They are ready with special halters. This time it doesn't struggle as much against the tether; it is as though it can smell the ocean, and knows the four maddening glass walls are gone for good. The call is given out from the Chamber that signals the descent of the sea mammals back into the ocean from the conference room vessel. As soon as the first two dolphins have plunged back in, Regan gives the go-ahead. They wade into the water, and lower the creature in. It stays dead still until the last bridle is loosened, then bucks away from the humans, its hefty tail pushing one of them over. The other dolphins sight it straight away, and begin orbiting it, sensing its insalubrious state. The whales are out now too. The freed dolphin surfaces again, sets its eyes square on Regan, and then is gone, lunging and gambolling through the salty liquid with the others.

The Queen turns to see Maen making his way down towards the beach. She thanks her guards and dismisses them.

'Everything all right with you?' Maen asks. Regan nods. The late afternoon on shore breeze is snappy. She realises she is shivering. Maen looks at her blue lips, removes his jacket, and places it about her shoulders. He senses she is affected by something, as well as she conceals it.

'Thank-you, King Maen,' the Queen says.

Maen and Regan watch the whale rise and submerge, like a small black sun slipping beneath the waterline.

'I believe that Keesa could be the strongest of all of us. We can afford to have faith in her,' Maen says.

'I agree. Still, we have yet to reckon with my mother.'

Regan looks into Maen's face. Simply beholding his hazel eyes and the way they sit between his tufty ears yields a sense of security in her. So easy it is, she thinks, to slip into false comforts, unproven self-assurances. But the part of her that wants to believe in the power of their pact bucks against the cynicism.

'Tomorrow we begin her training. But first things first. I believe cook has prepared an exceptional meal for this evening. Shall we go up, Queen Regan?' Maen glances quickly towards the Chamber to see who might be viewing them, and resists the urge to offer the crook of his arm.

'Never mind,' Regan says, allowing a frayed smile through her lips.

They walk towards the Chamber. Regan reflects on how much has come to pass since the last time they exited a beach together. Their daughter awaits them within. They will be happy for her tonight.

Lessons by the Sea

27/01/2051

Regan places her instruments one by one into the steel trays of disinfectant. Her consultations are completed for the morning. She is enjoying practicing without being frowned upon. She unrolls a muslin spool that holds the implements she had used during her initial years of learning medicine. She lays them out neatly on the blinking counter. Tomorrow she will begin Keesa's instruction in the basic principles of human anatomy. But now to a different lesson.

The area chosen for Keesa's training sessions is a strip of shore to the left of the Chamber. Guards are positioned at key points around it within a generous radius of a hundred meters, in order to maintain privacy. Regan's personal guards tail her to where Maen stands coaching Keesa, then retreat to an acceptable distance away. A row of objects in various states of disrepair form a line about 10 meters away from the King and Princess. Toekoums and Ninev sit a short distance behind them on the sand, watching the lesson. Two canopies have been set up to provide relief from the mid-morning sun. The beach is graced today with a vaporous zephyr.

Regan and Valtere quietly join the pair of spectators on the backline. Keesa is focusing on a dummy made of bundles of dried long grass held together with reeds. It has been staked into the sand on a stick.

'Now remember,' Maen coaches, 'concentrate on the left arm. Don't be too specific about which bones yet; we can get to that later. For now, the entire limb is fine.'

Regan watches as Keesa crouches her torso slightly at first, ears flat, head thrust forward, tail held low. She poises for a few moments, like a cat in the final stage of stalking its prey, so still it is as though she is some motionless ejection from the sand, bound to it forever. Then suddenly she breathes in, billowing her structure upright again, her ears pricking up, and lets the roar rip from her lungs towards the target. The left arm of the doll breaks clean away from the torso, and bursts into flame.

324

'Well done.' Maen is pleased with her progress; she is a quick learner. 'Next time we'll begin with isolation again. Then we can move on to heat.'

'Thank-you, Father.' Keesa curtseys quickly; the King dips his head, indicating that the lesson has come to a close. They turn, see that Regan has arrived, and head over to the second canopy.

'You seem to be improving, Keesa,' Regan comments.

'Thank-you.'

'I trust you're adjusting to your medical quarter?' Maen asks.

'Indeed, thank-you. It was a busy morning.'

Maen's eyes are glowing in her direction. Regan feels a smile blushing her lips, looks quickly to Keesa, and manages to quell the racing inside to an equable state.

'Shall we begin?' she says to the Princess.

Ninev chirps a few flat notes. Toekoums looks at her.

'I'm still getting used to her language, but I think she says she needs to sleep, and will be heading back to the Chamber now, if that is in order.'

'I believe you are right,' Maen says. 'Of course, Ninev, you must rest.'

Ninev bows her tiny head, and lifts her tail plume. She appears to have deteriorated rapidly since Elke's burial, which took place the day before. Her feathers are colourless and splintered, and her stick legs no longer seem as capable of carrying her own weight as they used to. She takes off feebly, manages to fly a few meters, then makes a stumbling landing again. Keesa is about to bolt over, but Maen holds her back with his hand. He knows the small bird will feel humiliated.

'I will take her back,' he says in a low voice to the others, and starts over to her. Before he reaches her, Valtere wings to her side, and fans his wide wing, placing its tip next to her claws. She hops away with surprise at first, then considers the offer. Cautiously, she picks her way up the length of the wing, and settles onto the eagle's thick back. He takes off slowly, and carries her towards the Chamber.

Maen rejoins the others. 'They say helpers usually don't last long after their masters have died,' he says in a hoarse voice.

———◦••———

The Queen's lesson is coming to a close. Night is better for this work, but with Keesa's age, Regan has chosen to start with day lessons. She stands to Keesa's side, a few feet behind the girl, and coaches the final attempt for the day.

'Once again, imagine that you are empty, feel the part of you that hangs in black space. You are the void. Lift your hands, and face them towards the clearing before you.'

Keesa poises her hands, loose, ready. She opens her eyes and fixes them forward.

'Now allow the light of time to wake within you. Then gradually feel it drawing counterparts from the ether towards you.'

Keesa permits the abyss to superabound inside her, inking through her arms, her brain, her heart. The image of the ocean before her seems to multiply out, as though she is seeing the million fibrils that make it up. This magnification is more harmonious, more fluid. The pieces move and sway, fitting together in a pattern that is at once what is and more than what is. Then blackness swells her sight. For the first time, she feels the magnetism, the sense of so many moments coursing their way towards her, voices to be heard, fragments to be seen. It is confusing, overwhelming. Her mind struggles to choose which moment to view as they race closer, switching from one instant to another. Determined to manifest something, she abandons the task of choosing, and allows the moment to choose her. Pieces of the scene constitute quickly before her: a burnt tree, a girl painted standing at a gate in a blue dress with white apron, a man's profile silhouetted against an ample window displaying an overcast sky.

Once the last piece joins, the tableau comes clear. It shows an office or study of sorts: a mahogany desk, a chair clad in red leather, a small bookcase that houses some latter-day books as well as volumes that look centuries old. The fair-haired girl with unpretended expression is part of a painting hanging on one of the walls. The man standing by the desk has cropped dark hair, and wears a deep, steel-coloured suit—rare apparel in these times. He appears to be talking to a younger boy standing in front of him. The window behind them shows a sweeping view of a burnt city. Mostly seared trees and charred remains of buildings. A stream that trickles through it catches Keesa's eye, and the tower that half-stands next to it. It looks like a larger version of the one Keesa saw in her dreams. It would have four clock faces on it, had two of them not been somehow lopped off. The scene begins playing.

'I have had word that Queen Signa's plan is complete. We leave for the south a day from now,' the man says.

'Yes, Father,' the boy replies. He can't be more than 15.

'The time has come to apply all the skills you have learnt, my boy.'

'I am ready, Father,' the boy answers, 'I will not let you down.'

The man's face shows a satisfaction in it, stern and determined. The scene freezes momentarily, then dissipates out, allowing the sea skimmed with glittering sun to rush back in.

'It came together,' Keesa breathes, slightly light-headed from the effort.

'I am impressed with your headway, Keesa,' Regan says, touching the girl's shoulder.

Maen enters their span of shade, followed by Toekoums. 'That's the first time I've seen anything like that. You do your Mother proud, Keesa.'

'Thank-you,' Keesa says, depleted, but glad of her morning's training. 'Do you know who it was in the scene? And what was outside the window? Do you think it was the future?'

'The man is older than I remember him, but I did recognise him,' Regan answers, 'He is Robert Northam, a Dark Lord. The last time I saw him he was barely in his twenties. He came to the Chamber with his father, the Duke. He was one of my marriage candidates.'

'I remember my Father mentioning the Northam family. They controlled a sizeable area, did they not?' Maen enquires.

Regan nods, 'Three countries.'

'What place do you think that was in my vision?' Keesa persists.

'I believe that must be the ruined city of London.' Regan's features are cast over with misgiving.

'Perhaps in our afternoon session we can analyse the emanation in more detail,' Maen suggests.

Regan indicates agreement. 'We might need to try draw it up again to find clues as to the date. My sense is that it takes place in the near future.' She sees her younger self in Keesa's face. A look of fatigue overridden by novel excitement, and a desire to try it again.

'Certainly. But for now, you need to eat something, growing girl that you are,' Maen says to the Princess.

They allow Keesa to take off her shoes and walk ahead of them with Toekoums back to the Chamber. She revels in sinking each footstep into the quaggy half-liquid, half-sand of the water's edge. Regan and Maen trail behind her, partial to the unassuming act of walking together in salty air, surrounded by quiet. No hoods, no disguises. Regan gets carried away in the soughing lap of the waves, like the blinking of an animal's eyes at peace. She bumps into him by mistake; their hands brush. Maen laces his fingers through hers. Blessedness spreads across her face.

Keesa looks back, notices the togetherness. Regan senses her gaze, gently drops her hand. The Queen and King keep in step side by side. Keesa turns back and advances into the matchless stretch of beach before her, Toekoums avoiding the water, but nonetheless pattering next to her. The Princess is content. Her future looms, black, unknowable, and bright.

GLOSSARY

Karoo
An elevated semi-desert plateau in South Africa.

Koppie
A small hill rising out of the African veldt.

Veldt
An extensive grassland of southern Africa with scattered trees or shrubs.

Fynbos
A distinctive type of vegetation found solely on the southern tip of Africa. It includes a wide range of plant species, particularly small heather-like trees and shrubs.

TRANSLATIONS

Afrikaans:
Die Hel (p.153)
English:
The Hell

Afrikaans:
'LAAT HULLE LOS!' (p.199)
English:
'LET THEM LOOSE!'

Afrikaans:
'Vok dit! Ons kry karre iewers anders. Dit kos te veel bobbejaans! Laat waai!'
(p.202)
English:
'Fuck this! We'll get vehicles somewhere else. It's costing too many baboons!
Let's go!'

Afrikaans / Xhosa:
'Jah, vokken amagqwirha are killing our stock. Hambani!' (p. 202)
English:
'Yeah, fuckin' witches are killing our stock. Let's go!'

Afrikaans
Eina (p. 241)
English
Ouch

ABOUT THE AUTHOR

Anita Berk lives and writes in Cape Town. You can contact her at:
anitaberk7@gmail.com